The Shepherd

The Shepherd

LELA K. KING

TATE PUBLISHING
AND ENTERPRISES, LLC

Published by Tate Publishing & Enterprises, LLC
127 E. Trade Center Terrace | Mustang, Oklahoma 73064 USA
1.888.361.9473 | www.tatepublishing.com

Tate Publishing is committed to excellence in the publishing industry. The company reflects the philosophy established by the founders, based on Psalm 68:11,
"The Lord gave the word and great was the company of those who published it."

Published in the United States of America

ISBN: 978-1-68270-395-3
Fiction / Christian / Classic & Allegory
15.12.04

I dedicate this book to God's Spirit, who guided me, encouraged me, helped me, and led me through every step of the way in writing it.

Also to my son Jeff, who said to get the story written and out there to help everyone who needs encouragement and knowledge that there is a God who made us, loves us, and wants everyone possible to trust him and be with him forever.

And to my daughter-in-law, Jessica, who put it all together for the publishers.

I also dedicate this book to everyone who has never heard or learned of God's purposes for creating this world and everything and everyone in it. It is a wonderful experience to learn that each and every one of us was and is created for a purpose. It's to have a personal relationship with our God and Father, who is our creator. He loves us and tries to be an integral part of our lives. But we can only have this by learning about him and seeing all that he has done to make a relationship with us uplifting, encouraging, strengthening, loving and protected; what more could any parent be and do?

He loves all of us, but will not tolerate evil, meanness, selfishness, and uncaring attitude. To bring us closer to him, he gave us his only begotten son, Jesus, to pay for our debts and receive forgiveness and eternal life with him in heaven and all the universes that we don't know exist.

My prayer is that this book will show how faith begins, continues—or not—and how we can all participate in a life that will never end in the glorious presence of our Father, who art in heaven.

May God bless all who read or hear this book. May God's light shine upon you no matter the troubles you have or have had. May his love bring you into his presence forever.

In Christ's name, I pray. Amen.

Prologue

The men shifted uneasily on the floor as Samaes Ben Ahimelek rose to speak. From the side, a whispered warning lingered on the dust motes. "Samaes, be careful what you say. Herod has powerful friends…"

"Brethren, I stand before you again to say if God is God, the law his law, and we are his chosen people, we must not compromise. Herod has usurped the law. We, the leaders of the Jewish nation, owe the responsibility of governing them rightly for God. If we fail them, we fail God. He is just and merciful. He won't fail us. But he will judge us. And be assured, he will judge each and every one of us. You hypocrites! You vipers! You are more concerned with your own well-being than your responsibility to our God and our nation. You are on trial yourselves today. Don't you see that your conduct is open to his eyes and the eyes of the very people he has given to us to shepherd? Again, I say, Herod must die!"

The din of men's yelling swept through the room as everyone rose to his feet. As they were shaking their fists at each other, spittle and musty sweat mixed with the dusty air. The clamor ricocheted off of the pillars and ceiling. Anger and fear permeated the air as the hot breeze stilled within the chambers. Tempers rose. Then joining the echo of voices, the clanking of armor penetrated the roar. As the new sound overcame the shouts, the men of the Sanhedrin, Israel's highest court, turned and watched as Roman soldiers ringed about the walls. Then everyone shuttered as Herod, the Idumaean, strode into the room.

"Go ahead, Samaes. What were you saying?" The young soldier demanded.

"I said that you had overstepped the law, Herod, and as such, should be punished. Surely, even you must know that the decision to kill Hezekiah rested with the Sanhedrin and not you. As far as I've heard, you haven't been given that power and authority yet!"

"Gentlemen, gentlemen, calm yourselves. Have we turned into animals that we cannot discuss things reasonably and calmly?" The high priest turned to Herod saying, "Herod, must you disregard all proprieties by bringing your Roman guard into a place of holiness? This is an open meeting, but for Jews only. Please send them outside. You will be safe in here." Hyrcanus turned and glared at Samaes. "I believe that you have had your say. And now I must add to this conclave more important news. I have just received a letter from the governor of Syria demanding Herod's acquittal. I think that we should adjourn until we have given all that has been said some serious thought. Herod, if you would, please remain. I would have a few words with you." Turning and straightening his robe, Hyrcanus, the high priest of Israel, left the court.

Herod walked over to Samaes and bent down to his ear. His breath was fetid and warm as he whispered, "I admire men who are not afraid to say what they think. However, one should always know who one's friends are and who his enemies are. I think we know where you stand." Then throwing his cape over his shoulder, he left the court and followed in the wake of the chief priest.

Pollio and Joseph crowded about Samaes, both trying to get his full attention. "You fool. Don't you realize what you've done? Herod is even more vicious than his father, Antipater. You will have to have eyes in the back of your head to prevent his attacks. If you had any sense, you would leave the country for a while. You won't be safe anywhere in Judea or Israel. Take your family and get out now while there's time."

"If it is God's will that I die, then I will die. But I won't run because of Herod. I am a Jew, and no one but God directs me and my life."

Pollio and Joseph shrugged and followed their friend from the courtyard. Both knew that he was a dead man, and for what? Of course, he was right. They shouldn't compromise, but there are times when it is more expedient to be quiet than rouse the anger of a lion. Samaes had aroused a young lion in calling out Herod. Where it would end, they could only guess.

Meanwhile, Hyrcanus had reached his quarters and had ordered wine and refreshments for Herod. He was just sitting down as Herod flung open the curtain and charged into the room.

"Hyrcanus, don't ever tell me what to do again, especially when there are people about. Someday these clods will be under me. Then I won't have to put up with their constant whining."

"Naturally, my friend. But in the meantime, I strongly suggest that you leave Judea for Rome. Let this blow over. You know that Marc Antony will help you. But at the moment, your absence is more important. I can smooth things over, and then when you return, who will be able to stand against you?"

"Hyrcanus, if I leave now, I will come back with an army and destroy everyone who has been against me. You do understand?"

"But of course. You are right. But the time isn't now. Go and return with your army. With Rome's backing and a legion or two of soldiers supporting you, you will have the power and authority. And you will need both if you plan to rule these people."

Herod downed his wine. His face was flushed, and the wine dripped upon his tunic. His cape lay heaped upon the floor. His dark eyes were almost black and glinted with hatred that lay in their serpentine depths. *They were all going to pay*, he thought. *And how shall I punish Samaes? It must be slow and painful. And it must last for a very long time. And that fair sister of his, she will be included. Maybe he would give her to his soldiers for sport, or even send her to Rome as a slave. Oh, well, the voyage to Rome is long. I'll have plenty of time to plan their futures.*

Hyrcanus cringed as an evil expression seemed to blaze up and then turn inward on Herod's face. *He's quite mad*, he thought. *But he's brilliant too. I must watch him carefully. He would have no compulsion at all in killing me. Yes, I'll have to be very careful.*

Lifting the urn, he refilled Herod's goblet. "How is your father? We haven't heard of him lately. Is he still in Antioch?"

"No. Antipater is in Damascus with the governor. Why do you think you received that letter so quickly? My father looks to the welfare of his children. You are right though. I'll leave for Rome immediately." Sweeping his cloak from the floor, Herod left.

Hyrcanus laid his head back on the divan. *This whole thing is too much strain.* He frowned. *Herod is going to be a power here in Judea. And if I'm to retain my position, I'll have to coddle the little snake. There must be some way to defang him.*

His absence will give me some time to make plans. First though, I've got to do something about Samaes. That little rooster is going to mess up everything. Every time he and Herod are near each other, there's a fight. Ever since the fair Hannah refused Herod and Samaes backed her decision, Herod has been determined to destroy the whole family. Yes, I must do something about Samaes, and soon.

Hannah stood on the roof and looked down the road to Jerusalem. She twisted her necklace and strained to see if Samaes was visible. Shortly, a figure appeared, and she raced down the steps and out onto the road as her brother grew closer. *His face is so strained*, she thought. *Will this fight never end?* Then she felt her brother's strong arms envelop her, and she grinned widely at him.

"Another fight, Samaes? Will he never go away and leave us alone?"

"Probably not, little one. Herod thinks he is royalty, and as such, can and does pretty much as he desires. But let's not dwell on him. I have a surprise for you. Tonight, Gideon Ben Shaul is coming to dinner. I met him in the marketplace today, and he wants to discuss some things with me. Naturally, I invited him for our evening meal. You will have to look especially pretty for him. How do you feel about him, Hannah? He's a good man and comes from a good family." Samaes inhaled the sweet scent of his sister and smiled. She was his life, and yet he was going to have to send her away. There was nothing else he could do. Herod would kill them both without hesitation if he could. The time was coming when he would be able to do whatever he wished. Samaes must be prepared.

Hannah's heart fluttered when she thought of Gideon. "I know he's nice. I want to marry him. But if I do, I'll have to move to Tarsus, and leaving you and our home makes the decision so difficult. I'd miss you so much. Since Mother and Father died, you've been my whole family. Oh, Samaes, I really do like him."

"Well, worry no more. Today Tamara accepted me. We'll be married right after Passover."

"Oh, I'm so glad. She is very loving and gentle. She'll make you a wonderful wife. I'm happy for you both. You've loved each other for so long." Suddenly, Hannah felt sick at heart. Looking into her brother's kind eyes, she knew something was happening, but what? Her brother was settling things as if he knew he hadn't much time left.

"Samaes, why are you doing all these things so suddenly? I know that you have sold many of your businesses, and today strangers were taken to the pastures. Are you selling the sheep too?"

"No. On the contrary, I've decided to concentrate on raising sheep. Times are going to be hard here. The Romans will eventually take over, and I don't want to be here when it happens. And why shouldn't I get married? I've been thinking about it for some time now, and today seemed the right moment. Besides, I'm lonely. I want a home filled with children and laughter, just like it was when we were young. I also plan to sell this house. I've bought a new home outside Emmaus. The land around it will allow for several sheepfolds. I knew you would be leaving and decided to start in a new place too."

"You're right. Tonight I will accept Gideon, and we'll both start on our own journeys. But, Samaes, be very careful. Herod will always seek you out." With this last thought, Hannah turned and went inside.

I must get her out of Judea, he thought. *Herod will soon have the power to do anything he wants, and I know that Hannah and I will be at the top of his list. I wish that I could get Tamara out of here too. I only hope that my plans will succeed and that Herod won't find us. Emmaus isn't very far, but hopefully, it will be far enough. Tamara's father has agreed to handle my businesses here. I don't think that Herod will bother him. I hope not. Dear God, take care of us all.*

Samaes slowly turned from the dock as Hannah's ship sailed from view. *Well, she should be safe now,* he thought, stroking his beard. *I should be afraid for myself, but I'm not. I wonder why. I do know that all of us are in peril and that I must somehow be here to help. But only God knows how I can do that.*

Turning toward Emmaus, he was again deep in thought. God had prospered him. He owned land, animals, vineyards, and a thriving trading business. But it wasn't important to him. Certainly, it was nice not having the day-to-day worries of making a daily living. Just so, it gave him more responsibilities and duties far and beyond that of a poor man. God did require more of those he abundantly blessed. *I guess it's because they have more time to pray and seek him,* he mused to himself. He left the port of Tyre on his camel and started the long journey back to Jerusalem. He hated leaving Jerusalem, but he knew as surely as he trusted the Lord that Herod would be seeking him out.

Two days later, he saw the hills where the city of God stood. How he loved the relationship he had with the Lord. He knew he had to leave, but he wasn't going that far, just seven miles. He had been making these plans for years, and now he would see just how well he had planned everything. Looking up, he saw that he was almost home—at least, his home for now, he mused. He would try to make his new home just as pleasant but not too obvious. Soon he saw the walls of his home in sight and breathed a prayer of thanksgiving to God for the safe trip he and Hannah were embarking on.

The outside of his house was plain in comparison to his neighbors, but inside, starting at the entry and into the courtyard and patios, was where the changes astounded people. The beauty and serene atmosphere was incomparable to any others in the whole of Judea. A waterfall cascaded down one wall, spilling out into several ponds, waterways, and fountains. Fish swam in their cool depths, and lilies scented the air. Pomegranate and orange trees grew in sheltered groups about the garden. Flowers and herbs lined the pathways. Visitors were more content to remain outside in the refreshing shade of grape-covered arbors than retire to the inner sanctum of the house itself. Samaes was saying his prayers in any one of the arbors that he might be near to when he felt the urging of God to commune with him. Grapes hung on trellises, and even vegetables were intermingled with the other plants. The whole area served to not only provide comfort and seclusion but also as a source of food for the family. It truly was "Beth Enajim, the House of Fountains."

Tamara was in the kitchen. She loved her new home, and Samaes was a loving, generous, and kind husband. She was so lucky to have him and this wonderful life, she thought. She had set her bread and was now making her soup for the evening meal. Samaes had dug a cellar as well as a cistern for their private use. As a result, she need not go for the household water to the central well in the square at the end of their street, and the wine and extra foods stayed cooler in the cellar's dark depths. Tamara had help over the household. Anna ground their flour and worked in the kitchen, Rachel and James worked in the gardens, and Eunice helped Tamara spin, weave, and clean. The servants had easily transferred their loyalty to their new mistress. She and Hannah were like twin sisters. They had grown up together, and each had been blessed with happy and loving spirits. Now they were young married women.

Hannah had gone to live in Tarsus in Celicia, but Tamara was here for always. She was loved and part of a family. Anna's daughter, Rhoda, had chosen to go with Hannah. At first, Anna's heart had been heavy with her absence, but she soon found her young mistress to be affectionate and comforting, so the pain of separation had ebbed. Anna fussed tenderly at her new mistress, but soon Tamara would have the older woman laughing with her.

Meanwhile, in the shade of an arbor, Samaes paced. *Hannah will be safe now. If only I too could leave. Who would stand with Pollio against this invasive corrosion of God's laws? He and I must be united.* As he continued his pacing, he stroked the phylactery on his left wrist. He was jarred out of his thoughts with the banging on the door. As he walked toward the pounding, the door flew open, and his mentor Pollio rushed in.

"Samaes, please pardon the intrusion, but have you heard? Herod has left for Rome. We should have known Hyrcanus would resolve Herod's crime this adroitly."

"Calm yourself, Pollio. Herod will return, and when he does, we will be here waiting. My dear teacher, would you like something to drink? And, of course, you will stay for dinner."

"No, no, Samaes, I can't stay. I've made an appointment with Hyrcanus. The man is a simpleton. Does he think he can be friends with Herod? Why can't he see what we see? Herod will not forget that meeting or those of us who sat in on it. And Hyrcanus, a Hasmonean catering to that Idumean offal offends the most basic of Jewish belief. How God tolerates us is a miracle in itself." And with a swift turn, Pollio was gone before Samaes could even decide what to say.

The splashing fountains lulled Samaes as he paced about the courtyard. He could hear Tamara preparing the evening meal in the kitchen. How he loved his home and its daily noises, he thought, its comforting, and even enjoyable, sounds of normality, of peace. Even in these times of turmoil, one needed routine. Samaes flung himself down on the cushions. His head began to throb as the face of Herod invaded his mind's eye. *Well, Herod, old enemy, you win this round. By the first of the month, I, Samaes Ben Ahimelek, will cease to exist, and in his place will be David Ben Shophan. May God protect us all and give us peace!*

Part 1

Chapter 1

All was quiet as Demas sat perched on his rock, watching the lowering sheep. The other shepherds lay sleeping about the dwindling campfire, even Joel. Joel was supposed to be keeping watch with him. *It's a good night*, he thought. *Let Joel sleep.* Joel's constant chattering was tiring. He hated his life so. Strange how children were frequently so different from their parents. Joel's father, Abel, was a trustworthy and hardworking man. And then there was Joel. He hated everything. He wanted to do his own thing—live in cities and travel. Where had these ideas come from? Demas marveled at the difference between himself and Joel.

The stars were so bright tonight, he thought. Suddenly, a radiant light danced above the horizon. It crept closer, and Demas slid to his feet as he gazed upward in awe. The air about him had changed. It was soft and gentle yet exciting. It was a star, brilliant and glorious, hovering over the nearby town. It grew in size and brightness. Frightened, Demas turned and ran toward the sleeping men.

"Wake up! Wake up," he shouted. The men leapt to their feet, staffs in hand, not knowing the nature of the danger. Then they too became aware of the brilliance about them. Falling to their knees, they peeked through their fingers, overcome and frightened. Suddenly, an enormous angel of the Lord appeared. He rose before them in dazzling light, and the glory of the Lord flashed all about them. They were cowering and trembling, trying to hide.

Then the angel spoke and told of God's child being born in the city of David. He told them that they would find him wrapped in swaddling clothes and lying in a manger. Suddenly, with the angel there was a heavenly host praising God and saying, "Glory to God in the highest, and on earth peace, goodwill toward men."

The angel and heavenly host slowly faded, leaving only the dazzling star in the soft spring evening sky. Jarius, Demas' father, staggered to his feet, and the other shepherds too began to rise. "We must go into Bethlehem and see this miracle from God."

Grasping Demas by the shoulder, Jarius stopped him and said, "No, my son. You and Joel must stay with the sheep. When we return, you can go into the city to see him. We won't be long. Come, brethren, let us go while the star still shows us the way."

Demas hid his disappointment as the others hurried away. "Please, Lord, let me see the holy babe too." Then he returned to his perch upon the rock. Joel sauntered over and leaned next to Demas.

"Well, that was something, wasn't it? Can you imagine grown men hurrying to town to see a baby? How ridiculous! Now to go to town and have fun, that's different. Of course, we got left with the flocks. I hate sheep. I detest being outside all the time. And I am especially sick of being away from people. I want to see things, travel, and talk about something other than sheep, fields, etcetera. I'll get a horse and travel in style like a Roman. I'll be important."

As Joel droned on, Demas wondered how many times he had heard his friend complain and talk of going away. He looked at the star, still bright and hovering majestically over the little town of Bethlehem. "Joel, how often have I listened to you? Do you really detest your life so much? What about your family?" Joel just shrugged and then flopped down on his blanket and quickly went to sleep. Then Demas heard the ram's horn. It was such a holy sound. It was like the sound of God himself.

The horizon was getting lighter when Jarius and his companions returned to their flocks. Demas saw them coming, and he ran toward them, tumbling and slipping in his haste. "Father, did you see him? What is he like? May I go to see him now?"

"Slow down, Demas. Yes, we saw the babe. He is a beautiful child, a true son of the living God. He may well be our Messiah. We will wait and watch. Perhaps, we will see this great thing that the Lord is preparing. Now you and Joel may go into town. It is the fifth inn at the end of the marketplace, in back, in the cave stable. Hurry but be careful. Return before noon. Now go."

Demas and the now awakened Joel fairly flew over the rocks and brush as they made their way down out of the hills. *Jarius's face had shone,* Demas thought to himself. *Truly the Lord's messenger had visited them.*

At the marketplace, Joel took off in another direction where the road was already becoming crowded with milling people and animals. Carefully, Demas counted the inns until he found the fifth one. Then skirting the building, he searched the stables and caves in the rear, but no one was there. He returned to the street and recounted the buildings. This was the right inn, but where was the babe? He went inside and, finding the innkeeper, asked, "Sir, where are the people who were in your stables last night?"

"They've left, boy. After all, who would stay in a stable with an infant any longer than necessary? Now get out! We've work to do."

Demas slowly returned to the street. *Where would they have gone?* he thought. *I wanted to see the Lord's child too.* He looked about anxiously, hoping to see a woman and a child, but the thoroughfare was a mass of jostling humanity. He could see nothing, so he turned and walked toward the end of the town, looking for Joel. Suddenly, he heard a shout, and Joel barreled out from between two stands. "Come on, Demas, they're right behind me," he yelled. Demas automatically started after him.

They ran until the village was hidden by the rolling hills that they had been climbing. "What's wrong, Joel? What have you done now?" Demas asked as he bent his head and tried to catch his breath.

"I was casting dice with some men. When I won, they refused to give me my money, so I grabbed the pile and ran. It wasn't right for them to not give me my winnings." Joel panted. "Let's get back to the flocks and don't say anything, you hear." He threatened.

Later that evening, Demas sat by the campfire, staring into the glowing embers. Tears glistened on his cheeks. Jarius sat down next to him and patted his shoulder. "Don't fret, Demas. I have thought of a way that you might see him yet. The child must be taken to the temple and presented to God. According to the Law of Moses, that would be forty days from his birth. We will go to Jerusalem then. You will be at the temple when they come. Then you will see him."

"Oh, Father, thank you." And Demas, unable to contain his joy, danced about the camp. Joel, who had moved closer to hear, shook his head in disgust and walked away.

Jarius was unlike most shepherds. These were his sheep, and the shepherds worked for him. He had many interests, but he kept a low profile so that no one, especially the Romans, took notice of him. His father, David Ben Shophan née Samaes Ben Ahimelek, had an important and dangerous enemy in Herod the Great. When Herod had returned from Rome, Samaes had already sold many of his businesses and his home in Jerusalem, changed his name, and moved to the town of Emmaus. Since that time, almost forty years, the family was known as Shophan. But all the children knew their real name and history. Whether Herod had decided against any aggressive move on the family or had already made attempts, they had no idea. However, they had shifted the center of their various businesses to Tarsus and lived quietly in Emmaus.

Samaes had made a deal with Hyrcanus, the then high priest, to leave his position in the Sanhedrin and leave Jerusalem if he could be the main provider of sheep for the temple. Hyrcanus was so relieved to be rid of Samaes that he readily agreed and also agreed to never tell Herod where the family had moved. Apparently, he had kept the agreement, for they were not aware of any Roman ever coming to their door.

Jarius had three brothers and two sisters, but they lived several miles west of Jerusalem. They all had a part in the family businesses, but Jarius as the oldest had stayed near the Holy City. Now he had been given the privilege of seeing God's newborn son, the Messiah. It was thrilling but at the same time very frightening. Herod was not going to be happy to hear that his replacement was on the scene. He had Demas to think of. His eldest son was so much like his own father—a gentle man yet stronger in faith and determination to be a true man of God. He must start teaching Demas all the facets of the family interests. Other than the flocks, no one could begin to guess the wealth that the family was accumulating. Demas would one day take his place as the head of the family, and he would have to be prepared.

For the wealth wasn't for them alone, but it was entrusted to them by God to share when times became harsher. Now that the Christ was here, things would begin to change. Of course, the child would have to grow up, but manhood came quickly in these times.

Chapter 2

The days dragged for Demas, even though the ewes were lambing and he enjoyed this time. But his heart was already in Jerusalem where he knew the Christ child would shortly have to come. Joel had taken off for several days and then returned bruised and beaten, but he never told anyone what had happened. It was soon forgotten, as he healed and worked harder than ever.

At last, the day came, and father and son left for the city. Joel came too, but he wasn't interested in a baby. He wanted to see, smell, and feel the sights of the town. As they walked along, Jarius was reminded to tell Demas and Joel how to behave. "Boys, remember. We must obey the Romans, so take care when they are around. Should one tell you to do anything, do it! By law, we are required to do so. But don't worry, it seldom happens. And if we get separated, go to the outer court of the temple and wait for me. The parents of the babe looked poor, so they'll probably sacrifice doves.

You might watch for them at the fowl dealers. Also, they were from the tribe of Judah, so you'll be able to identify those colors in their clothing. But whatever you do, beware of the soldiers. Joel, meet us at the Temple. And don't get into trouble."

"Yes, sir" rang out as Demas bounded onward and Joel raced at his side. As they approached the city gate, Jarius pulled Demas close to him protectively. The alleyways were already crowded as they made their way toward the temple. Joel was out of sight.

Upon reaching the temple gates, they made their way inside, and finding a place to rest, Jarius sat down and began to tell Demas about the different temple courts. Hours passed, and Jarius had begun to visit around. Suddenly, there was a commotion at the main entrance, and people surged forward to see what was happening. Demas was shoved to the outside when he was suddenly grabbed by the neck and hauled upward. Twisting his head to see what had gotten hold of him, he was dropped back to the ground.

"You! Boy, pick up that sack there and follow those other men down that street. Now hurry."

Demas lay sprawled on the ground as a huge horse and rider pranced about him. Then he saw that it was a Roman soldier. He jumped to his feet and backed away, but the horse and rider soon had him out in the open again.

"Do as I say, boy," the soldier shouted.

Demas had no choice but to grab the sack and start off after the others. *Oh, please, let it not be far,* he thought. The heat was oppressive and wearying as the group entered the gates of a courtyard. The men hurriedly dumped their loads and quickly retreated back outside. No one talked, for all were anxiously trying to return to the maze of streets and out of the sight of these hated Romans.

Demas stood rooted to the path, gazing at the fountains and flowers. The Roman soldier had dismounted and walked up to Demas. "It is awesome, isn't it? When I saw it, I knew I wouldn't be satisfied with anything else, so I bought it."

"Yes, it is a wonderful place. I haven't been here in many years," he said without thinking.

"You know this house? How is that possible?' the soldier asked.

"My, uh, grandfather's friend built it and called it Beth Enajim."

"The House of Fountains. Yes, that's very appropriate. I am Gauis Asti Attilo. What's your name, lad?"

Demas suddenly sensed his danger and, turning, said, "Demas Ben Shophan. I must leave now, sir."

"Come see me sometime, Demas Ben Shophan. You can tell me more of Beth Enajim," the centurion hollered after him.

Demas had no idea how much time had passed, but he ran as fast as he could to the temple. His father was worriedly looking about when he spotted Demas entering the courtyard.

"Son, where have you been? You missed the babe again."

"Oh, no, Father. A Roman centurion grabbed several of us, and we had to haul sacks to Beth Enajim. I returned as quickly as possible. Now I've missed the Christ child again. I'll never see him. Father, it's not fair. I wanted to see him so much."

Jarius put his arm about Demas's shoulders and guided him toward the outer court. "Don't worry, my son. God will answer your prayer to see his son. The Lord always answers prayer. But it will be when and how he wants to. Come, let's try to find that scalawag, Joel. He'll be at the booths, for sure."

As they neared Emmaus, Jarius was more determined than ever to start teaching Demas about the family. Demas was only fourteen, but the preciousness of time was something Jarius was always aware of. As they came within sight of their home, it was ablaze with lanterns. *This isn't right*, he thought, and they hurried forward.

The door swung open, and Mariam ran into Jarius's arms. "Oh, husband, come quickly. Samaes is deathly ill. We don't know what to do."

He ran swiftly up the stairs, for his father preferred having the roof room. As he pulled back the curtain, the moon shown on the pale face of his father as he lay on his pallet. Moving to his side, he bent down to his father's ear. Mariam could not hear what Jarius said, but she did see her father-in-law nod. Then she heard, "Herod." Jarius stayed at his side and prayed. Finally, as the sun rose, Jarius stepped from the room, tears streaming down his face. "My father is dead. Send for the preparers. We will bury him before sundown."

The friends, servants, and family members looked shocked. What was the hurry? Wasn't he going to send for family friends? This was not the customary way funerals were done. Mariam walked up to her husband and asked him why he was doing everything so quickly. But Jarius just walked past her and went into the garden. He sat under an arbor and held his head. Herod hadn't given up. He must be extremely cautious of everything and everyone now. And he must talk to Demas.

As soon as Joel heard that the master was dying, he realized that Archelaus had acted against the Shophan family. He panicked and ran to gather his things. Even though darkness had come, he knew he had to leave home for good. He threw the bag of silver and his extra clothes into a blanket and rolled everything together. Then looking from his doorway, he turned and walked into the shadows and swiftly made for the hills. He had hidden several sheep in a natural enclosure and would take them with him back to Jerusalem. Someday he would repay the family of his best friend, but for now he had to survive.

Stumbling through the rocks and trees, he found the pen. He would stay until midnight and then walk the sheep into the city and sell them as he and Demas had done before. No one would question him. Then he would be free. As he wrapped his cloak about him, the reality of what he had done suddenly overwhelmed him. Tears poured from his eyes, and remorse shook his body. But just as quickly, he roused himself, and his stubbornness and selfishness again took control.

The old man had lived a full life, he rationalized. He just died a little sooner than he normally would have. Jarius wouldn't miss these few sheep. The Shophans were rich. These sheep would be his lost wages. With these thoughts capturing his mind, he dozed off.

The funeral was swiftly arranged. Mourners hovered in the courtyard, and their grief was not unreal. Many of them worked or had been helped by the Shophan family, and their sorrow was a reflection of their loss as well as their sympathy for the master's kin. Now the master was dead, and his son was the new headsman. They knew Jarius and were assured that things would continue as in the past. However, why the rush for the funeral? This puzzled many, but the others just shrugged and said it was God's will. No one had noticed that Joel had again disappeared.

That evening, Jarius sat in his father's room and dictated letters to his brothers and sisters. The scribes busily dipped and wrote. He informed them that their father had died suddenly (since it was so quick, he had been buried immediately) and also that Jarius was coming to visit each of them, but could not state exactly when. The deed was done, and they must get on with the rest of their lives. They must lead their lives as their father had taught them: no excesses but moderation, care, caution, and faith. And lastly, that he, their oldest brother, and his household sent their love and blessings to them. As the scribes dropped sealing wax on the letters, Jarius bent and pressed his seal into each mound. The seal of the Shophan family was a menorah with a flame above each stick except the center one. It was blank. He had filed the flame off of the first candlestick too. He was using his father's ring.

Jarius sat back as the scribes cleaned the area and left the room. The deed was truly done. He must get these letters to his family, but now he knew that the family was being watched. How could he get these away without anyone finding out to whom and where they were being sent? The thought was provoking. Then Jarius sat up and smiled. Of course, it would be very simple. He would use the animals. Yes, he thought. That should be most interesting.

The next day, Jarius rose early and sent six riders off to various places. They did not carry the letters written the previous night, but only orders for merchandise and where to move some of the herds of goats and sheep. Earlier when his shepherds had gathered, he gave each a new coat, which was the custom when a new master took charge. He had spoken to each in turn. And now they left with their herds.

Then he heard Demas in the kitchen and headed toward the voices and laughter. As he entered the room, Mariam smiled at him and went out. Demas's hair was mussed, but he bounded to his feet when he saw his father. "I'm sorry about the laughter. Mother caught me off guard, and we both were being silly."

"Demas, laughter is always a good sign of healing. Your grandfather would be glad to know that you were at peace and had joy in your heart. I hope that I don't rob you of it. For now, you must learn why things are so. Come, we are going to the east hills and will be gone for several days. Your mother already knows and has prepared our supplies."

Late that afternoon, they reached the encampment of shepherds southwest of Emmaus. Their foreman, Matthew, came out to meet them.

"Has it been sent?" Jarius questioned.

"Yes, Master. It has left here," he answered.

Then Jarius and Demas went into a tent hidden in the shadow of the hill and sat down. Jarius looked at Demas intently and began to tell the story.

Chapter 3

"Back before Herod was king, he came to your grandfather and asked for your Aunt Hannah in marriage. Hannah had told her brother she was afraid that Herod was going to press his suit, and Samaes knew that Hannah loathed Herod. He terrified her. And he wasn't really a Jew, so when Herod came and was refused, he threatened to destroy the family. Herod was seeking a Jewish wife, for he already had great plans of ruling Judea and the surrounding country. He was of Idumaean and Arabian blood and, as such, was not Jewish. But his children would be. All they needed was a Jewish mother. Of course, it didn't hurt that Hannah was incredibly beautiful. He had decided on Hannah, but when she had refused him, he considered it a slap in the face." Demas looked on in amazement as his father continued.

"Later on, Herod had Hezekiah murdered, and your grandfather, who was in the Sanhedrin at the time, had him brought up on charges. You see, at that time, the Sanhedrin was allowed to judge and punish people who transgressed the laws. However, Herod's father, Antipater, had the governor of Syria pardon Herod. After this, your grandfather knew that there would be no peace between our family and Herod. So your grandfather transferred his businesses outside of Judea and Israel where it was possible. When your aunt married Gideon Ben Shaul, the two families entered a covenant with each other. The Shauls would combine our business with theirs. Both couples had hoped that they both would have large families. However, your aunt died in childbirth. Now her son, Joshua, his father, Gideon, and I head the families.

"Your grandfather sold Beth Enajim to your grandmother's father, Joseph Ben Ehud. You've met many of these people, but I want to clarify their relationship and put them in proper order for you. Your grandfather bought the land and house in Emmaus and built sheepfolds. He changed his name from Samaes Ben Ahimelek to David Ben Shophan. He made an agreement with then High Priest Hyrcanus to leave the Sanhedrin if he could have a contract to furnish the temple with animals for sacrifice. He also got the priest to promise to never tell where he or his family had gone and, of course, to never mention their new name. Hyrcanus was so glad to get rid of Samaes that he immediately agreed.

"Your three uncles, two aunts, and I were born in our home in Emmaus. As we grew up, we were taught to always be cautious and somewhat suspicious of strangers. My father knew Herod very well. When I was your age, we were having problems with soldiers and thieves taking our animals, so Samaes chanced a visit to Jerusalem to see some of his old friends in the Sanhedrin. He asked if it were possible to brand our animals so that they would still be considered unblemished. That is where our family seal came from. We use the menorah. Father represented the center flame. And our order in birth represented the other six candlesticks. Each has a flame. When we write to each other, we leave off the flame where our birth order is. We all have different names to the outside world, but our true names are listed in the family records. I'm the first candlestick to the right of the center. Across from me is your Uncle Samuel. Below me is Uncle Jacob, and below Samuel is Uncle Caleb. Then your Aunt Ruth and Aunt Mary are below Samuel and Caleb.

"Look at your ring, Demas." Demas looked down at the ring he had been given at twelve and continued to listen intently as he studied it. "See how the flame has split. That shows the family that you are my son. We have done similar things with your cousins' rings. Since the girls received bracelets and necklaces, their signs are on charms. It was Father's idea to make sure that the females in the family were taken care of. They receive a percentage of everything just like the boys. It is only fair. Anyway, we decided to start branding all the newborn animals on the inside of their hind leg in the crease. When an animal was brought for sacrifice, the priests would check to see if it had our mark. If it did, they checked to make sure it was purchased from a temple shepherd. If not, they would have the man arrested. You see, not only us but also the priests lost money from this kind of theft, so it has worked out for everyone.

"Four years ago, we grew lax in our scrutiny of the unusual. Remember when your Grandmother Tamara went to visit her father in Jerusalem? That was your Great-grandfather Joseph Ben Ehud she went to see. They decided to go up to see your Uncle Samuel in Tyre and then catch a ship back to Caesarea and then home. You heard how bandits attacked them on their way to Tyre. After the mourning period, your grandfather went to see Samuel. He suggested that men be sent to all the main coastal cities. They were to check all camel buyers and look for the camels taken in the raid. Included in the raid was your grandmother's almost pure white camel, which had been branded. The men knew what to look for. Every camel that was stolen turned up in Seleucia. The sellers were brokers for some Roman soldiers from Herod's household in Jerusalem. Your grandfather knew then that this wasn't a random act. Herod knew where we were. We increased our security measures, but not visibly.

"However, we were wrong. We found out that Archelaus, Herod's son, wanted Beth Enajim. When Joseph refused to sell, he arranged to have the caravan waylaid. Unfortunately, your grandmother was killed too." Jarius paused and looked at his son for a moment before continuing. "You said a centurion owned Beth Enajim now. He must be from an important family for Archelaus to sell it to him. Then, of course, Archelaus may have just needed money for his pleasures and just sold it. Still, a Roman owns it now.

"We truly failed this last time. Your grandfather's death was not a natural thing. When we got back, I rushed to his room. I stayed with him until he died. He was still coherent when I got there. He told me that he had been working with the sheep when his chest suddenly began itching. Then he felt very weak. He walked home to lie down and rest before supper. He hung his cloak on the peg by the door, but as he turned, the coat moved. Carefully, he opened it, and sewn into a crease, he found a carpet viper. He killed it and buried it, but he realized it was too late for him. There was no use alarming the household, but when he awoke the next morning, he started to check who had been near the house other than the regular people. A washwoman said that a stranger, a woman, had helped her with the wash by the stream. She was grateful for the help. She said that the woman's husband had come and that they had sat and eaten together. Then they left, and she brought the wash home. That is when the snake must have been slipped into the coat crease.

"Demas, your grandfather saw this as a real attack on our family. I buried him quickly and sent messages to your uncles and aunts. Tomorrow you and I will go and visit them. From now on, you are going to learn about every aspect of our businesses and their purpose. Son, we live in tragic and terrible times, but with the birth of God's son, I believe that things are going to change. Just remember that, like a storm, things get worse before they get better."

The next morning, Jarius and Demas rose early, but they did not wear their regular clothing. The clothing they put on was old and had been used, something that the poorest of shepherds might wear. Demas was curious and intrigued. He was only fourteen, but he was being treated as a man. He wanted to show his father that he could handle any situation as an adult. He knew that the purpose behind the disguises were serious. They ate with the other shepherds and then walked out with the others as they took the sheep to pastures. As he glanced back, he thought he saw a boy dressed in his clothes enter a tent, but he shrugged and followed the flocks.

Several hours later, as the flock they were with started to graze, Jarius took Demas's arm and led him behind some rocks. "We will wait here for a while and rest," he said.

"Then we will walk down to the stream and follow it. We are probably being watched, so we must be careful."

The head shepherd was watering the sheep before settling down for the night when two figures casually walked to the stream and disappeared. Jarius hoped that they had gotten away without suspicion. Since the stream ended in a spring, the two shepherds walked into a cleft in the rocks. Demas was getting tired and had so many questions to ask, but he remained silent as Jarius led them between the rocks. As they neared the end of the path, a large boulder blocked their way. Jarius slid around the huge rock, so Demas followed. Behind the rock was a cave, and they walked into its cool depths.

Demas was completely bewildered as he walked behind Jarius. It seemed that they walked forever. Parts of the cave were natural, but there were places that had been shored up with timber. Suddenly, there was light in the distance. As they walked to what was another opening to the cave, Jarius turned and urged quiet on Demas's part. Outside the cave was another trail, but tethered nearby were two donkeys.

Jarius relaxed and said, "Okay, we're safe for now. Let's eat and rest, and then we'll leave when the moon comes out. We must get to the sea by early morning. We're going to catch a ship to Tyre."

Demas knew why his father was taking precautions, but he was still amazed by his father's ability to plan so quickly. The cave was partially man-made. There were beams and columns in places keeping the walkway safe. And now here were supplies and animals to ride, just waiting for them. Demas couldn't help but be excited. And they were going to sail in a ship too. So much had happened in these past few months that sadly Demas realized his childhood was over and gone. He would be learning more than just a family business; he would be learning survival tactics.

It was around ten o'clock in the evening when Jarius shook Demas awake. "Quiet now. Eat and then we'll leave." The sun had long set, and now the stars were spread across the sky. Demas could see the moon rising and hurriedly ate the food spread out on a cloak before him. His father had packed the animals and watered them one last time before they mounted and left. The moon made the hills and sands a contrast of deep shadows and shining reflections as the donkeys prodded up and over them. Jarius did not encourage talking, so Demas just watched their trail. Occasionally, Jarius would halt and listen and then urge his beast on again.

As the horizon started to lighten, the two travelers stood on a hill overlooking the Great Sea. Jarius helped Demas down, for he was stiff from the ride. Demas stood gazing at the sea as the sun started to rise below the turning of the earth. Jarius put his arm on Demas's shoulders and spoke softly. "We must go down quietly and stay near the shore. A ship will be waiting for us."

Demas nodded, and the two led their animals down the sandy dune and onto the shore. This sand was totally different from the sand around home. It wasn't as rocky, and it clung to your feet and legs. Demas scooped up a shell and put into his cloak. He liked the sea air. It was brisk, whereas at home the air was dusty, musty, or scented by the wildflowers that grew about the hills and plains in spring. As they approached a hut, someone came out of the shadows and stood waiting for them. Jarius dropped the reins of his donkey and stepped closer to the man. Demas tried to hear, but the morning breeze whisked away the words being spoken.

"Come, son, breakfast is ready. We'll sail shortly." Demas entered the hut as a woman brushed past them. It was good to drink cold water and eat. Demas was tired now, and it was hard to concentrate on chewing the fruit and bread laid before him. He must have dozed, for suddenly his father was shaking him and helping him to his feet. "I know you're tired, but soon you can rest when we get aboard the boat."

Walking outside, Demas saw a small rowboat rocking in the shallow shore water. Hurriedly, he and his father climbed into it, and the man from the hut started rowing them out into the sea. Demas's stomach was beginning to rebel when he saw a larger ship approaching them. Before long, his father and he were hoisted aboard, and Demas watched as the small boat moved back toward shore.

"We are safe, Demas. This is one of the family's boats. Go up there to the small cabin and sleep. I'll join you shortly." Demas's head swirled from all the things he had seen and experienced. *Life sure wasn't dull anymore. Wouldn't Joel have enjoyed all this?* he thought as he drifted off to sleep.

The next morning, the brisk salty air made Demas feel exhilarated. The boat swept over the waves as the water splashed the decks. *I love this,* he thought. *It's so clean and cool.*

Later that afternoon, father and son were talking again. Jarius told Demas how Samuel handled the shipping business in Tyre and northward. Jacob handled the caravan trading in Damascus. Caleb lived in On in Egypt. He made up caravans of goods for Arabia and shipped goods to Crete and Rome. Ruth lived with her husband, Simon, in Antioch, and Mary and her husband, Andrew, lived in Aleppo. Everyone had a part in the business, and all were constantly aware of the danger that the family was in.

Still, the question was how had Herod found them? No one but the family knew the names that each brother used and where they lived. Jarius had gone over and over in his mind where the breakdown had occurred. Where had they slipped up? Samaes had lived untouched within eight miles of Jerusalem for almost forty years. Even Herod wasn't patient enough to wait that long to get at him. Where had they messed up? Or maybe who had talked unknowingly? They would have to find out how much Herod knew.

Maybe just the family in Emmaus had been compromised. If so, they had contingency plans for just this problem. The family was going to survive, this truth Jarius promised to himself.

On the afternoon of the third day, the crew and passengers saw the port of Tyre in the distance. Jarius put his arms about Demas's shoulders and thought how fortunate he had been to have this son. He was a leader. It was inbred in him. But he had also received the wonderful characteristics of his grandfather: gentleness but strength, kindness but discernment. He was intelligent and courageous. But above all, he had a strong faith in God. What more could a father hope to see in his child?

He hadn't told Demas yet, but a time of separation was coming. The lad was to apprentice at each family location for at least six months. He would be gone from home for years. Miriam was upset when he told her, but she had the girls and young Benjamin to fuss over. He knew that she would miss Demas. He was their first child. She knew that he would eventually take Jarius's place as the head of the family. He must learn everything he could in the coming years. Jarius had hoped that they could wait until he was sixteen, but these new events had accelerated the time to further his education.

Jarius had gone with his father and each brother to set up each working area abroad. His father had always been there, but now Demas must walk his own path alone. Jarius wanted to protect this boy, his son, but he knew that he had to go out into the world alone. He would have his uncles, aunts, and cousins, but basically all of whom he had known his whole life would be far away from him. Jarius bent his head and said a silent prayer for this young man whom he loved dearly.

Chapter 4

Herod leaned back against the cushions as he watched his sons eat. None of them were capable of ruling his whole dominion, so he would have to give them each an area. Archelaus would be given Judea, Samaria, and Idamea. Perhaps, something more. That's the least he could do for him after he had delivered Samaes Ben Ahimelek to him. Samaes had been quite clever to remain hidden this long. And to think he was just down the road in Emmaus. It took someone like his boy to be slyer and sneakier. Herod felt the pains in his body almost constantly now, and the voices in his head made it throb. But he was proud of his brood. It had taken ten wives to produce sixteen children. Of course, he had had to dispose of some of his wives and a few of his boys along the way. However, on a whole, he was quite happy with his family. He liked the boys. Girls were too conniving and argumentative. They were okay as ornaments and playthings, but it took men to rule, so he had married two of his girls off to well-placed relatives. That left him with two virgin daughters. He really should do something about them and soon.

As his thoughts traveled back in time, he thought of Cleopatra and Marc Antony. They were as close to being friends as Herod had ever had, but they were long dead. If he hadn't been as quick on his feet back in those days, he too would have been dead. Those were exciting times. Wars, conspiracies, politics, power, how he loved it all. And now in his last years, he could add revenge to the list. It was too bad that Hannah had died. Oh, well, she and her brother were gone. Now he had to concentrate on wiping out the rest of the family in Emmaus. He wouldn't be subtle with them. The men would be sent to Rome as slaves, and his army could have the women. The children would die. Then there was his dearest friend of all, Nicolaus of Damascus. Nicolaus had stayed with him through everything and had even written Herod's biography. Good old Nicolaus. He, who had overlooked his methods and yet had remained true to him and his family. With this last thought, he slurped his wine. *Funny how hard it was to get it all into your mouth*, he mused and then fell back asleep before his guests.

Archelaus watched his father under hooded lids. *The wretched man will die soon, and then I'll be ruler of Jerusalem*, he thought. He knew that the country would be divided between Philip, Agrippa, and himself, but he wanted Judea. What luck it had been when he had seen his soldiers beating a young Jewish lad. The boy was almost dead when he had stopped to watch. He had had no intention of stopping the soldiers' fun, but the boy had raised his head and offered information for his life.

"And what could you tell me that would compel me to save you." He had sneered.

"I can give you something that will prove invaluable to you. I can tell you where Samaes Ben Ahimelek is."

Those were the magic words. He grabbed the boy and almost strangled him demanding where the man was. But the boy was smart. He held out until he was guaranteed his freedom. Archelaus took him to the baths and had him cleaned up. Then giving him a bag of silver, the boy babbled about not being able to ever go home if he told him. Archelaus laughed and had asked him if he minded that so much. The boy hung his head and said no. He then told him where Samaes had been hiding all these years. Before he could grab the bag back from the urchin, the boy ran out of the building and disappeared.

After that, Archelaus had made up a plausible story to tell Herod. Of course, in his scenario, he had spent much time, money, and effort in the process of finding his father's hated enemy. He knew that it would please him if he could find the man that his father had endlessly searched for. Now he knew that he would be king of the country south and east of Jerusalem with this great city as his seat of power. What a piece of luck! Now, if the old man would just die.

When Archelaus told Herod where Samaes was, Herod had laughed. "Just think, Archelaus, he has been right under our noses." After much planning, it was decided that an accidental death would best serve their purpose. That way the rest of the Ahimelek family would not be afraid and disappear. The boy said that Samaes had only one son, Jarius, and that the family now used the name Ben Shophan. A spy here and there and the homestead was found and watched. Herod had thought of using the carpet viper. If an asp was good enough for Cleopatra, then a viper would be good enough for Samaes. Apparently, it had worked perfectly. The son returned home just in time for his father's death. There had been a quick funeral, and things had seemingly returned to normal. However, Herod wanted this Jarius watched. He would give it much thought on how he would take the family without too much talk. Naturally, he would confiscate all their property too.

The spies reported regularly, but said the headman and his son had gone with the rest of their shepherds to pasture their sheep. Herod wasn't too worried. The man had left his wife and other children at home, so he would return. In the meantime, all Herod had to do was wait and plan.

Archelaus grew tired of hearing about that family and soon returned to his more sordid interests. He liked gambling, drinking, and women and did all three things regularly. Actually, he had wished he could go to Rome or Capri for a time, but Herod's health was deteriorating, and he didn't want to be absent from Jerusalem when the old man died. He had to protect his rights. His brothers would not hesitate to usurp his claims if he was absent from the city, so Archelaus threw parties and spent his energies in as many past times as suited his cruel and selfish temperament, but all the while keeping a watchful and hopeful eye on his father's deteriorating health.

Archelaus's mother had been the Samaritan Malthace. Antipas was a natural brother, and Philip his half-brother. Malthace had wanted kingship for both her boys, and it looked like it was going to happen. Where Archelaus was somewhat dissipated in character and the way he spent his life, Antipas was more organized and instinctively good in managing his settings to get the desired outcome. Philip was laid-back and took life as it came. Nothing was worth getting overly excited about. What would be would be.

It was Archelaus's ambitions that would override any sense of what was right and good. If he liked it or it came first to mind, then that was the way he did things. He was sly but not as politically savvy as his father or as well-connected in high places or with important people. His knowledge did not include the experience to rule. He was, in fact, ill-suited to control and reign over anyone, much less a people that despised him. But his vanity was such that he felt he was liked by all that were necessary to him to step into Herod's shoes.

At this point in his life, Herod was in no condition to think sensibly or be practical. His sons in his own mind would be as good at ruling as he had been. However, he had never taken into consideration the differences of upbringing. Herod had learned at his father's feet. He had learned the art of war and rulership from Antipater. For all of Antipater's misdeeds, he had practiced a strong belief in the Jewish God and learned to exercise patience and justice over the people he served. Herod, on the other hand, had sent his sons to Rome as hostages of Caesar Augustus. They had received a basic education for that time, but not the instruction of leadership from their father. By the time the young men had returned home from Rome, their father was suffering from numerous physical and mental ailments. They saw him in the waning years of his glory and suffering from the many effects of social diseases. By that time, Herod had lost the keenness of mind that had served him so well in the past. Now he was an old man, dying and hardly able to take care of his most basic needs.

His occasional burst of energy would leave him exhausted. Herod was no longer able to figure things out to their probable end. Now he functioned by instinct, and that was clouded. Herod the Great had been a splendid builder. Except for a desire to kill anyone who interfered with his plans and an inbred tendency toward evil, his years and association with the might of Rome had brought peace and a semblance of balance and order to Judea. There were dissenters and always would be. No one in politics would ever be able to please everybody. His methods at times were excessive, but he did what he felt was necessary to accomplish his goals. The Jews did not appreciate him or his methods. His parentage had been his biggest hurdle with the people he ruled. His father, Antipater, had been an Indumean, and his mother, Cypros, was an Arabian. Herod was not a Jew. He was, therefore, unacceptable to rule the Jews as far as they were concerned.

And Archelaus thought he could follow in his father's footsteps. His mother was a Samaritan, and that was far closer to being a Jew than an Arabian grandmother. Unfortunately, he lacked the skills and abilities that had been inherent in Herod.

Chapter 5

While Demas rekindled his acquaintance with his cousins, his father and uncle spent the time closeted in discussion. Finally, Demas was summoned to them.

Demas entered the room and took a seat in front of his father and uncle and sat quietly as his father began to speak. "We've had much to consider since your grandfather's death. Demas, as the heir to my position, it was planned for you when you turned sixteen to spend time with each of our families learning our businesses. But we've had to move up our timetable. If there is time, and I pray there will be, your mother and I will be moving to Damascus. Unknown to everyone outside the family, we all have Roman citizenship. It was necessary to our businesses to be able to move freely about the Roman Empire. But now it seems certain that Herod knows where we are. Your uncle and I don't think that he knows about the rest of the family, so we feel they are safe to remain where they are—that is, all except your

Uncle Jacob. He is going to move into our home, and we will take his place in Damascus. His name is different than ours, and he's a widower now. We will make up deeds of transfer, and he will be a newcomer who has bought all our holdings. That way he will be able to blend in, even though he is a stranger. We will take each other's stewards and learn from them what the other knew and who they knew. That way, things will continue on except we'll be where Herod doesn't know our whereabouts. The hard thing is to get your mother and the rest of the family away from Emmaus. Jacob will be here shortly, and I'll return home. When we get back, you can come with us to Damascus, and we'll learn our new work together. Eventually though, you will travel to On in Egypt, stay here in Tyre for a while, and then go to Aleppo, Antioch, and Tarsus. I'm sorry you've had to grow up so fast, but it is out of our hands."

"Don't look so glum, Demas. I'm sure we can keep you busy while your father is gone. We can begin your lessons, and you can see how we do things here in Tyre. Consider it an adventure." His Uncle Samuel smiled.

Demas left the room literally in shock. He was never going home. And he had so much to learn. He walked out into the garden and sat on a bench. It wasn't long until Lydia, his cousin, found him and started to playfully tease him.

"Come on, Demas, don't be unhappy. You're here for a visit, so let's enjoy it. We haven't seen you in years. Now we're almost grown-up. There's so much to do and see. You'll enjoy yourself, even if it wears me out." And with this, she pulled him to his feet and dragged the young man down the path.

Meanwhile, Samuel and Jarius had more planning to do. Jarius would leave the next morning so that he could get home in the evening with the shepherds. The young boy that was masquerading for Demas now would continue to do so until the family got away. And so would his stand-in. They would play their roles until Jacob came and took over. Then they could work for him, or they could leave if they desired too. Jarius didn't think anyone would go, but their people were free to make their own choices in the matter.

As for Mariam and the children, they would have to leave late at night. They would go south and then cut back up west and north to the sea. A ship would then bring them to Tyre and then on up to Damascus. They would need camels to transport the family from Emmaus. They were faster and would be able to move on the desert more surely. It would have to be done quickly though before Herod could again act against them. They were in danger no matter what they did. It would be either Herod or possibly bandits in the desert.

Thank God these plans had been made long ago. Jacob felt sure that he would be safe. He had no children, and his wife had died, so there was no one but himself to be concerned with besides the shepherds and their families. But the shepherds would mean nothing to Herod.

Most of the family's things would be left behind and given to the poor. Jarius wasn't poor, and new clothing and necessities could be purchased in their new home. He and Mariam had talked of this possibility occurring, and she agreed that the safety of the children came first.

Dinner that night was somber, although Samuel and his family had tried to make it a joyous occasion. Demas was saddened that he had left his childhood home for good. Now his concerns for his family consumed his thoughts. Oh, if only he was older, then he could be of more help to his father. The idea that they might be caught and killed terrified him.

Around midnight, Demas walked with his father to the ship that he was leaving on. Jarius knew how heavy his son's heart was, but what must be done must be done. Standing on the wharf, he took his son in his arms and held him close. "Son, I know what has been going through your mind with all that is happening. Don't give in to these things. If it is God's will, we will be back here within a week. Always look forward and never behind. The past is gone and cannot be redeemed. If something goes wrong and I don't return, you will take my place. I trust God completely to see us through these times. I want you to trust him too. I'm so proud of you, Demas. I know that you will do everything that is expected of you. You always have. Your mother and I couldn't have asked for a finer son than you. I love you very much. Now dry your tears and show me what you are truly made of."

After blessing his son, he turned and walked up the plank. Lifting his hand in farewell, Jarius walked onto the boat. Demas rubbed his eyes and smiled at his father as the ship slipped out of its mooring and the sails bellowed, catching the evening breeze. He stood watching until the boat was hidden in the darkness of the night. Then turning, he walked slowly back to his uncle's home.

The next day, Samuel began showing Demas how his part of the family business was operated. At noon, they took lunch at home, and then Demas was freed to explore. Lydia became his shadow and teacher. She stayed with him and remained quiet when he seemed distant to her questions. She couldn't begin to imagine what he was going through and tried to be his friend when needed. On the third day, Demas had asked his uncle if he could go to the local synagogue to pray. Samuel agreed, but he would go with him. He cautioned Demas to say he was a distant cousin who had come to visit should anyone ask. He was from Jerusalem, and that was all that needed to be said.

On that same day, Jarius was on his way back to the pastures he had left days before. He kept a sharp lookout for anyone and was anxious to get through the cave and to the encampment. So far everything was going as planned. Late that afternoon, he rejoined the flocks, and in the evening, his stand-in became just another shepherd as Jarius moved about the campfire. The next afternoon, they broke camp and headed back to Emmaus.

Jarius's steward met them a couple of miles out. Matthan had been with the house of Shophan for over twenty years and was a friend as well as the steward. He and his master talked the rest of the way home. He knew that Jarius would have to leave but was sorry that he would have to stay behind. But he knew that he could go to his master eventually. Saddened but glad to know he would be summoned, he helped with the plans for the clandestine journey about to be taken. They decided on two nights from the morrow for the departure, as tonight was the beginning of Seder. Nothing could be done until then. There were already camels at home. He would make sure that they were well-prepared. They would be taken to a sheepfold just south of Emmaus and packed ready for the family when they got there. No one had seen any strangers, but they knew they could be watched without knowing it.

Mariam was so happy to see her husband and the children were jubilant. They had been told to call the young man, Demas, when he too entered the house. Mariam had tried not to worry the children but also had had to stress the importance of them acting normal around Jason. It was strange at first for him to pretend he was part of the family, but like most children, he soon joined in with the homecoming.

When everyone had gone to bed for the evening, Jarius told Mariam of Samuel and his plan for them to disappear. When she hadn't seen Demas, she knew the danger was for real and that they would have to leave their home very soon. She just hadn't realized how quickly. But her family was more important than a house. Memories could be carried in her heart. She was from a town several miles from Damascus, so it wasn't as though she was going to a totally strange land. Her parents were dead, and friends she had had as a girl would probably not remember her should she meet one. She would keep her name, but the family name would be changed. There was to be no connection to them and Emmaus. They would say they were from Tyre. The children would be taught to forget this home and learn about their new home as soon as possible. The girls were old enough to understand, and Benjamin would forget as he made new friends. For their safety, it had to work. Herod would not live forever, and she doubted any other members of his family would be as intent on their destruction as the king had been.

Lately, more often than not, Mariam had thought of the story that Jarius had related to her about the visit from God's angels announcing the birth of his son. She tried to visualize the young woman who had born him. All Jewish girls were told that one day God would ask one of them to bear his son, and now it had happened. Her husband had seen the child twice, but poor Demas had missed the event on both occasions. For his sake, she hoped that one day they would all get to see God's son. But for now, she prayed that God would protect her family and see them safely to their new home. She had not told Jarius that another child was on the way. Fortunately, she had only realized it herself recently. This journey should pose no problems for her, but she couldn't help but press on her stomach and pray for the safety of her unborn baby.

The night soon came, and Jarius and Mariam moved silently as they got the children up and ready. Matthan was worried, for there was a stranger in the town tavern. He wasn't the usual type of traveler that stayed around, and he had been there for several days. Matthan wanted to send an escort with the family, but Jarius said more people would arouse too much interest, so the family slipped out through the stables and down a cleft in the hills behind the main house. The children were cautioned to be very quiet, so like shadows, the Ahimelek family again disappeared.

At that moment, the innkeeper in town was kicking the stranger out into the street. "I told you no more wine. We're closing for the night," he yelled and then turned and slammed the door. The man struggled to his feet and staggered between the buildings. He was starting down a pathway when, looking up, he saw moving shadows at the top of the hill. Funny, he thought. Why didn't they stop here for the night? He made his way down the path and then crossed back over the main road to a stream hidden in the trees.

"Well, it's about time that you got here, you drunk. I suppose the inn is closed now. Did you bring anything for me?"

The drunk just mumbled and fell down on the grass. The other man walked over and kicked him in the chest and then returned to his own place near the low fire. He was sick and tired of watching that farm. What was so important about the family that lived there, he wondered. Then he too promptly went to asleep.

The next morning, the drunk's moaning woke his partner up. "Can't you shut up, you pig?" he whispered. "They'll hear you at the farm."

The drunk crawled over to the fire and began to vomit. "I think I must have broken a rib last night when I fell down," he said.

His partner just sneered at him. "You know what," he said at last, "something doesn't look right over there. The shepherds have left, but the kids aren't outside playing. And the woman is always outside and about by now."

"Oh, yeah, well, isn't that too bad?" The drunk whined. "I'm telling you I'm really hurt."

"You know, there is something wrong over there." The partner growled. "I'm going to check."

Pretty soon, the man was back, and the drunk was still whining. "You fool, the family is gone. The captain is going to whip us for losing them. Now get up, we have to report." With that, he strode off to the horses tethered in the upper glen.

That morning, Jarius and his family arrived at the sheepfold that his men used in the winter. There was food and bedding already there for their use. He would miss Matthan, he thought. The man was a wonder at getting things done quietly. The family ate, and the children quickly fell asleep. Jarius and Mariam sat quietly and talked. Jarius had a prickly feeling about staying here all day and finally brought it up to his wife. "You're just worried for us, husband. We've made it this far. Don't worry," she answered. Finally, he showed her in the dirt where they were heading. "If something does happen and we get separated, I'll send you this way, and I'll go in another direction. Travel as far as you can. I know it will be hard on the children, but you must reach this rock face near Abbas. From there, you will go through the pass to the sea. Then follow the shoreline until you see the cove where we meet our boats. Baca will meet you and take you and the children out to the boat. Samuel will meet you in Tyre."

"You really are uneasy, aren't you, Jarius? Do you know something I don't know?" she asked.

"It's just a feeling I have. If we have to part, put Benjamin on the camel with you. I'll try to obliterate your tracks and take the other camel in another direction. Promise me you won't hesitate. You and the children's lives will be at stake if this happens."

She nodded, and then they too lay down to rest. Around four o'clock in the afternoon, Jarius was up and had already packed the animals. Miriam fed the children, and they left again, hurrying the camels along. As evening came, Jarius stopped and listened. He heard horses far behind them, but they were coming on quickly. He turned and caught up Benjamin and placed him in Mariam's lap. "Hurry." He urged. Then grabbing his robe, he jumped down and started dusting the trail his family had made. Running back through the grass, he got on his camel and led the other camel on a rope with him. He whipped the camel, and they took off at a fast trot in a southern direction. He could hear the horses now. They had entered the wadi behind him. *Oh, God,* he prayed, *please keep my family safe.* He had not heard the small rocks rolling around him, but as he came around a bend in the trail, he was knocked from his seat. He landed hard and was disoriented, and when he tried to stand, he couldn't. Suddenly, he was surrounded by a group of straggly looking men. He was thrown over one of the men's shoulders, and they all disappeared up and over the cliffs.

When he woke up, he was tied to a rock, and his leg was in a splint of sorts. One of the men at the campfire saw he was awake and came over to him. "Well, my rich traveler, I see that you are back with us. Why your haste?" he asked. "Did the horsemen follow you?" questioned Jarius.

"The Roman pigs came and went. They looked around for a while but turned back. Why were they after you?"

"They're Herod's soldiers. Herod has been trying to kill my family for years. We were trying to escape when we heard the horses behind us. I came in this direction to lead them away from my family. Do you know where they went when they left here?"

"They went north back to Jerusalem, I'd guess. They might have backtracked the direction you came from. I don't know and really don't care."

"You don't understand. My wife and children are out there. If they find them, you can imagine what those animals will do to them."

"Well, that's too bad, traveler. We're quite satisfied that we got one pigeon. Let them have the rest." Saying this, the ruffian returned to the fire.

Jarius was bereft. Did Miriam and the children get away? Were they okay? He would have wept if he hadn't decided to pray earnestly for their safety.

Another man rose from the fire and brought some water for Jarius to drink. "I understand that Herod is after you. That means he would pay a reward to get his hands on you. How much do you think you're worth?" He spat. Tossing the water over Jarius, he too returned to the fire.

The rest of the night, Jarius dozed off and on. Eventually, everything was quiet, and he again lifted up prayers for the safety of his family. He had tried all his life to be decent, but these weren't decent times. Men were out for themselves. Nobody seemed to care what was going on. Now he would be sold to Herod. He had just about fallen asleep again when he heard a rustling in the grass. Suddenly, his ropes loosened, and he had to think hard to prevent himself from falling down. Then he heard a whisper. "Try to crawl around this rock. I'll help you from there." Jarius dragged himself around the rock where strong hands reached out and pulled him further into the shadows.

He could see nothing, but he felt himself being lowered into a shallow hole and covered with sand. "The soldiers are coming up the backside of the hills to attack us. We can't take you with us, so hide here. I'll tell the others that you escaped. Hurry now, I must warn my friends."

"Thank you, my friend. What is your name?" he whispered back.

"Amos," came out of the darkness. Then there was a shout, and the commotion got louder as armed men ran out of the blackness past him. He barely breathed, hoping that no one would discover him. Then the battle began, and with that, the screaming and clanking of swords pierced the night. Suddenly, it was over. Jarius couldn't see anything, but he could hear the soldiers talking.

"You stupid idiots, I told you not to kill everyone. Now we don't know what has happened to Ben Shophan and his family. Where could they have taken them? The camels aren't here, so they must have been taken to another encampment. We'll camp here until it's light and search the area."

Jarius didn't know what to do. Should he try to crawl away or stay put? This was the longest night of his life. Finally, he carefully added more sand to his hole, leaving a small space for air, and went to sleep. All was in God's hands now.

Chapter 6

Mariam had been absolutely terrified when Jarius had flung Benjamin into her lap and told her to go quickly. They had been traveling almost all night, and the children were exhausted. Now she reigned in her camel and listened. "Children, we can't stop yet. We must reach the rock face before we can relax. Are you okay?"

"Yes, Mother," the girls chimed together. Sarah held on tightly to her sister. She had dozed off and on, but poor Rebecca had had to guide the camel the whole time.

They started off again but at a slower pace. Just as the sun rose, Mariam could see the rock face of Abbas. As they went around the huge rock, the path was laid out in front of them. They kept on the trail for another mile, and then Mariam stopped and lowered her beast. The girls did the same. All of them were stiff and sore, but no one complained. They walked into a small clearing off of the trail and helped their mother get water and food ready for them.

"Do you think Father is okay?" the children asked at the same time.

"We can only trust God that he is. Now eat, and then we will sleep for a few hours before going on." Mariam got the children into the shade and asleep and then walked out onto the trail. *Maybe I should conceal our tracks too when we leave,* she thought. Then she went and lay down herself.

Late in the afternoon, Mariam led the camels out onto the trail and told the girls to walk down several furlongs. Then grabbing a bush, she rubbed out where they had stopped and back almost to the turnoff. She then ran back to the children. Mounted again, they headed for the sea. Mariam had been to the inlet where the family boats came in, but had no idea how far south of that area she was. Hopefully, they would get to the seashore soon and then look for a place to rest again for a while. She tried to not think of Jarius. First, the children must be gotten to safety, and then she would think of her beloved. She too habitually looked behind to see if they were being followed, but so far nothing.

Just as the sun was setting, they came up on the seashore. The children were fascinated by so much water and were eager to get into the water that lapped onshore. Mariam looked at the ground and then around the dunes carefully. Apparently, no one had been here as the sands were windswept, and no prints of any kind could be seen. Fortunately, the rocks came down to the shore, and she was able to find a place out of the wind and hidden from the beach. While the children looked for shells and ran into the water, she laid out a small fire and their bedding. Soon the cold brought the children back to their mother, and she fed them and got them to bed.

It was high tide, she reasoned. When low tide came in, she and the children would head up north toward the inlet. Adding the time that they had traveled south and then subtracting the northwesterly time they had moved in, she felt that they were about six hours from their destination. At last, she too lay down to sleep, praying that she was doing the right thing.

Around two in the morning, Mariam roused up and checked the tide line. It was definitely going back out. It was time to get the children up again. The travel was wearing the children down, and they were cranky when awaken. But they helped their mother pack again and climbed back up onto the camels. Mariam led now, for she wanted to make sure that they didn't walk into someone's encampment unknowingly. All the children slept, swaying with the camels in their seesaw motion. Mariam had taken the rein of the second camel too so that it wouldn't stop or wander away from her lead. On into the night they traveled.

Mariam had almost dozed herself, so she stopped to drink some water and wet her face. She was just starting again when she saw a brief light ahead. She shook her head to clear it, but there it was again. Making the camels walk slowly, she approached where she had seen the light. It was their bay. Praise God, she had made it. As she got closer, she looked around to make sure it wasn't a trap. Nothing! As she had the camel kneel, she could feel herself shaking. She had been closer than she had calculated. Now she could relax. She walked up to the door of the hut and rapped. "Baca! Are you there? It's Mariam Ben Shophan."

Slowly, the door opened, and Baca looked over the weary travelers. "Come in, come in." He motioned. As the children huddled against Mariam, Baca drew the bar down on the door. "So the master didn't make it, huh?" He slurred.

Suddenly, Mariam was wide awake. "You're drunk, Baca. What will the master say when he gets here?"

Baca leered at Mariam and then laughed. "What difference does that make? By the time he comes, you will be gone, sold to slave traders, and I will be rich."

"What do you mean sold? You can't do that! Jarius will kill you if you do anything to harm us." She bluffed.

But Baca only sat down and smiled. "Ever since he came through here and told me that you would all be coming, I started to make plans. Now I can get away from this hole and back to civilization. You can do nothing to stop me. Tomorrow I won't signal your boat, and it will move back to sea. Then the ship you'll be sailing on will come in, and I will be rich."

"Baca, you must know that we aren't poor. Our family will search you down and kill you if you do this terrible thing. And who forced you to stay here? You could have left anytime you wanted too. You asked for this job, remember?"

Just then, Yazir came into the room. She was Baca's Parthian wife. "Yazir, do you go along with your husband in this thing?" Mariam asked.

"I told him that we should do it. I hate this country. We're going to go back home. Your family won't be able to touch us there." She shrugged.

Later as the children and Mariam leaned against the wall, tied, Mariam thought of Jarius. If he was dead and she and the children were taken away, would the family be able to find them? She refused to cry. She would be strong for them all.

Baca went to the door and opened it just a crack. "Well, well, there's the old family boat signaling. Too bad they aren't going to get an answer." As he began to close the door, it was pushed open hard, slamming Baca into the far wall. In walked Matthan and some men from home. "Mistress, are you okay?" he asked.

"Yes, Matthan. Thank God you came. Hurry, signal our boat. It's offshore."

"I know, Mistress. We signaled it already. They are lowering a boat for you now."

"Matthan, how did you know to come? Jarius didn't say anything about you coming to the inlet."

"The morning after you left, soldiers rode through the village in a great hurry. I surmised that something had gone wrong. I tried to reason that the master would send you on and try to mislead them, so I gathered some men, and we came here. It looks like it was the right thing to do. Why are you tied, Mistress?" It had finally dawned on Matthan that the Shophan family was trussed up.

"Our friends, Baca and Yazir, were going to sell the children and me to slave traders. Their boat will come in when ours leaves. So, Matthan, you have my permission to sell Baca and his lovely wife in our place. Divide the gains between yourself and the men." And with this said, Mariam gathered the children and walked out into the morning sun.

Before she got into the rowboat, Mariam told Matthan to try and find out what had happened to Jarius. She knew that Jacob would not rest until he knew where or what had happened to his brother. Matthan promised, and she knew that if it were at all possible, he would find her husband. Stepping into the boat, she looked around one last time and then sat down and pulled the children close. Soon she would be in Tyre and safe, but what of her dearest husband? She would make plans when she knew for sure.

Chapter 7

Someone walking around woke Jarius. He was chilled and sick at his stomach. But he didn't move. He could hear muffled voices, but the sand covering his head prevented him from hearing anything clear. Finally, it was quiet, and Jarius wondered if he dared remove the sand from his head. He couldn't stay here forever, and he knew that he was going to really be sick if he remained much longer in this hole. Slowly he raised his head and the sand dust choked him. He pulled his arm up to muffle his cough. He could hear now, but it seemed he was alone. The silence was eerie. Slowly, he raised himself to a sitting position. By stretching his torso he could see over the rock that had concealed him. The sight was horrible. The soldiers had apparently just left all the bodies of the bandits laid where they had fallen. Then a shadow passed over him and he could see the eagle circling above.

He had to get out of here. Before long the stench of rotting bodies would be unbearable. This in turn would bring jackals. His leg had been numb, but when he pushed his body free of the sand, the pain almost caused Jarius to lose consciousness. He was so thirsty. Easing himself around the rock the full shock of the scene made him ill. How could men do this to each other? He found a pole and tried to raise himself to a standing position.

Looking around he found another broken pole and dragging a tattered cloth to him he made a crutch. But how far could he go and what direction? Then he heard or felt movement in the rocks behind him. Slowly he sat back down and clutched the staff. He couldn't hide he didn't have time. He would pretend to be dead.

"Traveler, are you okay? It's me, Amos." Slowly Jarius raised his head and there stood the young man that had saved him the night before. "Thank God, you're alive. I had to wait until I was sure the soldiers were gone before I could come back here for you. Here, drink." The water was the best that Jarius had ever tasted. The boy pulled the skin away. "You mustn't drink so fast, it will make you sick."

"I can't begin to thank you for all you've done. Can you help me get away from here," Jarius gasped.

"Yes, I can get you to my camp. There are just a few of us now since this raid happened. You'll be safe there."

Slowly, Amos helped Jarius up. He had brought a donkey and now proceeded to help him up on it. On the way back to the camp, Amos told how he had been sold into slavery. He had eventually escaped and ended up here with these bandits. His hatred of Herod was why he had decided to help Jarius. Anyone Herod hated was his friend. Up and down, skinning through tight passages in the rocks, they traveled. At last, they came to a large cave, and Jarius saw a few children and women outside, but only a couple of very old men were evident.

"Is this all of you?" Jarius asked. "Yes, the soldiers killed all the younger men. We still have your two camels and a few donkeys. Other than that, what you see is all there is," the young man answered.

Helping Jarius down, Amos moved him into the shade and brought him some food. Afterward, a woman came over and looked at the splinted leg. "They did a terrible job on that leg," she muttered and walked away. A few minutes later, she returned with some smoother boards and more rags. "This is going to hurt, so bite on this stick." And upon removing the splints on his leg, she suddenly yanked his foot, and Jarius passed out.

It was nighttime when Jarius regained consciousness again. His leg did feel better, but his stomach growled, and his head throbbed. Amos saw that he was awake and brought him water to drink. "You look like you are going to live now. Do you want something to eat?" Jarius nodded, so the boy brought him the same soup he had had before. When he was done, Jarius again dozed off.

The sun in his eyes woke Jarius. It looked like everyone else had been up for a while. Then Amos noticed him awake and came over. "Tell me, Amos, where did these people come from? And why live out here in the wilderness?"

"Some people don't have choices, traveler. Marta, the woman who reset your leg, worked sheep with her husband. When he died, she was kicked off the farm she lived on. The older men became old and were tossed out by their families. The children belong to the few younger women. Now their mates are dead. And like I told you, I'm a runaway slave."

"Are they good people, Amos? Do they care to live better? Or has life beaten them down too much?"

"Traveler, everyone likes a roof over their head and food in their bellies. Circumstances decide their condition."

"Okay, then I have a proposition for all of you if you will help me. I owned a large farm in Emmaus. I just sold it to a friend. If they are willing, I will send you down to the steward there. He will give you clothing for all of you and some more animals. Then they can live on the farm as freedman and work for their living. I can't go back, and I doubt if it would be safe for you. I will hire you to take me on down into Egypt to On. I have friends there who can help us both. You can stay with me and work for me, or I will give you money, and you can go on your way. What do you think?"

Amos stood looking at Jarius for a moment and then turned and went to the group of people who were watching.

He talked, and then they were all talking back. Finally, Amos returned to Jarius and squatted in front of him. "Are you sure this friend will accept these people, traveler? What can the old ones do? If you are sure about this, I'll go and meet this steward you talked about."

Jarius said that he needed to write a letter, so the steward would know it was from him. After much digging around, a sheepskin and some dark liquid were found and brought to him. He would have to write so that no one but Matthan would know who had sent it. It took a while, but he finally composed what he wanted Matthan to do. Looking at Amos, he waved him over and asked if they had any beeswax. Amos produced a comb of it, and Jarius softened enough to seal the letter and put his seal on it. Then he told Amos to bring the cloak that had been on his camel. Giving it to Amos, he told him to ride a donkey down near Emmaus but not to go through it on the road. Then he grabbed Amos's arm and pulled him down so he could speak more quietly. Finally, the young man stood and, waving to the others, climbed on his donkey and rode away.

If Jarius had figured rightly, Amos would arrive the next morning at the farm. Hopefully, the soldiers and the spies were gone. But he had warned the boy to scout the place before riding in. If the soldiers were still there, then he was to ride around behind the main buildings and wait until dark to approach Matthan's house. He told Amos what Matthan looked like, so anyone posing as him would be immediately exposed. He had looked at all the possibilities and hoped that he had covered everything. All he could do now was wait. Hopefully, Matthan would have news of his family.

Two days had passed, and Jarius was beginning to worry. He trusted Amos, but maybe the soldiers had gotten him. The people were beginning to watch him suspiciously, but they still gave him their sparse food and water. The day wore on, and he began to wonder what he should do. With a broken leg, he wasn't going to be able to get anywhere by himself. He needed Amos as much as Amos needed him. The boy was able, but what had he run into at the farm? Was Jacob there yet? The sun was low in the sky when everyone started toward the entrance in the rocks. Then in rode Amos and several asses with large packs. Amos slid off his donkey and walked up to Jarius.

"Well, you were right. The steward read your letter, and here I am," he exclaimed. For the first time in ages, everyone had a good dinner. Matthan had sent food, meat, and bread, plus a letter from his brother Jacob.

He told Jarius that Mariam and the children had made it to Tyre. The soldiers had come back to the farm and were about to pillage it when Jacob rode up with his caravan. When they learned that he was a Roman citizen and the new owner of the farm, they left for Jerusalem.

Jacob gathered they weren't too happy about what they were going to have to report to Herod, but that was their problem. Yes, he would take care of the people with Jarius when they came down out of the hills. And he was right to not come back right then. Amos would take him south, but not to On. He would swing back to the west and the sea. A boat would be waiting to take him to Tyre. He hoped that he would get well soon and that he would not worry, as Jacob rather enjoyed being the nabob of the area. Samuel would send news of his arrival. He hoped that Jarius and his family would enjoy their new home. His steward was as good a man as Matthan. Mariam would tell him what the good steward had done for her and the children when he saw her again. He wished him Godspeed and blessed him.

Jarius was so relieved that he didn't mind the others seeing the tears stream down his face. His family was well, and he would see them before too long.

When Amos walked over to him, Jarius grabbed him in a hug and thanked him. God was watching over them, and he was happy to know that all was working out for him and these poor people.

Chapter 8

"What do you mean the family is gone?" roared Herod when his captain reported the missing family. Herod stood and almost tumbled from the dais on which his throne stood. Not another hunt to find that accursed family. He staggered back and fell into his seat. "Archelaus, you found them once before. Find them again and get rid of them all. Don't bring them back, just kill the whole family. Do you understand?"

Archelaus stood there and glared with murder in his thoughts as the captain hung his head. Then he walked over to the man and, putting his arm around him, said, "Now, now, Father. Let the good captain and me go over what happened, and we will get the Shophans. Don't worry. We will find them and take care of the matter for good. Come, Captain, let's have a talk." And with this, Archelaus and the subdued captain left the room. They walked to his chambers where his men awaited them. The captain said nothing, for he knew his fate as soon as they had lost those people.

Upon entering the room, Archelaus turned and struck the captain before the door was closed. His men picked up the bleeding man and held him as Archelaus paced back and forth in front of him. "So you lost them? Do you mind telling me what happened?"

The captain told how the spies had come to get him when they found that the family was gone. They pursued them into the hills and, from the tracks, had been able to discern that robbers had taken the family. That night, he and his men crept up the hillside from the back. When they attacked and killed the men, they found that the family and their camels were gone. They waited until morning and searched, but they could find nothing, as it was all rocky terrain and there were no tracks. Upon going back to the farm, they found that a trader from Cyprus had taken possession of it. The man whose name was Titus Ben Tob had papers and deeds showing he had bought the property. He also showed proof of being a Roman citizen. There was nothing that they could do. The trader had more men than they did, so he returned to Jerusalem and reported.

Archelaus had sat down by the end of the tale and was deep in thought. Shophan had acted very quickly. He must have had this planned for a long time. "Captain, why did your men kill everybody? Wouldn't it have been more practical to save some for questioning?"

The captain looked up and said that he had told the men to save at least one man, but once the fight had started, nothing could stop them. It was as if the bloodlust had engulfed them all. Archelaus stood up and walked over to the man. "So, Captain, do you think that the robbers killed the family? Or do you think they have another camp in the area?"

The captain thought for a few seconds and then said that they had searched a radius of three miles and found nothing, no tracks, nobody, nothing. With this, Archelaus nodded, and his men instantly fell upon the captain and killed him. "Now I've got to go out there and find out what happened. Leave the spies in place. Tell them to look for anything out of the ordinary." He ordered then, dismissing his men.

As he poured himself a goblet of wine, Archelaus wondered if this trader was involved or if he had been just available when Shophan decided to sell out. He would have to go to Emmaus and see this Titus Ben Tob and decide just how to proceed.

Meanwhile in Emmaus, Jacob had had the area around the farm searched and found where the spies had watched. Matthan stood at his elbow and thought how much this man was like his brother. Matthan liked him. "Matthan, send some men to meet those people coming down out of the hills. I don't want them around the main buildings just yet. Where can we put them temporarily? Should those spies come back, I don't want things to seem unusual to them. If I know Herod, they'll be back and watching everything again. Also, since I'm supposed to be from Cyprus, the rooms will have to reflect that culture. I brought quite a bit from home, so we should be able to make the change quite easily."

"We can take them to a compound that is far enough away that they can be told what we can offer and then get them set up. It's not too far, and we can keep an eye on them too if needed. They'll be comfortable there, and we'll get them well. Does this meet your need, Master?"

Jacob thought for a moment and responded, "Yes, Matthan. And thank you. We're still going to have to watch our steps for quite a while. The family will be so glad when this ends. But with the Romans here, I'm sure something else will happen. It always does."

Four days later, Archelaus rode out of Jerusalem and headed for Emmaus. His head ached from all the wine he had drunk the night before, but he had to be done with this mess once and for all. His father had already written six wills, and he didn't want the old man changing his mind again. The old fox could still disinherit him at a whim. Why couldn't he just die? Archelaus pondered.

It was afternoon before they arrived at the farm. Jacob had known when they left Jerusalem, for he had spies too. The house had been transformed and was a mix between Roman and Cyprus décor. The colors were more brilliant and lustrous than the original style. Cushions and draping curtains were everywhere. Jacob and Matthan had both agreed that it looked a little like a harem. Then they both laughed, for neither of them had ever seen one. Jacob assured Matthan that this was how the Romans decorated their villas, so he felt sure that whomever Herod sent would recognize the décor as authentic.

Jacob was not careless. He had figured that Herod would send Archelaus to check on him. He had adorned himself with silks and jewels and had a large feast laid out waiting for the arrival of his uninvited guest.

Jarius had come too close to being killed for the rest of the family to be careless now. He knew as much as could be gleaned about Archelaus. He was cold-blooded, mean to the point of viciousness, but stupid. Jacob would enjoy sparring with him, but he would never let his guard down as long as Herod the Great was around.

He put on his turban when told that Herod's son had arrived and walked to the courtyard swiftly. Bowing in a wheedling manner, Jacob walked forward to greet his enemy. "My prince, you have come to welcome me to my new home. How very good of you! Come, come, I was just getting ready for lunch. Would you join me, Most Exalted One?"

Just as he had figured, Archelaus stood straighter and nodded to Jacob. Upon entering the main room, Archelaus was truly impressed by the décor. *This man could be my friend,* he thought as servants brought water for him to wash with. "I am Archelaus, son of Herod the Great. I understand that you just recently bought this home place. Could you tell me why? Wouldn't Jerusalem have been a better base for your business?"

"My name, Most High One, is Titus Ben Tob, a trader of everything. But come, let's dine and have refreshments. I will tell you all about myself if you are interested. But for now, let us enjoy the food and relax."

The servants poured wine and began serving the two men. The soldiers were already being taken care of. Normally, no one would care about someone else's servants or men, but Jacob wanted to make a good impression on everyone. He knew this was a wise approach. Make friends everywhere was one of his father's adages. He intended to keep his head firmly on his shoulders.

Archelaus had not enjoyed such an array of exotic foods since his days in Rome. *This man knew how to live,* he thought as he downed goblet after goblet of wine. And the wine, it was superb. "Tell me, Titus, how on earth have you managed such food and wine. It is wonderful." Archelaus slurred. Already the wine's potency was making him sleepy.

"Then I will send you two very large casks of it, my prince. Now what is it you wish to know about me?" Watching the drunken sod of a prince amused Jacob. *This idiot has no wiles at all*, he thought. The man reacted like he didn't plan at all. Power, yes, but he was nothing like his father from what he had heard. All the same, he wouldn't underestimate him.

Hours later, as Archelaus prepared to return to Jerusalem, he felt wonderful. He had a new friend and someone to supply him with anything he could want. And as far as the Shophan family, this man had never met them. His father had made all the arrangements months before exiling him to Emmaus. Archelaus felt as though he had a kindred spirit in Titus Ben Tob.

Jacob watched as the mounted horsemen headed back to Jerusalem. He frowned, concerned that he had overplayed his part. He had a feeling that Archelaus was going to be coming around regularly. Well, he would just have to be absent himself occasionally. After all, he was a trader and must be about his business.

Sitting under an arbor, he began writing a letter to Tyre. He was just finishing it when Matthan entered. "Master, the spies are back in the same place," he said. "Also, the people are down from the hills. They are really going to need help. Three younger women have five children between them. There are two elderly men and two elderly women. One has worked with sheep, so I'm letting her handle a few in the sheepfold there."

"I really don't know what to do with them, Matthan. Do you have any ideas?"

"Well, Master, two of the younger women want to go back to their homes. One is from Bethany and the other from a town in Samaria. Why not send them home with some money? They'll be happier, and they won't be around here. Also, the two older women say they'll take care of the men. That will just leave the one younger woman and one child. I can put her to work and give her one of the smaller houses in the shepherd's compound."

"Yes, let's do it that way. Also, Matthan, I don't want to be involved at all in this. I'm going to have to put up the persona of being a flippant, spoiled son of a foreigner. Let these people think that you are following the orders of the former owner. That way they won't be able to associate me with Jarius. I can't have that happening as long as Archelaus is around."

Meanwhile, Jarius and Amos were moving slowly toward the west. They had decided to use donkeys so that Jarius could mount with more ease. His leg was getting better, and it tried his patience to take it so slowly, but he knew it was important not to endanger his healing. Amos was truly excellent in his care of Jarius. He did everything, and in the evening when they stopped, they shared their experiences. Jarius was careful not to expand too much on his troubles, but that left plenty for them to talk about.

Amos had been sold into slavery by his uncle when he was nine. His owner hadn't been too bad, but when he fell on hard times, he sold Amos to another man. By this time, he was becoming a man, and his owner's wife had not failed to notice. Several times she had tried to seduce him, but he had remained careful of involvement. Finally, she had cornered him. He either did as she wanted or she would tell her husband he had stolen from them. Not sure what to do, he had run and had been running ever since. Six years now and his circumstances had continued to disintegrate until he had fallen in with the bandits.

And that more or less brought him up to the present. Amos's hatred of Herod had come from his slavery. Herod's law had overridden the Roman edicts in that Roman slaves could work for their freedom. Under the rules set by Herod, this wasn't so. Amos would always be a slave here in this country.

On the sixth day, they came to the Mediterranean Sea. Now all they would have to do was to wait until the ship came for them. Jarius was eager to join Mariam and the children and go on to Damascus. He had offered Amos a job, and the young man had eagerly accepted. Amos had liked the fairness of Jarius and felt a kindred spirit with the man. Right now, anything looked better than what he had experienced so far. With this man, he saw possibilities for a better life. He was as anxious as his new employer for the safety of the ship.

They had taken care to camp a short distance from the beach, but in the evening, they would walk down to the shoreline and look for a signal from the boat. So far, they had not seen anyone and hoped that it would continue this way. On their third night, a light blinked from offshore, and they returned the signal. Shortly a rowboat came in, and the two men got in. One of the seamen stayed behind to lead the donkeys up the coast to their usual landing. He would leave the animals there and catch the next ship that put in.

At last, Jarius could sleep and not worry. The boat was not stopping until it reached Tyre. His relief was such that he slept for two nights and a day. On the second day when he awoke, he was famished, and Amos, who had been watching over him, was there with food and water when he finally sat up.

"I was beginning to worry about you," he said as he settled down next to Jarius. "Guess you were tired and a little stressed. But this salty air, isn't it wonderful? I've never been on the sea before. It's so fresh and clean."

"Yes, but it has its problems too, my friend. Instead of bandits, there are pirates and storms that make you appreciate being on dry land. It's just like life anywhere. It has its good points and bad." And with this said, they both lay back and enjoyed the warm sun and refreshing wind.

Chapter 9

Mariam was spinning when Samuel found her sitting in the garden. It had become her haven. She could work yet still keep an eye on the children. Demas had been shocked when his father hadn't accompanied his mother to Tyre. The young boy was fast becoming a man with worries. He devoted his attention to his uncle's instructions. Even Samuel was surprised at how swiftly the boy grasped the dealings he handled. But ever so often when he was quiet, Samuel would see Demas look out toward the port longingly. The boy truly loved his father deeply.

"We've news at last. The courier just brought a letter from Jacob. That scamp has already entertained the king's son, Archelaus, and he says that Jarius and a friend are heading for the sea. They'll be picked up by one of our boats. I have the captain sailing up and down along the coast from Egypt to our landing right now, so he should be here within ten days. Praise the Lord, he is a good God.

He said that Jarius broke his leg, and that's the cause of the slower travel. But he's well and on the way, Mariam."

Deep inside, Mariam felt herself slowly breaking down. She had been strong for the children, but now she could no longer hold herself together. She bent over and began to sob. Demas came in just then and, grabbing his mother, rocked her in his arms as she had done so many times for him. Looking questioningly at his uncle, he saw the smile on his face and suddenly knew that his father was well. Samuel turned and walked into the house to let his wife know the news. The sun was setting before Mariam raised her head and looked into the face of her firstborn. He was so much like his father, strong and courageous. From now on, the men could carry the burden of decisions and heroism. She liked being a wife and mother. This role was the one she liked best. Helping her to her feet, Demas guided his mother inside, clinging to each other now out of joy and not fear.

As Jarius and Amos walked toward Samuel's home, Amos was awestruck at everything he saw. It was different from the places he had been to before. At last, they came to Samuel's house and entered the gate. Suddenly, Jarius found his arms full. Mariam had almost leaped into his arms, and the children were all clinging to him too. Amos stood off to the side, not knowing quite what to do. Then a young boy, who could only be the son of his friend, walked over to him.

"You must be Amos. Words can't tell you how much we owe you for what you've done for our father. But come, we offer our hospitality and our gratitude." Impressed by the young man's demeanor, Amos followed him and the family into their home.

The dinner was truly a happy and joyous occasion. Amos sat with all the Shophans and enjoyed the laughter and stories everyone had to tell. They were especially delighted with Jacob's description of how he had entertained Archelaus. Even though he was their enemy, his superficiality was funny to them all. Jarius was glad that Matthan had hit it off with Jacob. Jacob had always been the scamp of the family, ready to try anything. However, both Jarius and Samuel were worried for him. Just one slip and Archelaus would not hesitate to have him killed. They would have to keep in constant communication with him and protect him as much as would be possible from their distant homes. Jacob was loved by everyone, especially the children. He played games with them, and they felt they could tell him anything. He was more a friend than a kinsman.

Jarius's leg was almost healed, but he still used a staff to lean on when he walked about. They would soon be leaving for Damascus. The caravan would be well-guarded and quite large. Mariam had found many things in the Shophan warehouses to replace what she had been forced to leave behind. She was glad that the people who had aided her husband could use their things left in Emmaus. Jacob would be sending their more personal possessions directly to Damascus. Mariam was anxious now to go to her new home and get settled. She just wanted to feel safe again, if that were ever going to be possible. She still had not told Jarius about the new baby. It would not be long before he knew.

Samuel and Jarius had been talking about the next steps to be taken concerning Demas. He had an amazing memory and was already able to do many things in the business. However, Samuel said he felt that Demas preferred shepherding to trading. Jarius agreed, but the boy still had to learn about their whole operation. If he retained as well as Samuel said, he might not have to stay as long at the different cities where they had businesses. And if it became safe again to return to Emmaus, he could live there and run the sheep flocks; only time would tell when that could be.

Demas and Amos had become fast friends and did nearly everything together. Naturally, Amos was not allowed to know about the other Shophan families nor the extent of their business dealings. This was family business only. Samuel and Jarius did wonder, though, how Archelaus had found out about them in Emmaus. They would ask Jacob to see if he could find out from Archelaus, but only if he felt he wasn't endangering himself. They still didn't know if anything else had slipped into Archelaus's hands. They did feel sure that no one, including Herod, knew about the rest of the family. However, they would not let down their guard.

One of their sailors had taken over the house at their landing. He had been with the family for many years and was ready to stay on shore. Jacob was planning on going in a caravan to Egypt. He didn't want to be at Archelaus's every beck and call. Also, he said they were going to incur some high expenses for gifts that he would have to give to Herod's son. Not too many, but enough to make him think he was considered a friend. Otherwise, he enjoyed the sheep and animals for a change. He did like to go into Jerusalem occasionally.

This was somewhat worrisome to the two older brothers, but Jacob was Jacob, and they couldn't restrain him too much. He would be careful, only not as prudent as they would have desired. They really wished that he would find another wife. Since Ruth had died, he had lapsed into his wondering ways again. A wife would have a settling effect on him, so they decided to look around for a good woman for him. They could only hope that in the meantime, Jacob wouldn't underestimate Herod or his son.

Finally, the day of departure came. The field about the house was a maze of pack animals and people. Children were running about and screaming as Jarius and Samuel said their farewells. Mariam had already said her good-byes and was making sure that the children were firmly secured on their mounts. It was already getting warm, and the air was thick with dust and flies. Bells tinkled on the livery covering the camels. At last, the leader blew his horn, and the caravan of camels, donkeys, and mounted men started off toward the east and home. The caravan contained over 150 camels, donkeys, and oxen. There were one hundred mounted and armed men. The Shophans no longer took chances of having their caravans raided. They moved masses of trade goods, and they were able to keep their merchants happy by always having everything available. The guards were as much of an investment as everything else that they had. The trading part of the business was huge, and it took all of the family to make it work. They exported and imported from all over the known world—spices and silks from China and India; exotic plants and foods from Ethiopia and Egypt; frankincense, oils, wine, dyed clothes, and fish from all over the Mediterranean Sea. If people were willing to pay, the Shophans would find whatever they desired and bring it to them.

Several times, bandits had attempted to raid their caravans, but with permission from the various governors, sheiks, etc., the Shophans mounted their own protective cavalry and had prevailed against further attacks from happening. Even so, at all times when they traveled, they were always on the alert. The Shophans set up stations where the caravans could stop and rest. In many cases, retired employees managed these inns. Wherever there was a need, the Shophans tried to fill it. It was amazing that the Romans hadn't found out about them, probably because each brother or sister had a different name. The extent of their business was unknown, and they worked to keep it that way. Not even servants knew of all the family, perhaps, the nearest brother or sister, but never more than that. Their father, Samaes Ben Ahimelek, had arranged it this way, and they didn't plan to change it unless it became prudent to do so. Their main concern was Herod and his family and to avoid them at all cost.

Damascus was like many cities in the world,—not really too far away but still a long walk. From Tyre to this ancient of cities was less than one hundred miles, but it was over hills, rock, sand, and switchbacks. It was a long walk and one that took about five to six days. When the walls of the city finally appeared, everyone was glad the trip was over. Jarius had been looking at Mariam strangely the whole journey, finally coming up to her and telling her that their new home was very near now.

With much braying and commotion, the camels kneeled, and Jarius and Demas began sorting out what went where. At last, Mariam and the children were led to the gates of their new home. Although tired, she was curious what type of home Jacob had had. He was more contemporary than traditional. His wife had died the second year, so she wouldn't have made much of an imprint on the house. Mariam was the typical woman and wanted to see everything and began to make plans.

To her surprise, it was very similar to Beth Enajim. The house was built in a U shape. Sleeping quarters, which opened out onto the inner courtyard, were upstairs. A large fountain splashed in the center of a large pool filled with lilies and plants. It was very pleasant. As she turned to look for the kitchen, there stood the largest man she had ever seen. He wore a turban and a solid white jacket and trousers. He bowed to her and said, "Madam, I'm sorry I was not here to meet you. I am your steward, Baba. Come, I have refreshments awaiting you."

"Not right now, Baba." Mariam smiled to show her appreciation before continuing. "Where is the kitchen? Please show me the rooms of the house."

Baba smiled, for he liked Mariam's interest in the house rather than the care of herself. He led the way, smiling at the comments the children made. "Uncle Jacob sure has a big house, Mother. Where will we stay? Do you think he has a stable? I sure could use a bird or lamb for company. Is this going to be our new home? Is there anything to eat? I'm hungry, Mother."

Finally, in a back room near the kitchen, Baba laid out food and drink for everyone. The children sat down on the cushions, but they couldn't take their eyes off all the fruit, nuts, and sweetbreads. "We must wash children and wait for your father. He will be here shortly." Then to her surprise, young ladies brought in towels and basins of water.

"Baba, how many servants do we have?" Mariam asked.

Lela K. King

Baba responded, "For household duties, there are seven women. In the gardens are four men, and in the stables there are three more men. If you need more help, just tell me, Mistress, and I will get them for you."

"No, Baba," Mariam looked around. "I think that we have sufficient help for now. After I see everything, I'll know what is truly needed."

Just then, Jarius and Demas arrived, and so they all sat. The safe journey, food, and new house were blessed. Afterward, Mariam took the children to their rooms to rest, and she and Jarius sat down to talk.

"Mariam, is something wrong? You seem different somehow. You're not sick or anything, are you? I know this whole thing has been unbelievably hard on you and the children. But you can relax now, and we will have a whole new life here."

"Jarius, I am not sick. We are going to be blessed with another child in four months. And except for being tired, I feel very good, just curious of what surprises this new house holds for me. There are so many servants, but we may just need more here than we did before. Do you mind much?"

"Mariam, you can have fifty servants if you want them, anything for you, dearest. These past few months have shown me what we should treasure most, and that's our wives and children. All else are just extras. When I thought you were out in the desert alone with the children and I was helpless to do anything but pray for you and the children's safety, I was so lost. For myself, I cared nothing but only to get to you and protect you. And now we've come home, and a new child will be born here. God is continuing to bless us, sweetheart. Somehow, someway, everything will be okay."

Jacob had been to the temple, but as he left, he suddenly had an urge to see Beth Enajim. He had incorporated fountains and ponds in his Damascus home, but he found that his grandfather and brother had not done the same thing with their home in Emmaus. If he had not had to be a part of the family's businesses, he would have loved to have gone to sea and traveled. After his wife had died, he had thought about doing it, but days and then months passed and he was still a trader. Now he really wished that he had gone ahead and done what he truly had desired to do.

He didn't really care for Emmaus, and even Jerusalem wasn't that interesting to him. When Herod died and the family could relax, then he would go to sea. His bodyguard was never more than a few paces behind him. This was his one concession to Samuel and Jarius—a bodyguard. It would have been laughable if his brother's recent troubles hadn't made the whole family aware of the danger that they were still in. And he had Herod's son coming to see him regularly. The whole situation was ridiculous.

As he approached the gates to the old family home, he could see that it was being restored. How often he had visited his great-grandfather here and sailed boats in the various ponds. Time was passing too swiftly. He was only thirty-one, and yet he had been married, widowed, and operated a major trading center for over eight years. He wished that he would have had a few sons and daughters, but with the situation the way it was, maybe it was just as well that he hadn't. He was mobile and able to do some traveling, but not half as much as he would have liked to do. It really hadn't bothered him that much to leave Damascus. Actually, he wanted to go to Ephesus or Rhodes. Maybe he could yet.

Just then, a centurion rode through the gates and stopped in front of Jacob. "You like my house?" he queried.

"Yes, centurion. I was here several times when I was younger. I'm glad to see that it is being restored."

"My name is Gauis Asti Attilo, sir. And what is your name?"

"My name is Titus Ben Tob. I'm sorry if I've blocked your way. I'll leave if it's okay with you." Jacob turned to leave when Gauis called to him.

"No, wait. It's strange, but a few months back, a young lad said that he was familiar with my home too. It or its previous owner must have been very popular."

"His name was Joseph Ben Ehud, centurion. He was a member of the Sanhedrin, so he probably did have many guests. Thank you for your time. I'm a trader. If you should need anything, I would be glad to help you. I live in Emmaus now, just newly arrived from Cyprus."

"Do you know the Shophan family in Emmaus? The lad was from there too."

"No, I didn't know them personally. My father bought the land and house from the Shophan family. I was sent to manage it for him."

"Do you know where they went to? I rather liked the boy."

"No. When I arrived, they had already left. Good day." And with that, Jacob turned and walked back into the city. *Wonderful,* he thought. *Of all the bad luck to meet that soldier and he knew of Demas. I'm going to have to avoid this part of town from now on.* With this, he and his guard entered into the maze of streets and were swallowed up by the teeming life that abounded there.

Chapter 10

Demas enjoyed working with his father. Together they were learning how to manage the business in Damascus. Over a year had passed, and he had not only been to On in Egypt for six months, but he had been to Antioch and Tarsus. His new brother, Joseph, had been born, and the family had done some changes to the house. His mother was happier than she had been for a long time. The children liked their new friends, and he liked being treated as an adult. He still enjoyed the sea and liked taking boats to various places, but he missed shepherding his sheep more than anything else he did. They kept a sheepfold outside the gates, but he was so busy most of the time that he seldom got to go and tend the sheep. His father could walk without a limp now, and he seemed younger than before. The strain that he had been under must have been harder on him than he or the others had known. In Damascus, it was as if he had been reborn.

Just as Demas started out the door for home and lunch, his father joined him. He had a letter in his hand and seemed agitated. But Demas waited until they were in their house before Jarius turned and said, "Demas, do you remember the miracle we witnessed out in the fields of Bethlehem?"

"Yes, Father. I think of it often. Why, what has happened?"

"Apparently, some wise men from the east went to King Herod and said that a star had led them to the new king of Israel. Where was he, they asked. Herod had his soothsayers read up on the prophecies, and they said Bethlehem. He sent his soldiers to Bethlehem and all the surrounding towns and had all the male children under the age of two slain. The man is crazy. If we had still been in Emmaus, Joseph would have been killed too. Don't tell your mother about this. She would panic. In time, she'll find out, but not now."

"Do you think he escaped, Father? Surely God protected him somehow. Dear Lord, how can God allow that man to live with all that he has done?"

"His reckoning will come, Demas. And he will face God's judgment. I'm concerned with Jacob now more than ever. He has had to entertain Herod's son regularly. I fear for him. Maybe we should lease out the lands in Emmaus and get Jacob out of there. I have the same bad feelings that I had when your grandfather was murdered and we had to come here. I think that you and I had better go to Tyre and talk this over with Samuel."

Jarius mentioned a trip that he and Demas would take to Tyre to Mariam, and she was so content that she only asked when they would be leaving. He tried to be casual and said that they would leave the following week. Mariam looked at Jarius and nodded, but in that split second of eye contact, he knew that she knew something had happened. He was determined to keep it from her until he got back.

As they lay down to sleep that night, Mariam snuggled into Jarius's arms and hugged him. "Now, sweetheart, what has happened?"

Jarius thought of holding back again but couldn't. They had shared too much, and he couldn't stop as he told her what had happened and what he thought they should do. Tears flowed down her cheeks, and she wept as she rubbed her newly pregnant belly and thought of all those innocent babes being slaughtered. Then, she curled into his arms and told him that she agreed. It was time for Jacob to get out.

In six days, Jarius and Demas had reached Tyre. This time, Demas was present as his father and uncle decided it was time to get Jacob out of Emmaus. There was a farmer in Bethany who had often said he would like to lease their lands. The letter was written to Josias of Bethany, stating that the lands would now be for lease. If he was still interested, he could contact Titus Ben Tob in Emmaus and sign the agreements. Then they wrote to Jacob and told him what they were doing. Jacob could choose what he wanted to do now that he was free to leave Emmaus. That Josias of Bethany would be in contact with him. They felt that he should bring a caravan up the eastside of the Jordan and then cut across to Damascus north of the Sea of Gennesaret. He was to bring Matthan with him.

Chapter 11

Jacob stomped into the house and threw his turban across the living room. Matthan stood off to the side with a tray with a cup of tea on it. "And was the prince his usual pompous self today, Master?" He mused.

"Matthan, every time that man comes here, I want to scrub myself thoroughly when he leaves. And did you hear him when he justified Herod having all those babies killed? I wanted to go for his throat. I don't know how much longer I can put up with this, my friend."

"Maybe not for long, Master. Here's a letter from Tyre. Maybe they have news for you."

Jacob had just started to read the letter when they were told that soldiers had entered the courtyard. Jacob quickly put his turban back on, straightened his clothing, and smiled as he walked into the entry. There stood the centurion, Gauis Attilio. "Well, well, centurion. Welcome to my humble home. Come, sit and let my man get us some refreshments."

As Jacob motioned to Matthan to bring some food and drink, he turned to Gauis and asked, "Sir, we offer hospitality to all who come to our doors. Would you mind if we serve something to your men too?"

"That's a refreshing idea, Titus. Thank you. Yes, if you don't mind. It's been a warmer-than-usual ride today. We come from the King's Highway."

"The King's Highway! Then you've been in the eastern part of the country, haven't you?"

"Yes, and today I found out what your good King Herod has been up too. I'm going to be frank with you, Titus, for I've been checking up on you and the Shophans. Herod doesn't much care for them, does he?"

"You said you've been checking up on me. And what have you found that interests you, sir?"

"For one, I believe that you do know the Shophans. I also believe that directly or indirectly you and they are related to the Ahimelek family. Am I getting warm?"

"Please continue, centurion," Jacob answered calmly. His eyes narrowed, and he felt for the dagger at his waist.

"I am a Roman centurion. I am also from an old Roman family, which loved the republic when it was one. I still do my job, but thank the gods that I wasn't here for that slaughter that just took place. I don't know what I would have done to avoid carrying out the order. I know that you have no reason to trust me, but I would like to make a start at being friends. I have been all over the known world and met my wife in Ephesus. She is Jewish. No one else knows that but you. When I was given orders to come to Jerusalem, Hannah was overjoyed at coming to the Holy City of your God. She loves our house, but she fears for me because she knows I hate the Herods. She wants me to put in for duty somewhere else, or even quit and go back home. She feels that more terrible things are going to happen."

"That's quite a story, Attilo. But why should I believe you? You know that Archelaus comes here frequently. If I tell him and you are telling the truth, you're in trouble. If I say nothing and you're lying, then he will think just what you have stated. You can see that you have put me into a quandary of sorts. You will have to say a little more before I will believe you." With this, Jacob walked over and sat down. Attilo followed him.

"Okay, how's this? My father has businesses in Cyprus. When he checked into your story, he found that there is a Tob family. They have five daughters but no sons, and neither do they have a business here. Also, I know that you or the Shophans have a cove on the Great Sea almost directly across from here, and that they have boats that put in there regularly. I also know that you have contacts in Tyre that you correspond with. For your protection, we have paid the Tobs to say they have a son here and have bought lands that you are managing. That's in case your good prince makes any inquiries. Does this information help?"

"Okay. Apparently, you are a much better tracker than the royal family. I will tell you about the Shophans. Then you will realize what has been happening." With this, Jacob told Attilo about Jarius and his family only. He wasn't about to go into the relationships of the rest of the family. He told Attilo why the family had to leave so quickly and what had almost happened to them. He didn't tell him where they were. He did say they were safe now and hopefully out of harm's way.

Attilo sat and looked at Jacob directly into his eyes. "Yes, you look a little like Demas. Nothing that has been said here will go any further. I will tell you this. Herod is extremely sick, both physically and mentally. He will probably die within the year. When he does die, I believe that none of his sons will be given total jurisdiction like he has. My father, who is a senator, believes that Caesar will break the area up into tetrarchs for each of the boys that are still alive. Unfortunately, Archelaus will probably get Jerusalem, Idumea, and Samaria. He doesn't know how to rule. He gets out of control easily, and I'm sure that you have realized he's not smart but sneaky. He kills without thought. I don't believe he loves anyone and will sacrifice anything that stands in his way. He is even more vicious than his father is, if that is at all possible. I tell you this because I have already decided to leave here. My wife finds it hard being accepted by her people since she is married to a gentile. If I were you, I would get out of here too."

"Thank you, Gauis. For some reason, I do believe you. And I'm hoping that I will be leaving myself soon. I don't know when, but I will let you know."

With this said, the two men walked side by side out into the courtyard. When all were mounted, Jacob walked up and grasped Attilo in an arm shake. "Good-bye, friend. May God bless you and your family." And with that, the soldiers rode out and up the road to Jerusalem.

Jacob rushed back into the house and read the letter that he had received earlier. When finished, he sat down and smiled. *At last, I'm going to go to sea,* he thought. Then calling Matthan, he made plans for their journey.

He had liked Josias and, after signing the contracts, couldn't help but ask if he wasn't worried about the way things were politically. Josias had just smiled and said what would be would be. His son would actually stay in Bethany. The son was married and had a boy and two girls. He and his wife liked being closer to the temple, but he himself would be moving to take over in Emmaus. He liked working with animals, and with the seasoned shepherds that were staying, he knew he could make it all work.

With everything loaded, Jacob and Matthan mounted their camels, and the long caravan moved eastward across the desert toward the King's Road. For the first time in months, Jacob drew in a deep breath. He was almost giddy with the thought of no more sand, just water and lots of it. At first, he wondered what he would do about Baba, who had loyally stayed behind and served his oldest brother's family. But news had been sent that Baba was anxious for his master to get to Damascus so that they could go to sea. Good Ole Baba—he was only a few years older than Jacob was, but they had been together for years. Now they would be renewing their friendship and sailing like they had always wanted to do. Life was getting better every day as they got closer to Damascus.

Matthan was happy too. He missed his master. He liked Jarius's calmer and reserved attitude. Jacob was nice, but he lived on the edge of life, taking chances. Matthan was getting too old to enjoy this type of excitement. He wanted the joy and peace of the family that he had been with forever.

Damascus lay 175 miles from Jerusalem. Since they had to go to the east before going north, they had added another fifty or so miles to the journey. But before the month's end, they could see the city rising out of the sands on the horizon. Everyone was glad to see his or her destination. Wind, sand, and being on the alert constantly made the trip seem endless at times. But they were almost home. Tonight they would sleep in beds instead of on the ground.

Part 2

Chapter 12

The wind swept the decks as Demas grasped the rudder ropes tighter. Jacob stood off to the side, watching his nephew guide the boat on its course to Ephesus. How long had it been since he had been the captain of one of the family ships? The years had literally flown by, and now his nephew was a grown man. The family was doing very well, and he himself was married and had children.

He had met Gaius's daughter on one of his stopovers in Ephesus. He and Gaius had become very close friends, and then one evening he had seen and met Alyssa. He couldn't help smiling when he thought about his wife. She was lovely. But most of all, she was spirited. She would tease him, love him, but she never failed to speak out if she felt he was becoming too much of a tyrant. Their home in Ephesus was his Garden of Eden on earth. It was his sanctuary and his castle. And his twin sons were just like Alyssa—strong-willed but handsome and loving. He was truly blessed. Actually, he could see his seafaring days coming to a close soon. He wanted to be with his family. Mercy, he was becoming like his brothers. But then who better to emulate? His brothers and sisters were the biggest gift of all. When they got together, the joy and love that flowed between them all was almost overwhelming. He couldn't wait to get back home.

"You know, Jacob, if I didn't know better, I'd say you were excited about getting home." Jacob had become Demas's best friend. They had sailed together, fought together, and had some good adventures too. He knew Alyssa, and it wouldn't be long before she grounded him from the sea. Too bad, but Jacob deserved his share of happiness. Demas certainly wouldn't expect him not to enjoy his family on a more daily basis.

That evening, the sea had calmed and was only choppy, opposite to its earlier ferocity. Jacob and Demas were relaxing under the canopied shelter at the rear of the boat. "Demas, do you remember when our troubles first really began? It seems just like yesterday to me. Do you think that means I'm getting old?"

"Hardly, Jacob. I was fourteen at the time, and I still have nightmares about it. Not as often as before, thanks to the new adventures you've gotten me into, but memories are with you always. Just think of what has happened since we left Judea. Herod the Great died four months after having all those children slain. Then your good friend and prince became tetrarch of the area. Archelaus must have been insane to have all those people killed on Pentecost. Then he continued to do so many horrid things, and even tried to con Caesar into believing it wasn't his fault. Believe me, when Samaritans and Jews agree on something, it must be bad. They traveled together all the way to Rome to get Caesar to get rid of him, which he did. Even Nicolaus from Damascus couldn't help him. Now Archelaus is exiled to Gaul, and for the most part, our days of fearing the Herods are over. Now we only have to concern ourselves with the Romans, pirates, bandits, rebels, etcetera.

"I thought those bad times would never end. Now they're over, and I want to enjoy my family. Those boys of mine are getting to be a handful for Alyssa. Besides, the sea is losing its fascination. What are your plans? Are you going to continue to sail or help out your father? You've been fortunate in being able to see several places and their opportunities. Isn't it about time you started looking for a wife too?"

Demas just smiled as he remembered his mother asking the same question. She had cautioned him not to rush things but, at least, to be open to thinking about settling down. Demas, her firstborn, had always had a special place in her heart. He had been her strength many times over the years. She wasn't particularly happy to see him go to sea, but she knew that eventually he would come home to stay and to raise his sheep. Yes, she knew his dream of returning to their old home. One of these days, he would walk ashore for good. He had been sailing with Jacob for years now, but he had never given up hope of returning to Emmaus and shepherding again. Silly how something like tending sheep had always been his first love. His father knew this kind of life, and so had his grandfather. Shepherding was a calling and a love of sorts. Anyway, it was his hope. Plus, he was still looking for the Son of God. He knew he was out there somewhere, and someday he would find him. He must be around twelve years old now. One of these days, Demas would have his prayer answered. He knew it in his heart.

Demas stroked his short beard. He was built like his father—broad-shouldered and six feet tall. His eyes were light brown with green specks. The years of being on the sea had made him a deep brown, and like most seafaring men, he had wrinkles on the edges of his eyes from squinting out over the seas. He and Jacob kept their hair short. For a while, he had let his hair grow long and tied it back, but he couldn't keep it clean that way, and the ocean spray mixed with sweat made it wiry. So he finally cut it short and had kept it that way for a couple of years now. Both he and Jacob had enjoyed the Roman baths and frequented them whenever possible. Sometimes their Jewish friends would comment on their gentile habits, but neither man cared and paid no attention to the remarks. Jacob was leaner and somewhat taller, but he carried himself with such a demeanor of dignity that you had to look closely at their faces to see that they were related.

Demas lay back and gazed into the night skies. No moon showed, and the darkness was stygian black. Again, he remembered the night that he was on that hillside outside of Bethlehem. *I will see the Lord,* he thought.

Jacob looked intently at Demas. "Are you thinking again about the birth of God's son?" he asked.

Demas looked intently at Jacob and then said, "Why did he come? Where is he? And why was he born in a stable to poor people? I'm beginning to see something else in God's plan. I don't think he came to put his son on the throne of Israel. I think he's going to change our minds, our ways, and make us all aware that God loves us all, and it's time for us to have a more personal relationship with him."

Suddenly, Baba appeared and whispered to Jacob and Demas. "I saw the outline of a ship off the port awhile back. It was dark, but then I heard whispers and a yelp. I think we may have pirates about. What should we do?"

Jacob and Demas both reached for their weapons at the same time. "Quietly rouse the men. Tell them we may be boarded, so get ready," Jacob answered back. They put out the fire and slowly walked over to the port railing. The wind was snapping the sails, and the water was still rough as a breeze rolled across it. Straining to hear or see, they stood alert. The men all crept up onto the deck, their swords in hand. Too many times they had met these killing thieves who thrived on the ships that plied the trading routes of the seas. These were all experienced sailors, and they knew what to expect if captured. When it came down to the choice between being freemen or slaves, the answer was easy. And so they were able to dish out more than what they had received in the past. They all breathed softly, but that didn't stop the sheen of sweat forming on their brows. These barbarians could be ferocious. They appeared to have no fear of death, and yet they were usually surprised when they met up with men willing to fight to the death for their freedom.

Suddenly, the sound of heavy breathing assailed the men. The pirates were near. But where were they? The moonless night made it impossible to see in the darkness. All at once, flaming arrows filled the sky. Jacob and Demas were everywhere, dousing the fires and giving orders. Then the two ships rammed into each other, and the men were suddenly fighting a bloody battle. Demas climbed the mast to see what the other ship was like and how many were trying to board their own vessel. The sail and boat were black, and he could see that the pirates were a mixture of peoples. Their firepot was left unattended, so he decided to swing across and dump it over onto the deck. That would cause them to back off the attack.

Jacob looked up just as Demas sailed through the air to the other boat. *Good God Almighty,* he thought. *What is he doing?* Demas smacked into the spar and started lowering himself. Then he felt a searing pain shoot through his side. It was an arrow. As he landed on the deck, a pirate sprang at him and would have skewered him if he hadn't been alert. He grasped the rope and, using it, swung over the enemy's head. Then as he looped back, he hacked the pirate in the neck. His side was throbbing now, but he had to reach the firepot. So far, none of the other pirates had noticed him, and he wasn't staying around any longer than he had too. The pitch was still boiling as he slopped the pot over and lit the oil. It spread out like a flaming wave on the shore. As he turned to climb the mast, he heard a cry below his feet. Seeing a hatch, he chopped open the latch and raised the lid. There were people reaching for him. He started to leave but turned back and looked again. There were women in there too, and they didn't look like they belonged there. He reached down and grabbed an arm and pulled back. A young man came out of the hole first. Then they were both lifting people out.

"Jump overboard. It's your only chance. We'll get to you after the fighting is over." With flames leaping higher and higher, it didn't take them long to start climbing the rail and jumping into the sea. Some grabbed boards or anything that would float as they went over the side. Then the pirates saw what was happening and turned toward Demas. He joined the others as they swam around the prow of the pirate ship toward Jacob and their boat. Jacob had already had the pirate ship pushed away from their vessel. The pirates were too busy fighting the fire to resume the fight, and so the ships drifted farther apart.

"Ahoy. Jacob, look out here on the water. It's Demas and several others. Help!" he yelled. Finally, some of the people reached the ship and, reaching for oars or ropes, started climbing up. Jacob saw what was happening and directed some of the crew to pull the stragglers onboard. But he couldn't see Demas. Demas had suddenly cramped and then gulped too much water. He was drifting farther from the boat but couldn't seem to lift his arms and swim. Then something banged into his head, and all went black.

"I hope you're awakening, young sir. I have nothing with which to help you. Please wake up. I can't hear or see anything, and I'm afraid."

Demas heard the voice but couldn't seem to climb from the dark pit he was in. He could see nothing, and his ears rang. *And I thought dying would be more spectacular than this.* He mused and then drifted back into the darkness he had only just struggled out from.

The pre-morning chill swept through Demas. He tried to raise himself but could only moan.

"Oh, you're awake. I was afraid you had died."

It was the same voice from before, but he couldn't focus or find where it was coming from.

"Don't move. We haven't much space on this board."

There it was again. He reached out and felt cold wet flesh in his hand. "Where are we?" he asked.

"Sir, if I knew that, I wouldn't have been so frightened. Please just lie still until the sun comes up. It shouldn't be long now."

Demas could feel the throb in his side, but it had been wrapped. *Well, so much for death.* He shrugged. Together, he and the voice waited until the morning sun rays appeared on the horizon. Turning, he looked at his unknown companion. There, not two feet from him, sat a young girl shivering in the chill wind.

"What happened? Where are the boats? Here, sit next to me. Our two bodies will help keep us a little warmer," Demas said, as he scooted upright next to the girl. They were sitting on the hatch lid. It wasn't very large, so their feet were dangling in the water. "My name is Demas, and I was on the ship that the pirates raided. Do you know what happened?"

"Not really. I climbed on this lid and was paddling when it bumped into your head. I pulled you out of the water, and by that time, I could see nothing. The ships drifted into the darkness, and then everything became silent. My name is Roxanne."

"What language are you most comfortable speaking, Roxanne? I speak several languages."

"Aramaic, I guess. I speak Latin and Greek too." A shiver ran through her, and she coughed. "I hope that someone finds us soon. I tend to get sick if I get chilled too much. I'm used to a much warmer climate, and this morning breeze and wet clothing are beginning to get to me."

Then she smiled, and Demas almost fell off the lid. He had thought she was a very young girl at first. Now he could see she was a young woman. "If I know my uncle, he will be searching for us. Keep looking as we talk. We can't have drifted too far from where we were. If you see anything, let me know. I'll try to signal with the sun's reflection on my sword."

"What a clever idea. I know we are just flotsam in the water and couldn't think how to get someone's attention. You must have a lot of experience being out on the sea."

"My family is very well-versed in survival tactics, Roxanne. That's a pretty name. I don't think I've ever heard it before. How come you were on that pirate ship?"

"Family friends were bringing me from Crete to Ephesus. We were just out two days when the pirates attacked the boat I was on. My friends were killed, but the pirates threw the rest of us into the hold of their boat because they had gotten the wrong vessel. Apparently, they meant to raid yours. They didn't have time to harm us because they wanted to find your boat and get it too. I'm originally from Rome. I was going to Ephesus to see my older sister, Hannah. She's married to a Roman tribune stationed there. His name is Gauis Asti Attilo. Have you, by chance, met him or know of them?"

Demas looked up to the sky and laughed. "Your brother-in-law is my uncle's father by marriage. This is unbelievable. Two people meeting under these circumstances in the middle of an ocean. God most certainly performs miracles." And again, he laughed until his side reminded him that it was not putting up with his mirth.

"Then you must be from the family Ahimelek? You knew that Gauis and Hannah were moving from Ephesus back to Jerusalem, didn't you? I always wanted to see our holy city, so my sister invited me to come to Ephesus and help her with the move. I was so excited. I've been living with Gauis's parents for two years now since my parents died."

"No, I didn't know that Gaius was leaving Ephesus. Is he being ordered there by Caesar?"

"Yes. It seems many of our fellow countrymen are rioting more and more. With Gaius's experience, Tiberius thought he would be helpful to the governor. So as soon as my sister heard, she wanted me to come out and join them. And that's how I ended up on this piece of wood in the ocean. I always wanted to see Jerusalem. I just didn't envision my journey being so tempestuous."

Demas liked this woman more and more, and then she nudged him and pointed toward the west. "I hope that's your ship and not the pirates again." She sighed. Demas stood, holding onto Roxanne's shoulders. It wasn't the pirates. The sail and boat weren't black, but from this distance, it was almost impossible to recognize the boat. "It's okay, it's my ship, the Phalan." He assured Roxanne.

"Phalan. What is that?" she asked.

"Phalan was a son of King David. Since David was a shepherd before he became king, I named it after his son, who also became a shepherd. I'm partial to shepherds, if that's your next question."

Demas took his knife out and began flashing the sun off it. Within moments, the ship changed course and headed for them. They watched as the ship grew larger, and soon they were helped aboard. Jacob stood still for a moment and then grabbed Demas and hugged him.

"I thought we had lost you. But leave it to my intrepid first mate to get lost at sea with a lovely female." They all laughed and then turned to get dry clothes and some food.

Later that evening, all the recovered captives lay sleeping on the deck. Demas had been doctored by Baba and was relaxing as Jacob and Roxanne talked. She was so pretty, he thought. Her hair was like golden wheat, and her eyes turned up at the outer edges. Those eyes—they sparkled with delight as she talked about living in Italy. She was twenty-five years younger than her older sister, but they were all the family that they had since the death of their parents. Their mother was Jewish, and their father was Roman. Their marriage had been very happy, but for the sake of the girls, they did not advertise their mixed ancestry. The girls were taught their religion and followed the laws handed down to Moses by God. They were kept away from most of the population, especially the men. If Gaius's parents had not been friends with the girl's parents, Gaius would never have met Hannah. When they did meet, nothing could stop their attraction for each other. They married within three months of their meeting. When Hannah followed Gaius to Ephesus, the elder Attilos more or less adopted Roxanne. Then when the fever killed her mother and father, it seemed natural for Roxanne to become part of the Attilo household. She was eighteen now and missed her sister, so when Hannah sent for her, she left Rome immediately.

She was very well-educated for a woman of her times. She spoke and read several languages, had followed the senior Attilo's career in the Roman senate, acting as his secretary regularly. She had learned household arts from Helena Attilo as well as art and music. She was an accomplished woman. She had spontaneity and the sweetest laugh that seemed to bubble up from deep inside her. Demas was totally fascinated by her.

In the days that followed, Demas and Roxanne became almost inseparable. When he had work to do, she would help the other women wash and care for the wounded. And soon the port of Ephesus appeared. Jacob had watched their love flower and was interested to see how Gaius would take the news. There was no doubt that Demas would offer marriage for Roxanne.

When they landed, Baba took over the unloading at dockside, so Jacob, Demas, and Roxanne started up Harbor Street toward the Agora marketplace and the main part of Ephesus. It was late morning, so they headed toward the senate building where they felt Gaius would already be at work.

Roxanne felt rather wobbly from being on the sea so long, but nothing was going to stop her from enjoying the sights and sound of this new land. She was wide-eyed as they walked through the length of the marketplace. Everything seemed on display. It was a mixture of exotic foods, wares, fabrics, all balancing the loud voices of a dozen languages being spoken at once. It was like a quick short tour through several countries. As they turned onto Curettes Street, a squad of Roman soldiers met them.

"Citizen Ahimelek. The Tribune Attilo asked us to meet you and tell you to proceed to his home. He's awaiting you there."

"Thank you, Claudius." Demas greeted him. "How have you been? I didn't see you that last time I was in port. The tribune said you were in Tarsus."

"Yes, it was an interesting trip. However, I did meet a woman." The soldier responded with a glint in his eye.

"Oh, I can well imagine. But when haven't you met a woman of many talents and virtues?" Jacob laughed.

The officer grinned briefly and then turned, and he and his men went back into the city. The street offered a spectacular view of villas, temples, monuments, and fountains. At the meeting point of the hills sat the governor's estate. The main gate opened onto a drive lined with trees, and at the end was a beautiful fountain spraying its misted water over the stone-lined courtyard. Hannah, Attilo, Allysa, and Jacob's sons were waiting as the voyagers approached. Then Hannah forsook her dignity and ran to Roxanne.

"You've grown up on me, little one." Hannah gushed as the sisters embraced. Soon everyone was escorted into the house, and there was laughter and joy as everyone greeted each other.

After the noon meal, the women and children disappeared, and the men gathered in Gaius's office. As they lay relaxed on couches, drinking their wine, Jacob looked up and saw a frown on Gaius's face.

"Okay, my friend. We have dined. Now what has happened? When did you get posted to Jerusalem again?"

"The emperor ordered me to report to the governor next month. The Jews are clamoring with each other as usual, but some are becoming too aggressive for their own good. Groups are attacking soldiers and destroying our baths and anything else that they can get at. Soon they will try to rise up against the Roman army itself. I fear for your nation, Jacob. Rome will never let that happen, I can assure you." Gaius lay back and shook his head sadly.

"Surely there are clearheaded leaders that know this. Is no one trying to hold the population back? What of the Sanhedrin? Is the governor doing anything to cause more trouble?"

"I really don't know, Jacob. I just have to go and see if I can do anything to ease the situation. I did buy Beth Enajim again, but I don't know what condition it is in. I wanted Hannah and Roxanne to be comfortable and safe. I can easily protect them within its walls. However, something else has come to my knowledge. When they exiled Archelaus, the soldiers under his command were sent to other units in various countries. At first, I only heard what I thought was rumor, but then a couple of these soldiers were stationed here briefly, and I got the full story. Do you remember a boy named Joel, Demas? It seems he went to Jerusalem sometime just before your grandfather's death. While there, he got caught cheating in a dice game with these particular soldiers. Instead of just throwing him into the jail, they decided to teach him a personal lesson. I gather it was somewhat rough. Anyway, about midway through their lesson, Archelaus came upon them, and the boy called out to him saying he had some information he would give for his freedom. Apparently, it worked, and the boy got away. I assumed it concerned the whereabouts of the Ahimelek family. Then, of course, shortly afterward, your grandfather died. I'm sorry to have to tell you this, but I know that your family has tried for years to find out how Herod found your grandfather. It's always worse when you realize betrayal has come from someone you know quite well."

The disbelief on Demas's face said it all. "You do believe what these soldiers said?" Demas gasped in disbelief. "I remember that Joel came back from the city bruised and sullen about that time. He wouldn't talk about it, so we left him alone. Shortly after that, we went into Jerusalem ourselves. When we came back home, Grandfather was dying. Joel disappeared that evening. I haven't heard of him since. Of course, he took much of what didn't belong to him, but we were concerned with many other things, so we did nothing. *Joel! Joel! We grew up together. We saw the coming of God's son. What made you betray the family who cared and loved you?* Demas stood and walked to the veranda.

Jacob and Gaius felt Demas's pain but could say nothing. Betrayal by anyone is one of the most painful experiences a person can have. But to be given into the hands of your enemy by someone you loved was unthinkable.

Slowly, Demas coughed and then looked to Jacob, and Jacob nodded. "Gaius, I know this seems very sudden, but I would like to ask for Roxanne's hand in marriage. I know that we haven't known each other very long, but she and I share so many things in common. I have to go on to Damascus to see my family for now, but I'll be in Jerusalem for Passover. We could be married there soon after."

Gaius smiled and leaned forward. "If Roxanne is willing, I can think of no one I'd rather see her married too. What is it about these women? Hannah and I knew we were meant for each other almost immediately too. They are very special, aren't they?"

Hannah was taken aback at first with the news of the engagement, but she remembered how she had felt with Gaius. It had been a wonderful time of love and planning. She did not like what Gaius had chosen as his livelihood, but she loved him, and then the children came, and things had worked out. She hoped that Roxanne would be just as happy as they had been. Demas seemed like a wonderful and gentle man. He would take care of Roxanne very well.

However, Hannah wasn't thrilled to have to return to Jerusalem. They would keep their home here in Ephesus, and someday they would return to it. But how many years would pass before that was possible? The Ahimeleks had offered Gaius a job, but he was determined to put in his time before retiring from Caesar's service. Thank God that he had not had to fight in many battles. He was more involved in administration than being a warrior. For this, Hannah was eternally grateful. Jacob and Alyssa would watch over their property in their absence. She would still miss her home here in Ephesus, but fortunately Roxanne would be nearby. She would not complain no matter how heavy her heart was in leaving her daughter and grandsons. All was in God's hands.

The days flew by, and finally Demas had to make ready to sail. His companion and friend of so many years planned on staying ashore for good. Jacob had finally decided to set up a trading center in Ephesus and stay put. Demas had captained many ships by himself over the years, but he would miss his uncle. They had shared so many things together, but most of all, they could talk openly with each other. There was very little that they didn't know about how the other thought or felt. They were closer than brothers. Time brought changes. He chuckled to himself, he would be married before summer was over. He knew his mother would be thrilled to know he was leaving the sea too. She never said anything, but she knew that his voyages were dangerous, and she was always concerned for him and Jacob. And now he would also be giving her another daughter. She would truly be happy.

Jarius always knew that Demas would leave the sea, so he wouldn't be upset. Hopefully, Demas could set up their trading center near Jerusalem again. Too bad he couldn't go back to Emmaus. Oh, well, he was being blessed so much already. God would see him through whatever lay ahead.

The tides waited for no one, and the whole family stood at the docks to see Demas and Baba on their way. Roxanne clung to Demas and tried not to cry. In many ways, she was frightened, but she knew she had chosen right. If Demas's parents were like Jacob, she knew that she couldn't find a better family to become a part of. But she would miss Demas so much. Her life had taken so many twists and turns, and yet what could she say? She had moved like the wind, encountering some obstacles but always being moved on toward so many wonderful things. It stunned her when she realized that soon she would be married and setting up her own home. She had dreamed of this time, but it had seemed a distant thought. Now it was actually happening. And she was going to Jerusalem too. It boggled her mind when she saw how swiftly her life had changed over the last months. She was grateful that her new husband-to-be would not be taking her back to Rome. Even though she had been born and lived there most of her life, the people were alien to her.

Of course, her religion had played a large part in her thinking. The Romans had done many things, but at what cost to their souls? They lived as though nothing counted but their own desires and power. Power seemed to be the leading force in their plans and methods. They had gods, but they were like adornments with no purpose. They were recognized but not truly held in faith. It was strange how their lives seemed meaningless. She would always love and hold the senior Attilos in her prayers and memories. They had been very good to her, although her religion had seemed to keep them at arm's length. They had respected her right to continue to practice her faith but didn't truly understand how much it was an integral part of her life. For this, she was always grateful to her parents for the foundation of her thinking. They had put her on the path to God, and she knew in her heart that it was the reason for her deep faith.

Demas finally began saying good-bye to everyone and hugged Roxanne. "It won't be long before we're together again, sweetheart. Soon we'll be married and have our own home and be together forever. Be careful and don't forget me." Then he kissed her and was gone.

Roxanne stood on the dock until the Phalan had sailed out of port. Then she turned and, not looking back, hurried to her sister's home.

Chapter 13

Demas and Baba stood at the helm of their boat as the city of Tyre rose up on the horizon. Turning and looking at his companion, Baba knew that he might never see him again, this young man whom he had grown to love. But it was all in God's hands. Their paths might again cross through this haphazard life they shared.

"Demas, I want you to know how much you and your family mean to me. It has not only brought me into a secure and profitable life but a secured one in our shared belief in God. Should you ever need me, you know how to get in touch with me. I will come."

Turning to his friend, Demas grasped his shoulders and smiled. "Your time will come too, Baba. Someday you too will be fulfilled with a wife and children. I thank you for all you've done for me and my family. We consider you one of us. And the same holds true for me. If you need me, ever, I will be there as soon as I can."

At the dock, Demas again turned to look out at the sea. It had been his home for many years, but now it was over. He was going up to Damascus to see his parents and tell them of his planned marriage. His mother would be so happy, and he knew that she would love Roxanne. His father's message to come home had come at the right moment, but he had already planned to go to Damascus to tell his family of his plan to wed. He still wondered what his father wanted. They knew his schedule and that he would have been back to them in a few months. But his father had said that it was imperative that he come as soon as possible. Merciful God, please don't let anything bad be happening again.

Baba reached out and grasped Demas's shoulder. "It is time to go. The boat is loaded. We both must go our ways."

Again, Demas grasped Baba in a hug. "Go with God, Baba. And remember, we shall be there in case of need for each other as long as we both live."

Turning their separate ways, Demas walked toward his uncle's house, and Baba jumped onboard the Phalan. Turning briefly, they waved farewell to each other and then, turning back, left from each other's sight.

He had almost reached his uncle's house when he saw him and Amos approaching.

"Welcome, nephew. Amos and I saw the boat come in and decided to come down to the docks to see you."

"Well, this is a surprise. I don't think that you have ever come to see me at the docks before. What's happening? Is there some kind of trouble with Father and Mother? I got their letter in Ephesus when Jacob and I arrived."

"No, nothing's wrong. My daughter is with your parents and about to give birth to another grandchild for me. I thought that Amos and I would go with you up to Damascus. I'm letting him come along since it's his wife having the baby."

Demas relaxed and watched the two men joke with each other. He had always liked Amos. Then two years later, after he had been helping Samuel, he had asked Samuel for Lydia's hand in marriage. He was family now and a good addition to it and the business. "When are we leaving then?" he asked.

"If you feel up to it, we'll leave tomorrow. If not, we'll leave the next day."

"Why not now? I'm ready."

"Well, I'm not. I want one good dinner before that arduous journey. Your Aunt Elizabeth said that she would be making all your favorite things tonight, and I'm going to enjoy it." Samuel laughed and slapped Demas on the back. The three men turned and reentered the courtyard of Samuel's house. Samuel had his arm about his nephew whom he looked on as a son. Demas was so like his father. He would be a great leader of the family. "Well, what's happening, Demas? Have you left the sea for a while?"

"Uncle Samuel, I'm getting married. She's Jacob's sister-in-law. I'm going to Damascus to tell my family. Jacob and Gauis will be coming to Jerusalem for Passover. We'll make the arrangements then."

"That's wonderful, but we'll be with you when you do. Your Aunt Elizabeth, Amos, and I will be going with you. We want to see our new grandchild. We were already packed when we saw your boat come in to the harbor. Now we'll have a great get-together."

Later that evening at dinner, Samuel and Amos looked stunned as Demas related how he had met Roxanne.

"You mean you've been fighting battles like this all the time you've been at sea? We knew you've had run-ins, but this is ridiculous. There must be something that we can do to protect our shipping and crews. So far, we've been fortunate to have had so few losses, but this must be addressed. Jarius and I must see what we can arrange to protect our interests. But your betrothal sounds wonderful. It's strange how we've bonded to a Roman family. But Gauis has converted to Judaism, so we are family."

"Uncle Samuel, do you know why Father has sent for me?"

"Yes, but that's for him to tell you. I think that you will be pleasantly surprised."

Demas looked at his uncle, wondering what was going on. Then he said, "Who will be watching things here while you are gone?"

"Well, my steward, Isaac, and Gauis's son, Antonio. I believe that Gauis will be joining the family business eventually, and his son wanted to learn economics, so I've had him here learning the art of trade. He's quite bright. Then he may go visit his grandparents in Rome in a few months, but Gauis doesn't seem too happy about that. He doesn't want the boy to get involved in Roman society, so we'll have to wait and see how things go. He's a good young man, but he's going to have to think about what he wants to do. We hope he'll stay away from Rome, but only time will tell what choices he'll make. Well, it's getting late, and we have an early start tomorrow for our journey. Let's call it a night, okay?" And rising slowly, Samuel stood and left the room.

"Amos, since you married Lydia, you seem to be doing well. How is your family? This makes three children for you, doesn't it?"

"Yes, we have a boy, Steven, and a little girl, Esther. We really don't care what this child will be. Lydia thinks it's a boy, so she wants to call him Simon. Of course, you know her. She tells me what will be. I love her so much I just let go, but I do rein her in occasionally when she gets too rambunctious. What a woman! There's not another like her, that's for sure. She would have made a formidable man. Thank the good Lord she wasn't. And, yes, I'm doing very well. Your father has helped me more than I could ever have dreamed possible. What would my life had been if I hadn't met him when I did? He's as dear to me as any true father could be, so, yes, I'm happy and very content with my life."

With that, Amos said good night and retired too. Demas sat, wondering what his father's news would be. Apparently, Samuel knew and thought that he would be pleased when he heard it. *Interesting! What has he got in mind for me? I have news too. So we will get to surprise each other when I get home. Amos will be too when Father tells him what I'm bringing for him.*

Early the next morning, the sun had already heated the sand. Dust mixed with the grunting of camels and donkeys, the guards were sweating profusely, and the noise was growing. Finally, the caravan started off. As the day wore on, Demas realized he had never cared for land travel. It was tedious, dusty, and exhausting. The days passed, and other than the wonderful evenings of companionship with his family, everyone became more silent and just hoped that the journey would soon be over.

However, the landscape was already changing, and he could see the black hills and knobs of rock that indicated they would soon arrive home. Damascus was an interesting town. It had plenty of water, and the oasis-like valley that the city sat in was very pretty. But the surrounding hills were difficult to pass through, and in summer, harsh to bear with the heat radiating off of the black jagged rocks. However, his home and family were there, and soon he would be as well.

Suddenly, he began to realize that he would have to start planning for not just himself but Roxanne too. They would live with his parents for a while, but Demas wanted a farm. He wanted to return to shepherding. Hopefully, his father would help him now that he would be starting his own family. He would just have to see what was happening and what was available for him. He carried the responsibility of being the firstborn of the firstborn. This meant that he would have to take over for his father someday. That was okay just as long as he could live away from the cities and work the land. His mind drifted as he watched the caravan work its way through the ravines and cliffs.

Then there it was. Damascus. *It's good to be home,* he thought and urged his camel onward.

Chapter 14

As they approached the open fields where they would unload the caravan and reload with the next order, they saw a figure running toward them.

"Masters, hurry. The birth is eminent of the child to Mistress Lydia. They are at my master's house." Matthan, the Ahimelek steward, gasped.

Amos had already turned his camel toward the Ahimelek compound. Samuel turned to follow, but Demas dismounted and walked toward Matthan, who was bent over gulping for air.

"Matthan, you shouldn't run so fast. You're getting on in years. We'll get there in time." Demas smiled.

"I know, Master Demas, but I was so happy when I saw the caravan come down the road that I wanted you to know as soon as possible."

"When you catch your breath, dear friend, we will proceed to the house. How is everyone? Any problems?

Father sent a message for me to return as soon as possible. Is the family okay?"

"It's not for me to say, sir. As for me, it is good to have you back home."

Demas laughed, and together he and his father's steward headed toward the family home. As they approached the house, Jarius walked out to meet them. "Welcome home, my son. I didn't know how long it would be before you got my letter. It's good that you are back. And there is no catastrophe, but I think you will be pleasantly surprised by my news. But that's for later. Let's go see your new cousin first. As usual, Lydia has had her way and has another boy. Amos is very proud."

Amos was holding his new son as Jarius and Demas entered the house. Suddenly, Demas's mother was grabbing hold of him.

"Thank the good Lord that he has brought you home safely." She cried and clung to her oldest boy.

"Mariam, let the boy breathe. He's going to be here for a while. Let's go out onto the patio and have some refreshments."

Mariam didn't relinquish her hold on Demas until they had sat down under the trees and refreshments were handed out. She couldn't take her eyes off of her son. He was perfect in her sight. She just kept smiling and wiping her eyes. Her joy was as tangible as the sun peeking through the canopy of trees that overhung the little oasis in their yard. This was a perfect day for her. Her eldest child was home, and they had another baby to rejoice over. *God is so good,* she thought.

Jarius finally turned to Demas and said, "Son, the reason I had you come home is because we have gotten the property back in Emmaus. I know that you have always loved that place, and now it is yours. Josias of Bethany got hold of us and said that he would like to relinquish his lease on it if we were interested, so I went down to Bethany, and we have taken the property back. Josias says he is getting too old to handle it any longer. When Emmaus was burned, the property wasn't harmed, although the house and buildings suffered from the raid on the town. He and his son are traders of sorts. Mainly they have a lot of local and country people contributing to their trade goods. I decided that if you come back, you can continue with the farm. Since you will eventually replace me as head of the family business, Samuel and I decided to go into business with Josias and his son, Benjamin. They will start handling our caravans. They are closer to Jerusalem and have a large area to put the caravans together and send them on to us. This will free you to travel as is necessary to our other ports of call and yet have a home base from which to work from."

Demas was stunned. His dreams were coming true. "Yes, of course, I am pleased. Now my news will make you as surprised as I am. I have found a young woman that I wish to marry. Her name is Roxanne. She's the younger sister of Hannah, Gauis Attilo's wife. We met during a pirate raid on our boat two months ago. I know that this seems sudden, but I love her very much. She is coming with Gauis and his family to Jerusalem to live. Gauis has been reposted to the city of our Lord. He has repurchased Beth Enajim. You can meet her then, and we can sign the contracts of marriage. I am so happy now that I could jump for joy."

Jarius and Mariam were quiet for a moment, and then Mariam grabbed Demas and said, "Oh, honey, I am so happy for you. What is Roxanne like? Do you think she'll like us? What do Jacob and Alyssa think about her? Is she pretty? Does she love you as much as you love her? I'm so excited. Just think, we'll have a new woman in the family. God has been so good to all of us. The girls are married, and Sarah is expecting her first child. And now I'll have another daughter. You don't know how much I was concerned about you not putting down roots, and you won't be that far from us."

Then Jarius spoke up. "Well, I guess we need to go to Emmaus and see what has to be done. We will still be providing animals for the temple, but we need to see what the property and herds and flocks are like. Plus, you are going to need a steward. We've got a lot to do in the next few months."

After everyone left to go to bed, Demas sat outdoors for a while, absolutely delighted by the prospect of his future. Soon he would be his own boss, have his own home and a wife. It was almost too much to take in. Then he started thinking about the old house. If it was in too bad a shape, he would rebuild and try to copy Beth Enajim's style. And where would he find a new steward? Would he need more shepherds? What were Josiah and his son like? Maybe they could help him find everything he was going to need. Just then, he heard some footsteps and looked up to see his father.

"Things are changing quite quickly, aren't they, son?" Jarius said as he sat down opposite his son.

"Yes, sir, they certainly are. I have those documents that you wanted me to get. Amos's old master was quite happy to give them to me when I offered the money to him. He didn't even inquire how Amos was or where he was at. I don't think things have been going very well for him. When are you going to give them to Amos? Does he know that he is also now a Roman citizen? Father, I am so pleased by everything that I couldn't sleep. I know that you and Mother will love Roxanne. She's very intelligent and will be a great help to all of us."

"Demas, I am happy for you. I knew that when the time was right, you would find a good woman. It intrigues me to see how much our lives are involved with a Roman soldier. What does Gauis think about all of this? And why is he coming back to Jerusalem? I would imagine he wasn't too happy to be returned here. We must keep our eyes on Rome. I don't think things are going to end well for our people before all this is over with."

"I agree with you, Father. Gauis is mainly an administrator, not so much a soldier. He and Hannah were quite happy in Ephesus. Has he said how much longer he will be serving Caesar? They are keeping their home in Ephesus where he will retire to. I believe he's concerned with his oldest son now. The boy wants to go to Rome and see it and his grandparents. Needless to say, neither he nor his wife wanted to come back here. Also, Gaius accidently found out who betrayed us to Herod. It was Joel. He got caught cheating while gambling and offered the information to Archelaus to save his own hide. It broke my heart when I heard it."

"Joel! We should have known. I wonder where he's at. His poor parents were so ashamed of him. I tried to help them after he disappeared. By the time we had moved and made all those changes, both his mother and father died. I believe it broke their hearts the way he was. But God would have us forgive him. Forgiveness is never easy, especially from someone close to you who betrays your friendship and love. May God have mercy upon him. Well, now that mystery is answered. Your mother will be just as disappointed as we are in him. I know that you are anxious to go to Emmaus, so I thought that we would go down there in a week. When Samuel and Elizabeth leave, we'll go by way of Jerusalem and stop in and see Josias and his family. We'll need to see how they have prepared to handle our business when it starts coming their way. Also, what bride price did Gauis set upon Roxanne? We'll get the contracts ready so that we will be ready when they get to Jerusalem?"

"Father, if there are a lot of repairs to be made to the farmhouse, I would like to redo it in the style of Beth Enajim. With that stream nearby, water access will be near enough for what I want to add to the main house. And I'm glad that the caravans will be leaving from Bethany instead of Emmaus. Do they have the space to pack and unload the caravans as they come and go?"

"Yes, they do have the space, and they will have the advantage of being closer to Jerusalem. My main concern is drawing attention to them if the Romans see how much traffic they have. However, it will give you more time to devote yourself to the old homestead. And, of course, you'll have to travel to see how we operate in other areas. Truthfully, I think we may have to separate each trading center into individual businesses. My brothers and sisters have families that are learning the business, and it is becoming too big. Someone is eventually going to put it all together, and then we may have trouble with the Romans. It's something the family is considering. Each family will be its own entity. But we will still trade between ourselves, and the profit will stay with each family. I don't believe your grandfather could foresee how successful everything has turned out. Also, I think that you will eventually have to leave Israel for another country, but that won't be for a while. We have plenty of time to discuss that. But it is something that in all probability will eventually happen."

Demas was stunned at first but could then see the probability of this becoming a necessity. He could take over in Damascus when his father stepped down, but Amos was doing such a good job that Demas would have to look elsewhere for a new home. He shrugged. *That's for the future, and I've got enough on me to handle right now. Who's to say what tomorrow will bring. But his family had succeeded because they did watch and monitor the times and the Romans. These times were getting harder and harder to maneuver in. The Caesars were a sneaky bunch. They had no problem at all with killing their own family, much less other people. And then there is the situation of the coming of God's son. It would probably be another eighteen years before he would be coming into to his own. By then, he would be considered old enough to have status as a prophet or whatever he was coming to do, so I can stop worrying about that and start planning for my own home and family.*

With that, both men stood, said good night, and went to bed.

Chapter 15

In the morning, the men gathered on the patio; Amos was present too. First, Jarius turned to Amos and said, "We have a gift for you and your family. We wanted to reward your hard work." He handed Amos the rolled parchment, and Amos had a quizzical look on his face.

"I've been given so much. I can't imagine receiving anything else." He slowly opened the scroll and sat, stunned. "Is this true? I'm a free man and a Roman citizen now? How?" Then he just sat, totally stunned.

"We finally found your old owner. He gladly took the money offered and signed the papers in front of the city magistrate. I'm sorry, he said nothing about you. Then we had your citizenship applied for and have received it. Welcome, citizen Amos!"

Amos turned away as tears flowed down his face. "I've got to go tell Lydia. She's going to be so pleased," he said as he stumbled out of the patio and into the house.

"Well, that went well." Jarius chuckled. "I don't think Amos had any idea of this happening to him. Now I want to hear about this pirate raid. You're right, Samuel. We have to figure out some way to protect our ships and men. What do you think we can do to protect them, son?"

Demas was bent over with his hand cupping his chin. "We're going to have to double up with two ships when we're crossing over the open waters. Most raids happen away from the main lands. As long as we're close to the coasts, we're okay sailing alone, but when we have to cross large spans of open water, we need to have two ships sail together. Also, we're going to have to hire about five fighting men per ship and train our crews the real basics of fighting. Of course, eventually the pirates will double up too, but we can start now and get a jump on them."

"You're right," said Samuel. "And as you said, the pirates will start doing likewise, but eventually. Whenever good men take precautions, the bad guys will alter their ways too to overcome them. But it will give us a head start. Hopefully when the pirates organize, and they will, Rome will have to step in because they will be attacked as well."

Jarius sat back and nodded. "Well, we had to do it with our caravans, so why not our boats? Yes, this is a good plan. When our ships are loaded, they will meet up with another ship and sail together. We'll have to change our scheduling, but it can be done. Anything is workable. Also, we can schedule in such a way that ships will have home ports for a month's lay over each six months at sea so that the men can be with their families. Yes, I think this is a doable situation, and it is a necessity. Is this agreeable with you, Samuel?"

"Absolutely! I'll start redoing our schedules and look for men. I would ask you to help, Demas, but if you're going to Emmaus, you're going to be busy for several months. I will write Jacob and get his advice too. Now Passover is in two and a half months, and I believe we will all be fairly busy until then. Demas, when are you and Jarius leaving for Emmaus? And where will the wedding be held? I assume at Beth Enajim. I'm quite sure that your promised one will want to be around her family. I wonder if Attilo's parents will come from Rome. If they are able, I'm sure they will be here."

Samuel stood and went back into the house. "Well, son, when do you want to leave?" Jarius smiled at his son.

"Would yesterday be too soon?" Demas grinned.

"There's an awful lot to be done. Can we leave Monday?"

"I don't see why not. We have to go the inland route though. I have supplies for the two inns that we have out there. The road will bring us right to Bethany first. After we inspect the farm, we can go up to Jerusalem and see Attilo. The dowry requirements requested are very reasonable, so we'll go to Jerusalem as soon as we can and get everything signed and paid. Is that okay?"

"Yes, sir. I just want to get started. I never thought marriage could be so exciting, complex, and exhausting."

"Just wait until everything is on the final stretch, then you'll know what true exhaustion and happiness is." He smiled and left Demas, who was absolutely stunned.

The next morning, Demas sat on the patio, just enjoying the peaceful quiet. His mother came outside and sat down with a smile. "My dearest son, don't be upset or worried. I have already gotten a list made up for you. As a woman, it's mainly for your new home." She grinned knowingly as she continued, "I do know what's needed."

She pulled the list out to show him and then put it back. "The list covers the main things that you will need. When you get to Bethany, give it to your new partners and ask if they can start filling it. When Roxanne gets here, she, her sister, and I will go over it. Don't be upset. These are areas that the women will handle. Men have other things to consider, and so do women. We want to make our homes as comfortable as we can for our husbands."

Putting her hand on his shoulder she smiled. "You have your job, and we have ours. You said that Roxanne received training from Attilo's mother. She and I will discuss this when she gets here. You do your job, and Roxanne will do hers. We make our homes pleasant and comfortable, and our men allow us to handle any bumps that might arise concerning it. If you told Roxanne that she had to make sheep pens and do it right, she would feel as you do now. We each have our expertise in the jobs we do. Frankly, I think your father is enjoying your discomfort. He knows he was the same way when we were getting married. Men really do have a weird sense of humor."

She saw him grin and knew he was beginning to relax. "You will learn just as all the rest of us have. Now you're going to need a steward, a cook, and a house girl or two. Plus, you'll probably need a foreman to handle the men and flocks and more shepherds to help you work the sheep. Ask Joseph or his son if they can help you find these people. I'm sure everything will get taken care of by the wedding. As for things for Roxanne, I'll help her find the fabric for her wedding dress. Fine linen would be perfect. Ask Joseph if they have any. I think that a necklace, bracelet, perhaps, a hand mirror in silver or gold, a ring, or earrings would also be nice. Maybe a hair ornament or hairnets would be too. When we get down to Jerusalem, I will look for some things for her and let you see whether you want them or not. I can tell you now she will treasure everything that you give her. Love doesn't see with the eyes but with the heart."

Demas had tears in his eyes as he hugged his mother. "Thank you, Mother. I've never had this experience before, and I was overwhelmed. You've gotten me back on the right path. I guess I should think about the outside of our home and let Roxanne take care of the home itself. Father just surprised me when he dropped it in my lap. You're right. I think he is totally enjoying my foray into marriage and my own home. You know I love Father so much that I forget that he has had the same experiences."

"Jarius is very special, but he's human too. Sometimes I think that I love him too much. Then I realize that we both are equally blessed with each other. I pray that you and Roxanne will be the same. Well, it's time to eat, so I'll go and let you make your own lists of needs. The tea is ready. Do you want some?"

"Not right now. I'll come in too. I'm going to need a lot of things. Thank you again." Demas felt a load had been lifted from him. He rose and entered the house, somewhat overjoyed and relieved.

Chapter 16

Monday came at last. The caravan was packed, and the outriders were mounted, and the usual good-byes were given along with hugs and prayers. Demas and his father mounted their camels, waved to the others, and started off. This was when Demas missed being on a boat the most. Land travel was tedious, noisy, and dusty, and unfortunately this was a part of their work.

Several miles later, Demas asked his father, "Do you think he'll be in Jerusalem this year? He's twelve now and should be ready to go to the temple."

"That's what I'm thinking too, son. We'll just have to see."

Two days later, they reached their first inn and were received with relief. At least, they would sleep indoors tonight. Jehu was excited as they had their supplies unloaded. Demas was surprised to see a flock of sheep grazing in a field across from the inn's post.

"Since when do these inns keep sheep?" Demas asked.

"Well, this is their home, and they don't see many people. So when they asked if they could get some sheep and chickens, we said fine. But they have to keep the inns clean and welcoming. They're happy, and so are we. Jehu only has about twenty sheep, but Adam has about sixty. The inns are clean, and it gives them something to make it more like a home. You should understand. You're going to be a sheep owner soon too."

The next morning, they were off again on the long trail. They had had a very good lamb dinner the night before and a comfortable sleep. The next inn was three days away. Demas was already looking forward to the inn. One of their ex-sailors ran it, and Demas was anxious to see if Adam's oldest son still wanted to go to sea. They were going to need more ships and men if they were going to double up their fleet.

The third afternoon came, and they pulled into the second inn. Adam and his wife walked toward them. Demas was really surprised at the number of sheep up on the hillsides behind the inn.

As his camel lowered itself, Adam came over to them. "Demas, how are you? Figured you would come by one of these years. Time really flies, doesn't it? What's it been, four years since I left your boat?"

"Just about five years now. What's with the flocks of sheep? You've got quite a few."

"Yes, we do. We have about one hundred fifty. We sell them to caravans and travelers. It gives us something extra, and I enjoy it."

After dinner that night, the men were gathered, talking. Demas turned to Adam and asked him, "How do you handle such a large flock? You have three boys, but that's a large flock to watch over."

"Well, that's my secret. Come, I'll show you how we manage." He led Demas and Jarius through the back of the inn and were surprised to see a pen with several dogs in it.

"What are you doing with these dogs?" asked Jarius.

"Our first year here was a real test for me. One day, a large troop of soldiers came in. They camped across the road but came over to buy a couple of sheep. One of them was really interested in the small flock we had and asked if we would be interested in having help. I didn't know what to say, so I asked what he had in mind. He whistled, and two dogs came out of the bushes. He said he had just returned from being in a far northern country. While there, he noticed that they used dogs to work the sheep along with the shepherds. Anyway, he brought two of them back with him. But new commander doesn't like having them around, so he told him to get rid of them. I'll show you tomorrow how they work. I've got several now, but if you want a male and a female, I've got them. If you are planning on raising sheep again, this will be perfect for you."

Demas was amazed and really interested, so the next morning, as the caravan was reloading, he, his father, and Adam walked up the hill to the sheep cotes. About six dogs were already helping Adam's sons move the sheep to a still pond for watering.

"This is fabulous," he said, and his father agreed. By certain whistles and words, the dogs let the fringe of sheep out into the pasture. Adam's son would whistle, and the dogs would stop and circle the sheep. It was fascinating to watch. Both Demas and his father were speechless.

"This is great. Do you ever lose any sheep? The dogs don't damage or hurt the sheep, do they?"

"No, and they make good watchdogs too. They let us know that you were coming an hour or so before you got here. And no one comes near the inn that we aren't alerted to. What do you think?" Adam grinned.

Demas looked at his father and nodded. "I want at least eight of them, but I'll need someone to show me how to work with them. Jonah wants to go to sea. How about letting him bring them to me and show the shepherds and me how to use them. Then I'll put him on one of our boats and see if he does like being a seaman. If he doesn't like sailing, he can come and work for me in Emmaus or come on back home to you and your wife."

Adam looked at his son and saw the eagerness in his face. "Okay, it's a deal."

They got down and worked out the transaction. Also, Demas saw a smaller dog, which he was told was a runt, so he got that one too for a surprise for Roxanne. As they headed up the road, Demas couldn't get the grin off of his face. But even Jarius was somewhat excited. Jonah would come to Emmaus in a couple of weeks and bring the dogs with him. He would be helped by men whom Demas would be sending. However, he had the runt with him. She was a sweet little thing, and Demas was wondering if Roxanne would like her. He had a feeling that she would like this little gift the best of all that he was giving her.

"Demas, do you think the men will mind having the dogs to help them?" Jarius asked.

"Why not? The dogs will prevent any sheep from wandering off. Plus, they will alert the herders of anyone or anything approaching. I think this is really going to be a good help. Also, we won't have to have as many herders, and they will be good company for the men. I got what I wanted, five males and three females, and when I have to leave on trips, Roxanne will have protection. Yes, I think God has just answered my prayers."

The next few days flew by, and they finally arrived in Bethany. As they crossed through the large gate, a young man walked out to meet them.

"You have come. My name is Lazarus. Go to the right side of the house. We have structures for all that you bring. Just unload into them! My father and grandfather will be here shortly. We will bring water and food to refresh you in the meantime."

As the camels were led to the side of the house, Jarius and Demas dismounted their camels. Demas tied a rope on Runt's neck and walked toward Lazarus with his father.

"You have grown, Lazarus," said Jarius. ""Do you remember me from my last visit about three years ago?"

"Just a little bit, sir. I was still pretty young, and my father didn't want me to be in the way. Now he lets me help him more and more and has been teaching me how to handle the caravans that come and go. Please come in and relax. Our household will start bringing water and food to refresh you and your men."

Jarius and Demas followed him into the house, and it was immediately cooler. As they sat down on mats, two little girls brought them water and towels.

Lazarus again spoke up. "These are my sisters, Mary and Martha. As you can see, they are being taught too. Martha, where is Joshua? He needs to help these men."

But just then, a young man came in. "I'm sorry to be late. I was helping your men unpack the animals. Please, sirs, let me wash your hands and feet."

Mary was by Demas's side and said, "May I pet your dog? She is so cute."

"Yes, but let her smell your hand first, and then she'll be comfortable with you. We call her Runt. She's going to be a gift to my bride-to-be. She'll probably rename her."

Then out came Martha and an older girl from the next room with trays of food. Demas smiled and thanked them.

Then Demas turned to Lazarus and asked, "How do you keep it so pleasant in here? It's very comfortable."

"We put tent fabric along the back of the house and along the front. A friend in Nazareth built the supports to hold the fabric and to keep the sun from shining on the doors and windows. Not having the sun heat the sides of the house makes it cooler too."

"What an original idea. We will have to try it."

Just then, two men came in. "Well, you've finally come!"

Jarius and Demas both stood up. "It is good to see you. Your son was just telling us how to hold the heat out of our houses. We're going to try it too. How are you?" Jarius said as they all sat down.

"That's my grandson. He is always trying out new things, and they usually work," commented Josiah of Bethany.

His son smiled and said, "We're sorry about the property in Emmaus. What are your plans?"

"Well, tomorrow we're going to look at it. Demas, my son here, is getting married after Passover, so he is going to work the farm. But we're going to need a head shepherd. Also, we have some lists of things we're going to need. We thought if we gave the list to you now, you would be able to determine if you have most of it. Also, Demas will need a steward, cook, and her assistants," he said and handed the list to Benjamin.

Scanning the list, he nodded and then said, "You would be better off going into Jerusalem for the jewelry. As for the head shepherd and housekeeper, there is a very good one here in Bethany, and his wife is a great cook. Just a minute—Lazarus, please go get Joseph and his wife if they can come. Tell them we have the owner of a sheep farm that is in need of help."

"Yes, Father." Then Lazarus left.

"You have everything that we were short of. I appreciate getting it now. On your list, you have linen for your bride's dress. We just happened to have a bolt of the finest white linen right now, the household goods too. You know what we carry, and with this new delivery, we should be able to fill it. Where is the wedding going to be?"

"That's something we're working on. Do you have any ideas?"

"Yes, I do. A friend of ours has a nice villa coming up to rent on short-time lease. He's going to Rome for a visit. Will you need it for longer than three or four months?"

"That would be perfect. The bride is going to be at our old house, Beth Enajim, with her sister and brother-in-law, the Attilos."

"I know him. He was here several years ago. He's one of the few Romans that we liked. His wife is Jewish, isn't she?"

"Yes, but it's not really known to most people. He's a converted Jew too, but we want to keep this low-key for his sake."

"How long will you be in Emmaus?" We can go up to Jerusalem when you come up and go and see my friend about his place."

"Demas is staying in Emmaus, but I should be back in a few days. How is the place doing, Josiah? Will it need much work?"

"It will need a little work to freshen it up. Right now, we're running about ten flocks of sheep. You will probably want to increase that, but you're going to need more men."

"That's something else we want to talk to you about. We stopped in at one of our inns coming here and got a surprise. Do you have any trouble with break-ins? We may have a solution for you."

"Well, for a while, we did, but Lazarus came up with the idea of putting briar hedges all around the property like many vineyards have. We made them pretty dense. Since then, the guards we have to patrol at night have kept down most efforts of infiltration of the compound. What are you thinking about?"

"We came across the most amazing dogs. A Roman soldier had been up in the far north and came across dogs that were used to guard and help to herd the sheep. They knew that we were coming an hour or so before we got there. We're getting some of them as soon as we can and use them at Emmaus, but we ordered extra ones in case you wanted one or two for guarding. The soldier's centurion told the soldier to get rid of them, so our innkeeper took them.

He showed us how they worked, and Demas and I were truly amazed. He's been breeding them and has several, so we'll pick them up in a few weeks. Runt here is too small, but Demas thought his wife-to-be would enjoy her, so we brought her with us. Think you might be interested?"

"It's a thought. Besides, my daughter Mary would love to have one. By all means, bring them by when you get them."

Just then, Lazarus appeared and said that Joseph and his wife were coming. The men stood as a man and woman came in.

"Hello, everyone! Your son came to tell us we were needed, so here we are. This is my wife, Shela. What's happening?"

"Joseph, these are the owners of the property in Emmaus. This is Jarius and Demas Shophan. Demas is getting married soon and moving to Emmaus. He needs a head shepherd, cook, and housekeeper. I thought that you might be interested."

Joseph looked at his wife, and she nodded yes. "Well, there's your answer. We loved the property in Emmaus. You built it and lived there for years, didn't you?"

"Yes, but we had to move. My son, Demas, loves raising sheep. With Josias retiring, Demas is going to take over now that he is getting married. Shela, will you need any girls to help you? If so, how many?"

"Well, sir, maybe one or two at first. Then we can always get more as they are needed. There are already families living there, and there are several girls, so we can see who would like to work at the main house."

"That's perfect. We'll be going down tonight, and you can come as soon as you're ready. Thank you for coming. I'm sure everything will work out."

Joseph and Shela left, and the men went out front. Their camels were already saddled and waiting. Demas picked up Runt and climbed onto his camel. Jarius climbed onto his camel and said, "I'll be back in three days. If you would check on your friend to see if he'll rent his house for three or four months, I'd appreciate it. We'll talk when I come back. Thank you for your hospitality and the food that you are sending with us. Have a good day."

Then turning their camels, they headed northwest to Jerusalem.

"I'm sorry that I did all the talking back there. You'll be doing most of the talking from here on out. He knows that you will be in my position eventually, and I wanted to get to Emmaus before dark."

"Father, you are the one in charge, and I'm still learning. If we had been talking ships, I would have spoken more. I may come back with you when you come. Remember, I need a steward too. How do we find one of those?"

"We will look around and ask. God will direct us to the right one, I'm sure. I want to see this villa that I may rent, and then I can bring your mother, sister, and brothers down right away. Your mother wants to be here when Roxanne gets here. She wants to make sure you have chosen well. Anyway, that's what she said, and I nodded. Frankly, I think she's just plain excited about your bride-to-be. I would imagine that Attilo is already here. If he is, we'll get to go see Beth Enajim. I loved that place."

"Me too! I would like to put similar things in my house." Having said that, Runt reached up and licked Demas's chin. "You're excited too, aren't you, Runt?"

An hour later, they arrived in Emmaus. They sat at the entrance and just stared at the house and then urged their camels on into the courtyard.

A man came running and then stopped. "Master, is it really you? It's been so long. I'm Andrew. My father was Eliazar."

"Of course, Andrew, I'm sorry about your father. Is your mother still alive?"

"Yes, sir. Mama lives with my wife, Ellyn, and me. Come, we tried to clean as much as we could, but I'm usually busy in the fields with the sheep."

"How are things here, really?"

"Well, as you can see, the yards are pretty wild, but the house was well-built and structurally sound. However, it will need a lot of cleaning and filling. Otherwise, it stands like a rock. Come, come, my wife will be bringing water and food shortly."

As they lowered the camels, Demas put Runt down, and then she was off running and checking out everything.

"Well, I think Runt is happy. Look at her checking everything out." Demas smiled. Then they opened the door and entered.

"Your mother would have a fit if she saw her former house right now. But she would just gird up her robes, grab a bucket and towel, go get water, and start cleaning. You definitely see there hasn't been a woman in charge for a very long time." Jarius smiled.

"I hope that Shela is prepared to work. She seemed nice, and she and her husband were clean and very polite. Oh, well, it takes time to get new servants and learn what each person's needs and wants are. I wonder where I can find a steward." Demas shrugged and then looked around. His father had gone up to the roof room, so Demas headed through the kitchen to the backyard. He just stood and stared at the barren spaces. Yes, his mother would be disappointed. What had it been, almost twelve years since they had fled from their home. *Times and things change,* he thought. Then he turned and headed for the sheep pens.

That evening, as they settled down, his father said, "Well, what do you think?"

"I am grateful to God for you and Mother. I really feel blessed."

"Yes, all of us are." Jarius spoke quietly. "Good night, Demas. We'll talk in the morning."

Then quiet settled over the house. The Shophans were back home again.

Chapter 17

The next morning, both men got up, rolled up their mattresses, and headed outdoors.

"What's on your agenda today, Demas?"

"Well, right off I will get a head count on the sheep and talk to the men. What about you?"

"I made some lists yesterday. Today, I'm going to see what we have in supplies. Then I'll come over to you and hear what the men have to say."

With that, the men went out in different directions. At ten o'clock, they were seated in a circle, listening to the shepherds. Most were content and eager to start working again. Five, maybe six, of the men didn't seem content. That could be addressed later. Right now, they had to organize and start fixing the sheep pens and cleaning up the yards. The wells were in fair condition. They needed new lids. But cleaning up was a top priority.

At lunchtime, the two men headed for the main house. They saw two donkeys tied by a tree, and smoke was coming from the back of the house.

"Now what?" they said at the same time. They walked in the front door. Joseph was scrubbing the walls down, and Shela was cooking.

"This is a great surprise and a welcomed one."

"We saw you out with the shepherds, so Shela and I thought you could use some help here. Figured this was your first meeting with your men, so thought I would let you talk to them before I was introduced."

"That was a wise decision, Joseph. I'm rather discouraged by the condition of everything, but we'll get it worked out. Did you look around when you got here?"

"Well, a little bit. It's a great place in truth. Yes, it needs help, but isn't that what we're here for?"

"Absolutely." Jarius nodded and washed his hands.

As they ate, they talked. Joseph said he had been here before but wasn't too happy with the attitudes of some of the shepherds and the condition of the grounds, so he didn't stay. Apparently, it had been too much for Josias to handle by himself, and the homestead had become rough and overgrown. All the fields needed to be cleaned and the sheep carefully inspected.

Demas turned to Joseph and asked, "How many men do you think we'll need to clean up and everything else?"

"Right now, at least twenty. We've got to get busy before the ewes start birthing. I know of about that number of men or so who would be good at their jobs."

"But right now, you've got something to do. You've got to get rid of the shepherds who are not doing their jobs."

Jarius agreed and added, "If the outside is any indication of their lack of dedication to their work, let's do it now. The sooner they are gone, the better. Then tomorrow Joseph can go talk to these shepherds he has mentioned."

"That sounds good. Well, are you ready to face these men and clean house?"

The men stood and reached for their rods. Demas was determined to get things settled. As they approached the first shepherd's home, Andrew came out with four other men. "I think you are going to do some cleaning. Do you mind if we come along?"

"Not at all," said Demas.

They walked to the first pens, and six men were sitting or lying on the ground. The one whom Demas had met earlier and didn't like stood and glared. "Well, what do you want? It's our meal time."

Demas walked directly to him. "I want you and these men and your families off this land immediately."

"Who do you think you are? We work and live here."

"Not anymore. I own this place. I don't need sluggards like you adding to the clutter. Now start moving, and I mean right now!"

The bully looked at Demas and the six men with him. They all had staffs and didn't look at all intimidated. He and the men got up and went to their houses. Within two hours, they were gone. Demas had paid them one month's wages each and gotten their names.

"Well," said Jarius, "that went well. Let's go look at the houses now so we can get it over with. I can only imagine what condition they are in. This used to be so clean and pleasant around here. Oh, well, it will be again."

The next morning, the men had already saddled the camels. Demas walked over to his dad and handed him a scroll. "These are supplies that we will need to restock the houses. Also, I need a gardener, carpenter, plasterer, stone mason, and tent maker. I may as well get it all done as soon as possible. Do you think you can get three or four caravan drivers? We need to send for the dogs as soon as possible. You'll be coming back today, won't you, Joseph?"

"Yes! Hopefully with plenty of men."

"God be with both of you and keep you safe."

As the men and camels left, Andrew walked up to Demas. "Where do you want to start first?"

"The sheep and their pens are first, Andrew. They will be birthing soon, and they need to be washed, watered, fed, and checked out. Then we will start on their pens. I've ordered in supplies, so we'll have food and other things shortly. Whatever is needed, let me know. Are your houses okay? I'll have workers here soon, and everything is going to be repaired, replaced, and put in working order."

"Thank goodness. This farm had always been so pleasant and comfortable. It broke my heart to see it going to rack and ruin. The men and I tried to keep things working, but Josias and his men did nothing to help. I'm so glad that you are here again."

"So am I, Andrew. Well, let's get started."

By late afternoon, Joseph was back with fourteen men and some women. Demas walked toward them and was surprised by the number.

Joseph dismounted and walked toward him. "Well, this is all I could get for now, but I believe more will be here in the next few days. Come, I'll introduce them to you."

After meeting each man and learning something about them, he told them what he wanted and needed. He told the wives who had come about the houses. "They have been neglected for years. We'll let you pick your own place, and I will pay you to clean it. If anything is broken or needed, let me know, and I will have it looked after. Supplies are coming, and I am only now checking everything out. If you also want to do yard work, you will receive pay for that too. I am getting married in three months, and I want my bride to see her new home looking as it did when my grandfather built it."

Chapter 18

Five days later, Jarius returned to Emmaus and the farm. He stopped just as he turned to enter the property. He was absolutely stunned. The brush and weeds had been cleared away. Palm trees had been planted along the road on the property. A grove of fig trees had been planted on the hill behind the main house. He was absolutely stunned. What a transformation! He went on in to the house and directed the caravan of camels to stop across from the house in an open field there.

Demas came out of the house, smiling. "Well, what do you think, Father? Do you like what we have done?"

Jarius slid off his camel and kept looking around. The fountain in front of the house was splashing into its different bowls, and a small rainbow hovered over the waters.

"How did you do all this in such a short time? It's absolutely beautiful."

"Well, I got the help I needed, and we've been quite busy. Come on into the house for refreshments."

Just then, several men came down the path from the sheep pens. Demas waved at Joseph. "Here are the supplies. Please put them in the storehouse and then come to lunch."

Demas guided his father into the house, but Jarius just kept looking at everything. "What did you do, hire an army? Look at the tile floors, the new lattices on the windows. The walls were clean, and there were couches along the walls."

Well, not an army but quite a few people. Come, let's go up to the roof. I fixed up Grandfather's room for you. It's very pleasant in the evenings."

Jarius followed Demas up the stairs. At the top, he stopped. It was literally shining, and potted plants stood against the low walls. "Son, I know you were able to command sailors, but this is unbelievable. It makes me homesick and to want to stay."

Demas walked over and opened the door to his grandfather's old room. "Well, does it pass inspection?

The room was clean and airy with a bed, table, chair, and lamp. Tears blinded Jarius's eyes. "It is just wonderful. I think your mother would be as dumbfounded as I am." Jarius walked back outside and looked where the sheep pens were. Men were clearing weeds away, and the sheep were clean and drinking water from a trough. "Okay, tell me you didn't make me a poor man while I was gone."

"No, Father. All the people pitched in and have been working to surprise you. I gather that you are pleased. And, Father, I have paid for everything myself. You know I never spent my money but saved it."

"Pleased! I am absolutely amazed."

Later after the caravan had been unloaded and the houses inspected, Jarius was still stunned. "How did you do this in five days?"

"The men that you sent out worked wholeheartedly. The men that Joseph got went right to work. Some of the men's wives came with them, and they started cleaning too. I'm paying them also, but they were so happy to have homes again. Plus, I think they are excited about me getting married. Everything is going well, and all of them seem happy."

"Your grandfather would be proud of you just as your mother and I have always been. Let's go see the sheep."

As they walked down the road to the sheep pens, women came out and bowed to Demas and his father. Then Jarius started checking the sheep. "How many are there? Are there any sick or diseased ones? How many will be bearing? How many males and females do you have?"

Demas reached in his belt and handed his father the whole inventory. Jarius smiled and started reading it. "Not as many as I had hoped for but more than anticipated after seeing the condition of everything when we first came. I am still stunned by how much has been done in such a short time. Do you have any other flocks in the western valleys? Surely Josiah had more sheep than this."

"Andrew says there are a few flocks out there, but he couldn't leave here for fear of the men we kicked out. He has a sweet young wife and two children that he feared for."

"I can well understand that. You have surpassed and pleased me. It makes me homesick for this old place, but I know now that you will bring us honor and a new family for your mother to visit. And believe me, she'll be visiting as often as she's able."

They laughed and headed to the house. That evening, Jarius told Demas what he himself had accomplished. He had rented the villa from Lasion's friend.

"It will be perfect for the wedding. After the initial start and prayers at the wedding, you and Roxanne can leave and come to Emmaus. A week later, your mother and I will visit old friends, and then we will head back to Tyre and then on to home in Damascus. Four of the caravan men that came down with us said they would be glad to go back to the inn for the dogs and Jonah. Jonah can go back with Samuel to Tyre and be put on one of our ships there to be trained as a seaman. Also, I met a very nice man who might make you a good steward. He'll be down after Passover. He's been in training for several years and wants to try it on his own. I met him, and he reminds me of Matthan when he became our steward. But you will have to make the final choice. Were the workers houses in need of much work? It was hard to tell because of the filth. I amused myself while going to Bethany, thinking of our bold confrontation with those men before I left. I felt somewhat young again. I'm so sorry that we will be so far apart, but I imagine your mother will be down at least yearly from now on, especially when the children start being born."

Demas just stared at his father. *Children! He was just getting married.* He hadn't thought past that point. *Children! What next?*

His father just laughed as he grinned at the look on his son's face. *Oh, yes, my son is really in for a lot of surprises.*

Chapter 19

Seven weeks had passed since Demas had first arrived at his old home in Emmaus. He had hired James as his steward, and many things had been lifted from his shoulders.

The dogs had come, and he and the shepherds were trained how to work them. At first, the shepherds weren't too excited about them. It only took them a few days to see how beneficial they were going to be.

They had gone to the old pastures in the hills and found over five hundred more sheep scattered all over the hills and in the small valleys. Some of the newly hired shepherds agreed to help bring them back to the farm. The shepherds who had been out there the whole time were glad to be relieved and able to come back to the main homestead. They were so happy to know that the owners had returned and had returned things as they had been like before.

The sheep were folding, and so far they had 355 lambs. With James's handling of the houses, women, and getting the stores in order, Demas was freed to do his work with the shepherds and sheep. They had over a thousand sheep now, including the lambs. Demas had added six teams of oxen, six bulls, and twenty cows, plus, chickens and a couple of mules. He had had three ovens built for the wives to bake in. And there were also several children playing in their yards. It reminded him of the times when he had been a child here.

He had widened the stream around the spring so that all the women could wash their clothes safely. And gardens had also been planted.

Runt was growing up and followed Demas wherever he went. The children really had fun with her.

Shela had put all the things away that he had ordered from Benjamin in Bethany. Benjamin was very pleased with the dogs that Demas had given him. His guards were pleased too. The dogs had routed or killed the creatures getting into the stock goods, and Mary loved having them around to play with.

Demas's parents were in Jerusalem now and had visited him. His mother was so happy to see her old home. She said it looked just like it was when she had been there. Demas and his father just smiled and agreed. She really liked the awnings in the front and back of the house. She said it made the house so pleasant inside in the heat of the day. She and Shela got on very well too. And she was very proud that Demas had put in good ovens for the wives of the shepherds. The new gardens thrilled her as did the fig orchard, date trees, and vineyard planted on the hills behind the main house. She hadn't decided about the banana trees that had been planted mainly because she had never tasted their fruit. All in all, Demas felt that she felt she was home again. He was so glad she hadn't seen it before all the work had been done.

He was going to Jerusalem the next day to see their house and hopefully Roxanne. She and her sister were expected at any time. He had seen Attilo when he and his father had gone to pay the betrothal fees. It was good to see his friend again, even though Attilo seemed stressed. So much had been dumped onto him by the governor that he barely had the time to get Beth Enajim ready for his family. Also, he found that the senior Attilos were coming for the wedding. He knew that his oldest son would want to go back to Rome with them when they left Jerusalem. He truly had a lot of concerns to deal with, and more were being added daily.

The Shophans didn't stay long and left as soon as courtesy allowed. Jarius was going with Demas to look for the animals he wanted to add to the stock already on the farm.

"Why do you want horses?" he asked Demas. "Won't donkeys work better?"

"Probably, but I want to get Roxanne and myself each one. I've ridden them, and for the closeness of Bethany and

Jerusalem, they are more comfortable. Father, have you ever ridden a horse?"

"Truthfully, no, but then I've never eaten certain things either. But I guess it would help your status around the Romans. You and Roxanne will be around them when you go to visit. What else are you getting?"

"I want to get a flock of goats, six more donkeys, and more cows. The priests said they need the calves for the sacrifices offered at the temple. They have been happy with the sheep we've taken in, but they need more. Also, I'm having a large cistern built in the back of the house."

"Need I ask why? You've put in so many things, but they've proven to work well. It's your home now, son. Do whatever you want."

They then began looking for the animal enclosures and finally found them on the outskirts of Jerusalem.

"You look for the donkeys, and I'll look at the goats, and then we'll meet at the cow pens," Jarius said.

"Good. That will cut down our time. I want at least two dozen goats. Make it ten males and eight females," Demas said. Then they went into different directions.

At the donkey enclosure, Demas was pleased to see that they had a good selection. A man came up and asked what he needed.

"I want at least ten males and ten females under three years old," Demas replied. The donkeys were quickly selected, and then the haggling began. An hour later, Demas had what he wanted and said that he was getting goats and cows too. The man asked how many cows he wanted. Demas said that his father was picking out the goats at that time, so they went to a pasture. His father was already there and had been looking the herds over.

"I've got some fine goats. Did you get your donkeys okay? Now how many cows are we talking about?" Jarius asked.

"I'm thinking about forty for right now. Do you see any that you like?" Demas was talking softly.

"Well, this field right here has the best selection. How many cows and bulls do you want? I would suggest about six bulls and thirty-four cows. And don't get any over two or three years old."

"That's the plan," he said and, turning to the man, asked if he owned all the livestock. The man said that he did, and they started separating the ones that Demas and his father had selected. Again, they had about an hour of haggling before Demas and the seller concluded the transaction. It was agreed that the man would have them brought to Emmaus the next day.

Then Demas asked where the horses were, and the man said they were over the next hill, but he didn't handle horses. He recommended a seller and then started separating the cows and bulls that Demas wanted.

Walking up the path of the hill, Jarius and Demas were relating how their haggling had gone. They were pleased with the prices that they were paying. At the top of the hill, the horses were scattered in small groups. Then Demas saw a beautiful white stallion off to himself. Again, a man walked up and asked what they were interested in. Immediately, Demas said he was looking for a good horse for himself and one for his wife-to-be, and he asked how much the white stallion was.

"You have a good eye for horses," the man said. "That stallion is two and a half years old and from good stock. Do you see a mare that you like?" I have one that I actually bought last week that might meet your needs. There she is." Standing in tall grass and behind a tall shrub was a beautiful golden horse with a white mane and tail.

"She seems pretty good," Demas said casually. "I haven't seen one with those colors before. Has she been gentled?"

"Yes, she has, but I don't think her previous master was very good to her. She has some marks that look like she might have been abused. Come on, we'll go catch her, and you can look her over."

The mare didn't run when she saw them coming, but she looked like she might bolt if they got too close. What she didn't see were two men coming from behind her with ropes. Before she could run, they had her roped.

Jarius stayed back. He didn't want to get into the way. Truthfully, he had never really been around horses very much. Demas walked right up to her, talking gently, and rubbed her nose. She still looked a little uneasy, but he could tell that she was relaxing. By the time that Demas had walked completely around her and was back at her head, she was nudging his hand. The man asked what he thought.

"She has definitely been whipped, but I would like to ride her and see how she behaves."

Quickly, a saddle was produced, and Demas had mounted her. He trotted about the pasture, stopping and then starting again and again. Then he trotted back to the group who were watching him. "I want to ride the stallion too."

The stallion was quickly saddled, and Demas worked him a little more vigorously. He then approached the men who were watching him, "Okay, let's see if we can reach a deal. These will be the only horses at my farm, so I'm going to have to find a place for them away from everything else."

The dickering took two hours, but finally they agreed. Demas would take the horses with him, and they would each come with a saddle. As they walked back down the hill to the dealer's tent, Jarius nudged Demas and said softly, "Where did you learn to ride horses like that?"

Demas just smiled and winked.

Indifferent to his father's lack of enthusiasm for riding horses, they walked to his father's temporary home.

"Okay, what is your first question, Father? I know you have several," said Demas.

"Yes, I do. First, where are you getting all this money you're spending? Second, where did you learn to ride horses? And thirdly, when did you become such an excellent barterer?"

"Well, I learned how to handle money from you. I invested it and saved it. I really didn't spend much all these years as I was traveling or at sea. I began to accumulate quite a bit, so Jacob helped me accumulate even more by investments and loans. I am wealthy by today's standards. Secondly, I had to develop skills similar to the people we dealt with. Riding and learning about horses was one of them, and surely you know that I learned to barter from the best teacher I was around the most. You, my father, are a master when it comes to bartering."

Jarius stopped and gaped at Demas, and then he started laughing so hard that tears came to his eyes. "Oh, my son, you are one of the biggest blessings that God has given me. When you were haggling with those men, I was actually jealous of you. I couldn't believe that you were so capable and able, and even better than I am, in some things. Now I see and understand. I helped you become an adult by handing on the same things that my father taught me. I'm sorry I didn't learn to ride a horse. My father didn't teach me or think it was necessary, but the times have changed, and we must adapt. That's what you've done. And I would imagine that when you have children, they will do the same."

They entered into the house, both laughing and hugging each other. Matthan stood and just stared at them. He had never seen his master or his son so happy. Then he came over as they sat and started washing their hands and feet. This family had always surprised him. Their joys and happiness spilled over and blessed those around him. He found himself smiling as he served them their lunch.

Father and son were still enjoying themselves when Mariam rushed into the house. "Whose beautiful horses are those out front? Do we have visitors?" she asked.

"No, Mother, the horses are mine. I got one for me and one for Roxanne as a surprise," said Demas."

"Mariam, what do you know about horses?" asked Jarius.

"Well, my husband, I learned quite a bit about them when I learned to ride." She smiled.

"You know how to ride? And when, may I ask, did you learn to ride?" Jarius stared at his wife.

"Well, a few years ago when you had left to check with your brothers, a man with horses stopped by our house. He was taking the horses that he had to a buyer up north. We got to talking, and he said he had a very nice mare that he was taking with him so that the new buyer could have a choice. I told him I had never learned to ride, but I thought that it might be interesting to learn. He said he would teach me and that if I found that I enjoyed it, he would sell the mare to me. He stayed for three days, and I found it especially entertaining, so I bought it and rode her every day. But after five weeks, I knew that you would be returning anytime, so I decided to sell her. However, the very next day, the man returned and said two of his horses had gone lame and would I sell my horse back to him. I thought, why not, so I resold the horse to him and told the servants not to ever let you know. And that's how I learned about horses and how to ride."

Both Jarius and Demas sat with their mouths open.

Finally, Jarius asked, "Why didn't you tell me? You make me sound as though I wouldn't understand."

"My dearest husband, after all these years of marriage, I do know many of your thoughts on things. You were adamant about your feelings about the animals, so I just let it pass."

"Tell me one thing, Mariam. Did you get the money back that you had paid for it?"

"Oh, no, my husband, I got twice what I paid for it."

By this time, Demas was gagging, trying to not to laugh out loud.

"Mariam, please don't hide anything from me. What would I have done if you had been thrown and hurt badly, or even killed?" Jarius said.

"Jarius, women never tell their husbands everything. Just think how bored you men would become if you knew everything about your wives. We have to maintain some mystery, or you would start looking at other women. Now that would be unacceptable to us. Besides, you never would have accepted the horse. But I am glad, Demas, that you thought of your betroth. Women will do their jobs so much more happily when they know that you don't know everything they are thinking."

Jarius just sat there looking at his wife, as if she wasn't whom he had always thought she was.

Finally, Mariam turned to Demas and said, "I have found some lovely things that I think you would like to give to Roxanne. We can go now and look at what I have laid aside. But before we go, I want to show you something. Matthan, would you bring that basket I keep on the shelf of our bedroom?"

A few minutes later, Matthan returned, carrying a basket and then handing it to her. "At your wedding, both you and Roxanne will wear head coverings. These were worn by your grandparents, your father and I, your sister and her husband, and Amos and Lydia at their weddings. If you want, you may carry on the tradition or get your own." Saying this, she took off the cloth covering and took out two white silk turbans. They were decorated with pearls and other gems. One was smaller than the other one. She handed them to him.

"Mother, these are beautiful. Of course, Roxanne and I will wear them. It's a family tradition. I wouldn't think of breaking it. But these are priceless. Thank you. And, Mother, if you like, you can ride the golden horse when we go to the bazaar."

All this time, Jarius just sat and looked at his wife. Then he told them to go ahead and that he had letters to write.

Later when Demas and his mother returned, Jarius arrived, coming from the stable. "Are you leaving for the farm today or tomorrow, son?"

"I'm going now. I want to be there when the animals arrive." He bent down and kissed his mother. He then hugged his father and left.

Later that evening, Jarius and Mariam retired to their room. She knew that he had something to say, so she sat and waited.

Finally, Jarius sat down and looked at her. "Why is it, Mariam, that you always amaze me? I guess I really think about you the way you really are in my thoughts. Today you really opened my eyes. I am so proud that you love me so much. When we get home, you can buy another horse if you like. But one thing I must ask, will you teach me how to ride so that we can ride together?"

Meanwhile, Matthan was locking the doors when he heard the laughter coming from his master and mistress' room. Then he grinned and thought, *I love these people so much.* He then said aloud, "Thank you, God, for allowing me to be here." Then all was quiet.

Chapter 20

It was the third day since Demas had returned from his parents' house. He looked up the road and saw some men on horses coming down the road. As they got nearer, he realized they were Roman soldiers. He remained on the front patio. They were slowing down, and they entered his gate.

"Hello," he said as the centurion dismounted and walked toward him.

"Demas Shophan?" he asked.

"That's me. What can I do for you?"

The centurion reached into his leather tunic and removed a letter. He handed it to Demas.

Demas opened it and smiled. "This is from Tribune Attilo. He says his family has arrived. Also the senator and his wife."

"Yes, sir. The tribune says that he hopes that you can come for lunch with them tomorrow. He has also invited your parents.

"Tell him I would be honored to come. Now let my man water your horses, and I offer refreshments for all of you."

The centurion nodded, and his men followed Andrew to the water troughs. "I appreciate your courtesy. It's getting hot already."

"Yes, it is." Shela came out of the house with food, drinks, and a large container of water and towels."

"Thank you, Shela." Turning to the man, he said, "Would you care to wash the dust off from your ride?"

The centurion and his men washed their hands and faces and then sat on a bench under a tree. "This is very pleasant. Thank you. How many sheep are you running?"

"I just took over this farm, and the sheep were scattered. But right now, I would estimate about a thousand."

"That's a lot of sheep. I'm coming up on retirement and am looking for something to retire too. My wife wants to settle down, so I'm looking at some options."

"If you've never done this before, you better look around and try farming with just a few animals. It looks very placid and easy, but it is work. Good pasturing is the biggest problem. Sheep will need to be watered daily and from still water. Then there is shearing time. The sheep are placid animals and can fall victim to almost any meat eater, so you have to have men around them at all times."

"I'm from a farm and know it's a lot of work. I don't know if I can handle the continuing work of a farm life again. For thirty years, I've been a soldier. Truthfully, I would like to just work a small place that didn't require constant work and vigilance. I know that my wife doesn't care what we do as long as I'm always near. She's always followed me wherever I've been ordered, but that doesn't mean I was around regularly."

"Then I suggest that you don't jump into anything too quickly. Find a place to live first that will give you time to figure out what you would truly enjoy doing. Then ease into it slowly and add to your place as you need to expand. Are you going back to Italia? If so, you will find your options in time."

"That's what is strange for me to figure out. I've been in this part of the world most of my career. Both my wife and I are comfortable here. We've become used to the customs of the people and speak several languages. I suppose that's what makes it difficult. Romans aren't that popular around here."

"I understand. I was a sailor for many years, but I began on a farm and always knew that someday I would return to it. Now I'm back doing what I always wanted to do."

"I know that you are marrying the tribune's sister-in-law. I wish you the best of everything. When I retire, may I bring my wife to see your place? This is much too big for us, but if she could see one, maybe we could get a smaller one like this."

Demas stared at the centurion and then said, "Of course, it would be my pleasure."

"Well, we must leave. Thank you for your hospitality. I don't meet very many people who are truly friendly. But then why should they? We're not here as friends. But again, thank you." Then the soldiers rose, mounted their horses, and rode out.

How do I get into these situations? he thought, *Well, if he comes back, I'll deal with it somehow.* Then he went into the house and told Andrew that he would be leaving for Jerusalem shortly and asked if he could have his horse saddled. *She's here at last,* he thought. *At last, Roxanne has come.*

Demas reached his parents' home in time for the evening meal. They greeted each other and then washed. As they ate, Demas told them of the centurion and his desire to come back with his wife when he retired. His father shook his head and asked how Demas always attracted so many problems. But as he said, what else could he do under the circumstances? They would ask Attilo the next day.

They discussed the fact that Attilo's parents had come. All three were curious as to how they would react to a Jewish wedding. Then his father said, "By the way, my friend, Zacharias, a priest at the temple, is coming with his wife and son, John, for your wedding. He will be giving the blessing for your marriage. They are a very devout family. He and Elizabeth were in their late sixties when they had their only child, John. Apparently, John is being raised as a Nazirite. We seldom hear of that these days. What's really interesting is he's about the same age as God's son. Now that makes you wonder what God has planned. I've been trying to figure out what's going to take place when they reach the age of thirty."

"Father, this is interesting. Well, we'll find out in about eighteen years, right?"

"Yes, we will. There has to be something in the works, and God will reveal it in his time."

They talked about these unusual things and then retired for the evening. Demas lay on his bed for a long time, thinking of Roxanne. In three weeks, they would be married. Passover was in a week and then their marriage two weeks later. He twisted and turned a long time before settling down to sleep.

The next morning, they were up and dressed in formal clothes. Mariam was as antsy as Demas. She found it difficult to relax. At last, they decided to leave. He was very surprised to see they had a chariot and horses to carry them.

"Where did you get the horse and chariot, Mother?"

"The chariot and horses were here, so we decided to use them. The owner said that we could before he left for Rome."

His father just nodded and helped his wife to be comfortable and then sat next to her. One of the stable hands jumped in and started toward the gate. Demas followed but couldn't help grinning. He was looking at his parents in a new light. They forever surprised him.

They rode into Beth Enajim and were immediately helped out and taken into the house. Gauis and his parents stood to welcome them. "Mr. and Mrs. Shophan, Demas, these are my parents. Father, Mother, these are my good friends, and Demas is Roxanne's husband-to-be. Please come in and have a seat."

At another table sat the ladies, so Mariam said to Mrs. Attilo, "Come, ma'am, let us sit with the other ladies. I know you'll want to hear of the wedding plans."

"Yes, of course," said Helena Attilo. "I'm very interested about the arrangements!"

The ladies rose as Helena joined them. Soon the women were engaged in their ideas and plans.

The senator turned to Demas and looked at him sternly. "Attilo has been friends with your family for sometime. My granddaughter and your uncle Jacob have been married, and he has provided very well for her. Now there's to be another alliance with your family. I'm quite fascinated by this turn of events."

"Demas looked straight at the senator and said, "Please ask anything."

"Before I ask anything, I will tell you about our family. We have always been in the Roman government. My father was a senator before me. We've tried to hold our position as a true responsibility to the Roman Empire and have always served that position as honorably as we could. It has not been a pleasant situation. You could say in a few words we went against the grain of our government. Attilo went into the army, much to my chagrin, but in his own way, he has made me very proud. I know that he won't be following in my footsteps. However, I would like to see an Attilo there again once I am gone. All people need good leaders. Now, Demas, ask your question." Gauis just dipped his head but remained silent.

"Sir, what did you think of Herod the Great?"

"I think, in your vernacular, that he was a pig, absolutely and totally mad. My father fought against his reigning here, but it was Caesar's desire, and so you people were stuck with him. Does that answer your question?"

By this time, even the ladies had stopped talking and were listening intently. Jarius almost dropped his cup, and Gauis's head shot up, and he was staring with his mouth open at his father.

"Please, my son, don't gape. You know me, and I will never pervert the truth."

Gauis looked hard at his father and then smiled and nodded.

"I have to go back to help you understand my family's plight. My grandfather was a farmer, but he was also a Pharisee in our faith. His sister, my great-aunt, was a very lovely girl who inadvertently attracted Herod's attention.

She was terrified of him. She knew that he wanted her as his wife to cement his position as a Jewish leader, even though he himself wasn't one. He had to marry a Jewish woman. He hated my grandfather because my grandfather continually fought him in our synagogue. When Herod left here to go get his position as ruler of Israel confirmed by Caesar, my great-aunt married and left with her new husband to his home in Tarsus. My grandfather changed his name and moved to a farm near Jerusalem. For years, Herod searched for him, and finally through betrayal by a friend, his son, Archelaus, told him where the family was. They had my grandfather killed. Before they could come after us, we fled. My father's brother, Jacob, handled a trading post for the caravans, so we went to Damascus and lived in his home under another name.

"When I was eighteen, I too became a sailor. I was captain of the ship that the pirates attacked. Seeing that they had left their fire unattended, I swung over and tipped it over. As I started to leave, I heard people screaming under the hatch. I broke it open, and seeing women and men, I helped them get out and jump overboard to swim for my boat. I had been shot with an arrow and was dizzy. When I fell into the water, something hit me in the head. Much later when I awoke, I was on the pirates' hatch lid with Roxanne. Like me, she was wet and cold. The ships were gone, but I knew that Jacob, my uncle, would search for me. When morning came, we saw a ship in the distance. I flashed my knife and saw that it was Jacob. We were taken onboard and then sailed on to Ephesus. That's when Roxanne and I became friends. After two weeks, I was well, and we had grown to love each other. I asked Gaius for her hand in marriage. He agreed, and I sailed to Tyre to tell my parents. Father had sent me a letter to come home anyway, so I went to Damascus. I told him I wanted to marry Gaius's sister-in-law, and Father handed me the deed to our old farm. I've been fixing it up ever since then in preparation for my bride, and now here all of us are."

"Yes, I had put that together when my last report came in. Now I'll tell you what I know. I've been researching about you for years. I know that Samuel in Tyre is your brother. I suspect the one in On is too. I know that you have a sister in Antioch too. You have a brilliant business in trade going on, and I have to applaud your decision to separate the businesses from each other. Once family growth reaches this position, it's best to cut back. You can't control and maintain this much growth and keep it secret. Also, times are changing, and so are attitudes, so breaking it into separate companies is very good. Besides, Jarius, you're like me and getting older. It's time for you to cut back and let the younger ones take over. Also, your rings won't work any longer. It took me quite a while to figure that out. Your father was a genius in putting all this together. And don't worry. Everything I received concerning you has been burned. Learning about you has become more than a hobby. It's watching a panorama of life unfold. You've been able to coexist with a power determined to break you and destroy you, and yet you plod on avoiding the pitfalls and living, and I mean truly living amongst all of us. Did you notice the name on your friend Amos's citizenship papers? I had a fellow senator and friend sign it. I assume there is another story behind it. I would like to hear it someday."

By this time, everyone was gaping at the senator. How had he done all this with no one noticing? It was inspiring yet frightening. The patience required was awesome.

"Well, everyone, I believe we've had enough surprises for the day. Demas, my wife and I would like to come see you this Monday. I'm sure that Gauis can send a detail with us to lead the way."

With that, everyone stood and started outside. The senator stopped Demas. "I have something for you and Roxanne. It's very old, but she will recognize it. Please! Take it with you now so that she can see it when you take her home." With a nod, a servant walked up and handed Demas a well-wrapped bundle.

"Thank you, sir. Whatever it is, I know that Roxanne will treasure it."

Good-byes were said, and everyone started leaving.

As Demas settled into their chariot, he smiled and said, "Well, Father, how is your headache?"

"Son, I'm so stunned I haven't comprehended it all yet. That old fox. And here I was so smug that we had fooled the Roman Empire. How he managed all that he has done is so brilliant that you can't fault him. I would like to really sit down and talk to him. Would you mind if I come with them on Monday? I'm sure the women will be busy getting things ready for the wedding."

"Of course, you can come. I've done even more since you were last there. Besides, I think you and the senator will want to talk more. Isn't it amazing how he has tracked us for years? That man is so much more astute than we ever imagined. But you have to admit, he had to be to be in the Roman senate as long as he and his father were. At first, I was shocked and then scared and then awed by his tenacity. I'm sure glad that he's on our side. Aren't you?"

"More than you can ever know."

Just then, Roxanne came out and stood, waiting for Demas. He glanced at his father who smiled and nodded and then turned and left with Matthan at his side.

Demas walked to Roxanne and clasped her hands. "I missed you so much. It seems like forever since we saw each other. I love you so much, but like I wrote to you, I've been busy getting our home fixed up."

"Oh, Demas, I've missed you too, though I was frightened when the senator said all that he did. I told you before that he was a fantastic man. I think Gauis was just as awestruck as everyone else. He will probably allow Severus, his oldest boy, to go back to Rome with his grandparents now. Even he was awed by his father. They really are wonderful people.

I know you weren't convinced when I told you about them, but I lived with them for years, and they are truly amazing, both him and his wife. Now you can understand why I was so defensive for them when we talked. I just didn't realize how amazing they were. Just think, he has been tracking your family for years. It boggles my mind. I had no idea that he was doing it."

"If you are surprised, just think how my father feels. He was rattled. He has tried to be so careful, and here is a man whom he had never heard of slowly and consistently following our every move. Thank God it was him and not someone else."

They walked through the gardens and then sat in the backyard on a bench surrounded by trees and flowers.

"You realize, don't you, that he knows your grandfather built this villa?"

"Yes, I do, but it still left me shaken when he said all that he did. I knew he probably knew about us with the way he talked. That's why I told him everything about us. And that's why I asked my question first before saying what I did. But then you probably knew that I had checked him and his family out too. After knowing Gauis and your sister and then Jacob marrying their daughter, I felt compelled to check out this Roman family. I didn't dig as deep as he has, but I did research on the Attilos. Everything I found out was interesting and surprising, but I never told my family. It just never came up."

"Demas, you mean you knew about me too?"

"Oh, just a little bit. It surprised me that a Roman senator and his wife would care for two Jewish orphans who weren't their slaves. I admit it intrigued me. I just didn't realize that he was doing the same thing on us. It's strange when you think about it."

"Oh, Demas, if these last fifteen years are anything but extraordinary, what will the next fifteen be like?"

"Just plain wonderful, my love. Now go see all the ladies. I'll see you soon."

They kissed, and then Demas strode away.

Demas dropped by his father's place to see how he was doing. He found him on the back patio with his eyes closed.

"Father, are you all right?" he asked.

His father opened his eyes and smiled. "Yes, I'm fine, just thinking about the senator. I'm completely relieved. Does that make any sense?"

"I don't know truthfully. I can understand you feeling as you do, and yet it makes me wonder. He's a sly old fox, but, I can understand what he did. It was originally done because of his concerns for the girls and Gauis. Now we see the brilliancy of his actions. I think in part he holds our family in high esteem. He understood our position and how we managed to weave our way through every possible setback. I don't think he knows how much I've studied him and his family too. In many ways, he has had to do the same things."

"Really! I guess I haven't thought too much about him and what he has had to do to survive. In essence, he is just like us. I think I'll take him to the Tabernacle at Passover. Then he'll understand our faith in the one true God. Who knows, maybe he'll convert to our faith too. And if not, he'll understand where we came from. Yes, I do believe that this is the thing to do."

"As you say, Father, at least, he'll see why we trust God so much. If he refuses, so be it. Just a moment, I want to get something." Demas went to his room and brought out the bundle that the senator had given to him for Roxanne. He took it back to where he had left his dad. As he opened it, he was startled. "Father, look what the senator gave me to give to Roxanne."

"Oh my good God." Jarius gasped. "It's a very old menorah. This must be very ancient. Do you think their mother's family were either very rich or someone was a priest? This is not a common thing for regular believers to have and pass down. I wonder if Roxanne or her sister knows its history. It's magnificent." Jarius took a cloth and scrubbed the candlestick. "Demas, look where I rubbed! It's solid gold."

Both men looked in awe at the sacred menorah. "This couldn't have been in the temple that Solomon built, could it? Are the girls descendants of priests? We are going to have to talk to the senator about this. He may have researched its origin." Jarius was visibly shaken.

Demas carefully rewrapped the candlestick. "I'll take this home with me and put it away until we know its true origin. If anyone has tried to trace it, the senator has. Can you imagine its history and its trek through the years? Father, I can tell you right now, I'm not giving it to the temple. May God forgive me, but I will not let those priests have it. I love and trust God but not the temple hierarchy. If the Romans saw it, they would take it."

Both men were visibly shaken.

Chapter 21

On Monday, Demas had everything ready for his father and the senator's visit. He had hidden the menorah. He was still shaken up by seeing it.

Shela was in the kitchen preparing the meal that would be served. As far as he could tell, everything was ready for the visit. He had even bathed runt and brushed her down.

He looked up at the road and saw a cloud of dust coming. *Well, here they come*, so Demas sat down and waited as riders became visible. Gauis had sent soldiers to escort the senator and his father. It was a good idea.

"Shela, here comes our visitors. Andrew, please bring out the towels and water for our guests."

As before, the soldiers were in front and back of the group. Stepping out to greet them, he waited as they dismounted.

"You must have left early to get here so soon," said Demas as he walked toward them.

The same centurion that had been here before dismounted and helped the senator and his father dismount their animals. Demas grinned at his father and greeted them.

"Come, my men will help you as before, centurion."

Then several men appeared and led the soldiers and their mounts to water that had been put out for them.

"Greetings, sir. Welcome to my home. Hello, Father. It's good to see you again so soon."

"This place is quite nice," said the senator. "When you said you had a farm, I assumed it would be quite a bit different than this. It almost reminds me of rural homes in Italy."

Demas led them into the house. "I know that you've been seated for quite a while. Would you like some refreshments before touring the grounds?"

"Just something to drink, I'm anxious to see everything." After the men had refreshed themselves, Demas showed them his home. The senator seemed very pleased at it and the surrounding gardens and orchards.

"You surprise me, young man. Let's see the rest of the place."

As they walked down the walk to the shepherds' homes, even Jarius was surprised at the new changes.

"These people aren't servants, are they?" the senator asked.

"No, I have no unpaid workers here. I provide housing for them and their families. The single men board in the houses at the very end of the path."

As the men walked down the path, the women bowed to them, and the children watched for a minute and then went back to playing and enjoying themselves.

"I am very pleased. Everything is very neat, and I like seeing children playing and enjoying themselves.

They continued down the path and then followed it up a hill. When they reached the top, the senator was stunned. Flocks of sheep grazed on one side of the fields, and there were also free-range cattle and donkeys on the other side. Shepherds with dogs walked through the flocks, checking them.

"How far does your property extend?" he asked.

"About two days' walk to the west and south," Demas said.

"You call this a farm? It's like a whole village," the senator said. "And what are all the dogs for?"

"Let me show you." He nodded to the head shepherd, who turned toward a flock and whistled. Two dogs were running around a flock of sheep and herding them to the water troughs when a couple of sheep started in another direction. The shepherd whistled again, and the dogs ran and stopped them and barked as they turned them back to the rest of the flock. They never touched the wayward sheep, but the sheep obeyed them and went to their flock and started drinking too.

"I have never seen anything like that," said the senator. "How did you train your dogs to be so obedient? We have dogs too, but I've never seen them work sheep like herdsmen before. With them so alert, you probably won't lose any sheep, and you won't need as many shepherds."

"That's right, sir. They protect them and keep them from wandering away. So far, every one of them is accounted for each evening. In the farthest fields, the shepherds are rotated weekly so they aren't away from home for months on end. They're happier, and so are their families. Shepherding in distant pastures was very hard on them. This way, whether married or not, they get to see their families more often and aren't exposed to the loneliness and harsh weather for weeks at a time. And like most people, they like to be home."

The senator then turned and saw the orchards and vineyard on the hills. "I see the vineyard and its tower."

"There are figs, olives, dates, and pomegranates. On the other side of the hills are my barley and wheat fields. Behind my house is an herb and spice garden, and farther away are my bee colonies."

"You are as totally self-sufficient as a village, aren't you?"

"I will be as soon as everything becomes viable crops."

The men turned and walked back to the house. The senator was quiet but still aware of all the activity going on all over the farm.

As they stepped inside the house, Andrew was there with water and towels. They washed and sat down at the table. Immediately, food and drinks were served.

"You have the most efficient and happy people surrounding you that I have ever seen. I believe my Roxanne will be very happy here. Thank you, Demas, for showing me your farm. I envy you the quiet and peace. There isn't much of it in Rome anymore."

They ate their meal and talked of many things. Finally, Demas turned and said, "I looked at your gift for Roxanne. Needless to say, I was stunned. My father and I both agree it is very old and extremely valuable. May we ask where it came from?"

"Yes, I figured you would be interested. It belonged to Hannah and Roxanne's mother. I tried to trace it but had difficulty doing it. I offered it to Hannah, but she said that since Attilo was a Roman tribune, they wouldn't be able to display it in their home. She said to give it to Roxanne when she married, and so I have. Where do you think it came from?"

"My father and I believe it was in our temple when Babylon captured the city. Someone took it at that time. Did Roxanne or her sister know anything about their ancestry? We're curious if her family came from our priesthood."

"That is my theory too. Her mother once said something like that, but she never expanded on it. She said that God would sort everything out in the end. I'm pleased that it has come back to its home in Jerusalem. You will be keeping it, won't you?"

"Yes, sir, we will. Our present situation and the attitude of those in the temple don't really make us inclined to justify our giving it back. As her mother said, we'll let our God be our guide. We aren't in a position where we can guarantee its safety there, so we will guard and protect it for now. But again, thank you for your protection of it until now."

Later after the meal and some relaxation, the senator and Jarius returned to Jerusalem. Before he left, Jarius congratulated Demas on the condition of their former homestead. He said it had become everything that he had always hoped it would be again.

Demas smiled and nodded. *Well, that's all over with,* he thought. Now he had to get the animals ready to be taken up to Jerusalem for Passover. The temple had holding pens close to town. They would need about three hundred lambs this time. Next year, they would double it. The temple was still buying them, but they were glad that Demas had improved their quality. He would also be taking more for the other feasts celebrated by his people. But more than anything, he and Roxanne would be together. It seemed he was always smiling no matter what he was doing. He did notice that the wives of the shepherds would smile and laugh with others when he walked by. Whatever. He was just plain happy.

As he thought back on everything, it made him wonder if the senator really would go to the temple. He would be restricted to the gentile's court, but he would see their faith in God in practice. His mother had done him the favor of asking Hannah if Roxanne could ride a horse. He needed to know so he would take the right animal for her to ride home on after their wedding.

They wouldn't stay for the feast, but he sensed that all of his workers and their wives were planning something to be part of their marriage celebration. Roxanne would really enjoy that if they did.

Chapter 22

All the animals were doing well as they were being led through the hills toward Jerusalem, so Demas talked to Joseph and rode his horse ahead on to Jerusalem to get the men expecting them prepared for their arrival. He had managed to fill all their requests. It was fortunate that he had bought enough cows, which calved, to bring them too. He even had three calves penned and being held at home if he needed any for personal use for feasts.

It looked as though Gauis was going to let his two sons return to Rome with his father and mother when they left. He didn't like it, but he realized their education should include studying in Rome, especially if one of them had the desire to follow in his father's profession in politics. He would miss them, but his wife would truly be lonely when they left. It might be years before they would see them again. He figured the eldest son would join the army, but the younger boy was more studious and would probably be the one to get involved in government. Only time would tell. Truthfully, Gaius wanted to return to Ephesus. He and Hannah loved it there. It would be wonderful if he could be the governor again. They missed their home and friends.

Roxanne was in a whirl of preparation for her wedding. Her sister, Hannah, and Demas's mother, Mariam, had taken her shopping several times. She was being fitted for new clothes. But she missed Demas. She guessed he was just as busy. But it was somewhat frustrating, if not exciting, as the time neared for their wedding.

Then one morning, her sister took her out to the rear gardens and sat with her. "There are some things that I want you to know, Roxanne, about you and me. I think now is the time to tell you. Our mother told me these things long ago and said that I must tell you when the time was right. I feel that that time is now. Even though we will be near each other, these are things you should know about our family." Roxanne listened intently in near disbelief as the story unfolded.

"Mother said we were from the priestly line of Aaron, Moses's brother. Being women, we weren't normally included nor mentioned in the priesthood lineage. It was up to the mothers to tell their daughters of our history. Men do as God commands, and women keep the records of their own background. Mother gave me those records, and so I'm passing them on to you. I've married a Gentile and had the two boys and Allysa, and she didn't want the added responsibility of knowing our history. However, you are marrying into a Pharisee family and, the Lord willing, will have a daughter or more to carry on our history. The Jewish women were especially careful to keep our lineage recorded. Most of the time it was memorized, but then one of our ancestors started recording it onto scrolls. Mother did not have those scrolls but had memorized them and then dictated it to me so that we would have our history recorded. I am giving you these scrolls to perpetuate our history. Sometimes it seems like we women are unnecessary, but we have a history the same as the men. I have memorized this lineage, and I would suggest that you do the same. You can use the scrolls to do that. If ever things or times become overwhelmingly dangerous, you know what to do. I believe you are marrying a very fine man of God. His family has persevered just as we have. I am sure that you will carry on the history of the women of God."

Roxanne was stunned over her sister's revelation, and yet it made sense. She was confused and yet felt very thankful to God for allowing her ancestors to keep this history alive. She would do the same. Hugging Hannah, they walked back into the house arm in arm together.

By late afternoon, Demas rode into his parents' gate. Both his parents were relaxing in the shade of the fountain. It was good to see them both enjoying the coolness of the day.

"Well, my goodness," said Mariam. "What has brought you to town today?"

"I just delivered the animals requested by the temple," Demas said and sat down with them.

"Were they satisfied by the quality?" his father asked.

"Yes, they were, sir. They said these were much better than the ones in the past few years. I told them that the next ones would be even better."

"Did you visit Roxanne yet?"

"No. I plan to see her tomorrow before I start back for the farm."

"Demas, I was just telling your mother again how good your place looked, and we were bantering back and forth about the menorah. I'm still amazed by its reappearance."

"We would probably be amazed to know how it just reappeared after all these years. It's like seeing a dream of the past come alive in our hands."

"Yes, I know what you mean. I put it away in the roof room. I thought it was the best place. I don't think anyone would recognize what it truly is and represents. I covered it again where we scratched it. It's under the flooring. Only someone truly familiar with antiques would ever imagine its real origin. Sometimes the best place to hide something is in plain sight. Besides, no one really goes into that room anymore."

"Yes, you are right in this case. I do want your mother to see it, though, when we come to visit you again."

They sat quietly, relaxing, until Matthan came out and said that dinner was ready to be served.

The next morning, Demas said his good-byes and rode over to Beth Enajim. Roxanne was relaxing in a side patio.

"Hello, Roxanne," he said as he walked toward her. "How are you today?"

"Just as you are, Demas. Looking forward to being with you in our new home. Only ten days more."

"Roxanne, I wanted to ask you a question while I can. We will have to travel a little ways after the ceremony. Can you ride a horse?"

"Of course, I can. I enjoy it very much. Naturally, I had to use a chariot in town because I was always escorted, but at the Attilos's estate, I could ride on a horse whenever I had the time. Why are you asking? Did you think that I would need a special means of conveyance?"

"No, dearest. I just wanted you to enjoy the trip to the farm. I'm so anxious for you to see it. I think that you will be pleased and happy when you do."

"My dearest love, wherever you are, I will be happy." She smiled.

After a while, they heard a servant girl sneeze. "Well, I guess that's my cue to leave," Demas said, and they walked back to the front patio, and he left.

Passover started the next evening, so Demas decided to stay with his parents until they went to the temple. He would leave at sundown. That evening, some of his shepherds were waiting to go to the temple to offer their sacrifices. Then they would all go back to Emmaus together. Demas's father tried to get him to stay longer, but he was ready to go home.

Chapter 23

The night of Passover, everyone was participating in the feast. They had the fatted calf that Demas had brought for them from the farm. The menorah was lit, prayers were said, and the meal was eaten. Demas was subdued by the holiness of the ceremony. The next day, he and his father took their sacrifices to the temple. It was unbelievable how many people were there. There were literally thousands waiting to give their sacrifices to the Lord. As they completed their ritual, Jarius leaned close to Demas and whispered, "If he comes, we would probably not realize it with so many people here. But I will be here every day until it's over though."

Demas nodded, and they headed home. The next day, he saw Roxanne briefly and then left for Emmaus. It was quiet at the farm. Even the children were subdued. Demas could feel the presence of the Lord the rest of the day.

Three days later, he returned to his parents' home. His father was excited as he told Demas what happened. Jarius had been walking in the courts one late afternoon when he saw several men sitting around a young boy. "They were putting question after question to him, and the boy gave them scripture after scripture to prove that they were missing the true intent of God's Word. Then Zacharias the priest came and took him away. I wanted to catch them, but another young man stepped up to me and said, 'Jarius, you will not see Jesus here again.' Then he followed them. The next day, I went again but got there late. The young man wasn't there. He had been there earlier, but then he left. What do you think about the second boy saying I wouldn't see him here again? And when I came, he was gone. I found that the second young man was Zackarias's son, John. How do you think he knew that I would just miss him? And when I came, he was gone. 'Demas, God's son is a genius. He knew scriptures like he had written them. He had to be the son of God, whom I saw as a babe."

"Father, calm down. Apparently, this boy, John, was saying you may be farther away when the next Passover comes. You may not be close enough to Jerusalem to come every year as you have in the past. We know that things are changing, but you, at least, saw him this time. I never have yet."

"Of course, you are right. It was just so exciting to hear him. The Pharisees constantly asked questions that most people wouldn't have considered that there might be a deeper meaning to. It was so intriguing. Can you imagine how he will be when he's older?"

"Well, as the son of God, he would know all the answers. He has been with God forever. Now how would you like to come to Bethany with me? I ordered some things, and a caravan should have come in lately."

"When do you want to go? It's getting late now. Let's go in the morning when we will have more time."

That settled it, so they walked home.

That next morning, they left for Bethany. It was a wonderful day. The dogs started barking before they could turn into the gate and dismount. Lazarus came out and met them. He went over to Demas first.

"Hello, Lazarus."

"I want to talk to you, sir. I have some ideas that I think you will like. You bought a horse for your wife-to-be. I was thinking of a way for her to be safer and more ladylike when she's astride. Would you like to see what I'm talking about?"

"Certainly, Lazarus. What have you come up with?"

"Let me show you. My father gave me a saddle to try it on." With that, Demas and his father followed him to one of the sheds. "Here it is," he said and took a saddle down off a saw horse. "I took this piece of wood and covered it with leather. Then I took the right stirrup off. I attached the horn to the front of the saddle. Then I put the shortened stirrup on the same side as the other one. When she mounts, instead of straddling the horse, she'll put her right leg over the horn and her foot into the shortened stirrup. Her other foot will be where it usually goes in the longer stirrup. I had my sisters try it, and they liked it. You are still balanced on the saddle, but ladies can drape their robes more nicely. What do you think?"

Demas and his father looked it over and just looked at Lazarus. "How do you figure these things out?" Demas asked.

"I just think of a problem, and it comes to me how to fix it. Would you like to try it out?"

"Yes, I would. If it works well, may I give you money to buy two more new saddles and redo them? I'll borrow this one for now. When you have the others done, I'll return this one. And I'll pay you for your time," Demas said. "Do you have anything else that I could use?"

"Well, yes. It's rather embarrassing but extremely useful. When Mary had to learn to use a bucket to relieve herself, she kept falling into it. But if you build a box about a hand's width wider than the bucket and put a top on it with a hole cut out and leather straps on the back to hold it in place, it makes it easier for girls to use. All you have to do is raise the lid to remove the bucket and dump it and then put it back. Here, I'll show you." Then Lazarus drew a sketch in the sand.

By this time, Demas and his father were smiling broadly at the boy.

"Lazarus, you're a genius. We are impressed. Have you anything else that you've created?" Demas grinned.

"Not really, sir. I think all the time, but I do a lot now for my father. I'm always thinking, but no time to see if any of my ideas will work."

"Well, you've sold me. Here, is this enough for two new saddles?" Demas handed the boy the money.

"Oh, sir, that's too much."

"That's okay, Lazarus. A man is worthy of his pay. Anything extra is yours. Now do you have my order yet?"

"Yes, sir, it's already packed on the donkey that you brought here last week. I saw you coming and loaded it. I'll add the saddle to it. My father and grandfather are at the temple now, so I'm in charge."

"Well, my man, you are doing a wonderful job. God always rewards those who work hard. We have to go now, but thank you so much. May God bless and keep you."

"Thank you, sirs, and may God bless you too."

All the way to Emmaus, Demas and his father were laughing over Lazarus's industry.

"Are you going to build the box, Demas?" His father grinned.

"Of course, and I'll use it too. Don't laugh. You know you'll be doing it also." Demas grinned.

"That boy is one of the most creative persons I've ever met. Wouldn't it be something if all the world's leaders were as smart?"

The trip to Emmaus was the best that either of them had ever experienced. They were sharing their joy and peace.

When they got to the farm, they unloaded their load. Then Demas took the saddle and put it on the horse that he had bought for Roxanne. Then he called Shela from the house.

"Yes, master," she answered.

"Shela, have you ever ridden a horse?" Demas asked.

"Yes, sir, but not in years. What is it that you need?"

"I have a different kind of saddle for my bride, and I would appreciate it if you would try it out for my father and me. You will sit sidesaddle with your right leg looped around the horn. Put your right foot in the shorter stirrup and your left foot in the regular stirrup. I'll help you up, and my father will hold the horse's head. Are you willing to do that?"

"Well, I guess. You won't let me fall, will you?"

"No. I just want your opinion of it. Once you are up and feel secure, you can walk around, or we will walk the horse. It seemed like such a good idea. I want to know what a lady would think. If you want to try it on your own, you can, okay?"

"Okay, Master Demas. Let's do it."

Demas helped her up. She kept her robe together. She put her leg around the horn, her feet in the stirrups, and held on. She went out to the gate and came back. Then she trotted around for a bit. "Oh, master, this is very nice. My robe covers me, and yet I feel very comfortable. Yes, I like this saddle very much."

As she dismounted, she thanked him and then returned to the house.

Jarius grinned at Demas and said, "It's a winner. But why did you order two saddles?"

"One will be for Roxanne and one for Mother, of course."

"I should have known. Now you're going to have to teach me how to ride."

"I planned to do so tomorrow. It's a great experience. Besides, when you buy your horses, you will able to show Mother how quickly you can learn." He grinned.

They were still laughing when they went inside. "And when are you going to make your box, Demas?"

"I told Lazarus to send a carpenter tomorrow. I want one for every house on the farm."

Jarius was still laughing later that day when they sat down for dinner. He was so happy to have his boy to share things with. They had missed so much time together that now every day was a treasured joy.

Chapter 24

Two days later, Jarius and Demas were ready to return to Jerusalem. Two fatted calves had been sent up to Jerusalem for the wedding feast. Demas had given the other to Shela to cook for all the people on the farm to celebrate his and Roxanne's marriage. Three more calves had already been penned to be fattened up too.

The carpenter had finished his job. At first, the women had been leery of this new thing in their houses, but by the end of the first day, they were all thanking him. The carpenter wanted to start making them at his business, and Demas said that Lazarus should get five percent of everyone made for one year. The carpenter agreed.

Now it was time for the wedding. Jarius had caught on quickly to riding a horse. He was riding Roxanne's horse as he and Demas left Emmaus for Jerusalem. They were talking the whole way.

By afternoon, they arrived at Jarius's home. It was Tuesday, and the villa was already being decorated. Thanks to Mariam and Matthan, the place was neat and shining.

"Well, I wondered if you were coming back." Mariam smiled.

Matthan took Demas's wedding clothing into the house.

Finally, it donned on Mariam that her husband had been riding a horse. "My husband, how was the ride?"

"I liked it. I'm a little sore because our son has had me on a horse for three days. But you were right, it's quite enjoyable."

Time flew by, and Thursday came at last. Demas couldn't sit still. He kept asking if everything was ready. His mother would pat his cheek and hand him another cup of coffee. Tables covered the large patio. The aroma of roasting beef filled the air.

Musicians were playing softly. By noon, people were arriving. Demas was dressed and still pacing. His mother had gone over the whole course of the way things would go at least a dozen times. Then a great noise came from the street. The bride and her family were arriving. Demas and his father stood at the entrance to the yard. Mariam was waiting to escort Roxanne and her sister to their room. At last, Demas could see her. She was so beautiful he could feel tears in his eyes, but she was immediately whisked away. He greeted all of the Attilos and helped them get seated. By now, the yard was full of people. The canopy barely rippled in the light breeze. The last to arrive were Zackariah, Elizabeth, and their son, John.

Finally, he was called into the house. His mother took him to the side of the entryway, and then his bride was led out of a room. Demas felt like he was floating and hovering as Roxanne was handed to him. They walked out to the canopy and Zackariah started the ceremony. After he finished, others stood and blessed them, their marriage, and their future. Lastly, his father stood and said a blessing for them and hugged them both. Then they went back into the house to their own rooms. Demas removed his turban and gave it to Matthan, who already had Roxanne's. He put on his outer robe. Then there she was. The veil covered her completely, and she was like a shadow in it. They joined hands and walked out to the guests and were presented as husband and wife. People clapped for them, and then they withdrew into the house and went out the back door to the stable. The horses were ready, and Roxanne twisted the veiling to cover most of her face but left her eyes bare. Demas had sent the horse and saddle over to Beth Enajim with his father, who showed her how to sit in the saddle.

Demas started to help her mount but stopped, pulled her veil away, and took her into his arms. He kissed her lips, her eyes, and then her lips again. "I love you, my darling wife," he whispered. She grinned back and said, "I love you, my husband. Now can we go home at last?"

He grinned, hoisted her into the saddle, mounted his own steed, and said, "Let's go home."

As they left the stable gate, they were greeted by the centurion and three other men. "The tribune has ordered us to take you home. It's for your safety."

"Thank you, my friend. Let's go."

Demas and Roxanne rode side by side, talking most of the way. The soldiers had dropped back to give them some privacy. Before they realized it, they were home. The place was decorated and the shepherds and their families had set out a feast to welcome them. The soldiers started to turn back, but Demas told them to wait and enjoy the feast before going back to Jerusalem. They came into the front court, and the party began. Roxanne was enthralled by the house, the people, and their joy for her and Demas. At last, the soldiers left, the men took the children home, and Demas and Roxanne went into the house. They climbed the stairs to the upper room, and he showed her the farm.

"Well, dearest, what do you think?" Demas grinned.

"I think that I'm the luckiest girl alive," she answered.

Then Demas took her into their room and shut the door.

Back in Jerusalem, Jarius and Mariam had visited with every guest and thanked them for coming. When Jarius came to Zackariah and his family and asked if he could come see him the following Sunday, he agreed.

Dusk was approaching as the guests began to leave. Lanterns were lit, and the tables cleaned. Wine, coffee, tea, and juice were poured. Everyone was sated and tired. Jarius and Mariam stood at the gate and said good evening to every guest. The senior Attilos came to them and thanked them and said they admired the whole ceremony and reception. Then they left.

At last, Jarius and Mariam went inside and sat down. "Well, my dear, our first son is now married. I think they are well-paired and will be very happy. You did a wonderful job of organizing, as always."

"Thank you, dearest. It reminds me of us when we were first wed. Poor Demas. He looked as uncertain as you did when we were married."

"Yes, he did. I believe that all his people were holding a feast for them, so they are probably just now alone. I pray that they are every bit as happy as we were then, and even more so now. I'm tired, Miriam, let's go to bed."

Hand in hand, they went to their room, and Matthan shut the door and blew out the lanterns.

Demas lay in bed, just looking at Roxanne sleep. He was so happy, and he loved his beautiful wife so much. She was everything that he had hoped and prayed for. He could understand his parents' relationship now. He hoped that when Roxanne and he had been married as long as them, they too would have as strong a bond. He got up and went out to watch the sun rise. He wanted to show her the farm today and give her Runt. He knew that she would love her.

Suddenly, she stood beside him. "Good morning, my love. And how are you?"

"I'm just wonderful," he said. "Are you hungry? Let's eat, and then I'll take you all over the place. I have another gift for you, but it's downstairs."

"Demas, how many gifts are you going to give me? I have you and this wonderful home. I don't need anything else."

"Well, this gift is different. When I saw it, you came to mind immediately."

"Let's go then. I can't wait to meet our people again. Yesterday was somewhat overwhelming, but I'm ready to go again."

As they came down the stairs, Shela met them. "I have coffee and hot bread for you. There is also honey and fruit."

"Thank you," they said in unison. They ate and talked and held hands and then got ready to go outside. Just as they opened the front door for the day, a bundle of energy ran to them.

"This is my other gift for you. We call her Runt because I wanted you to name her."

Roxanne hugged and petted Runt. "I love her. I even like her name. Thank you, Demas. Now I have a horse, a dog, a home, and a wonderful husband, plus, a big family. Demas, aren't we blessed?'

Demas took her out to the workers' homes. Roxanne met and talked to the women, held some of the babies, and tried to remember who was who and all about their families. Then they walked to the fields, and she was amazed at all the animals.

"You didn't tell me how big your farm was. And look, we have orchards, gardens, and animals. It's like a town of its own."

Demas was so happy at her enthusiasm.

The days passed into weeks. They spent a lot of time together, but each had their own things to do. Roxanne and Shela became close friends as well as the other women.

Then one day, a rider came riding into the yard. "I have a letter for Demas Shophan," he said and handed the letter to Demas. "Do you have a reply to send back?"

As he read the letter, he was saddened and surprised. "Yes. Please relax. My steward will get you some food and water and see to your horse." Then he went into the house to get Roxanne.

Apparently, his Uncle Samuel had received the news and sent it on to his father.

"Demas, what's wrong?"

"I've just received a letter from Father. My aunt in Antioch was killed in an accident. Her husband wants to return to Tarsus with his two children and asks what to do about our place there. Father and Mother are getting packed now to leave. Would you like to go with me to say good-bye?"

"Oh, Demas, of course, we should go. I'll get ready immediately."

Demas paid and dismissed the rider. He then asked Andrew to saddle their horses and then went to tell Joseph that he and Roxanne had to go see his father and mother immediately and that they should be back in a few days. Then he and Roxanne rode out.

Chapter 25

There was a flurry of activity as Demas and Roxanne road into his parents' courtyard. Jarius came out and smiled. He then turned and hollered, "Mariam, they're here!"

Demas and Roxanne dismounted and hurried over to his parents.

"I told you, Mariam, that they would come."

"Yes, dearest, I was so hoping that they would come to see us off. Come, let's go out to the patio in the back where we can visit."

As they settled down, Jarius spoke. "First, apparently, a viper spooked Ruth's camel, and she fell. She hit her head, and she was dead before anyone could do anything. Now Simon wants to quit our business there and go back to Tarsus and take over his father's tent-making business. He'll take his son and daughter, Cassia, too. "

"You know that your mother and I were wondering what to do in Damascus. This could turn a tragedy into a blessing. Amos is more than capable to take over in Damascus. Samuel's boys are old enough to take over in Tyre. They plan to stay there to be near their children and their families anyway, so your mother and I are going to go to Tyre. We'll catch one of our boats to Antioch and move up there ourselves. In a few years, your younger brothers will be ready to handle the business. Then we can retire too. Things will change, I know. I just didn't think that it would be sooner than later."

"If you are leaving tomorrow, why don't we go to Emmaus and see if those things that I ordered are ready. Then you'll have them."

"Yes, let's do that. We'll only be in the women's way here."

They got a couple of donkeys ready and left.

"Well, the next week after the wedding, I went to see Zackariah and Elizabeth. I asked him about the boy whom we think is God's son. He asked me why I thought that, so I told him all about what we had seen in Bethlehem twelve years before. Then he told me that his name was Jesus. His mother had been a virgin, that his mother was betrothed to Joseph. They had both received guidance from angels sent by God. Joseph went ahead and took her home as his wife. Then they had to register in Jerusalem as ordered by Rome. The place was teeming with people, and that's why they ended up in Bethlehem. They left the next morning and found a place to stay. Later they were warned by angels to go immediately to Egypt to protect the boy. They left immediately that night. The next day, Herod had all the male babies under three years old killed. They stayed in Egypt until an angel again appeared and told them it was safe to go home, so they went home and live there even now. He said he wouldn't tell us where he lives. That in eighteen years, we will recognize him when he starts his ministry. He also said that an angel had foretold their own son's birth and that he would be a Nazirite. He knows that he and Elizabeth will probably die before the boys reach thirty. When they do die, their son, John, will go to the Essenes to live and learn."

Demas was quiet for a while and then said, "Now you understand why John said that you would not see Jesus here again. He knew that you would be living farther away and not come to Jerusalem every year. It's unbelievable how our Lord works everything out according to his timetable."

They rode on to Emmaus. Lazarus had the saddles ready. Another caravan was loading, so they thanked him and left.

As they returned to Jerusalem, they hadn't talked very much. Both were deep in thought.

The women were getting dinner ready when they walked in. "Mother, I have something for you and Roxanne." He presented the new saddles to each of them.

"After you told Father and me about your experience with a horse, I knew you would be needing one of these too. This is the same type as the one Roxanne used on our wedding day."

His mother walked over to Demas and hugged him. "You are, as always, so thoughtful. Thank you."

Roxanne was just as pleased as Mariam and smiled at Demas and nodded.

Dinner was pleasant as everyone tried to be happy with the changes that were happening. Then they retired early, for the caravan would be leaving at dawn.

Demas and Roxanne waved and watched as the caravan went over the hills and disappeared from sight. Then they turned their horses and headed home.

"When will we see them again, Demas? I truly love your parents. I lost my parents so quickly, and now Jarius and Mariam are leaving. They are so wonderful. I am going to be lonely without them. Thankfully, Hannah is fairly close. But your parents are very special to me."

"When they get settled, we'll go to Antioch for a visit. In about a year, I would imagine."

"A lot can happen in a year, Demas." She was quiet as she reflected that in a year, they would not just be a family of two anymore.

Part 3

Chapter 26

Twelve years had passed since Demas's marriage. He had four children now—three boys and a girl. He and his family had arrived in Tyre two days ago on their way to Antioch. Roxanne was at Samuel and Elizabeth's house visiting. They were waiting for his father, who was due in anytime. He had gone to Ephesus to see Jacob and Gauis. Gauis was governor of Ephesus now. He had retired from the army three years previously and had been given the governorship of Ephesus. Both his boys had returned to Rome with their grandparents after his and Roxanne's marriage. Just as Gauis had predicted, the oldest boy, Severus, had joined the army, and Antonio had followed his grandfather into politics. Both the senator and his wife, Helena, had died a few years ago.

However, they had come back about six years ago and stayed with Roxanne and him at their farm for a couple of weeks. They were happy with the farm and the boys. Little

Rebecca hadn't been born yet. The farm had matured, and they spent every day out walking and visiting with the workers and their families. Demas had invited them to stay, and even offered to build them a house there, but the senator said no. He had to get back to Rome and guide Antonio through his growing and maneuvering career as a politician. They were great grandparents for the boys. He and the senator had enjoyed long conversations about the way Rome was getting tired of the Jews and their constant aggression with the Romans. He told Demas that he felt Rome would eventually be the death of the Jews or, at least, most of Israel. He felt sure that Demas didn't have too many years left to stay in the area. Even his father and mother had come down from Antioch to visit with all of them. His youngest brother Gabriel had been studying at the temple to be a Pharisee.

They had stayed on the farm most of their visit. Gaius was so busy that he really didn't have much time to be with them. They truly enjoyed their time with Roxanne and the farm wives. Helena had brought two looms for Roxanne and then spent sometime teaching her and the other women how to use them. They turned out to be a blessing for everyone. There were very few dry eyes around the place when they said their good-byes and left for Rome.

Then two years later, they had died within a month of each other. Gaius had already retired and moved back to Ephesus. Their passing had saddened everyone. Gaius's boys had inherited their grandparent's estate in Rome, but Antonio was the only one there now. Severus was in Greece at the time, serving in the army. He was already a centurion.

Demas had left the farm in the good hands of his steward, James, and his head shepherd, Joseph, while they were gone. Demas and Roxanne planned to go with Jarius to Antioch when he arrived in Tyre. Jarius was a little late arriving but not overly so, so no one was worried. Demas had spent the day with Jonah, who was now a ship's captain. When he had left his father's inn to sail, he had loved it immediately. Demas had put him under Baba's tutorage. Now Jonah was married to Esther, his Uncle Samuel's younger daughter. They lived in Tyre near her father and mother. They had a little boy, Reuben, and a girl, Ruth. His father and mother were still living at the inn and were semi-retired. Jonah's two brothers ran the inn and were also married.

It was getting late, so Demas headed back to Samuel's house. It was chaotic, as there were children everywhere. Esther and Jonah rounded up their family and left for their own home. Samuel was in his element as he kissed the children good-bye.

Turning to Demas, he raised an eye and said, "They haven't landed yet?"

"No, not yet, but they're only two days late. When sailing, things happen. He's on Baba's ship, and he's one of our best captains. They'll be in by tomorrow, I'm sure."

After dinner, everyone headed to their rooms. It had been an exhausting day for all. Jarius would be in soon, and then Demas and his family would be sailing with him to Antioch for a visit with his mother, brothers, and sisters. It would be another hectic family gathering, but he loved it. A year had passed since he had seen all of them. They were married and had families too.

Just before the first light of a new day, Demas woke up. Something wasn't right, and he didn't know what had caused him to be so unsettled. Sometimes you get a sense that something's amiss. He dressed quietly and left the house for the docks.

The sun was just peeking over the horizon as he walked out to a dock. Everything seemed okay, but he had a bad feeling all the same. He heard something behind him, and as he turned, his Uncle Samuel came toward him.

"You too, Demas? I awoke and felt something wasn't right. I heard you leave, so I decided to follow you. You had the feeling too?"

"Yes, Uncle Samuel. I don't know what caused me to awaken. I just knew something was wrong. Well, the sun is showing clearly now, but I don't see anything on the horizon yet. It's strange that we both got the same sense of foreboding."

"I know what you mean. It's as if something is wrong."

The two men stood, looking out over the water. Then they saw two specks on the horizon. The two specks got larger as the sun rose more, and then they could see that two boats were heading to Tyre. They watched, not moving or talking. All they could do was watch and wait. About an hour later, they could see the ships more clearly.

"Oh, dear God, they've been in a fight. See the listing of Baba's boat and the burn marks. They've had a fight with pirates. The sails are scorched and torn."

Men were coming down to the docks now and pointing at the boats. Everyone knew that they had been in a fight. As more time passed, they could see the sailors on the deck but not real clearly. It seemed forever when they could see the terrifying condition of both ships.

Demas saw Baba first. He was wrapped up and had a bandage on his head, but he didn't see his father. "Oh, Lord in heaven, please let my father be okay. I love him so much, as does the rest of his family. Please, Lord!"

The boats finally docked, and a board ran out to the dock. Baba came off first, and Demas caught him as he stepped on the pier. Baba's tears were running down his face, soaking his bandages.

"Demas, I'm so sorry. I tried to protect him, but he was the first one killed. We were talking and an arrow struck him in the chest, and he fell overboard. Then the pirates swarmed all over us. When we finally got rid of them, we searched for your father for two days, but nothing! I believe he was killed immediately and was dead before he hit the water. Oh, Demas, please forgive me. I tried. I really tried to find him, but he was gone." Baba stood there, crying like a child.

Demas grabbed him and helped him walk to their building. Samuel was holding up Baba on the other side. All three men had tears flowing down their faces. The rest of the crew were being helped by the dock workers.

"Bring everyone to the warehouse. We'll tend to everyone there." Demas ordered.

Benches were put up all over the building. Water was being boiled. Samuel had gotten out a bale of soft wool and was helping to wrap the wounded sailors.

Jonah came running and took over the boats and the unhurt men. Women came with coffee, water, food, and wine. They made bandages to rewrap the wounds. Everyone was crying, and a wailing began for those who were killed. Samuel came to Demas and nodded. They left the building, taking Baba with them. As they approached Samuel's house, the women came out with tears streaming down their faces. Samuel went to Elizabeth and held her, while Demas took Baba inside. He and Roxanne got him comfortable and then went out into the garden. As they sat, tears streamed down their faces, and Demas told her what had happened. Then he told her he had to write letters to Uncle Caleb and Uncle Jacob. Boats were leaving soon, and he wanted to let them know what had happened. Demas went to the table and took a file and scraped off the flame over Jarius's candle on his ring. Then he wrote the letters and sealed them. He kept thinking, *Poor Mama. Let her be strong, Lord. She and*

Father had been married more than forty years. How she would miss him, as they all would.

He checked on Baba, who was still weeping even as he slept. Then he went in search of his uncle. He needed to go pray. Samuel stood waiting for him at the door. As they walked to the synagogue, crying and wailing echoed everywhere. The mourning seeped into everyone's souls. Sailors had died too. As they stepped into the synagogue, they covered their heads and wept. Praying together, they called out to God.

"Oh, Lord, please comfort each and every one of us. We know that our loved ones are no longer here and not suffering. Please give us peace, comfort, and strength to endure this separation from them. They were very much loved. We will miss them sorely until we ourselves are reunited with them. Please give us peace and strength to carry on until we are united again. Blessed be the name of the Lord. Amen."

An hour later, they returned to the house.

Turning to Samuel, Demas said, "It's awkward for me to take Father's place. You are older, but I know that this is how we must continue. Roxanne, the children and I will leave tomorrow with Jonah. I must get to Antioch and tell Mother and my family what has happened. Here are the letters for Uncle Caleb and Uncle Jacob. I don't think Baba will be able to leave for a few days, but please send him and his crew home as soon as possible. The wives of the men who have died will need to know too. I want you to give a year's wages to each widow. I will pay for it myself. I'm concerned for Mother and my siblings. I think that I may have to move to Antioch myself. I'll have to see if my brothers are able to handle the business there. My men on the farm are capable of running it. Right now, Mother and the family are foremost in my thoughts."

"You are so much like your father. He too took over the transfer of responsibility when our father died. Actually, I'm glad to have you in charge. I've been moving toward letting my boys take over for me. Also, I'll write and let Amos and Lydia know what has happened. Thank God you will step right into your father's shoes. They will fit well on you, my nephew. And, yes, I will do as you say about the families of the men who were killed. But don't worry about them. Your father and I set up a fund of sorts to cover these families many years ago. They will be taken care of. Baba had to commit the bodies of the killed sailors to the sea so there won't be anyone to bury. I'll see to every family as soon as possible. And if any wounded men can't go back to sailing, I'll make sure that they will have work or a pension of sorts. It is only fair and right."

"Thank you, Uncle. I'm so concerned for Mother right now. She's always been sort of prepared for this eventuality, but didn't truly think it would happen after all these years. And now it has. Please say a prayer for all of us. We'll need them from now on."

The men hugged and entered Samuel's home.

Chapter 27

That evening, Demas went to see Baba and how he was doing. Baba's eyes were swollen and teary.

"My dearest friend, don't despair. You did everything possible. It was just time for Father to be with the Lord. Yes, be sad, but don't take or carry any guilt. Death comes to all of us eventually. It's the one surety that we all have. Physical death comes, and those left behind can be sad, but the reality of death is a fact. We go on with the memories of those we love and have parted from. Nothing can take those away. I'm sure Father told you about seeing God's son at the temple. Did he also tell you that John, the son of Zacharias and Elizabeth, told him that he would not see Jesus here again? At first, we felt that he meant at the temple. Now I believe he meant that Father would be with God the next time they would meet. I am comforted by that more than anything else. So must you."

"Thank you, Demas. I can believe that. I was so angry and upset that we didn't just escape from the pirates. We killed all of them and sank their boats. At least, they won't be terrorizing anyone else again. I've never felt such raw anger and hatred like that ever before. I pray God forgives me."

"He has, and he won't hold it against you. Those men chose their way of life. Now they have paid for it. But don't feel too badly over your actions. I'm sure there will be plenty more of them in the coming years. Evil surrounds us, and from evil great sorrows result. This is where our faith and trust in God protect us. It envelops us with the understanding that though our bodies will eventually die, our spirits will live with the Lord forever. Now these are the plans that Uncle Samuel and I have made. Your boat is being repaired as we speak. Replacement sailors will join your crew for those killed. In a few days or whenever, you will sail on home. Years ago, apparently, my father and his family set up a fund to help out the families of our killed or hurt sailors. Uncle Samuel will get your information on who will need it and send the funds with you. My family and I are leaving for Antioch early tomorrow morning. I must go and tell my mother what has happened. There's going to be some changes, that's inevitable. But I am sorry I have to leave you for now. I'm now the head of the family, so you will be seeing me more often. Get well and strong, and I'll be seeing you soon."

The men hugged each other, and Demas went to find Roxanne. She had let the children play for as long as she could and had fed them dinner. Now they were playing quietly before going to bed. "I thought I would get everything packed before morning. I know that we will be leaving early."

"Yes, dearest, at sunup, we should be at the boat. Is everything ready?"

"But I am so sad to know that we must tell Mariam. Your father and she had such a wonderful relationship. I hope that I never have to experience her heartbreak."

Demas took her into his arms and prayed the same thing. "You do understand that we may have to move there, don't you? It depends on my brothers. The last time that I was there, I wasn't very happy how they were doing things. If I think it would be best for us to handle things, then we'll have to leave the farm. I'll have Joseph take over for me and let Andrew become the head shepherd. It'll work out, I'm sure."

"I had a feeling that everything would be changing, but as long as we're together, that's all that matters. We'll have a new home and new memories to make. Don't worry! At least, we'll have each other."

Demas and Roxanne woke up early. She started waking the children. Demas walked into the main room and found Samuel and Elizabeth sitting and drinking tea.

"I figured that you would be ready to go. We wanted to be up when you got ready. I had most of your things taken to the boat already. Elizabeth and I will help you with the children."

"Thank you, Uncle Samuel. I know that we have to go, but I'm concerned if I will have to move to Antioch."

"Cross that bridge when you have to. Just take one step at a time. We'll be waiting to hear from you. Don't worry, nephew. Everything will work out in God's time and way."

Demas carried Esther, David and Andrew held hands, and Roxanne held Joshua's hand. They crossed the boards and stepped onto the boat. Then they turned and waved as the boat started moving. They took the children and sat on a bench on the other side. Everyone looked at Samuel and Elizabeth as the boat turned and headed out to sea. There were tears in everyone's eyes.

Roxanne then wrapped each child in a blanket and had them lie down between her and Demas. The wind was picking up and carrying them away from Tyre and home. They just sat and watched as the shoreline changed, and then nothing was in sight.

Chapter 28

The days passed, and Roxanne and the children were bored and tired. Finally, Roxanne asked Demas when they would get to Antioch.

"We'll be in port tomorrow. I'm sorry that it has been so hard on you and the children. Now you see how tedious it is to sail. Just be glad we aren't going to Ephesus."

"I know. It's just so hard on the children. But this journey is not as good as the others I've taken. It's so hard trying to keep the children occupied and out of danger."

"Someday the ships will be larger, possibly with two decks for passengers to have more space to walk around on and with rooms for privacy. I think that's why it takes men to do this now. We don't require the space that women and children need. And we're always alert for danger. It will soon be over. I'm anxious to get to Antioch, and yet I'm so sad for mother and my brothers and sisters. I know what these trips are like, but I am proud of how well you and the children have handled it."

"I'm sorry, Demas. I didn't have a family when I had sailed before. It's amazing how tedious it is. I can't understand how you endured it all these years. I keep wondering if my stomach will ever be the same."

You'll get your land legs back in a couple of days. Plus, you'll have help when we get there. I know that you've been thinking about if we have to move there. If we do, I'll leave you in Antioch and take care of it. Mother will enjoy the company, and the children will keep her on her toes."

"You mentioned that possibility. Do you really think that we will be there from now on?"

"Let's just say that it's a good possibility. With me being responsible for the whole business now, I believe it will be a necessity. I know you love the farm, but, dearest, you do see why I'm strongly considering it. It's not necessarily a choice at this point. I need to live in a port city so I can freely sail when necessary. I'll be gone more frequently, so living in a port will cut my time to travel inland to get home. Father and I shared the traveling, but now it's all on me. But I think that mother will be a great help to you and help you to adapt to your position. She'll help you with the children too. I truly am so sorry. We had a wonderful life on the farm, but things out of our control have caused us to adapt to changes. This is a major one. I've had to make changes most of my life."

"I know, Demas. We just had such a great life, and now it's shifting. I guess I really never believed that anything would change. It's rather childish of me, isn't it?"

"No, not really. No one really likes being uprooted. But all things are in God's hands, and he has done a wonderful job so far. I would imagine that there will be even more changes but probably not as drastic as this one. I really don't see why we would at this point. I try to take one day at a time. Besides, what point is there in fighting it? I have known all my life that eventually I would have to take over. Now it has happened. So be it!"

They sat with the children and watched the sun going down and then took the children below to sleep.

Demas was awake as he felt the boat turn. They were approaching Antioch at last. He went onto the deck and saw Jonah by the oarsman.

"Up already?" Jonah asked.

"Yes, I felt the shift in direction. We should see Antioch in the next hour. You've been a great sailor, Jonah. When your dad first told me that you wanted to sail, I felt that you would like it. I'm glad that everything has worked out for you. Now we're family too. Seems strange, doesn't it?"

"Strange but wonderful. I'm sorry this trip is going to be hard for you. I love your mother. She's one of the kindest and most thoughtful women that I've ever met. Did you know that she never forgets birthdays or special days? I don't know how she keeps track of everything. Your father was the same way. He never forgot the name of anyone. They were an amazing couple. You have mine and my family's deepest sympathy."

"Thank you, Jonah. He left a tremendous legacy. I just hope that I can be as good as he was."

"Well, there's Antioch. You knew today that we would arrive, didn't you?"

"Yes. I've traveled these waters many times, just not under these circumstances. I feel so inadequate at times, but my father trained me well. Hopefully, he will be proud of me. That's my hope and goal."

"Don't worry about it, Demas. You're just like him."

"Guess it's time to get my family ready. Are you going back to Tyre or to Ephesus?"

"Back to Tyre. Samuel wants the ships to go in pairs from now on, even when sailing close to land."

"Yes, we used to meet up when we got midway, but the pirates are already anticipating our plans. It's becoming a regular ongoing war now."

Roxanne walked over to Demas and put her arm through his. "Well, there's our new home. It seems like a nice town, doesn't it?"

"Yes, it is. I think you will like it once you've gotten familiar with it and have made friends."

An hour later, they were docking, and there stood his mother and brothers, waiting for them."

Mariam helped Roxanne and the children, and Demas took his brothers aside. "Father is dead. He was instantly killed in a pirate attack three days from Tyre. I know this is a shock for you. We got here as soon as possible."

All three hugged each other and trudged to their parents' home.

"Why isn't mother asking about Father?" Demas queried.

"We'll let Mother tell you when we're home," they said.

Then they walked arm in arm up the hill to their home. Mariam turned to her eldest son and said, "Jarius is dead, isn't he? How?"

"The boat was attacked by pirates. Father was killed by an arrow. Everything happened so quickly. It was night, and he and Baba were on the deck. They didn't know that the pirates were anywhere near. They both took arrows in the chest. Father fell overboard before anyone could catch him. Our ship was alone at the time. Then when the second ship arrived, the fight turned into our favor. When it was over, both pirate ships were sunk. Baba's ship and sister ship searched for two days for Father. Baba said he knows that he was dead before falling into the water, but they looked for him anyway. Then they came on home. I was there with Uncle Samuel when they reached Tyre. We lost eight men and Father. Baba said that no pirates survived. Mother, I'm so stunned by all of this. Everything and everyone has been taken care of. I can't begin to tell you how much I'm heartbroken. Samuel has already accepted me as Father's replacement. I wrote letters to Jacob and Caleb, so they know what has happened. But how did you know? We left the next day for Antioch."

"Two weeks ago, I was sleeping when I heard your father call me. I sat up in bed, and it was like he was there with me. He said he loved me but had to go. In the morning, I just knew that Jarius was dead. I told the boys what had happened, and we have all grieved. I believe that God allowed your father to come and say good-bye to me. Now it has been confirmed. He will always be in our hearts, and we will miss him. Now what are your plans?"

"Roxanne and I have talked about this and think that we should move here. I have good men running the farm, and I will let them continue to do so. I will go there every three months to check on things. My wife and I had twelve wonderful years there, but I have to step up just as Father did when Grandfather was killed. So we'll find a home here to live in."

"No, you won't. This house is big enough for all of us. You will live here with me. I need Roxanne and the children around me, so that's settled. What about your brothers? Your father talked to me about them. He felt they needed more training and some travel experience. I believe he was right. Is that your plan? I know you and your father have been thinking about it. Have you made any decisions?"

"Yes and no. I'm going to talk with them both and see how they feel about the work here and then traveling south.

Neither of them seem dedicated to the company, and I really don't know what to do until I spend time with them both. I'm going to need your ideas and support when I've made some decisions."

"That's good. Now let's have breakfast and relax a little. A caravan is due tomorrow, so you can see how your brothers work. I know you won't be harsh with them, but they must mature and be responsible. You were grown up by the time you were twelve. Unfortunately, they aren't as dedicated as you. They need your help and guidance. Be gentle but firm. They will see you as their teacher. Patience will be needed, and that you have. Now let's dine and rest. Roxanne looks like she could use some relief. Also, here is a letter that your father wrote for you should anything happen to him. I believe he knew that something would happen to him on one of his trips. He wanted you to have some guidance from him if and when it did."

Demas took the letter and put it in his robe. "I'll read it later," he said.

After eating, the women took the children outside to burn off some energy and to see their new home. Demas went into the room that his father used for business. Matthan followed him; Demas sat down and nodded for the steward to sit too.

"Well, old friend, how have you been? I wanted to talk with you and see if you needed anything. As you've probably guessed, my family and I are moving here as soon as possible, and I want your input on what plans I should make. You have known all of us for years. I knew this day would eventually come, but no one is truly prepared for it when it does happen. I'll bring my steward, James, here, but you are still the head steward in my heart. But what would you like to do for yourself?"

"I've been mulling this over myself. I'm slowing down, there's no doubt about that, and I love this family as much as is possible. I know all that you've done on the old farm. Your father and I frequently talked about it. I would like to stay here while you get moved. I will help James get settled in and learn what he needs to do. Then maybe next year, I would like to go see the farm. And if things work out with James here, then I'll be your steward in Emmaus. I've missed the old place, and I'll have a slower pace down there. Yet I will run it for you as I did for your father and Jacob. Would that be okay?"

"I have thought about this too. When I go back there to move our things here, I will let my head shepherd know that you will be coming down. You will be my representative there. You ran it before, and you can do it again. James is used to our growing family, and he is also younger. You have been a good and faithful friend, Matthan. I believe that you deserve a happy and quiet life for a while. But just know that if you want to come back to us here to live, you will always have a home with us. When you are settled there, you will be my voice in all matters. You will have my authority to conduct business as my overseer and manager. We've made a lot of changes, and I will feel comfortable knowing that you will run it as you did in the past. The people on the farm will like you and trust you as I do. You already know my uncles. By having you in charge, it will lift a large burden from me. You will live in the main house. All I ask is that the roof room, which was my grandfather's, be kept locked. That's where I'll stay when I come down. The head shepherd Joseph's wife, Shela, will cook, and some of the women will be helping her to clean and work in the gardens. I pay all of them now, but you will be the paymaster to them when you take over. Is that acceptable to you?"

"Yes, Demas. It's more than I could ever imagine possible. Thank you."

"Now, Matthan, what is going on with my brothers? I've been so busy that I really don't know them. That's terrible to say, but it's the truth. Please tell me all about them."

"Your brothers are good men, but they weren't trained as you were. They need to see how things work and to be more reliable. Your father was too slack with them. I don't think they really understand the tremendous responsibility and commitment necessary to running the business. Your father handled most of it, but they need to be more knowledgeable of how things are run and maintained. But they can learn, just as their cousins have in other cities. It would probably be a big help if they spent time with your Uncle Samuel and go see your business partners in Emmaus. Also, a trip to Damascus would give them plenty of experience. It will be hard for them, as they are already married, but it will make them aware of how everything is done. I think it will give them a sense of appreciation to get a view of the whole business that they are a part of. They'll mature quickly when they see what your family has done and is still doing. Send them to Tyre for two months and then to Emmaus. Then I can send them up the eastern route to Damascus. They'll see our two inns on the way. There's nothing that will teach them better than experiencing what you and your father have been doing for years. By the time they come home, they'll appreciate not having to travel again. Of course, you'll have to send them one at a time. You'll need one in Antioch when you have to travel. Your mother can handle helping them with the caravans. She's always been a part of that anyway. She would have been a tribune if she had been a man and we were Romans."

"Yes, that's what I've thought too. I'll be leaving in two weeks. I'll take Benjamin first and leave him with Samuel. Then I'll go to Emmaus and see if Lazarus will teach Benjamin how he does things. He should be there for about a month. Then I'll go to the farm and let my men know that you are coming and will be my manager. I want to bring some dogs back here, our horses, and Roxanne's loom. I hope to be back in six weeks or less. I'll have to bring James back then. Also, Matthan, send the boys by the eastern route as you suggested to Damascus. Let them get to know our trade routes and innkeepers. They may as well see how much Father and I have had to travel. By the time they are both home again, hopefully they will realize how good they've had it. Tomorrow I'm going to our compound and see how it looks. Didn't you say that Benjamin lives with his in-laws? We may have to build him and his wife a home on the compound. It will be similar to how Lazarus and his family are situated. I never did like the compound being without someone there most of the time. That's what the dogs will be for. But we do need someone on it at all times."

"Yes, Demas, I agree. Your brothers don't always get to it as early as they should. With Benjamin living there and having the dogs, we won't have any more losses."

"Are we experiencing losses? Father never said anything about it."

"Well, they weren't too much, but they did happen. Your father made up for it from his own money. I didn't say anything to you because I knew you would find out when you saw it and the missing goods from the inventory."

"Thank you, my friend. I've always appreciated your tact and honesty. I believe my brothers are in for a hard lesson on life, don't you?"

"Yes, I believe they are, but they'll learn and be better men for it. They've needed you but weren't aware of it."

"Well, they've got me now. I only want things to go well for all of us. Believe it or not, I don't enjoy traveling so much, but it's my way of life for good or bad. Thank you, Matthan."

Matthan left, and Demas pulled out the letter from his father from his belt. He was anxious to read it but then sad to realize his father was thinking of him, knowing something could happen to him and that he needed to help Demas in case it did.

Demas held it for a little while and then unrolled it.

My dearest son, if you are reading this, then I was wise to heed God when he put it in my mind to do so. I'm leaving for Ephesus next week to see Jacob and Gauis. I don't think it's about anything of too much importance, but they asked me to come visit, so I am. Jacob is teaching his boys the business as well he should. I don't know what Gauis wants, but if nothing else, it will be pleasant to enjoy their company for a while.

Now to business—should anything happen to me, I leave your mother, brothers, and sisters in your hands. I've had many wonderful blessings in my life. You have been one of the best. As you grew up, you more than met my expectations. Your grandfather would have been so proud of you. You've always done any and everything that had to be done, usually without being asked. Sometimes I coasted on your shadow as you continued to do whatever needed to be done without questions or complaints. In so many ways, I see myself in you. I think that when I saw the farm and what you had accomplished, my pride of you was boundless. But I knew in my heart that you would have to leave it someday, just as I have had to leave special places again and again. You too will probably experience it. I will assume that you are in Antioch and that I am gone and you are now the head of the family. That's one reason that I went to see Caleb and Jacob. I've talked to Samuel too. He is so glad to know that you are ready to take the lead. He's like me and ready to retire. Caleb has already done so more or less, and Jacob is looking forward to his boys stepping into his shoes within the next few years.

But I've failed you and your brothers in several ways. While you were gone on the sea, and Gabriel was studying, I should have worked more with your other two brothers. They needed a firm and guiding hand many times, and I didn't do it. Now they are married men, and you will have to do my job. I have no doubts that you can and will do it. They are good men but can become much better. With your experiences, patience, and goodness, I believe they will meet their fullest potential. In their youth, they were jealous of you. But then they saw so little of you that they didn't think or care what you thought of them. Now they are men, and you will have to lead, drag, and pull them into full maturity. I'm sorry to drop this on you, but I know that you can and will do it. You are in full control of my estate because I know that you will take care of your mother and them. I love you, my son. It was you and I out on that hillside when God's son was born. You were always there for your mother and me whenever we needed you. And you will get to see God's son. I know it in my heart. Be strong. Enjoy your family. Love Roxanne as I've always loved your mother. And never doubt that you are fulfilling all my hopes, dreams, and thoughts of you and for you. Don't waste time grieving. Take each day as it comes, for as with all things, that's how we should live. Praise God for his many blessings. Keep being patient and kind, but foremost, know that I love you so very much, my son, forever.

Your loving father,
Jarius Ben Shopan (Ahimelek)

Demas was crying as he finished the letter. He would miss his father so much, but his memories would always be with him: the times they had shared together, the joys and the sad ones. He carefully rerolled the scroll and put it in his chest. Then he leaned back and started planning for tomorrow. The boys weren't going to like what he had planned for them, but hopefully when it was over, they would respect him. Like his father had reminded him, they really didn't know each other very well. But they were brothers, and they could and would learn to accept their own place in the family and to do their part for its continuance.

Chapter 29

The next morning, he and Matthan walked to the field where the compound was. It was a mess. It was overgrown with weeds. The tents were in terrible shape, and the whole place was wide open to anyone and anything. As he walked, he stacked rocks to show where the boundaries for the planned enclosure would be. There would be plenty of room for a nice house for Benjamin and his family. He would definitely be bringing dogs here to protect the place and his brothers.

"Matthan, what time do the boys usually come here? Isn't a caravan due in? Surely they are here when the caravans are near?"

"No. They usually send someone else to be here until the caravan is seen. Then they are told, and they come here to see that they get unloaded and reloaded. Then they go back home."

"And what do they do with the rest of their time?"

"In truth, I don't really know."

"Well, they're in for a rude awakening, aren't they? I can't believe they haven't learned anything, especially how to work and be responsible. Well, they will learn, or they won't be eating very much or lazing around anymore. I'm the paymaster now, and they will work, or they can look for jobs elsewhere. How did they fool Father for so long? Truthfully, I'm appalled."

"I knew that you would be, but it wasn't my place to tell on them."

Just then, Benjamin walked up. "Well, hello, brother. I came to get ready for the caravan coming in today."

"And what and how do you do that, Benjamin? This place is a mess. Where do you sell merchandise to the local people? Where is the merchandise that is to be reloaded and sent out? Where do you let the men rest and feed and water the animals? I strongly suggest that you go bring our younger brother here as soon as possible."

Benjamin glared at Demas and then started to say something. But he stopped and started back the way that he had come.

"They are not going to be happy and compliant, are they, Matthan? I am so shocked by his attitude. Did they act like this to our father?"

"I think that they kept him away from here as much as possible. One would be at your parents' almost constantly in order to keep him unaware of how little they were doing.

You know that your father was wearing down in his last years. He would come back from trips, and it took a lot of time to regenerate his strength. Between the two of them, they managed to keep him in the dark, so to speak!"

"Well, let's get to other matters until they come back. I need to see some tradesmen. I need carpenters, gardeners, and tent makers for now. Where is the well on this property or some kind of water source? Also, go back to the house and have Mother and Roxanne prepare food and bread for the caravan men. Please send some men with buckets so that the camels can be watered. I'm going to start looking in the tents and see if there is anything here. Oh, and I need field workers out here to start cleaning as soon as possible. Please hurry, Matthan, and thank you."

Demas started looking for a well. He finally found it and uncovered it. The water was almost to the top. There must be an underground stream or spring feeding it. *Thank you, Lord, for that, at least.* Then he searched the tents for the food for the animals. They were all a mess as were all the tents that held merchandise.

Father, I would like to take a whip to these brothers of mine. But instead, they are going to work with their hands until they are blistered. Then I'm going to set them down and let them know that they will get paid like the other laborers until this place shines. They won't be allowed to come to the house until I say so. I don't want them whining to mother. How could they be so disrespectful and lazy? Well, they're going to learn to work and be responsible men and husbands, or they can leave the family and make it on their own. He looked up just in time to see Benjamin and Joseph stomp across the field.

He sat down on a rock and waited. They finally got to him and almost laughed. They thought that they could intimidate him with an attitude. This was going to be interesting.

"Well, boys, welcome to my workplace. Of course, until I say so, you may not come to the house. Have a seat!"

"Where? There's no place to sit!"

"What are you talking about? There's ground all around you. We are going to have a talk, and you are going to listen. First, you will not receive any money from our mother and me until you've earned it. I am the sole heir of our father's estate and assets. That means everything! You are sneaky, spoiled, useless, and very poor excuses of supposedly grown men. You used Father, never realizing how hard he had to work to provide very well for you. Well, either you are going to learn or you can leave and go provide for yourselves and your own families. Mother can't give you anything because it's all mine now. And I assure you that I will use it to find real men willing to work and proud to do it. All your life you have learned nothing but how to avoid doing anything. Now you are going to have to make a choice. Grow up and be responsible men, husbands, and fathers, or starve and become beggars and thieves. Apparently, you have no honor or pride, and you won't have any extended family either. If you decide to leave to go, our whole family will never recognize you again. Your cousins are already starting to take over their father's businesses, and then there are you. What's the matter? Have you no honor or pride? You may not have liked me when you were children, but while you were playing, I was working. I honored our parents, and they had pride in me. What have you given them in return? They are ashamed of you. Father is dead now, and our mother has agreed to not see you until you commit to working as responsible men, or if you refuse, you will never be admitted into our homes or lives again. The choice is yours. So start deciding because I have workers coming and a caravan due."

"We hate you, you know. You were always the best in Father's eyes. We could do nothing to please him. It was always 'Demas will do it and not complain,' or 'Your brother does this or that. Why can't you do anything right?' So now big brother is home, and we have to be obedient to your wishes or lose our inheritance. How is that fair?"

"First, did you complain when asked to do things? Did you even try to earn his respect? I've been working like a man since I was nine. I worked for all our uncles as a laborer from the time I was fourteen years old. At eighteen, I became a sailor until I was twenty-five. You mean while I was off learning, working, and lonely, you were still jealous of me? Why? You've never had to suffer exhaustion, loneliness, pain, and fear. I have, and now I'm finally able to reap the reward of all that effort. No, I never argued with our parents because I respected them. Did I cheat or lie to them? No, because I couldn't or wouldn't have, even if I had been nearby them. They were my parents. I love them and respected them. They were sorry to never see me. You've been like babies wanting more and more and giving nothing in return. Well, now you are reaping what you've sown. You do nothing, so you won't get anything. Sorry, brothers. If you don't sow in the fields of your life, how do you expect to reap crops? You're not that ignorant, are you? A man is known by what he does or doesn't do. What have you ever done for anyone? I'm willing to give you a last chance to redeem your wasted lives, or you can leave forever and go wherever and do and be nothing but poor and all alone. It's up to you. You are adults now with families. What about them? What fine models of sluggards you are to them. I've had my say. You are responsible for your own choices and lives. I'm expecting a caravan and have work to do. Let me know what your decision is. I haven't the time or desire to put up with two lazy, worthless men. Make up your minds quickly. I have to make arrangements for people who are willing to work and will reap the benefits of their labors."

Without another word, Demas stood up to meet Matthan and several men with him. His brothers just stood there, gaping at him. Then they turned and walked a little ways from him.

"What are we going to do? We don't have a trade and no money. Demas will never acknowledge us again nor the rest of the family," whispered Joseph.

"I think he's serious. Well, I guess we are going to do what he says. We haven't any choice. We can't ignore our family's needs. Let's go and find out what we have to do. It galls me to admit it, but we have been selfish, mean, and lazy. Guess it's time for us to grow up!" Benjamin answered.

They turned and walked back to Demas. "All right, we want to be part of the family. What do you want us to do?" Benjamin said.

"Go out there with these men and start cleaning up this place. Do not tell anyone what to do because you have no position or authority to do so. Start cleaning out the things in the tents. Inventory everything. I will be checking up on you. You will eat when the rest of us do, and you will rest when we do. So get to work!"

With this said, his brothers took off their cloaks and got busy. Demas watched them as they worked for the first time in years. *Well, boys, you're going to learn the hard way, but you will learn. You are Shophans, and I'm going to teach you to respect our name.*

By late afternoon, the area was cleaned. New tents had been erected, and all the workers had been paid except his brothers. He needed to talk to them about his future plans for them. They finally came to him and stood there, waiting.

"Well, brothers, what do you think of your first day of working? It's really quite satisfying, isn't it? I am glad the caravan didn't make it in today. We'll be more ready for them tomorrow. Do you have the inventories? I want to go over them tonight."

Benjamin handed him the inventory list and he paused momentarily to look it over. "When the caravan comes in, I want to add to our inventory, but be able to send out what is needed elsewhere too. In two weeks, Benjamin, you and I are traveling south. You will work for Uncle Samuel for a month or so. The time there will be determined by how fast you learn. Then you will go to Bethany and work for our partner there. You will learn how a real business is run. Then you'll travel up our eastern trade route and supply our inns as you go on to Damascus. You will work under Amos for a few weeks, and when he deems you're ready, he'll send you back to Tyre and home. I think you will be gone at least three months. Mother and Roxanne will check on your family while you are gone. When you get back here, then it will be your turn, Joseph, to go. You will copy what Benjamin had done."

Both men looked at him in disbelief listening to what would be required of them. "You may not be gone as long, as you and I will be working together here in Antioch. Apparently, you think traveling is an adventure that you've been cheated of doing. I want to make up for that by letting you see what Father and I have had to do our whole lives.

Here are your wages for the day. Be here tomorrow at sunup. We have to work on enclosing our trading center. I'm bringing dogs back to work as guards. We will not be losing any more stock. See you tomorrow!"

Demas rose and walked home with a smile on his face and thought to himself, *Not a bad start, was it, Father, for the first day? Let's see how tomorrow goes.*

His mother was waiting for him when he walked into the house. "How did it go today, Demas? I saw your brothers working. Did they grumble very much? When can I see them?" she asked.

"Mother, it will be six months before you can talk to them. Their wives and children can come anytime for visits. My brothers aren't being punished. They are learning to be responsible men. And as such, they will see and experience what Father and I have done for years. They will learn to appreciate their labors and the benefits of them. They are spoiled brats right now, but I know that in the end, they will appreciate all that they learn. It's too bad they're having to learn the hard way now, but better late than never. I have great hopes for them. Benjamin and I will be leaving for Tyre in less than two weeks. He is going to appreciate being at home instead of traveling regularly. While we are gone, builders are going to build him and his family a home in the compound. I think that when Joseph sees Benjamin's home, he'll want one too. So when he and I leave, a new home will be built next to Benjamin's. Then, my dearest mother, almost all your roosters will be with you. Does this make you happy?"

"Demas, you are forever surprising me, and the good Lord forgive me for my pride in you. I knew that if anyone could help them, it would be you. I think that Jarius knew what you could and would do. It will build a good bond between you and them that has never existed before. Thank you on behalf of your father and me."

"No, Mother. Thank you. I want you to relax and enjoy yourself. You know that I'm going to switch out Matthan with our steward, James? Matthan and I talked about this. He wants to retire, so he will be my manager in Emmaus. He has earned this retirement. He can come anytime for a visit. It's a good thing I know how to maneuver things like Father did. It's never easy but challenging. Someday, I'll be able to sit back and watch my children take over. Isn't that what life is? Doing the job we were taught to do? Then teaching our own children to take over for us? My only sorrow is that Father won't see things evolve and continue."

"Don't worry, Demas. Jarius knew you would do what you would do. My regret is that he didn't stop sooner. He was truly worn-out, but he did get to see all of his brothers first. For that, I am grateful. Well, what is happening tomorrow?"

"Caravan day! After they leave, we're going to start enclosing the compound and building stronger storage units. Tents are great temporary storage, but we need something more durable and safer. I haven't figured it out yet, but I will."

"I know, my dear son. What are you bringing from Emmaus?"

"I'm bringing the colts of our horses, dogs for guard duty, Roxanne's loom, plus other odds and ends. If I forget anything, I'll be back there again shortly when I go to see how Benjamin is doing, and then again when I switch him and Joseph out. And I may have to go to Ephesus too. I'm expecting a letter from Jacob when I get to Samuel's. I also want to see how Baba is and how our new plans for our boats are working out. We're increasing our security again, but you know me, I'll be busy. I'm really going to miss you and my family. Roxanne has enrolled David and Andrew in the synagogue to continue their studies. Then next year, David will start learning the business with me. We'll be going to the various businesses, and he will get an understanding of them and what will be expected of him. By the time he is eighteen, he will travel on his own. It's the same routine that I learned. Life goes on, and we do what is necessary."

Mariam hugged Demas and walked away. Now he had some time for his wife and family.

Chapter 30

Demas stood watching Benjamin wretch over the side of the boat. He had to have eaten quite a bit before they left, but he hadn't listened to him. He was determined to do his own thing. Well, he was learning the hard way.

Jonah walked up to Demas and nodded. "He ate a big breakfast, didn't he? I know that you probably told him not too. He's one very stubborn and opinionated young man. How long will he be staying down south?"

"Oh, I figure he'll be there for about three months. Then I'll take him back and bring our younger brother down to get the same training. They will learn and do it, or I'll cut them loose. But I'm not too worried. They have nothing to fall back on. I made that clear. Also, they can't see their mother until they've successfully completed their training. I think Samuel is going to work them into submission. I'm still amazed what miserable little stinkers they are. But hardship is a good trainer. By the way, how is Baba? I hated to leave him, but I had to be with Mother when she heard about father."

"Was she okay, or has she had problems with his death?"

"You would be surprised how well she's doing. She told me that when it happened, our father came to her to tell her good-bye. When I told her, she said she already knew. It was kind of odd, but they really loved each other. It was a gift from God to let him tell her good-bye. I'm not going to question it. I've got enough to do for now. I don't want Samuel to give these siblings any leeway. They've got to learn first and as fully as they can. I've got too much to do myself to raise two adults to maturity."

"I can't this trip, but I'll work with them too. It's too bad that they didn't realize that all they had to do was grow up. It comes to all of us eventually. We become adults and mature, or we just give up. They're as much a part of your parents as you are. But they'll learn. What are you going to bring back with you when you come?"

"I'm bringing horses and dogs. Think we can do that okay? It'll be messy, and my things will be about all that you can handle. I'll drop Benjamin at Uncle Samuel's and then head to Emmaus. We'll be shifting my home base to Antioch. I've got to go see Lazarus and get his okay to school my brothers. Then go on to the farm. Then back to Tyre and you. Or I can take them straight across to our cove. Only problem with that would be getting the horses onboard. What do you think?"

"It'll be easier bringing them to Tyre. You were going to put a dock at the cove but were afraid it might bring uninvited and dangerous people there. Sorry, it'll have to be Tyre."

"That's what I figured. Oh, well, it was a thought."

"Think we should ask Benjamin if he would like some water? He looks a little green around the edges."

"Of course, I'm not here to punish but to teach."

By the time they reached Tyre, Benjamin was still feeling queasy. It turned out he was seasick too. Demas almost felt sorry for him but not too much.

Samuel was at the dock when they came in. "Well, my nephews, you made good time. What's wrong with you, Benjamin? You look a little green."

"I just need to lie down for a while. I hate sailing."

"We'll go up to the house then. By tomorrow, you'll be ready to go to work."

Benjamin glared at his uncle and then saw Demas and saw his eyebrows raise. "That will be fine. I'll be ready."

He staggered into the house and greeted his aunt, and she took him into a room to lie down.

Samuel and Demas went outside to the patio.

"What do you want me to do with him, Demas?"

"Teach him what you taught your boys and me. I figured it will take him at least four to six weeks to get stronger and be able to do his share. He's in terrible shape. He and Joseph haven't done an honest day's work in their entire lives. You'll not only have to teach them but also get them physically stronger. Right now, neither of my brothers particularly like me, but by the time I'm done with them, they will respect me. Anything else will be an extra boon for everyone. How is Baba and the other wounded sailors? I hated to leave it all on you, but I had to get to Mother. Are the boats okay? Did you find replacements for the dead sailors?"

"Everyone and everything is fine. Baba is already anxious to work again, but I told him to get completely well first. He was so broken up over Jarius's death. He's okay now. The families of those killed have been taken care of too. Don't worry, Demas, your father and I did what was necessary whenever things came up. I don't know why I'm saying this, but you're being just as concerned and involved as he was over everything. Oh, and I've heard from Jacob. He was heartbroken too, but like me, he knows that you'll do everything like your father. He did ask if you wanted your brothers to come to him too. But looking at Benjamin's condition from this trip, he would never make it that far on a boat."

They both laughed and reentered the house.

The next morning, Demas checked on Benjamin, who was still bumping into things. "You'll be fine shortly, Benjamin. I'm leaving today for Bethany to see if Lazarus will work with you. Then I'm going to the farm. I should be back in a few weeks. In the meantime, get stronger. Do whatever Uncle Samuel tells you to do and enjoy your education. Think about your children and what you want them to be like. You're a man now, so act like one!"

Benjamin just glared at him.

Demas made good time getting to Bethany. Lazarus was already out of the house as he entered the compound.

"I saw you coming. It's good to see you. I heard about your father and want you to know that we're all very sorry about his death. He was a very good man. Come let my people take care of your caravan and men. My father isn't doing very well. He's resting now, but come on into the house. Remember, it's cooler in there."

"Thank you for your condolences, but I have come to ask you to do something unusual. First, I would be glad to pay you. It is reference to my brothers. My father was so busy he messed up on their training. What I would like you to do is show them how to run this trading center. I have the older one at our Uncle Samuel's place now. In about six weeks, I would like to have him come here and train under you for about a month. He can live at my farm, but he should be here each morning, and you can show him how to turn the merchandise over, store the things from the caravans, and meet merchants. When you feel that he has learned how to do things and keep everything organized, send him on in a caravan up the east route to Damascus. He'll work with our people there and then go back to Tyre and come home.

Then I'll bring my younger brother down to learn too. I know it's an imposition for you, but I've got to do all the traveling now, and I need them to handle things in Antioch correctly. Would you be willing to do this for me?"

"Of course, and don't worry about paying. Having him here will allow me some personal time. I'm sorry you have to do everything now, but where God leads us, we must follow. It's too bad that your brothers aren't ready, but they will learn to be good traders. I think they will be happier once they learn and benefit from hard work. Are you moving permanently to Antioch? Actually, living in a port city should make things easier when you travel."

"Those are my thoughts too. I'm going to Emmaus now to get our things and apprize my people there of my plans. I'm going to bring my family's older steward down to be my manager there. He ran the farm for my father for years. He's getting older and needs to slow down. I'll take our steward, James, back with me when I leave. Then bring Matthan down when I return."

"As always, you'll be very busy. I think this is a wise and practical decision for you. I'll miss you, but maybe I can start thinking of new things to try out. I'm like you, always on the go."

"Thank you so much, Lazarus. You're certainly like me. When things need to be done, we do them. May God guide, guard, and strengthen you. Be well until I see you again."

Demas mounted his mule and left for his farm. As he rode, he checked off the things he still needed to do. He must get the candelabra too. He had forgotten all about it over the years. He had yet to give it to Roxanne. It definitely had to be taken to her. As he reached the gate, he sat a moment just looking at the farm. Everything was mature and producing. Sheep were all over the western hills. *Well, Lord, I'm going to miss this, but you gave me twelve wonderful years, and I am grateful.*

Joseph and James both stepped from the house and waited until he had dismounted. "Well, it's good to see you. We heard about your father and want to tell you how sorry we are to hear of his death. Is your family well?"

"Yes, I've come into more work than I had planned for. Let's go inside, and I'll tell you what's going on." Immediately, Demas was saddened. He truly loved this place, but first, of course, there will be some major changes. "My parent's steward wants to retire, so, James, you'll be replacing him in Antioch. Matthan ran this farm for many years, so he'll become my manager. You will like him, Joseph. He's fair and industrious. You will continue to be over the animals and farm products. I have had to take on the added responsibility of making my younger brothers into men. Right now, they are beginning to learn how to work. The older one, Benjamin, is in training with our Uncle Samuel in Tyre. When he's been taught how things are done, he'll come here and work with Lazarus in Bethany. He will only board here and has absolutely no say or authority on the farm. You and Matthan will be autonomous here, answering only to me. Benjamin will be a guest. When he's finished up learning what he can, he'll return to Antioch. Then I'll bring Joseph down, and he'll repeat all the training that his brother got. Hopefully, they'll do well. And as I'm sure you've guessed, I won't be living here. I need to take the colt and filly back with me and the rest of our personal things. Joseph, you know my family and I truly need you to help me. I'll have to travel more and will be comfortable knowing my friends will be carrying on for me. Is this acceptable to you both?"

Joseph spoke first. "We will miss you and your family, but Shela and I are happy here. And, yes, it sounds fair to me. I've heard of Matthan, and I'm sure everything will work out just fine."

James smiled and said, "I've missed you all. You're my family, and I'll be happy to move to Antioch with you. Are you going to need dogs? One of Runt's families has whelped. Do you want one from her and a couple of the older dogs? You didn't say whether you would be raising sheep there. We have quite a few to choose from."

"Is any of Runt's pups a runt too? With Roxanne and the children, they'll want a dog around. And I'll take three older ones for guard animals. I won't have time to raise a lot of animals, so for now that's about all that I can handle. Then I need to take Roxanne's loom and other things.

There's a caravan going to Tyre next week. James, you can come with me. Joseph, do you need anything? Matthan will be a big help to you and me. You are all more like family than just friends. I know that everything will continue to go on as though my family and I still lived here. And it's not as if we won't see each other regularly. Until I get my brothers trained, you'll be seeing me quite often."

Five days later, everything was ready to go, and the men were loading the baggage. Joseph had made up carriers for the dogs, and the two horses were readied. He and James climbed unto the camels and, with a final wave, started down the long road to Tyre.

Demas kept wondering how his brother was doing at Samuel's. He knew if anyone could get Benjamin in line, his uncle was the man to do it. His brothers had begun badly, but he had high hopes for them. Whether they deserved it or not, he loved them.

Chapter 31

As the caravan arrived at Samuel's place in Tyre, Demas sighed with relief. The trip had been longer than usual because of the horses and dogs. But as he lowered his camel and dismounted, Samuel came out of the building.

"You're right on time, Demas. Was the trip productive? You brought a lot of things, I see. Jonah should be here anytime. He had to go to On. The merchants here wanted several things from there. The women love the linen, and the men need the parchment. Your Aunt Elizabeth likes the wheat and barley from there too. She says it's finer and better to cook with. Frankly, I can't tell the difference, but she says she can. And the merchants love the wool from your farm. They always take most of it when you send it here."

"Well, I brought everything you requested plus my own things. Tell me, how is Benjamin doing? I got the okay from Lazarus to handle Benjamin when you send him to

Emmaus. I'm having him send Benjamin to Damascus when he finishes there. I want him to see what Father was doing all these years. He probably isn't even aware that we have inns out on the eastern route. Think he'll appreciate all that our business has been doing all these years? Tell Lydia to not cut him any slack when he goes there to learn."

"Come with me, and I'll show you. Don't let him know that we're watching him."

They went inside and stepped into a side area where they could see and hear the workers.

"Why do we have to move all this grain and then put the new shipment where it was? Why not stack it in front of the other grains?" Benjamin asked.

"Because we sell the best and freshest grains available in this whole area. We can only do that by rotating the older stock first. Don't you do it in Antioch? We stay in business by having the best and freshest products available. You don't know very much, do you?"

"Well, not like you. Did Demas do this?

"Are you kidding? He's worked at every one of our centers since he was fourteen. Then when he turned eighteen, he went to sea. He's been to a lot of places and brought in a lot of new things from other lands. We have silk and rugs, which we sell very quickly, and lots of other stuff. The merchants in Tyre and Jerusalem buy everything that we import. Why do you think we have so many caravans and ships coming in all the time? Your brother speaks several languages because of his need to communicate with the different peoples and places that he has been. I heard our fathers discussing it when Demas came back to get married. He bought your family farm outright and paid for it out of his own pocket. Then he paid for its total restoration. Your father wasn't out of any money. He said he hadn't realized how rich your brother was in his own right. Believe me, he's earned everything he has. I bet it broke his heart to have to leave Emmaus. But he's like your father was. He works harder than anyone I know of. It must be really great to have a brother like him!"

"I really can't say. Joseph and I never saw much of him. He was on the go most of the time."

"Well, he is very smart. You would have to be to do what he does. I truly admire him. I hope that he and his family will be living happily in Antioch. Is Antioch a nice town?"

"I guess. I live there, but it's just another town, as far as I'm concerned. What's there to know?"

"You're jesting, aren't you? Don't you know anything about the people that you deal with and live among? What have you been doing your whole life? Just existing? You must be very bored or just plain boring yourself. Don't you deal with the merchants and seek out new business to provide for? No wonder you are so dumb. It's a wonder that your father didn't kick you out. I guess he loved you an awful lot to put up with your lack of interest in business and your neighbors. You are one very sorry human being."

Then Samuel and Demas quietly left the building and headed for Samuel's home. "Well, that was interesting, wasn't it? I hope and pray that Benjamin will appreciate what he's learning," Samuel said.

"Me too. I have higher hopes for Joseph. I think that he is more than aware of how selfishly he and Benjamin have been and wasting so many years."

"Now I can see why you had to come down on them so hard. They're really pathetic. All I can say is your poor father was just too tired, worn-out, and busy to deal with them when he did get home. Thank our good Lord that you will be present in their lives from now on. I wonder if they'll ever know what you have sacrificed to give them a good life. I don't know if I would have been as generous as you are. Truthfully, they should be whipped. But they are family, and I know that you are giving them a chance to grow up. I hope for everyone's sake that they take this last opportunity to realize what they've been missing. I never realized what Jarius was sacrificing so that the rest of us could be successful. And, Demas, I thank you for all that you're doing for all of us. I hate traveling. Now I understand how much my oldest brother did for the rest of us."

"I do know, but it's my responsibility. I do it out of love and appreciation for all of you. It has been difficult at times, but look how much God has blessed all of us. Sometimes I wonder what Grandfather would think of us. I want to believe that he would be proud that his family has fulfilled his dreams for us. Just think where we would be today if Grandfather hadn't had to leave his prior life. Where and how would our lives be? I like to think it was God who has been guiding all of us these many years."

"You're a good man, Demas, but learn from your brothers. Don't let your relationship with your own children be affected by work. Love them, enjoy them, but help them learn the value of hard work. Then they won't become like your brothers. I truly pity them in a way. I think they felt that their father didn't care for them. What you need to do is hire men to be your representative in each of our ports. Then you won't have to travel as much. They would report to you, and you would only have to travel once a year. Yes, I think this is a good idea. Think about it, and if you agree, we'll start looking for them now. I don't want what happened to your brothers to happen to you and your family. I wish Jarius had done this. He might still have been alive if we had."

"It's something that has crossed my mind too. I just thought you and my other uncles wouldn't agree to it. But the reason I have considered it was because of what Gauis's father told us before the wedding. He said that Rome was becoming more hostile toward the Jews and that if we kept on antagonizing them, they would retaliate by killing all of us. What have they to lose? They rule the world now. And the first to face their anger will be the destruction of the temple and Jerusalem. With us farther away from

Jerusalem, the safer all of us will be. The port cities we work from will be fairly safe from their wrath, but not Jerusalem. The prophets foretold its total destruction again. It very well may happen. We do a great trade in the cities where we are now living. If our people foolishly think they can keep rebelling, they are going to pay a very heavy price. God's son will be known soon. We should prepare for the worse."

"You're right. I hadn't thought of that. Yes, we had better get prepared. When he does start working among us, the Jews will really get angry. Even if he comes peacefully, the Romans aren't going to welcome any more trouble from us. Yes, it's imperative that we be ready for the worse. Demas, you have given me much insight. I'm going to give this a lot of thought. Also, I'll notify Caleb and Jacob to start looking for men to be your representatives in each of our areas. I'm certain that we will find men eager to do your job in those places."

That evening, Demas was waiting to see Benjamin. He hoped and prayed that they could build a new and good relationship with each other. Then in walked his brother.

"Hello, Benjamin. How are you doing? I hope that you are impressed by how hard and how much we all work to maintain our livelihood."

Benjamin stood and studied his brother. Then he walked up to him and threw his arms around Demas. "I am so sorry for how Joseph and I have been in the past. I promise that I'll work hard to gain your respect and love. I've spent so many years being jealous of you, and all the time, you were doing all you could to help all of us. I am ashamed."

Demas was stunned, and then he returned the hug. "I'm sorry too. We never had the time to truly be brothers. I love you and Joseph, but I'm sure that you can see why I wasn't around for you both. I had no choice. Father had to prepare me to take his place one day. Sadly, it came sooner than any of us expected. But don't dwell on the past. It's over. Let's enjoy where we are right now. I didn't want you and Joseph to have to do what I had to. But life is hard, and you only get back what you put into it. I had a job and position to fill, and so do you. Now you owe the same things to your children. Raise them right so that they won't be like you and Joseph have been. Teach them about God and how to serve him as worthy, loving, and hardworking men. That's our duty. Having you understand now how things are is a blessing for me. Let's build our friendship on the time that we have left."

Demas left three days later for Antioch. He carried a letter for Joseph from Benjamin. He had high hopes that they could be a loving and caring family from now on. James, his steward, was faring well, but he was looking forward to being back on land again. I suppose it takes a more adventurous type to enjoy sailing. He couldn't deny that he himself loved it. But he loved his farm and family too. *I guess I try to be content wherever I'm at. Things change constantly, and you have to adapt.* Right now, he was thinking of Roxanne and the children. If he could get some good men to do his traveling, he would truly be a happy and contented man.

Chapter 32

Demas got the workers he needed to bring their things from the boat. He felt badly about the mess the horses and dogs had made, but having them with him was a need and desire for him. James had grown fond of the dogs, so he had them. Demas was leading the horses.

Before they got to their house, the whole family was coming to meet them. What a wonderful surprise. He let the older boys ride on the two horses and let Joshua carry the small puppy. Roxanne carried Esther.

"Well, this is a great surprise. You all look wonderful. And, my beautiful wife, did you miss me?"

"I'll show you later, my handsome husband," she grinned deviously at him before continuing. "We had someone watching for you. That's how we knew you were here. And you brought your colt and my filly. Thank you. Did you get everything else? It looks like you brought everything but the house itself."

"Well, I just couldn't figure out how to get it on a camel. Sorry, but if I did miss anything, I'll get it the next time when I return there."

Joseph stood to the side of the group alone. When Demas saw him, he walked over to him and asked him how he was doing.

Joseph smiled and said, "Very well, brother. You won't recognize the trading compound. And Benjamin's house is finished. Grandmother moved Benjamin's wife and children into it already."

"Very good, but how are you? Benjamin's doing well too. He sent this letter to you. I think his biggest problem was seasickness and sore muscles. He seems to be getting used to the hard work. And he's making friends with his cousins and fellow workers. He's doing fine as I'm sure that you will too. You and I can go see the work yard later."

As they approached their house, Joseph excused himself and walked away. Then his mother was there as beautiful as ever. "How are you, Mother? So that you know I didn't kill or harm Benjamin, he did a good job doing that to himself by eating a big breakfast before we sailed from here. I can tell you he doesn't like sailing at all. Your little chick will be home before you know it. He and I have improved our relationship. He'll be fine when he comes home."

"Thank you, Demas. I knew that you could and would bring him around. Joseph is doing much better too. Matthan has been helping him. I think he actually is enjoying the work. A caravan came in while you were gone. They really appreciated the changes that have been made. We'll put your horses in with your father's and mine. Now whatever did you do to make Benjamin accept you?"

"It wasn't so much me as his cousins. I heard them talking, and Samuel's boy asked him what his problem was. Then he began telling him all about our businesses. He was so proud to be a part of it, that it actually surprised Benjamin. He isn't stupid. He just had no idea of the scope of our trading. He might be back home sooner than we thought he would be. I think that Samuel and Elizabeth have been an influence on him too. I know that when he gets to Damascus, Lydia and Amos will finish his education. You know Lydia. She'll polish off the rest of his rough edges."

Matthan and James had gone out together. James was so glad to be with his family again. Matthan was happy too. He was going back to Emmaus and the farm. Everyone seemed happier now. Eve was thrilled with having her own home. She was anxious for Benjamin to see it too. All in all, things were working out for everyone. Matthan would take James into town to meet the local businesspeople and tell them that they were improving their stock and adding new things too, and that they would get whatever they wanted or needed as long as it was available somewhere. Demas stressed to them that over half of their business should come from the local businesses. Within a year, the center here would be very busy.

The next morning, Demas and his stewards went to the compound. It did look good. Joseph was already there. He walked up to Demas and asked him what he thought.

"It's becoming what I visualized it should be. What do you think of it?"

"It makes me ashamed of how much Benjamin and I ignored it. I read his letter, and I had to agree with him. We have been totally useless all these years. I know that I'm looking forward to going south and learning more. May I ask you something?"

"Certainly, what is it?"

"Well, you built this great house for Benjamin. My own place is really pathetic, and I was wondering if I could have one built here next to Benjamin's house?" I can sell my very small house or fix it up and rent it. I want to be here with everyone else. All of our children can play and grow up together. We could be a whole family again. Do you think that's possible?"

"I was just waiting to see if you men would change, so if you can handle learning everything that your brother is learning, then, yes, I think it will fit right over there. That way, the caravans can come in here and leave down the trail between you. At the same time, you'll each have privacy. Is that what you wanted?"

"Demas, I can't figure out why we became so jealous of you. Here you were out working and learning and probably saw father less than we did. Benjamin told me what you had to do. I see now how stupid and selfish we have been. Anyone else would have thrown us away. It's what we deserved. Thank God you and our parents loved us in spite of our laziness and attitude. I am so ashamed!"

"Thank you for being my brother again. I thought I had lost both of you. We're going to have to start over and renew our ties with each other. Now I need gardeners. I want to line the whole property in palm trees and briar bushes. When the briars mature with the help of the dogs that I brought with me, no one will get onto the property without us knowing it. The area is growing. I may want to raise sheep out on the hills behind us. But that's a different idea that I've been considering. I do like sheep, you know. Wait until you go down to Emmaus. I'll have you see why these dogs are so useful."

"Really? I like working with sheep too. Benjamin thought I was crazy. But Father and you liked doing it, and I think that I would like doing it too."

"Well, you had better get the carpenters back if you want to live here too. It will be very good to work with all of you every day."

By dinnertime, the carpenters had laid out the new house foundation. The gardeners had planted a full side of palms, and Demas had his workers out gathering young briar bushes. He had also asked for several fig trees, date trees, and olive trees and anything else that could be grown in their area that was useful. He wanted to plant a vineyard too. He wanted to plant wheat, barley, and rye. For the first time, Joseph wasn't anxious to leave and go home. His wife was going to be overwhelmed by all that they were planning to do. His big brother was hard to keep up with. The man thought about things and then put the plan in action.

Joseph was excited every day when he came to see what Demas had planned for that day. He missed their father, but now he realized how blessed he was to have a big brother. Demas showed him the benefits of work. It made impossible dreams come true. Every day was busy and never dull. Benjamin was really going to be surprised by the changes being made.

Chapter 33

Four weeks later, it was time to take Matthan to Emmaus. The second house was built, and Joseph and Mary were already living in it. They seemed happy. Joseph followed him around, asking why he did this or that. Why did they lay bricks on the floors as well as the sides of their storage buildings? Why did they put canvass along the front and back of their homes? How did the dogs know when someone other than family had come? How had he found places for new wells?

At this rate, Joseph would be home much quicker than Benjamin. He sucked up information like dry earth did with water. Demas was pleased but ready to sail again. Apparently, his uncles had already found men to do his job at their business sites. He hadn't had time to even think if he should get one too. After all, he would be home now. He would have to see how his brothers would do once they finished their training.

Mariam was delighted by everything that had been done. She really liked the new houses and compound. They would ride out in the late afternoon to see what had recently been planted. His brothers' wives had their own ovens to bake bread in, and Roxanne was teaching them how to weave. The last caravan had brought in bolts of silk from the Asian countries, but one of the men had shown him something new. He had a couple of dried bushes and puffs of something called cotton. Then he showed him some material made from it. He liked it, but he would have to see how it was grown, harvested, and made into cloth. The man said the seeds could be made into oil, but he hadn't found out what it was good for yet. Demas was always interested in new things, but he wanted to know everything about it first. The man said that he would bring a bolt of the fabric the next time he came. It was getting late as Demas walked into the house. No one seemed around, so he walked on out to the patio in back. The women were relaxed and watching the children play.

"Well, this is a pleasant sight. How are my ladies doing?"

"We are doing splendidly. We thought we would let the children play before having dinner. They have so much energy," said Roxanne.

Demas sat down and chatted for a while. He told them that he and Matthan would probably be leaving by the end of the week. He figured it would take about four weeks before he returned. Did they want anything while he was down south?

They shook their heads and said they had all they needed. *Well, that was unusual,* he thought, *women who didn't need or want anything.* He smiled, and then Roxanne said, "Oh, Demas, I forgot. Here's a list for a few things they might have, if you don't mind, dearest."

"Not at all." He grinned. "Do you need anything from the farm too?"

"No, I think that will be all. Oh, Mariam, didn't you say you wanted something too?"

"Well, it's nothing, just some things that I can't find around here." Then she handed him another list.

He smiled at them and then went to play with the children.

That evening, when everyone was settled down to sleep, Roxanne sat down next to Demas and said, "I was putting things away and came across a bundle in your office. It was heavy, but I didn't open it. What is in it, Demas?"

"That is a gift to you from the senator and your mother. Frankly, I had forgotten about it again. I had put it in the floor of our room in Emmaus since our wedding. I only remembered about it this last trip to the farm. Would you like to receive it now?"

Demas went and got it and set it on the table. "It's quite heavy, so be careful."

She opened it and sat, stunned. "Where did this come from?"

"The senator said it belonged to your mother. He gave it to your sister, but she said to give it to you when you married. She said that she couldn't put it out in view because of Gauis being a Roman. It wouldn't be safe too. My father and I both checked it out. It's made of solid gold. We think that it came from the temple that Solomon built."

"Oh my, what should we do with it?"

"For one thing, don't clean and polish it. Let it keep the blackness to hide its true contents. Frankly, I think we should keep it wrapped until we know what's going to happen for a while. Father and I both felt that it shouldn't go to the temple or displayed. Things are building up to imperil our people with Rome. In a way, I think God was protecting us to make us move here to Antioch. The senator and I talked about this several times. He said the Caesars were getting more stupid and power-hungry. That we should probably move out of Israel eventually. Now that this has all happened, it's forced us to move up here. You know about Father and me being told that God's son had been born. Well, we figured when he's thirty he'll become publicly known. I know the Romans won't like that, so it's good that we're farther away from Jerusalem now. The senator had you and your sister registered as Roman citizens too. Our children will automatically be registered as well as any future children. All of my relatives are Roman citizens too. It was done originally because of our business, but, it doesn't hurt to be farther away from Jerusalem as we all are now."

"But what of the people on our farm and Lazarus and his sisters?"

"When they went into business with us, the senator made sure that they became citizens too."

"That wonderful man thought of everything, didn't he?"

"He was a very astute man. There's no doubt about it. He told us how the attitude of Rome was changing and that we should all be prepared for the worse possible situation. I truly miss the old fox. He was a man ahead of his time. I think that's why we became such good friends. He could see firsthand the shifting of the politics and attitudes of the hierarchy in Rome. I wouldn't be surprised if, at the end, he and his wife both had come to believe in God."

"Oh, I hope so, Demas. I pray that God has accepted them too."

"I think he has. They were as much God's children as are we. I like to think of him and my father being together and talking just as they did when we were all on the farm."

"That's a wonderful thought. It gives me so much hope that we will see them again someday. And, Demas, when you return, I want to tell you something about my sister and me. But let's do it when you come home. Right now, there's just too much going on."

"That's fine. I can wait. By the way, did you see that we're preparing the far back end of the property to plant wheat, barley, and rye. If this keeps up, this place will be just like the farm in Emmaus. Right now, I'm curious to see how Benjamin is. If he is learning as fast as Joseph has, this whole thing will be quickly over. For that, I am grateful. Today Joseph asked if we could raise sheep too. He says he likes doing it, but at the time, Benjamin had laughed at him. So we'll see about that. Of course, we wouldn't raise large flocks. The temple in Jerusalem gets most of the sheep there. But meat and wool are needed everywhere. I'm not going to do much else until things with the family are settled."

"Do you know how much I love you, husband?"

"Oh, maybe a little. I often wonder what would have happened if that whole pirate raid had never happened. That's why I try never to question God. He can and does everything in the best way possible for all of his children. Okay! That's enough talking. Let's go to bed!"

Chapter 34

It was time to go back to Tyre. Matthan had tears in his eyes as he said good-bye to Mariam and the rest of the family; even James was sad to say good-bye. They saw Jonah and his boat waiting on them.

"Well, here we go again, Demas. How are things going? Samuel said to tell you that Benjamin may be ready to go with you to Emmaus. He's waiting to see what you think."

"I hope he is right. I'm getting tired of making these trips. Matthan, you know Jonah, don't you?"

"Yes. How are you, Captain? And I didn't eat this morning, so you won't see me too ill on this trip."

"Good. In the case of sailing, it takes a while to get used to ocean movement. But you'll be fine. Well, we're loaded, so we can leave before the tide goes out."

The trip went well, and Matthan seemed eager to get back to the farm. Demas was anxious for him to see everything that had been done. He was glad to leave things in his hands. Matthan deserved this retirement of sorts. He knew he would like his job as Demas's representative.

It was perfect sailing weather. Demas had given Matthan the official scroll with his new title. Demas had to admit that he was anxious too. He hoped that Benjamin would be ready to go with them to Bethany.

When they arrived, Samuel and Benjamin met them. "Welcome back, Demas. You made great time this trip. The caravan will be ready to take you on to Jerusalem tomorrow."

Benjamin walked up to Demas and then hugged him. "Thank you for saving me, big brother. I am so sorry for all I haven't done, but I have learned, and I only wish that Father was here so that I could apologize to him too."

Demas looked him over. He was filled out and definitely stronger-looking. He certainly didn't look like the young man he had brought to Tyre a couple of months ago. "Well, are you ready to go with Matthan and me to Bethany?"

"Absolutely! Our little brother has written to me to tell me that my family has already moved into the new house. He says he can't wait to come here too."

"Well, tomorrow we leave again. I think you will like working with Lazarus. He's about your age, but the man is a hard worker and a thinker. You should enjoy his approach to business. You'll stay at the farm at night but go to Bethany to work every day. He'll help you meet the businessmen in Jerusalem and work with them. Then you will know how to deal with our customers in Antioch. You look good and healthy now. Oh, here's a letter from your wife. I'm sure it will fill you in on the changes there."

That evening, Samuel told Demas of all the changes in Benjamin. He was quite stunned himself with his nephew's improved behavior. "Shortly after you left last time, he came and talked with me. I told him everything he hadn't known. From that day on, he has become as good as my own boys."

"I am absolutely gratified. He hated me for so long and then to find out that I wasn't what he had thought I was. He's been able to get rid of the unnecessary baggage and see that we're truly family. Thank you, Uncle Samuel. I believe you'll enjoy having Joseph. He's already changing. They needed to be separated. Now I think they'll really enjoy being friends as well as brothers. I understand you've found a representative for yourself. Will he handle getting business in Jerusalem too?"

"Yes, he knows Lazarus already. He'll combine the businesses here with those in Jerusalem. He'll report to me, and then I'll send his reports to you. With Matthan in Emmaus, that should take care of your coming here on a yearly basis. Jacob's man is going to be used to find the things we'll need, so his contact will be mainly with producers. Jacob will get his own reports to you. Caleb has the same type of man working for him and will do like Jacob's man. All you will have to do is put it all together. Now instead of traveling so much, you can spend your time going over all these reports. Not to change the subject, but it sounds like you are remaking your place into another farm like the one in Emmaus."

"Well, yes and no. I am going more slowly there than I did here. I'm not that familiar with the area and what will grow there, but I'll learn. You and Elizabeth will have to come up next year and see it. Mother would be thrilled to see you. She misses Father, but she misses all of you too."

"Next year it is then. I gather you don't think Joseph will have to be here very long when he comes?"

"No. I'm making him work hard at home. I think it will just be for him to see how all of the places work together. He almost doesn't want to go home at night. In ways, he reminds me of Lazarus. I'm quite proud of both of my brothers now. While I'm thinking about it, can one of our boats pick me up at the cove? I should be ready to return in a week. Then I won't have to caravan back here."

"That's fine. It will probably be Jonah who will pick you up."

"Well, I'll see you in a week then. Who's at the house now? It's been hard finding someone to stay there because of its isolation. We might not need it for too much longer. I'm concerned about someone landing there who isn't friendly. What do you think?"

"We really don't need it anymore. Jarius used it when he lived on the farm. We could close it easily now. Talk to the man there and see if he wants to leave and work elsewhere."

"I'll let you know when I get back."

The next morning at sunup, the caravan left for Bethany. Demas was quite pleased at how much he and Benjamin could talk together now. He was sure that both Matthan and Benjamin would like the farm. And he was certain that his brother would like working with Lazarus. He was comforted to know that his family could all work together and enjoy each other's company. Joseph would probably only be away for less than two months. He was working well at home and wouldn't need to learn as much as Benjamin had to. He hated having to do what he did, but his brothers needed to learn the facts of their business and to realize that they were men now and not children. As for himself, he wanted to go home too. He missed Roxanne, the children, and his mother.

The trip passed quickly, and they were in Bethany on the third day. As they entered the compound, Lazarus was waiting for them.

"Well, how was this trip?" he asked as the camels were led down the path to the sheds.

"Very pleasant," said Demas as he, Matthan, and Benjamin dismounted their camels.

"This is my farm manager, Matthan, and my brother, Benjamin."

"Greetings! Come, my sisters are bringing water and food. I have two men who help me now. They'll take care of the caravan and check the new merchandise."

"We'll only be here for a short time. Did the men bring the donkeys from the farm?"

"Yes, they brought them up a few days ago when they brought the animals for the temple. Well, Benjamin, what do you think of the business now? It's quite extensive, isn't it?"

"Yes, much more than I ever realized. I like your place here. Do you go into Jerusalem very often? I haven't been there for a very long time. I would like to go with you and see how you handle doing business there."

"We will definitely be going there. Once you leave, you probably won't be back for quite a while."

After everyone had been refreshed, they mounted the donkeys, said their good-byes, and left. Demas wanted them to see the farm. He especially wanted to see Matthan's face as they rode up this first time. He knew he was proud, but he wanted to see again himself. He would forever love it.

As they came up the road to the entrance, Matthan stopped and just stared. It was breathtaking. It was better than he had ever seen it. "Oh, Master Demas, it takes my breath away. It is wonderful. Your father told me it was beautiful, but this is like a dream. I feel like I'm seeing a picture of how heaven looks like right here on earth."

"Thank you, Matthan, but from now on, it's just Demas. You aren't a steward anymore. You are a businessman now. Benjamin, what do you think of the old place?"

Benjamin was in awe too. "I was so young when we left, but this place looks like a rich man's estate—or, at least, what I think a rich man's place would look like. How many servants do you have?"

"There are none. Everyone gets paid here. It was always my hope to live here forever, so I made it my home. Roxanne and I had twelve blessed years here, but times and circumstances change. Come on in, and I'll show the whole place."

They rode on in and dismounted. Joseph and Shela came out to greet them. "You've come at last. Come on into the house and get refreshed."

"Joseph, Shela, this is my dear friend and new manager for the farm, Matthan. He has known me since my birth. And this is my younger brother, Benjamin. We left here when he was a very young lad, so he won't have many memories of the place. He'll be working in Bethany every day for a while, so you won't see very much of him. But I want him to see how the farm is run. We may do a similar project in Antioch."

They entered the house and, after refreshing themselves, started touring the farm. Everywhere they went, he introduced them to everyone, and they were happily greeted. It was at the fields, where the sheep were grazing, that Matthan was totally enraptured. They watched the dogs guide the sheep to water and then back out to the pastures to graze.

"Your father told me about using dogs to work the sheep. I knew it but couldn't truly conceive it as working. You never lose any of them, do you?"

"No. The sheep are used to them but obey them when they start moving them. The dogs never hurt them but will nip them if they try to do their own thing. Also, we aren't troubled with any wild animals or trespassers. They've made it so much better for the shepherds. It was truly a blessing when I learned about them"

They went back to the house to relax. Matthan was beside himself over the changes. He literally couldn't stop smiling. Benjamin had a puzzled look on his face and finally asked Demas. "Father said that you paid for everything. Are you rich? I don't understand how that happened. Joseph and I are paid but not that much. Do you get that much more as the eldest?"

"No, Benjamin. My wealth came from my own labors. I worked, traveled to many places to procure new goods, was a sailor, and invested my money. By the time I met Roxanne, I was quite rich. Father was just as stunned as you are now when he found out. Perhaps, now you can understand my frustration and anger with you and our little brother. You were two of the most useless excuses for men that I had ever seen. You had nothing and wanted everything others had without paying for it from your own efforts. I've fought pirates and caravan raiders. I've been beaten, stabbed, and marooned in the middle of the sea. Benjamin, do you know how to fight with a sword or shoot an arrow? If not, we had better get you and Joseph prepared. What if raiders had attacked our parents' home? It happened to your aunt and her family in Allepo. They were all killed. No one is exempt from an attack. How would you like to watch thieves rape and murder your wife and children? What would you do? Just stand there and wait for your turn to be enslaved or killed? Even now, your uncles and I are preparing for eventual takeover of all of Israel. The Romans are going to reach a point where they will completely destroy the temple and kill every Jew that they can. We will be dispersed again to other nations. It's a scary thought, but one that will happen. It may not happen for years, but it will happen. When it does, we will be prepared. The family Ahimelek will survive. We trust in our Almighty God to protect and deliver us, but we do our part too!"

Benjamin stood still as tears dripped from his chin. In that moment, Demas realized his brother had, at last, grown up.

"I think I'll go for a walk, Demas. I'll be back later."

Matthan stood there looking at Demas with pride. "You certainly got his attention, Demas. I don't know of anyone else who could have reached him as you just did. I've always loved working for your family, but right now I'm spinning. Lord, please forgive me for loving this man beside me."

Demas clasped Matthan's arm and smiled. "As do I love you, my dearest friend."

The next morning, Benjamin was mounted and ready to go to Bethany. "Demas, thank you. I'm going to make you proud of me."

"I already am, my brother. Life isn't always wonderful and beautiful, but it gives us enough to appreciate where we are. Have a good day. Oh, for your information, Lazarus is a thinker and an inventor too. Talk to him. He may have come up with something else that we can use."

A few days later, Demas was headed to the landing. He and Matthan had gone over all that he felt Matthan would need to know. Then Joseph surprised him by asking if he could go to the landing with him. Demas had assumed that Joseph had heard him when he had had that hard and serious talk with Benjamin.

"Well, Joseph, what do you have to say?"

"I know this is an odd question. Shela and I have talked before about it. We were wondering if we could eventually move to Antioch too. You were thinking about raising sheep there, and you know me. I could help you. We don't want to go now, but eventually we will. Your talk with your brother truly astounded my wife and me. It's so much like what I've been thinking too. I hear talk and keep my ears open. It's just as you said, the Jews are getting more belligerent. The younger men are especially frustrated. I've watched the outward hatred of the Romans build. It amazes me at our people's stupidity. We have no army. Most aren't as ardent in their faith to God. And frankly, I'm ready to get away from here."

"I was thinking about having you come up anyway to look the land over. I won't be raising as many animals there, but Antioch is a big town and growing. We can raise enough to meet their needs and sell the wool. I'm going back home now, but I will return in a month with my younger brother. And take Benjamin back home. I'm trying now to estimate how many sheep the area can sustain. I'm just not that familiar with the area yet. We'll talk more about it later. Andrew can take over for you while you are gone. How do you like sailing?"

"Don't know, never been. But I like to try out new things every chance that I can."

"Well, you'll either love it or hate it. The experience seems to pick and choose who it will get along with."

Demas's stay in Tyre only lasted a day before he was back on the boat and headed to Antioch. He and Samuel agreed that the next time he came down, they would close the landing down. Boaz and his wife were in agreement too. Their daughter lived in Tyre, and they wanted to be near her and her family. He said he would dismantle the buildings and have them all gone by the next time that Demas came back again. So that was taken care of. Now he was ready to be home with his family.

Demas was amazed with how many changes had been made. Both houses were finished, and Joseph and his family were living in theirs. He had sold his old house in the city and was busy getting things ready for business. People were already coming from the town to buy their supplies. The hillsides were lush with grass, and Joseph had marked the whole area that they owned. His mother was her old self and busy as ever. Roxanne was thrilled to have him back, and he already had his oldest boy ready to be blessed and welcomed into manhood at the synagogue.

Benjamin's wife was ready for him to come home too. A few days later, he and Roxanne went for a long walk. She too was happy to know he wouldn't be making many more trips once he had both his brothers at home and handling the caravans. Roxanne was surprised that they were closing the landing. She asked what they were going to do about the tunnel that they used to get back and forth from the farm. He told her that when he made his next trip to get Benjamin, Joseph and some of the men would collapse it. Again, it was a security issue—it was to prevent it from being used by anyone friendly or unfriendly.

Roxanne sat down on a rock, and Demas asked if she was tired.

"No, Demas. I want to tell you something that only my sister and I know. You must never tell anyone else. This is a secret that has been handed down to the females in our families for hundreds of years. But you need to know should anything happen to me. I, myself, didn't find out until my sister told me before our marriage. We are direct descendants of Aaron, Moses's brother. We are Levites. The menorah was my mother's. The senator knew but was sworn to secrecy by my mother. I have memorized our lineage from then until now. Since Hannah had two boys and a girl who didn't want to learn our history, she has passed everything on to me. When Esther is old enough, she will memorize our heritage line too. It's written down, but we also need to memorize it. Our ancestor and her husband hid several things from the temple before it was raped and destroyed. The menorah went with them into exile and then was brought back to Israel when we returned. However, none of the women in our lineage felt it was safe to expose it. Even now, you and your father don't trust our priests or the temple, so we will keep it hidden for the time being. I would have told you sooner, but when you gave me the menorah, I realized I hadn't told you yet. We've been so busy, please forgive me."

"For what? I am very pleased that you told me. It makes me proud of you and your ancestors to see what you've overcome to carry your traditions forward. Our little Esther is very fortunate, as am I." A frown crossed her brow, and Demas saw it.

"There's more? What else, my beautiful wife?"

"I wanted to be sure, and now I am. Our family is going to get bigger soon. Of course, it could be another boy, but I'm hoping for a girl so that she and her sister can share growing up together. You've got three boys, so you wouldn't mind having another female around, would you?"

"Every child that God gives us is a blessing. I love my girls. You and Esther are my treasures. I hope it's a girl too to keep their brothers on their toes."

They laughed and then returned home.

Demas told his mother and Roxanne about expanding their property further. They were going to need pasturage for the animals. He also told them about Joseph and his wife wanting to come here. Then he told them about the political conditions that were growing worse each day. They were shocked and worried for the Jews in Israel.

Mariam said, "Your father often mentioned his concerns but didn't expand on them. Sometimes I would get frustrated with him over him not explaining his thoughts. He was protecting me from worry. But most of the time, what you don't know is even worse than the facts. He carried too many burdens on his shoulders. I'm glad that you and Samuel are already planning for probable eventualities. And thank you for including Roxanne and me with your thoughts and plans. We may be women, but we have thoughts on many things too."

"I know, Mother. That's why I want to share everything that will affect us all. Right now, I'm waiting for Jesus to begin his public life. He and the Lord have something planned. I haven't a clue what it is, but I don't think it will make very many people, Jew or Gentile, happy. When I hear of him openly talking, I'm going to send scribes to follow him and take down everything he says and does. Then we'll know what his presence will mean for everyone."

"That's a splendid idea, Demas. I'm surprised that your father hadn't thought of it."

"Well, he, at least, got to see him. I haven't yet, but I hope and pray that I will someday."

Demas and Joseph had pushed their land boundaries out for several days' walk and registered ownership papers on them. Joseph was absolutely elated that there would be sheep and other animals on the property, and he found that he really did like to farm. He put a garden in for his wife, and Demas showed him that they could grow their own grains and orchards. Joseph had even asked him to teach him how to ride a horse. He knew that Benjamin would be home soon, and then he would be gone for a while. But he knew he wouldn't be gone for very long. Demas was teaching him so much. He was happy, and his wife was even happier. All the children played together, and the boys went to the synagogue together. The girls were learning to cook, sew, weave, and make breads. There was laughter all over the place. Joseph thanked God every day for sending his big brother to help them to really have purpose. He hoped that Benjamin had found the same joy. His wife loved their new home and having so many cousins around for the children to play with, and he felt good. He looked forward to each day now. He was tired at night, but every day had purpose and something else to learn. He could not even think of how his life had been. He was working hard, but the townspeople treated him with respect now. And he liked it.

Today Demas and he were going riding to look at the property that they had bought. Demas wanted to look at all the soil and see if they could grow wheat and barley. He wanted to see about grazing areas for the sheep too. Joseph was glad to get away from the house. There was a lot of activity and noisy children. He felt the need for some quiet time for himself.

They mounted his parents' horses and rode off. He had been taught to ride and enjoyed it once he got used to the horses' motion. Every day it seemed that Demas taught him something new. He marveled at his brother's abilities. The man knew about everything. He couldn't imagine where Demas had been. But once, when they were rinsing the dirt, grime, and sweat off of themselves, he saw several scars on his chest and arms. He wondered then of all the things his brother had endured. And yet he was kind and gentle but firm. He was sorry now for the lost years when his big brother hadn't been around. But they were making up for it now. He and Benjamin had treated their father badly and selfishly. Now Demas showed them what his life had been like. Every day Joseph asked the Lord for forgiveness for his attitude and behavior toward his parents. Then he thanked him for his big brother coming and teaching them the values of duty, responsibility, and how to work. He prayed that Benjamin was learning too.

As they rode through a cut between the hills, Demas rode quickly ahead and then halted abruptly. "Come look, little brother. I think that we have an underground river below here. See how the grass is more abundant and the reeds are thick. The water must run close to the surface. If it's there, then this is where we'll keep the sheep cotes. When I come back with my head shepherd this next trip, I'll bring him here to check it out. He would like to come here and see it. I'll let him find the best place. You'll like him. His name is Joseph too."

"Guess I can be little Joseph then." He laughed.

They headed back home. Tomorrow Demas was going down to Tyre to pick up Benjamin, and then it would be his turn to go. He was excited, though he planned to enjoy his experiences. He truly wanted to know all he could and to learn and see from a new perspective what life had to offer.

Chapter 35

When Demas arrived in Tyre his Uncle told him it would be a week before Benjamin came down from Damascus. He said that he had gone from Lazarus's up to Damascus on the eastern route.

Lazarus was well-pleased with his attitude and his work. He wrote that he was at work by sunup every day and stayed busy the whole time he was there. But Lazarus was surprised that he didn't care much for Jerusalem. He liked meeting the merchants, but it was too crowded for him. In a way, Demas was glad to hear that. Maybe his brother's niche was in a smaller community. He hoped that Benjamin was as eager to learn as Joseph had been. It sounded like he was.

Demas decided to ride the boat on down to the landing. He could go right to the farm from there and see how things were there. Then he and Joseph would go back to the landing and return to Tyre and then on home. He would be on the ocean more than the land this trip. However, he would be bringing Joseph down right away. But when he went home, he would have to see how Benjamin and he would relate to each other. Hopefully his angst with him was gone, and they could work together as well as he and Joseph did. It sounded like it was a good possibility.

Demas told him what he was planning, and his uncle became as enthused as he was. Then Jonah came to the house and said he would be leaving to go south in the morning, and Demas said he would be coming with him.

The next morning, Demas was again on the sea. Actually, he enjoyed it. He had time to make plans and just relax. Soon all this would be behind him, and then he would be able to get on with his plans. If Joseph liked Antioch, he could help Demas plan everything out. Demas was happy to have the help.

A week after getting home, he would be leaving again to go with Joseph down to Tyre. He was doing so well that all he needed was to see how the different families interacted with each other. He figured that at most, it would be just for six weeks, and most of that would be spent in traveling. That was the part that took up most of their time.

They finally got to the cove, and he told Jonah that he would be ready to go back with him in five days. He said that this would be the last time he would be stopping there, that there would be four passengers going back. He was bringing his head shepherd and Boaz and his wife too.

He hoped that they were ready to leave. Matthan would have the tunnel destroyed and the entrances caved in. Then Demas would have another problem solved—or, at least, he hoped!

When he was rowed to shore, he had to study it to make sure it was their cove. The buildings were gone, and only a tent and some tethered animals remained. He waved to the sailors in the rowboat as it headed back to the bigger boat. Boaz came out of the tent, smiling.

"Well, does it look different?"

"Yes. At first, I thought I was in the wrong place. You have done a great job. I'll leave now and go to the farm. I should be back in a couple of days. The boat will be back shortly after that, and then we'll all sail for Tyre. Thank you for doing such a good job."

"This was a good experience, but we're ready to live near our family again."

Demas was alone again as he made his way to the farm. Joseph saw him coming as he came into the lower hills of the farm.

"Shela said I could go for a while, but she can't imagine me not being underfoot. My return will give her something to look forward to."

Demas asked how everyone was getting along with Matthan, and Joseph laughed. "That man is a treasure. Everyone likes him, and there is nothing that he misses. The other day, he took in a bag of salt for Shela. She asked him how he knew she was in need of it. He told her that her last batch of wonderful bread was needing just a little more salt. He comes out to the sheep and can spot things that others had missed. He keeps all of us on our toes."

"That's Matthan for sure. He has always been like that. Is he feeling okay? I've been concerned for him."

"Wait until you see him. He looks ten years younger. You were right. He's flourishing here."

Matthan came out to greet them before they reached the house. Joseph was right. His dear friend looked healthy and happy. Being here had revitalized him.

The next day, they discussed everything. Matthan said he would go with them to the landing and then bring the donkeys back to the farm. The men would seal the tunnel as he went through it. Demas told him all the news and asked him what he thought of Benjamin now.

"He's a true Shophan now, Demas. He just needed guidance and the realization that you weren't as bad as he had always thought that you were. When you had that first talk, he was terrified. Now he understands why you were so disappointed. It's like he has been reborn. And how is little Joseph doing?"

"He is doing very well. I had two houses built in a line with the main house. Benjamin's family has already moved into theirs. Joseph was moving in as the carpenters were leaving. I think you would be surprised to see the place now."

"Not after being here. You did everything that it needed and more. When I go into Jerusalem with Lazarus, the people already know that we can meet their basic needs and extra and unusual things too. As your manager, I have a lot of prestige that I've never thought possible. I am grateful to you for letting me be here. I am very happy."

The next day, Demas picked out three young female dogs. With the property expansion in Antioch, they were going to need several more to protect and herd.

They left for the landing several hours before sunup. Andrew would stay at the farm, but they took three more shepherds with them. By the next afternoon, they arrived at the landing. They said their good-byes, and Matthan took the donkeys back the way they had just come. They slept on the beach, and the next morning, Jonah was there. It took two trips to the boat, but as they left, Demas could not see anything in the cove. The landing was gone.

In Tyre, Demas handed Boaz a bag with a year's pay in it. The man was almost in tears, but Demas assured him that he had done a good job and, if he needed work, to seek out his Uncle Samuel, and he would be taken care of.

He and Joseph walked to Samuel's home, and Samuel, Elizabeth, and Benjamin greeted them. Benjamin looked so much better. He acted proud of the whole family.

After dinner, Demas and Samuel went out on the patio to talk. Demas wanted to know if there were any more raids on their ships.

"Two were attacked, but they came on through just fine. Why? I think I see another idea coming. What is it?"

Demas smiled. His uncle could read his mind. "Since I'm living in Antioch now, why don't we drop sailing over open seas? The ships can come through Antioch from Ephesus and the other Grecian seaports. Then come straight down to Tyre. It will be safer, and we can open more areas to get more things. What do you think?"

"It's a great idea. I can't understand why we hadn't thought of it sooner. You'll be back in, what, ten days? I'll send Jacob a letter about doing that. He and his sons can go all over the Grecian ports and find out what's available. That way, Jacob can distribute it from Ephesus to you and then on down to Caleb in Egypt. That should take care of a lot of the troubles we had sailing on the open seas. As always, nephew, your fertile brain and seamanship experience will guide us into new directions."

Three days later, they were on their way to the main house. Benjamin handled the voyage much better than his first one. He laughed when he came onboard and told Demas that he hadn't eaten breakfast this time. The voyage was over—more quickly, it seemed, this time. Baba had brought them and was his old self again. He was interested in the changes that they were going to make. He would be up later for dinner and the Seder. Demas had invited all the sailors too, but a couple of them had to stand watch, and others were going to see old friends in the city.

Tomorrow they would rest, and then Joseph and he were going over the grounds. It looked like they would be raising sheep again. Not as many as in Emmaus but enough to sell in Antioch.

Mariam asked how Benjamin had done, and he told her that he was a man now, nothing like he had been when they had left.

Early Sunday morning, Demas and Joseph looked at the fields and the spring that he had discovered.

"It looks good, Demas. You can probably run about five hundred to a thousand sheep. I like these fields. When you get them under cultivation, it will be similar to your place in Emmaus," said Joseph.

"That's what I thought. Having the water available more or less settled it for me. The next few years should make it a reality. Do you think that you and Shela will like it here?"

"Oh, yes. I like having those cool ocean breezes in the evenings. It smells fresher too. Who knows, I may even learn to fish!"

They laughed and headed back to the house. Joseph loved the children and was amazed at how much they had grown, especially David. It wouldn't be long before he would be traveling with Demas. Actually, Demas was thinking of taking him to Ephesus on his next trip there.

The week went quickly, and the following week, Demas and both Josephs would be heading to Tyre again. The two Josephs were inseparable. Little Joseph was constantly asking questions, and Big Joseph patiently answered every question. He told Demas he was fascinated by all things that little Joseph could think of. He told Demas he was a natural shepherd.

Benjamin loved his new home and was happy to be with his wife and children again, but every morning, he was up and preparing for another caravan that was due. He read the orders over and made suggestions for new items that he had been asked for even in Jerusalem. He had found his niche in life at last.

Chapter 36

Little Joseph handled the voyage very well. Baba had him help the sailors do their jobs. He didn't suffer any seasickness, so he was in good spirits when they got to Tyre.

As always, Uncle Samuel was glad to see his nephews. He wasn't surprised at all of hearing Demas's plans for their place in Antioch. "Once a farmer, always a farmer," he told Demas. He had sent a letter to Jacob explaining their new sea routes. He was waiting for a reply.

Demas and Joseph said their good-byes and headed for Emmaus. On the way there, Joseph had to ask how Demas and his father had stood up to all the traveling that they did. Demas told him that you did what had to be done. It was just part of what they did. Joseph nodded. He could understand that their lives were dictated by their jobs. He was glad that he did what he did. Traveling was exhausting. He could certainly appreciate Demas's dedication to his job. He thanked God that he could be home every night with his wife.

Everything was fine at the farm. Matthan was inexhaustible as he went over the farm and flocks. And then he went into Bethany once a week. His semi-retirement was a joy. He was a grandfather to all the children, and he bloomed from all their love for him. He felt he was glimpsing at what heaven would be like.

Demas visited Lazarus to find when the next caravan was headed to Tyre. He was saddened to hear that Lazarus's father had passed away. But Lazarus was okay. He said that his father had been very sick for so long that it was a blessing for him and his sisters to know that he wasn't suffering anymore. Demas caught a caravan back to Tyre three days later. He took three more trained dogs with him.

At Samuel's, he was told that Joseph would be ready to go down to Bethany in a couple of weeks. Demas had taught him well. It was really just a tour to see how and what came into the different businesses. Every region had the basic things available, but each wanted other things not easily found in their area. Demas was glad to know that his younger brother hadn't had the problems that Benjamin had encountered. But then they were different personalities too.

Demas told his uncle that he would probably be going to Ephesus soon. He missed Jacob and wanted to see how his former sailing companion was. He also said that he would be taking about six sheep back with him when he came back for Joseph. Otherwise, he would see him again in six weeks. The trip back to Antioch was uneventful, and he was happy to be home again.

Early the next day, Benjamin was already outside feeding the dogs. He looked healthy and stronger. "What are we doing today, Demas?"

"We'll walk the property, and then I'm going to teach you how to use a sword and bows and arrows. Everyone needs to know how to defend himself and his family. The dogs can warn you, but they can't be your only defense. Joseph likes using the bow the most, but swords and spears are necessary too. You never know when or how danger is near. You have to be prepared for anything."

"I thought I knew so much. Now I see how stupid and arrogant I've been. Let's go see how much the trees have grown, and then you can teach me the manly arts of self-preservation."

They both laughed as they walked the tree lines. Naturally, the briars were growing quickly, and there was no doubt they had enhanced the protection of the property. It would be years before the trees would produce, but they added a comfortable elegance to the former bareness of the land. Right now, the people came to them for supplies, but Demas hoped that more businesses in town would come and open. He didn't like too much outside activity around their homes. He preferred that the businesses in town would grow, and then they wouldn't have so much traffic in and out of the grounds. In time, it would happen. Everything took time.

Naturally, Benjamin liked the sword and spear best. That afternoon, Demas realized he was getting older. He was sore all over. His brother had had a natural feel for sword fighting. With practice, he could be quite efficient with the weapon. *Good,* Demas thought. *My brothers can do the protecting, and I'll do the thinking.*

For several weeks, Demas and Benjamin went over the stock lists and made new lists of especially asked-for new things. The caravans still came regularly. Sometimes they stayed the night, but most of the time, they headed out again the same day. So far, bandits hadn't attacked, but they had a full company of guards with their caravans for protection. And a lot of times, smaller groups joined their larger one for safety. As a result, Demas saw more goods from the Far East and the northern countries. Then one day, the man who had brought those strange seeds from before came in.

"Well, I found out what these seeds were. It's called cotton. It grows well in dry climates, so it will do okay here. Then he proceeded to tell Demas how it was planted. The man was a walking storeroom of information. Demas suddenly saw an opportunity with this man. Here was a traveler who went everywhere. He would hire him to find unusual things from the other regions, so he invited him to come home with him. The man had also brought spindles of how to spin the cotton into thread and a loom of sorts to weave the cloth. He also brought three bolts of cloth. It was softer and more pliable than linen. When Roxanne saw it, she wanted to try the spindles too. Reznik looked at her loom and said it would work just fine. Then Demas made an offer to him, and Reznik accepted it. He said that it might be a year before he came back again. Demas said that was okay, and Reznik went back to the caravan. Demas had given him half of the money agreed on and promised he would put the rest into investments for him while he was gone. Demas was excited to see what Reznik would find for them in the years to come.

Roxanne wanted all of the cotton fabric. She and his mother were like two birds chirping with each other. Oh, well, they were happy, and so was he.

The next Monday, it was time to go get Joseph. Time was passing so quickly. Roxanne was rounding out much more than she had with their other babies. At least, he would be here when this child was born. He knew she would appreciate his being there when it was her time to give birth. Going to see Jacob would have to wait for a while.

Baba picked him up, and they left within a few hours. The trip went swiftly, and it was the most quiet and peaceful time that Demas had had this past year. He helped where he could; otherwise, he enjoyed the sea again. When they landed, Samuel was there, as always. Demas had sneaked some of the cotton so that he could show it to his uncle.

Then he told him about Reznik. Samuel, who was so used to his nephew's creativity and his far-reaching ideas, just sat and smiled. His only thought was how much he truly enjoyed this man and his ideas. He made him laugh, think, and enjoy everything each time he visited. Two days later, Demas was on his way to Emmaus.

Joseph was excited to see Demas. He told him everything that he had seen and done, but like Benjamin, he didn't like Jerusalem. It was interesting to see so many people, but the Roman soldiers bothered him. Now Emmaus was a different story. He loved it. Matthan had shown him everything, and he spent off time outside looking into every nook and cranny on the farm. He really liked the shepherds and their families. He told Demas that was what he truly enjoyed the most. He was born in Damascus, so he had never known about his parents' former home. As Matthan showed him how Demas had improved the place, he hoped that they could do the same thing in Antioch.

By the time they had gathered the sheep, they were taking the route back north to home, and Demas had stopped talking and just nodded occasionally. Demas went to Emmaus and had told Lazarus that they were changing their sea routes. He also told him of his and his uncle's fears about the possible destruction of Jerusalem and the Jews by Rome. Lazarus agreed with their observations and then said that he had heard about Cyprus and that he would like to see it someday. Demas said that if he was truly interested in it, he would look it over on his next trip to Ephesus. A small caravan was leaving in two days, so Demas told him that they would be back then to return to Tyre with it. No one would ever travel alone that far these days. He also had Lazarus hire extra guards for the trip.

They said their good-byes at the farm and headed for the caravan in Emmaus. When they got there, Lazarus showed him a temporary sheepfold that he had made for their trip. Also carrying pens for the sheep too while they traveled. As always, Demas was amazed at Lazarus's ability to think up things that were needful and unusual. And then they were on the road again.

In Tyre, Demas told Samuel of Lazarus's desire to go to Cyprus someday. Samuel looked at him, grinning. "Do you think Cyprus would be a good place to open a smaller trading post in? It could be quite handy someday, but if we do that, we won't need his compound in Jerusalem or the inns on the eastern route from Damascus."

"Yes, I know. As soon as Roxanne has our next child and everything is going okay, I'm going to Ephesus to see Jacob. I'll stop in Cyprus and look it over. Right now, I just want to go home and rest. Oh, what did you and Elizabeth think of that cotton fabric I brought?"

"What did we think? We want to find a regular source of it. Elizabeth really liked it. And as far as this man, Reznik, he sounds ideal for finding us new kinds of merchandise. Between him and Jacob, we could really expand the types of merchandise that we can offer. You know, nephew, I really look forward to your visits. Every time you come, I can't wait to know what else you're planning. It sure takes boredom out of our daily routines."

"Well, sir. I'm glad to be able to keep you satisfied. But I have to tell you, I'm tired of traveling for a little while. Roxanne and I want a sister for Esther, so I'm happy to be there with her when this baby is born. I missed all the others. And I have a few things to do to our place while I'm relaxing."

"Relaxation! Yes, you should try it sometime. It will be a new thing for you." He laughed.

The trip back home went well. They used the portable sheepfold to contain the sheep and the mess they created. Jonah was sure happy that they had it. Demas let Joseph take care of the sheep on the trip back. It gave him a chance to enjoy the voyage.

The whole family was waiting for them. They were having a feast at their house for everyone. The boys could talk to their mother again and were excited as they exchanged their experiences with each other.

The meal was over, and everyone headed to their own homes. Demas headed for the patio to relax and enjoy some silence. He wasn't quite used to being with so many people, especially children. He was thanking God for making him a man when his mother joined him.

"Thank you, son, for helping your brothers to become good men! Yes, they are very different from you, but you helped them mature. Your father would be so pleased. I know he knew that you could accomplish it. He just didn't have the time or energy to handle it himself. I'm so happy to have my family together again."

"I know, Mother. Frankly, I'm glad to be able to stay home myself. I am truly exhausted. How is Roxanne really doing? She looks so tired herself. She's not overdoing it, is she?"

"No, dear. I make her rest every afternoon for a few hours. She's just tired more because of the new baby that's coming soon. Men should have to carry a huge boulder tied to their waist for three months. Then they would have an idea of what it's like. She'll be fine once the baby is born."

They said good night, and Demas just sat and enjoyed the quiet and coolness. Big Joseph was right. These cool ocean breezes were quite restful. Then he went in and went to bed.

Four nights later, Roxanne woke Demas. "Dearest, would you go get Mother? I think our new daughter is about ready to meet her family."

Demas staggered to his mother's door and called to her. She immediately came out and went to their room. Demas stood confused, wondering what he should do.

His mother reappeared and told him to go to his office to sleep. Then several women were with his mother, so he did what he was told to do and went to his work room.

After much activity and several hours, his mother came to him. "Well, son. You are a father again. Roxanne has given you a son and a daughter. They are all fine. I'll bring the babies to you as soon as we've cleaned and swaddled them. You can go see Roxanne now."

Demas walked quietly into their room. Roxanne was resting. "Darling, are you okay?" he said. Roxanne opened her eyes and smiled at him. "I think we have ended adding to our family. We both got what we wanted. I know that fathers prefer boys, but I got my little sweetheart too. I thought I was getting awfully big. Now I know why. Are you as surprised as I am?"

"At this point in my life, no. Well, we picked little Ruth's name. What shall we name our boy?"

"Let's name him Aaron, after the head of your family. Would you like that?"

"That will be perfect. When my sister Hannah hears, she will truly be pleased. Thank you so much."

I'm going to go see my new son and daughter now. You rest. You did a great job, my little mother."

His mother was walking toward him with two little bundles in her arms as he stepped out of their room. They were asleep but swaddled completely. Only their little faces were visible. "Are they okay?' he asked.

"My son, they are perfect. Have you decided on a name for Ruth's brother?"

"Yes. He will be Aaron. Roxanne liked it right away."

"Aaron and Ruth, yes, those are beautiful names. Oh, how I wish at this moment that your father could see his new grandchildren. He would be so happy. He did love all of ours so much, but he always found time to see and talk with his grandchildren. He had more time by the time they came. Of course, these two would have been a wonderful blessing to him." She took the babies into Roxanne, and Demas went to his office and went to sleep. This whole thing had worn him out.

Chapter 37

Two months had passed, and everything was going smoothly. The dock on the Orontes River had been built so that the company boats could dock just a little ways from the compound. Benjamin and Joseph handled the compound and the caravans very well. They had hired a shepherd to help with the sheep, although Joseph checked on him every day. It was time to take his oldest son, David, and go to his Uncle Jacobs in Ephesus. Roxanne had heard from her sister, who was happy for them with the birth of the twins. And his wife was settling down to motherhood with the new babies and the other children. Lazarus had sent them two cradles for the babies, and his mother had hired two Jewish women to suckle them. He could leave on the next boat heading for Greece.

Merchants were buying more of their stock, and not very many people came to them personally to purchase their things. It was just as Demas was hoping would happen. He had bought some mules, cows, and goats, so it was growing as a farm too. The wheat, barley, and rye were planted, so summer would see all of that maturing.

It was time to do some traveling. He also wanted to make a stop in Cyprus and look around for another compound site. But mainly he just wanted to travel again. He had done so much of it in his lifetime that he actually missed it now.

At dinner, he told his family his plans, and David was jubilant. He knew he would take his father's place someday and was anxious to start his travels.

Baba was their captain, and Demas looked forward to seeing Jacob again. He told Baba that he wanted to stop in Salamis for a day and why. He was surprised when Baba asked about the property he was going to be seeking and why. Then he surprised Demas even more by asking if he could go with him. David had taken to the sea as his father had. It was a good trip. When they landed in Salamis, it didn't take long for Demas to find someone who directed him to a man who might be interested in selling his warehouse and home. It was close to the port. So off they went to see him.

As they approached the house, Demas was surprised to see the similarity to his Uncle Samuel's place. As they approached the gate and entered, an elderly man came and met them.

"Yes, sirs, how may I help you?" he asked.

"My name is Demas Shophan, and I was told that you might have property for sale?"

"Yes, I do. My name is Lemuel. I own this house and the warehouse next door. I've heard of the name Shophan. Let's see, I believe the man I talked to was Jarius Shophan. Was he any kin to you?

"That was my father. We're traders and wanted to see about opening a place here. That's why I'm here, to find a place if I can."

"Well, come on in, and we'll talk."

He led them to a large patio on the side of the house. It was really a nice place. It had a large fountain, and there were benches around the area. They were treated to the normal amenities. Servants washed their hands and feet, and water and coffee were offered.

"As you can see, this is a pleasant place to talk. Now what is it you need specifically?"

"It looks like you've got just what I need. Do you want to sell this place?"

"Yes. I only had one son, and he's died. My wife wants to move to a quieter area and wants me to retire. Let me show you everything. I gather your business is doing very well if you need a place here!"

"Well, we're traders, and we need a place away from the mainland."

"I do okay, but with your connections, you could do much more." They were shown everything. It was about the size of Lazarus's compound in Bethany, and it was on the fringe of the city. It would be perfect. Then the usual haggling began. They were served a meal, and finally an agreement was reached. Lemuel seemed quite satisfied as was Demas. Lemuel agreed to take half the price now and have the transfers of ownership drawn up. When Demas came back from Ephesus, the rest of the monies would be paid, and Demas would have the ownership papers. Lemuel said he would stay on until Demas had someone to take over. It gave him time and the money to find a new home for him and his wife. Demas had his receipt, so everyone was satisfied.

The next morning, they sailed for Ephesus. Demas liked the property. Now he had to find someone to run it until Lazarus was ready to move there. He would have to talk to Jacob about getting a new manager. He would keep Lemuel's workers.

The rest of the trip went quickly, and they were soon in Ephesus. Jacob was very happy to see all of them.

"Well, nephew, it has been a while since we were together. Samuel writes to me all the time about the changes you're making. I like them. They really are such simple things, but they will really expedite our trading. I wish you could take this new place over. We would be a little closer to each other. Now who is this trader you've found? I believe Samuel said his name is Reznik?"

"He's an eastern man. He goes up into the eastern and northern areas. He probably won't be back for a while, but he's found some interesting things that will add to our inventories. Here's a new fabric that I think will catch on. It's called cotton. He brought me seeds to plant and spindles and looms so that the women can make it into thread and then weave it into cloth." With that said, he handed Jacob a yard of the fabric.

Jacob felt it and ran his hands over it. "It's light, isn't it? And I don't think it will wear like our woolen garments."

"That's true, but if the women like it, they'll have to buy more, won't they?" Demas smiled.

"You know, Demas, you've become quite devious. Of course, profits would increase, but that is the whole idea, isn't it?"

"Yes, but in the warmer climes, it's more comfortable. We must never forget the women are buying or encouraging their husbands to get them more and different things that appeal to them. It would be nice for babies and young children too. Anyway, he brought me some seeds, so I've already planted them. I even bought spindles for the women to make the thread and then weave it. It intrigued me as well. We'll just have to wait and see. Like you, the men thought it was too light, but all the women at home loved it. I'm anxious to see what Reznik brings next year. He goes into all the northern and eastern regions. Who knows what he will bring back then."

Just then, Baba came in. "I'm sorry to interrupt, but before I left, I remembered that your Uncle Caleb gave me a letter to give you. I found it when I was loading to leave. The next boat will be here in two or three weeks. Be blessed by God."

"You too, dear friend, be careful and alert," they both answered and walked out to the gate with him.

Time went quickly, and David loved his extended family. He worked with his cousins during the day, and then they went fishing in the late afternoons. He loved his Aunt Allysa, and he helped her when he could. Both his cousins were betrothed to young women and would be married the following spring. He thought they were crazy to take on wives, but he liked being thought of as a young man instead of a boy. Jacob and Demas went over different ideas and otherwise enjoyed each other's company. Gauis and Hannah came regularly to visit. Their younger son, Antonio, was planning to marry the next year, so he and his wife would be going to Rome for a visit and the wedding. Hannah wanted to go and visit Roxanne in a few months. She and Demas had talked about her sister's activities and the children. She couldn't believe that they had six children now. Demas could tell that she missed being with them. Gaius could go to Rome for his son's marriage, but he would have to wait for a while longer before he could go for a visit to see them too. Their oldest son enjoyed being in the army and was gaining recognition for his campaigns. But he hadn't found anyone yet and apparently was too busy and active to even plan it. Unlike his father, he was a warrior and enjoyed it. Demas could see how lonely Hannah was. He made a point of inviting her anytime.

Soon it was time to leave when Jonah walked up to the house. He was greeted, and he handed Demas a letter from his Uncle Caleb in Egypt. While Jonah refreshed himself and talked to Jacob, he read the letter.

"Well, Jacob, I think I have received an answer to my prayers. It seems that Caleb's youngest son wants to leave Egypt and move to the north. He really isn't needed that much at home, and Caleb thought he might like it better here. I guess I'll invite him to come on, or I can go down there and see him personally. Yes, I think I'll go see Caleb and talk to his son. It will give David a chance to meet this part of the family too."

"You know what, Demas? I think God is taking care of you. We have a problem, and then suddenly it gets solved, and you keep thinking, planning, and expanding. I think that you are more like our father than Jarius. Your father did so much, but he didn't read the times like your Grandfather David did. He put this whole thing together and then evaded Herod while living only eight miles from him. Your dad was fantastic, but you have the same insight as your grandfather did. The way you maneuver and gain more business is truly awesome. I salute you, nephew, from my heart."

"Okay, that's enough. I'm just doing my job. So what do you think of bringing Abel up to Ephesus? He's a good man, and if he likes Cyprus he should be fine. Since Lazarus has never married, the eventual changeover should go well. Who knows, Lazarus may not want the whole responsibility of doing everything again. They could share managing the new place. Time will show us which way to go. You know, one thing I've never done is find Joel. I've had feelers out, but so far nothing."

"Why in the world are you looking for him? If he doesn't want to be found, so be it. Anyway, he's probably dead by now. And good riddance! I can't believe you still think about him."

"Jacob. I do understand how you feel. It's just he's kind of an unfinished business for me. I guess I just can't help wondering about him."

"My dear nephew, if I saw him, I would more than likely spit on him. He was the cause of my father's death. I can't forgive him. That's just how I feel. Sorry, but I loved my father, and he had a right to die of old age and not sooner because of a useless parasite."

"I do understand. It's just that he's a piece of unfinished business. Oh well, David and I are leaving with Jonah tomorrow. I'll write and let you know what's happening."

The next day, they were off to Tyre to see his Uncle Samuel. David loved sailing. That was good because in a few years, he would be doing it quite often.

Chapter 38

They were approaching Tyre, and David was eager to see Samuel's family. He was like Demas. Each day was a new thing to be anticipated. The boy loved his extended family as much as Demas did. It would be good for him to build his relationship with his cousins. One day, he would be like him and travel to keep things flowing and profitable.

As always, Samuel was at the dock when they pulled in. "Well, nephew, what's new? With you, something is always happening. David, you are growing up too fast. It won't be long before you will be the boss man."

"Not for a while, Uncle Samuel. I've got a lot to learn. Where are Steven and Joshua? I got something for them."

"They are at work, but you'll see them this evening. Come on to the house. Your Aunt Elizabeth is anxious to see you."

"Well, Demas, what is new? Every time I see you, there are changes coming."

Demas and Samuel sat out on the patio, drinking coffee. He told him he had purchased property in Salamis and that he was waiting to see Caleb's son, Abel.

Samuel was surprised that they already had another property, and he was even more surprised to hear that Caleb's son might be running it. "How do you accomplish so much, Demas? Even your father didn't cause things to happen so quickly. And what surprises me is how things work out almost immediately."

"You aren't the only one, Uncle. These past things just seem to have fallen in place, the way I hoped that they would. If Abel works out, he will be running the Salamis property within six weeks. I'm sending a letter to him with Jonah tomorrow. David and I are going to see Lazarus and the farm as soon as I talk to Abel. I was going to Egypt with Jonah, but I think I'll wait until I hear back from Uncle Caleb. The man that I bought the property from said that he would stay until I brought someone to take over. It's not really big, but it will help us to take on more merchandise from the other ports around Jacob's area. If we think Abel will work out, why don't you come with us when we move him in there? As soon as I know definitely it's a go, I'll write Jacob to meet us there too."

"Yes, plan on me coming. The boys are doing nearly everything now. I want to see what we've got there. See, I told you so. Every time you come, it's like a new adventure."

They laughed and went in to tell Elizabeth about their plans.

Two weeks later, Abel was there at Tyre. He was very affable and anxious for an opportunity to leave Egypt. He wasn't married, so it wouldn't take him long to get ready to move. He hadn't done much traveling, so he was eager to get started. Naturally, his father wasn't eager to see him move so far away, but he could always go and visit Abel. He could even see Samuel and Jacob more often. Samuel and Demas liked the man. They explained the possibility of his sharing the business with Lazarus. But that wouldn't be for a long while. He thought that would be just fine. They could share responsibilities equally. Since neither was married, that made it even more acceptable.

They agreed for him to be back in three weeks, and then they would all go to Salamis. In the meantime, Demas and David were going to Bethany and the farm. They were both eager to see their old home again, and David had a hard time containing his excitement. First, a boat ride, and now he would be in a caravan. For a young man, this was a totally pleasing adventure. Demas just smiled at him. Then he thought about how tiring and boring the constant traveling could be. Oh well, his son had to learn just as he had. Hopefully, his life wouldn't be as turbulent as his father's and his own had been. At least, he hoped it wouldn't be. David had to be trained, and he would be. He prayed that nothing catastrophic would happen for a long time. Times were changing, and he hoped it would give him the opportunity to enjoy his wife and family more.

Demas never knew someone could talk so much and ask so many questions constantly, but after a couple of days, David quieted down. And then they were in Emmaus. Matthan and everyone were thrilled to see them. Joseph asked how everything was doing in Antioch. The sheep were producing lambs and loads of wool. David was everywhere, checking things out. He loved their old farm as much as Demas. They were taking back lots of fruit, nuts, and honey. David said how much better this farm's honey was. Demas and Matthan went up to Bethany to see Lazarus and tell him about the new compound that they had bought in Salamis. He and his sisters were excited about the possible move in the future. And then it was time to return to Tyre. Abel would be there, and then they would go home to Antioch, leave David, and then sail for Cyprus. Samuel had already sent a letter to Jacob telling him about when they would be there. So the journeys began again.

David had enjoyed himself but was glad to be home. Samuel was surprised by everything done in Antioch and was constantly comparing it to the farm in Emmaus. Abel was just speechless. Apparently, his father really wasn't into farming, so he had lived in the city most of his life. But he really had a good time making friends with his cousins, and seeing how diversified the rest of the families were. A caravan came in while they were there, and he was surprised at how much was brought in, sorted, and sent on its way to Damascus. He loved the new farm surrounding the property. Even Antioch itself was totally different from Alexandria where he had lived. The people were friendlier, and it was literally a pleasure to walk the area and talk to perfect strangers. He even enjoyed all the children. His own family wasn't as prolific or as interesting. He loved his Aunt Mariam and Roxanne. There was so much camaraderie and industry going on among the wives too. They were weaving cloth and teaching their daughters how to cook. His sisters and brothers' wives had servants and did very little around their homes, but they still socialized and shopped. These women were always busy and enjoyed themselves. If he could find a woman like them, he might reconsider marriage after all.

Then it was time to leave for Salamis. Sailing, he enjoyed and fishing too. So Abel was really anxious to see his new home. Samuel told the ladies that he and Elizabeth would be back in the spring. Good-byes were said, and the three men were off again.

Demas told Abel that they would have to go through all the goods in the new warehouse and get rid of everything that was just taking up space and not being sold. He said to keep an inventory record of what they had and what was needed at the other facilities and to find new markets in town and list what was wanted or needed there. Each month he was to send him a complete listing of what came in, sold, or shipped on to him and Samuel and a report on how the business was doing. If he needed help, he was usually available as were Jacob and Samuel. He also said that their man in Bethany might come there eventually and would be a co-owner with him. However, it wasn't a certainty. It was something that might happen if they ever closed the Bethany business. They were constantly watching the Romans to judge how things were. Right now, the Jews were getting unruly and asking for trouble if they didn't settle down.

Abel just stared at Demas, and then he said that he hadn't realized the extent of the family involvement and watchfulness. Samuel told him that's why they had been so successful. He realized that Caleb didn't have the troubles that they had. But then they were living in or near Jerusalem, and the Jews represented a larger population than anywhere else.

Abel was still shocked. He had never fully understood the extent of the problems and overall size of the holdings that his family was part of. No wonder the oldest son of the whole family was so busy. Jarius was dead, and his son had stepped in admirably to keep the businesses going. And he sure seemed capable. There was nothing that he asked that Demas couldn't answer. The one time when he asked about how they knew the Romans so well, Demas simply stated that they knew them and watched them carefully. Abel didn't even know that all of them held Roman citizenship, even he himself. His father had never said anything to him about it. He could understand it, though, because it made sense. How else to safely travel the various countries and be protected? It made him proud to be a part of something so big and functioning. He was happy to really be one of them. Demas assured him that there was a large community of Jews on Cyprus if he wanted to go to the synagogue. Of course, that was something he hadn't considered before. His family only went on the Feast Days, but this man lived his life according to God's commandments. He felt that he could trust Demas for anything. It amazed him how different these families were to his own. They were godly people using God's precepts but being obedient to their conquerors too. It was inspiring to be accepted so completely.

The journey ended, and they walked to their new home. As they approached the house, Jacob came out. "What took you so long? I've been here for five days. Lemuel and his family have already moved to town, so I stayed here. Demas, this place is perfect. It needs cleaning and organizing, but it will work splendidly. You must be Abel. It's good to see you. The last time I saw you was over twenty years ago. Like it's said, time flies when you're enjoying yourself. Oh, by the way, I'm your Uncle Jacob from Ephesus."

"Hello. I'm kind of catching up to our family everywhere else. Things move at a slower pace in Egypt. You men are much more energetic than we are."

"That's probably true, but we have more fun."

"Yes, and more time to get into trouble. So you like the place, huh?" Samuel joked.

"Yes, I do. It's on the edge of the city, but far enough away for privacy. Also, we can get to the docks by this road here and not have to go into Salamis at all. The stock needs a lot of work, but I'll go with Abel to meet the businessmen in town and to help explain why they should come to us for anything they need or want. It's a pleasant town and area. I think you'll like it, Abel, once you're in full operation."

Abel just nodded. These uncles of his were fun-loving but very resourceful. He felt he had been crawling through life and now had to run to catch up. It literally made him breathless but excited. And he liked all of them, which surprised him. His father was so much more reserved than these men were. These men enjoyed life, and he was ready to join them.

Demas went with Jacob to settle up with Lemuel. He had the papers signed and witnessed. Everyone was content, so they returned to the business. Abel had a stack of bags of something that was rotten, so they had the men who had worked with Lemuel scatter the bag contents on the ground. Then he had them plow it under. He told them it would enrich the soil. Half of the building was emptied and cleaned. Then the things that Jacob had brought were sorted and labeled.

Demas asked the workers what basic things were needed or requested the most, and they said just about anything edible for people or sheep. So he had them start plowing the fields behind and around the buildings. He asked about a well and finally found and uncovered it. He sent one the men for a carpenter and a mason. He found several bushes like their burr ones and had them replant them all along the sides and back of the property. The land was more than he had originally thought it was, so he marked it with the bushes. They wouldn't have caravans here, so they didn't have to worry about water and food for camels. Samuel was supervising several people who were cleaning the house. Jacob had gone to town to see the competition and what they sold. Demas had hired a servant and his wife to clean and cook for them and Abel. At six o'clock, the weary family stopped for the day to rest.

The dinner was excellent, and they enjoyed the freshly caught fish and bread. Abel loved the camaraderie between his uncles and cousin. He listened as they talked of the past, present, and future plans. Demas was definitely gifted in his role as the head of the family's business. He couldn't get over the life that Demas had led, the things he had done, and the way the older men listened as Demas talked of new merchandise that they were going to have. And then they discussed the political situation. They even had a former tribune and governor of Ephesus as a friend and partner. His Uncle Jacob was even married to Gauis's daughter and had two sons. They all spoke several languages, and yet they weren't involved or interfering with each other's lives. They truly loved each other.

It saddened him when he thought of his own family. He and his brothers didn't get together except at work. Otherwise, they didn't enjoy gathering as a family. He was so glad to have left Egypt. And tomorrow they were all going to the synagogue. On Monday, he and Jacob would be visiting the local businesses again to just get acquainted and acquaint them of the many things they could have available. They had their own fleet of ships and caravans that were bringing goods in from all over their known world. It had awed Abel how much Demas could talk about. Apparently, he had a regular traveler bringing things that he had not heard of before, and they were polite and friendly as they brought him into conversations. He felt he belonged and was part of them. He actually felt loved.

Then the uncles asked Demas about someone named Jesus, whom they considered the son of God. When he and Demas were alone the next day, he asked him who this Jesus was, so Demas told him the whole story and how he was waiting for this Jesus to begin his ministry. He explained that Jesus would be bringing new ideas to not only the Jews but the Gentiles too. Then he talked about a young man named John and the miracles of his birth to a very old priest and his wife and how he was raised as a Nazirite and had gone to the Essenes community when his aged parents had died. Abel hated being so ignorant of his own religion, so Demas patiently explained how a Nazirite lived. Abel vaguely remembered the story of a judge named Samson, but that his family wasn't very acquainted or regular participants of his own religion. Demas suggested he meet the rabbi at their synagogue and start learning about God and his chosen people. Once he became acquainted with God's Word, Demas felt he would understand why he himself was so involved with this man called Jesus.

At first, Abel thought this whole change to moving here would become routine, but he could see how he was ignorant of his own origins. Demas told him the whole story of how their family had been moved to different areas to avoid Herod originally, how the business had grown so exponentially, and how the oldest son and then himself were to lead it. He had heard that Demas's father, Jarius, had been killed in a pirate fight, and that Demas had to step into his place to continue as the family's head. Abel hadn't understood about that at all. Now he saw why Demas had brought his oldest son, David, along to teach him. The boy would be trained and experienced by the time his father stepped down or died. The families and businesses would continue. He could see the benefit of having Roman citizenship now. It was protection and allowed freedom of movement.

Demas and each of his uncles had made notes on what to ship to Abel. Before very long, his warehouses would be filled, and he would be busy. They reiterated again to not discuss family connections. As far as others were concerned, he had good contacts and would be regularly supplied. They all had different names, so the relationship would be protected. Abel was learning how to make friends with the local people: to be fair in all business dealings and not show partiality to anyone. First and foremost, he was to be fair and friendly. He did ask about Lazarus and what he was like. Demas told about Lazarus's inventions and that he had two unmarried sisters. But when and if Lazarus came, they would be equal partners. If and when Abel married, another house would be built if it was needed. He could get in contact with their uncles and/or him. All he had to do was send a letter by one of their boat captains. They gave him a schedule of the boats and their captains. He could replace any workers or add more as he saw fit. His decisions were his own business, but at all times he tried to be fair and treat them the same way that he wanted to be treated. He would be responsible for the property and its condition. Any question only had to be asked if he wasn't sure. He could send his letters to anyone of them, but Demas wanted the reports monthly. They outlined how the profits were his except for the cost of goods, which he could outline in his reports. For the first time in his life, he was the head of his own house and business. He was truly excited to be his own man. He loved these men so much. They were all different and yet the same. They were family. Demas and Samuel were the first to leave. Jacob stuck around for the first few boats to help Abel get organized. Then he left for Ephesus.

On the Sabbath, Abel was in attendance and really learning about God and his heritage. In ways, he felt sorry for his own family. How could they exist without a relationship to their creator? He and the rabbi were becoming very good friends. Of course, they were eager to introduce him to the family females, but he didn't want any involvement at this time. He was a businessman and had plans to make. He kept on the gardener and his wife. His needs were met, and business was picking up. More businessmen were coming to him. Also, being part of the active Jewish community was a new experience for him. He had discovered God and was literally thrilled to read the books of the prophets. He was beginning to understand about Demas's interest in this man called the son of God. He was becoming very interested himself.

Chapter 39

Demas and Samuel had long talks on their boat ride to Antioch. Samuel seemed the most surprised by hearing about the lack of interest in God by his brother, Caleb. Samuel liked Abel as did Demas. They said he was like a dried-up field, which was suddenly being watered and coming to life again. They both believed that Abel would do very well in his new home. The way he soaked up information and worked gave them relief and confidence in him. Demas was curious to see if he would get the reports he asked for, but he also felt there was no need to worry. Abel would do just fine. Right now, Demas was anxious to get home and see his family. Thank goodness he wouldn't be traveling as much anymore. He wasn't concerned at all about his brothers. He knew that they would be doing their jobs well. They had learned their lessons, but in all ways, he still missed his father. It was difficult to be the family leader. With so many around him, he missed the vacancy caused by his father's death. They had so many good times and conversations with each other. Now Demas understood how his father had enjoyed their times and conversations. It would be a while before David and he could have the same type of relationship. Well, Grandfather and his father had endured it; so would he.

The babies seemed twice their previous size when he held them. They took a while before they were comfortable with him again. Hopefully, they would be walking before he had to leave again. The brothers were doing very well with the business. The sheep were having their lambs. Everything was growing, and his family was happy. Roxanne was excited about the coming visit with her sister. His mother was busy with all her grandchildren, and wives of his brothers were doing nearly everything with Mariam and Roxanne.

Sometimes he would take long rides or walks to get away from the noise. He had about two years before Jesus would be heard of. He would have to have about four or five scribes following him when he did begin his ministry. He would probably hear of John before he heard of Jesus. Lazarus was content to stay in Bethany for now, but he was looking forward to going to Salamis. It struck Demas then, why hadn't Martha or Mary ever married? He guessed they were content with their brother. Both were nice and kind but apparently had no desire to change their circumstances.

Hannah was due in for her visit with Roxanne. She had gone to Rome to see her younger son, Antonio, get married. Then when they had returned to Ephesus, she had boarded one of their ships coming to Antioch.

Abel was doing very well. He had become an active member of the Jewish community and had tripled his income as a result. The only thing bothering him was that he had met every single female on the island. Maybe he was a born bachelor. He said that his father was planning to come visit him. In a way, he was excited and also concerned. He wondered how Caleb would feel about his regular devotion and attendance at the synagogue. Demas had tried to encourage him in his studies of God's Word. Surely, his father wouldn't criticize his interest in God. Demas and Samuel had been surprised to hear of Caleb's lack of faith, but each man was responsible for his own walk with the Lord. Abel was a grown man and had made his own choices. Hopefully, Caleb wouldn't criticize him for that. Then again, maybe once Caleb saw how well his son was doing and his active part with the whole community, he himself might renew his own faith in God. Demas could only hope and pray so.

There was a boat due in tomorrow from Ephesus, and he hoped Hannah would be on it. Roxanne was cleaning the house constantly, and the children were running away every time she came at them with a wet rag. Children could only handle so many face and hand washings. Several times they had hidden from her in his office. Finally, they had begged him to talk to her. He did, and now she was very quiet toward him, so he had gone for a long ride. He couldn't remember his mother being that way, but she probably was. He was in his early forties now, and he really couldn't remember things like that in his childhood. However, he did remember that his father was always busy somewhere else. That's how men took care of many problems. They would just disappear for a while. He couldn't help smiling with those memories.

At last, Hannah arrived and constantly had a child in her arms or a couple in her lap. She was teary-eyed as she hugged and patted each one. She and Roxanne were talking constantly. Then they went for a walk with Esther. He figured that Esther was saying their lineage by memory. It was a feat to remember hundreds of years of ancestors. Demas saw Hannah clap then hug Esther, so she must have done it well. The visit went quickly and ended much too soon for Roxanne. They had tears in their eyes as they parted. Hannah promised to come every year. She had the time. Her boys were gone and between the governorship of the area and his business with Jacob, Gaius was always busy somewhere. So she was going to come visit her sister regularly.

Roxanne was sitting on the patio when Demas found her. "She wasn't here very long. It was so sad to see her go. I've missed her so very much. She loved the children and was so proud that Esther has already memorized our lineage. She feels it will continue on now that the next generation is prepared, but I think the twins truly captured her heart. I hope that Antonio and his wife will give her some grandchildren quickly. I could tell she envied us the whole family, and she loves our new home. She figured you would be fixing it up as you did our other place. I think she kind of envied us." Then Roxanne began to weep again.

"My darling wife, don't be sad. She'll be back. I've already told her this would be her home if she ever wanted to live here, and that you and the children can go see her when the babies are older. It will all work out."

Roxanne cuddled in Demas's arms. "You're a good and great man, my husband. You do so much. I will always love you, trust you, and admire you. Thank you."

Then they went inside.

Chapter 40

Demas sat on a seat, looking at the calendar that he had written. It was time for Jesus, he thought. Just then, James came in. "You wanted me, sir."

"Yes, James. I need four or five excellent scribes who are free to travel. Will you be able to find them here in Antioch? Or will we have to go farther afield to find them?"

James smiled. "I have already found them. Do you want to see them now?"

"Yes, James. It's time to send them out. John is down on the Jordan baptizing people already. That means it's time for Jesus to appear. When can you get them here?"

"I'll get a hold of them and see. They may be able to come anytime. I'll go see them today."

"Good. David and I are going down to Damascus next week and then to Bethany and the farm. Joseph sent a letter saying Matthan isn't feeling well, and I'm concerned. I would like to see the scribes before we leave."

"Yes, sir, I'll make sure they come as soon as possible. I hope that Matthan is okay. He's getting old now, so I guess we shouldn't be surprised. He writes to me and says he has truly enjoyed these past years. I hope he is better. He and I have been like brothers for years now."

"He was like a second father to me. I'm probably going to have to find him a helper to ease his workload. Time constantly brings change, doesn't it?"

"Yes, it does. Mistress Roxanne has the girls learning how to weave right now. The boys are in school, so I'll go now and talk to these scribes. Is that okay?"

"Yes, of course. I want to get them on their way as soon as they're able to leave." James left, and Demas sat back, musing over everything that had been happening. Abel had done a great job in Salamis. When his Uncle Caleb had come the first time to visit his son, he had ended up staying for four months with him, and then he had rededicated his life to the Lord. That had been a wonderful surprise. Now he came to visit Abel every year and stayed for months. His wife, Leah, had died several years before, and he had, more or less, retired. He even visited his brothers, Jacob and Samuel, each time he came north. Samuel was fully retired too. Sometimes they stayed with Demas and his family, and they would all go fishing. To Demas, Roxanne was as beautiful as ever. His mother, Mariam, was slowing down some but not much. She, Roxanne, and Demas went riding every few days. Even his brothers had learned to ride horses and seemed to enjoy it. He was truly blessed. His brothers handled all the business now in Antioch and the caravans. He only traveled once a year, so he handled the paperwork for the most part. He had partnered with Reznik and given him his own caravan. He still brought things that were new to them to determine whether they would be wanted or not. For some reason, he and Reznik had become truly good friends. He always brought gifts for the family, and all the adults enjoyed his stories as much as the children did. But he never stayed long. Demas could never understand how he could enjoy traveling all the time. He didn't have a home or any family, so traveling brought him the contentment he needed. Demas shrugged. He liked being home with his whole family. *To each their own,* he thought.

The farm here was maturing, and they were selling their own wool, animals, and fruits to the local people. His flocks averaged around five hundred ewes now. He had about fifty goats, twenty dogs, twelve horses, and a herd of cows plus oxen and donkeys. He had about thirty workers tending to everything. He had ended up buying most of the land around him and had had more homes built out on the farther edges of his land for the workers. This place was now larger than the one in Emmaus. And with all this, he still missed his father. *Well, sir, I'll be sending out scribes soon to search for Jesus,* he thought. *And David and I are going to go see John. He's down on the Jordan River.*

Jonah's parents had retired from the inn and had moved to Tyre to be near him and his family. So far, the inns were doing okay, but in Jerusalem, the Jews were acting up more than ever. Lazarus and his sisters were fine. Demas had gone down and had run the business, so Lazarus could go see the new place in Salamis. He loved it, liked Abel, and was looking forward to eventually moving there, but not quite yet. He said the Lord would show him when it was the right time to leave. So things were going along just fine. Other than requests for merchandise, which he still handled, things were running quite smoothly. Just then, James entered the room.

"Sir, all five men will be here after midday. All five can travel, and I looked at their work, and they are more than adequate for what you will require. None of them are married, so they really have nothing to be concerned about in leaving for long periods of time. I think that they will more than meet your needs."

"Thank you, James. I appreciate all of your effort and forethought. This is very important to me."

That afternoon, the scribes came. He sat them down and explained what their jobs would be. He said that Jesus was a new and powerful prophet, and he wanted an accurate account of all that he said and did. As far as he could determine, Jesus lived in the area of Nazareth, but he felt he could be in the towns in that general area. He said that every two months, he wanted to see what they had. He would provide a donkey for each of them and what he would pay. He asked if this would be sufficient for their needs and requirements. He also would provide any provisions and tents if needed.

They asked why this seemed so important to him, and he said that he strongly felt that Jesus would be greater than all the prophets in Jewish history. The men were young and unattached, so after talking together, they agreed to his proposition. They said they could leave after the Sabbath. He asked them if they needed any guards to go with them, but they felt they would be safe traveling together. He told them that they could take the scrolls to Tyre and his friend Samuel, who owned a trading business there. He would send them on to him here in Antioch. If they needed anything, Samuel would provide it for them. He would settle up with Samuel for any supplies that they needed. He was sending a good supply of pens, inks, stylus, scrolls, etc. with them as well as other things that they might need. He stressed the importance of this job for them. If any one of them wanted to quit, he would find replacements for them. But this was very important to him, and he was depending on their abilities to fulfill the work. He said the man they would be seeking was called Jesus and that his parents were Joseph and Mary. He would also send two men with them to care for their personal needs.

Out of curiosity, they asked how long the job would last. Demas sighed and then said at least three years. By this time, they were excited about the prospect of the trip. Then he asked when they would be ready to leave, and they said at least two weeks. He said that they had a caravan coming in then, which could travel with them to Damascus. Also, he asked them to be careful and not tell anyone anything but just that they were travelers and wanted to visit all of Israel. He told them when they were ready to come back and that his brothers would have everything ready for them. That he had to go to Damascus and would be there but only briefly. His work as a trader required him to travel frequently too, but he would be anxious to know if and when they found Jesus. He suggested that they go to synagogues along the way and quietly see if Jesus had visited them. It might help them find him sooner. They agreed and left.

The next week, Demas and David caravanned their way to Damascus. From there, they would visit the inns and seek out just where John was at that time. He had told his son why they were going and that he wanted to hear and speak with John. David was just as excited as his father to see this new prophet.

The inns were doing fine. Jonah's brothers ran both inns now. They had found wives and were settled and content out by themselves. At the southern end, they left the caravan, taking five guards with them, and headed for the Jordan River. Two days later, they found John surrounded by people. They sat down and listened to him talk. He certainly wasn't the young man that Demas had remembered. He was filled with the Spirit and was aggressive as he spoke. He didn't mince words, and when he started baptizing, Demas, David, and their guards stood up to be baptized too. David was first, and then his father followed him. When he stood up, John looked at him and said, "Demas, I know what you have done, and it is good because in your heart, God has shown you the way. He whom you seek has come and gone, but be assured that you will see Jesus when the time is right. Don't despair. God has been watching over you and your family, and he is pleased. The men you have sent to write all that he says and does will be shown to them. Keep on serving the Lord and you and all your family will be blessed. You are one of the few men that God has shown to me. Keep the faith and your wish will be granted." With this, he turned and continued baptizing "these wretched sinners," as he called the people all around him.

"We can go, son. I found out what I needed to know. Let's go to Bethany and Emmaus." David and the guards followed him.

They had talked with Lazarus. Then it was decided that David would be working with Lazarus for the next few months. Roxanne would be surprised and sad to not have David around. She knew this time was coming, but she would dearly miss their oldest son. Well, she would know soon enough. Lazarus was told of their baptizing by John.

Lazarus then admitted that his sisters and he had also gone to John and been baptized too. He also told Demas that he knew Jesus, but that his visits were sporadic. He never knew when he would come, and he seldom stayed very long. This surprised Demas, who then said, "His father was the one who did the carpentry for you, wasn't he?"

Lazarus nodded. "They came for Passover and stayed with us. Did you know that Joseph was dead? Jesus had been the head of his family now for over five years. Now his brothers have taken over, for he has left his home to start his ministry."

"That's what I figured. He had to wait until he was thirty to begin his work. I have scribes looking for Him now to transcribe everything that he says and does."

"He knows. He told me about you and what you would do."

"He's not upset, is he? I can't leave all my responsibilities right now, but I truly want to hear all that he says and does."

"He understands and will see them soon. Be patient. He knows all things."

With these last words, Demas, David, and the guards left for Emmaus. When they arrived, Matthan walked out of the house and greeted them. "Master Demas, it's so good to see you and David."

It wasn't long before Joseph and Shela appeared. "Well, it's about time you showed up." He laughed as he hugged his old friend. "I knew you couldn't stay away for much longer. How are things in Antioch?"

"Everything is grown and producing. When are you coming up to go fishing?"

"I was just waiting for you. Shela wants to come see the new farm. I've been training Andrew to take my place, and he's training one of the shepherds to take his. Also, I think I've met someone to take over Matthan's work. Matthan's putting on a good show, but he's wearing down. Do you want to meet Theo? He's young, about thirty, but he has a good head for business. I think you will find him capable. He's amiable and has a quick mind."

"Can we see him soon? I can't stay for too long. David is going to live here and work daily for Lazarus in Bethany. That's already arranged. As soon as we get Matthan's helper trained, then you and Shela can go to Tyre and sail up to Antioch. Believe me, you don't want to ride a camel for weeks at a time. Roxanne will be thrilled to see you and show off our twins. You haven't seen them yet."

"It sounds good to me. I'll go to Jerusalem tomorrow and see if Theo can come out as soon as possible. He knows all the businessmen, so he'll blend in really quickly. One problem though—he's married. His wife is very pleasant. They have a son and a daughter under seven. That shouldn't cause any problem, should it?"

"Not really. There are plenty of children here to play with. Have him bring her and the children too. Tonight I'll tell Matthan my plans. I just hope he won't be hurt. He's not being replaced, just being helped."

"I kind of think that he has figured this might happen. He'll be okay though. Let's see how he and his wife get along. Then we'll know for sure."

That evening, after a wonderful dinner, the men retired to the patio to enjoy the stillness of the ending day.

"Demas, who are you replacing me with?" Matthan suddenly asked.

"First, you are not being replaced. You are going into semi-retirement. You are my second father, longtime friend, and business partner. You came here to retire but have worked the whole time. Now you are going to pass the torch onto someone else. A man and his family are coming tomorrow, and you and I will interview him. Shela will take the wife around the farm while we talk. If we both like him and feel he can help you, then he and his family will move here. You will have the upper room and roof area for yourself, but I'm letting you decide what you want."

"The roof room? But it's always been yours."

"Yes, and it's the best place for you, my friend. It will give you privacy, and yet you will be close to train the new manager. They are coming tomorrow for both of us to see and talk too."

"What about Joseph and Shela? Are they leaving?"

"Just for a while, Joseph likes Antioch but wants to show it to Shela. She has to like it too. You know how wives are."

"Things are changing again, aren't they? When you get old, you really appreciate the earlier times when you were younger."

"That's why we will both be interviewing them. I know I can trust you to really see what I might miss. I hope she's as good a cook as Shela and will care for you accordingly. If you feel you wouldn't be comfortable with them, you can take one of the other houses. I want you to relax and let the new man do most of the work. You'll be free to come and go as you please, but his wife will be cooking for you. Let's see them before we decide anything."

Chapter 41

The next morning, they had just finished eating when the little family arrived. After introductions, Shela took the young wife and the two children out to meet the other wives. The men sat down and started talking. Demas let Matthan lead with most of the questions, since he would be working and living with them. Theo was young but very knowledgeable, and Demas was quite impressed.

Then he took over and explained the basics of their business, what they provided, and they worked together with partners in other areas. Relationships were not given, only that they worked to be able to meet any demands or special requests. Also, that the farm itself provided most of the animals needed by the Temple. That he himself was the senior partner and lived in Antioch. His job was to receive inventories and requests, which he would then appropriate and have sent to each trading center. That he would take a percentage of the business done in Jerusalem. However, it did not include anything pertaining to the farm. It had been in his family for almost sixty years.

Theo sat back and then asked, "So my job will be solely about merchandising and providing for the businesses in and around this whole area. How about the food grown here? That will be totally separate?"

"We provide animals for the temple and do sell food too. But as for you and your family, there will be no concerns. The food that you need is provided, just as it is for the farm hands and the shepherds and their families. The women are given wool after shearing, which is their wages for working in the gardens, but Matthan will show you how it all works. Some looms are provided for the women to weave and get pay for that. When you talk to your wife, she can explain it to you. You will get to live here, but the upper roof area is Matthan's. She will cook for him too. He's a good man and one of my best friends. He's been with me since I was born. I think you could do well here. If you have guests, the farm and staff are off bounds. That is a separate area, and I don't want to have strangers wondering around and causing any trouble. You and your family can go anywhere here. And if your wife wants to visit and work with the other women, she too will be paid in wool or produce. It will be her choice. The farm is mine, and the workers go to Matthan if any problems arise. Well, what do you think? Does this seem fair to you?"

"If I understand this correctly, I get a house, food, and a percentage of the trade goods that I sell. My children can play with the others, and my wife will have access to the women and be able to even earn materials to make our own clothes and make friends. This sounds wonderful to me. Let me see what Sarah says."

That's fine. I'm glad that you consider your wife's opinion. It will be a change for her, but I think she will be content. We are Jews, and we keep the Sabbath. Also, I've been thinking of bringing a teacher here to school the children. I've always liked being able to meet the needs of the families, so this is something I've been considering. I'll be looking into it."

Just then, Sarah came in with the children. You could tell she was excited.

Theo said he would let us know the next day as they left.

"Well, Matthan, what do you think?"

"He's smart, and he considers his family. Let's give them a try if they want to do it. I think I just might enjoy taking it easy a little more."

Shela came in and told them that she liked Theo's wife. The young woman was entranced by the activities, the fresh food available, the whole farm in general. And she loved how all the women shared the work and caring for all the children. She asked about Matthan, and Demas told her that he was like a grandfather to the children. He thought they would come back.

The next day, Theo was there early. He agreed to the terms and asked when they could move in. Matthan and Demas had already moved his things to the roof room, so they said that they could come anytime and offered them the use of camels or donkeys to help move their things. The next day before noon, they came with all that they had and settled in. Matthan had made the front room into his office. Satisfied with the family, Demas spent the day out with the shepherds and flocks. He started packing fruit and other things. He knew that Matthan would train Theo well. He and Joseph planned when he and Shela would be coming to Antioch. He said his good-byes and headed to Bethany. David had decided to stay with Lazarus and his sisters instead of the farm. This was fine with Demas, so joining the caravan that was waiting for him, he returned to Tyre. Briefly visiting with Samuel and his family, he was back on a boat to Antioch. Now he was waiting for the first scrolls from the scribes that he had sent out.

Four months passed, and David had moved on to Tyre and would then go to Salamis and then on to his Great-Uncle Jacob's for a while. He loved the travel and business, and like his father, he also loved to sail. It would be a while before he returned home.

Chapter 42

Two years passed quickly. Demas was receiving scrolls from his scribes. He read and reread everything that Jesus said and the miracles he performed. His wife, mother, and brothers discussed his words and were amazed by his fearlessness of the Romans and the Jewish hierarchy. Benjamin challenged some of his parables, but after an explanation, he agreed that Jesus was the son of God. Demas sent copies to his uncles and his cousin in Salamis as well as to Matthan and Lazarus. However, he too feared for Jesus, not so much of the Romans but of the Jewish leaders in Jerusalem. They didn't like Jesus's comments about them and were already planning on killing him. Lazarus wrote to Demas too and told how Jewish leaders were keeping Jerusalem stirred up. So far, the Romans were leaving him alone. They didn't want to get involved with Jewish doctrines.

Demas's sisters had married and lived in Antioch. He had given them houses for wedding gifts. Gabriel, his youngest brother, was studying to be a Pharisee in Jerusalem. Joseph and Shela had a house out near the grazing areas of the sheep and were semi-retired. His brothers handled their caravan trading center. David did most of the traveling now, so Demas's job had been boiled down to doing paperwork. Reznik had brought an Asian girl to teach them about cotton. This item was becoming very popular. His daughter Esther was getting married in a few months. The twins were growing up, and he was beginning to feel his age.

Then out of the blue, he received a letter from Theo saying that Matthan had taken a bad fall and had broken his hip. So Demas's life as a traveler was beginning again. He wanted to see how his old friend was. He asked Roxanne if she wanted to come, but her sister was coming for a visit, and Roxanne felt she should keep an eye on his mother, Mariam. Mariam was still active, but she was resting more and more. But she was so happy and content. When they talked, she didn't mention Jarius much. But at times, he would hear her talking to him. He never said anything because he himself did the same thing.

When he got to Tyre, his Uncle Samuel was very happy to see him. They talked and laughed as always. He said that Abel had gone to visit Lazarus and was quite taken with Mary, the younger sister. This surprised Demas. But then anything could happen. Time would tell. Then he took the next caravan to Bethany.

Lazarus was as interesting as always but also very concerned for Jesus. He said that the high priest wanted Jesus silenced, period! And even though he moved constantly, crowds of people would find Jesus wherever He was. Demas couldn't begin to imagine being constantly hounded like that. But he had his work to do and would continue until he had finished the job that his father had given him. Demas seemed to be praying continually for him. Then Lazarus got his full attention. It seemed a man named Joel had been caught stealing and thrown into prison. He had asked one of the guards to bring a message to him for Demas Shophan. Lazarus said that he had given the guard some money, and then he handed the message to Demas. Demas was stunned. Joel! And after all this time. He thanked Lazarus and headed for the farm. Well, he thought, his life was coming full circle. Joel, who had caused his family so much grief, wanted to see him. This would take some thought and lots of prayer.

As he rode in, Theo greeted him. "I'm glad to see you, Demas. Matthan isn't doing as well as we had hoped. He doesn't come down from his room very much. He's tired and hurting. We tried to get him to move into a room downstairs, but he said he feels closer to God on the roof. I visit him regularly, but…"

"I know, Theo. Thank you for caring for him. He's the oldest friend that I have now, and I love him. I'll go up and see him, and then we can talk later.

Sarah came out of the kitchen with a tray with juice and fruit. She handed it to Demas and smiled. "Make sure he drinks his juice. It's his favorite."

"Thank you, Sarah, for taking good care of Matthan."

"He's our good friend too and a grandfather to our children," she said.

Demas went up the stairs, glad that they had hired Theo and Sarah. They were very good and caring people. Matthan was resting in bed as Demas entered. "Are you asleep or just resting your eyes?" he asked.

"Just waiting for you, I heard you come. Please tell me it's isn't because I fell!"

"No. It was time for me to pay a visit. Everyone at home said to tell you they miss you and love you."

"I know. I've been thinking of all of you, but especially Jarius. He was a great friend. Guess it won't be long before I'll be seeing him again."

"Not for a while, okay? What do you think of the scrolls that I've been sending to you?"

"They are such sincere and wonderful things to read. They give me hope, Demas. You know, we live our lives as God has told us to, and then to make it clearer, he has sent his son. I've read and reread them many times. I know now what to expect, and I'm not doubting or fearful anymore."

Demas sighed. "He must be a great man. I hope that he knows how much I want to see him."

I think God will be very pleased with you as I've been. You are an honorable man, friend, and very kind. No one who has met you has ever said anything bad about you. I believe God is very pleased with you."

Demas smiled and paused before continuing. "To change the subject, I stopped at Bethany before coming here. A soldier had brought a note from the prison in Jerusalem. It's from Joel!"

"Joel! What a blatant thing to do. What has he to say for himself?"

"I don't know. I haven't read it yet. I thought that you should hear it too." Demas pulled the wrinkled papyrus out of his robe and straightened it.

"Demas, I know that this will surprise you, but I'm in prison and want to see you. Come see me if you will," Joel said.

"What do you think he wants besides getting out of there?"

"I thought about this the whole way from Bethany. I'll go see if I can find him tomorrow. He must be in the jail in Jerusalem. Jesus says to forgive, and I probably will end up doing it. But I can't really talk myself into trying to get him released. He caused Grandfather's death, disappointed and embarrassed his parents, and then stole from us. Jesus says to forgive all things. I think more than anything, I want to know why and whether or not it was all worth it."

"Yes, it will be interesting to know. I would go with you if I could, but I too want the answers to your questions. His parents were so ashamed of him. I think they really died of broken hearts. He was their only child, and he had no concern for them at all. He probably doesn't know that they died shortly after he took off. They are buried near your grandfather's grave. Demas, their names were Jeremiah and Naomi. Remind him of them. I'm curious now whether he has changed or is just trying to play with your sympathy. Hear him out. Then pray about it and let God guide you."

"I will, Matthan. Here is food and drink from Sarah. I'll come up after dinner. We'll sit outside for a while."

The farm was in excellent condition. Andrew was doing a great job with everything. His children were gown now, and he had grandkids. Some of his shepherds were related to him by marriage, but he expected more from them than the others. The sheep were being herded into their cotes for the night. He missed the farm, but he had a good one where he was now. If Matthan were to die, the men he had would carry on here. He might have to sell it eventually. Everything really depended on how Rome would deal with his fellow Jews. They were causing more and more troubles. Only time would tell how and when the Jews again would be facing the results of their actions and attitudes. They never seemed to learn. They had Jesus here trying to teach them, but the actions of the Jewish councils indicated their concern was more for their own positions than in helping the people to let Rome rule and be obedient. *We are a stubborn and often stupid race,* he thought.

The next morning, he left early for Jerusalem. He and Matthan had eaten dinner outside on the roof. They talked about everything, and then Demas had helped his friend back to bed. He himself slept well, but curiosity over Joel had him up early and on his way.

He went directly to the Pretorian. A soldier approached and asked him what he wanted.

"I would like to see the officer in charge of your prisoners."

"That would be the tribune. Come with me!"

They walked down several corridors until they reached a shut door. Knocking, the soldier waited until he heard, "Enter!"

He told Demas to wait and then went in. A few minutes later, the door opened again, and the soldier came out and told Demas to enter.

"Well, I'll be." The tribune stood and walked to Demas. "Do you remember me, Demas?" he asked.

"You made tribune. Congratulations. I figured you would have retired by now. I know, they made an offer you couldn't refuse, huh?"

"Well, you know how it is. I couldn't say no." He laughed. "But what of this prisoner, Joel? He can't be a relation!"

"No. He and I grew up together. Then he betrayed my family and almost got us all killed. But God was watching over us, and we survived. Unfortunately, my grandfather was killed by Archelaus. But the rest of us survived."

"I would imagine if you had found him sooner, he would have paid for his folly."

"Probably, but God has taken the bitterness from my heart. I guess I still just want to know why. That's why I've come. He sent a note saying he was here, so here I am."

"Yes, I had the note sent to you. I can tell you right now that he is going to be our guest for at least two more years. But if he messes up, he'll be hung up on a cross. He is walking a very thin line."

"Can I provide anything for him? I probably won't come again."

"Well, if you want to have him given better food, I can make that possible."

"That's fine. Whatever the cost, I'll pay. However, I would like to talk to him now. May I? I have to ask why he did what he did. His parents died of heart break shortly after all that happened. He has never asked about them that I know of."

"He's a real winner, isn't he?"

"Let's just say that he made some very bad choices. His present circumstances say a lot."

"Yes, it does. I'm having him brought up now. You can talk to him in a room down the hall. There has to be a guard in there with you."

"That's fine. I just want to ask why he did what he did." Demas laid a bag of silver on the table. "If you need more, see my headman, Theo, at the farm. He'll give you whatever you need."

"This will be fine. I'll make sure he has better food, but it won't be banquet quality."

"Good. And thank you so much. I live in Antioch now. My son, David, will be keeping me abreast of the farm. Should you need to contact me, leave a letter with Theo, and he'll get it to me."

"That's fine. Maybe we'll meet again one of these days."

"Probably. It's all in God's hands. Good-bye, tribune, and give my good wishes to your wife."

Demas gripped the tribune's arm and then stepped back out into the hall. A soldier nodded and led him to a door. He entered, and there stood Joel.

"Well, Demas. Do you want to kill me?"

"Not anymore. From the looks of you and your surroundings, I would say that you're doing it to yourself quite well."

"Yes, I have to agree. You came sooner than I expected. You must have been on the farm."

"Of course. My old steward, Matthan, has been my manager there for years. He broke his hip recently, so I came to see how he is. He's in his seventies now, and it will take sometime for him to heal."

"Yes, it will. You know that over the years I've kept tabs on you. Don't know why, just curious, I guess. I am sorry about your father though. At least, he didn't suffer."

"Joel, what do you want? All I want to know is why you told the Herods where we were. Grandfather was killed by them, and we barely got away. Of course, your parents died of broken hearts. They are buried out on the farm with my grandfather."

"I was just plain scared. I got into dice game with some of Archelaus's soldiers. They caught me cheating and were beating me to death. Archelaus came in and was watching, so I yelled that I knew where you all were. Archelaus gave me money, and I ran, self- preservation and all."

"That's it? You were getting what you deserved and wanted out. That really is the lowest thing anyone could do. Then you came home that night, stole a flock of sheep, and ran. If it's pity or sympathy that you want, you won't receive it from me."

"Yeah, I figured that, but I had to try. I am sorry, but I was just a kid."

"You haven't changed any, have you? You are what you are—a petty thief, a liar, a cheat, and indirectly a murderer. Well, you've made your choices. Now I get to make mine. I've paid to have you fed better, but you're stuck here for two more years. If you make any more mistakes in here, it will be the cross."

"You're a hard man, Demas!"

"Why? You made your choices. Aren't I entitled to do the same? Oh, I forget, you didn't have the same opportunities. That is a lie straight from hell. Everything that I have, I've earned by honest hard work. Now I'm able to enjoy all those years of work. And I'm hard? I guess we'll never understand each other, so let's put it this way—stay away from me and my family. If you don't, believe me, I will take care of you in ways you've never thought of. I'm not interested in you. Don't ever get in touch with any of us again."

Demas stood and walked out of the room. He was shaking when he left the prison. *Dear God, I'm sorry about my anger with Joel. After thirty years or more, I hate Joel. I ask forgiveness, and I will try to let go of it all. I even pray that Joel will have a change of heart and attitude. I don't believe he will, Father, but have mercy on him.*

Chapter 43

As Demas rode back to the farm, tears streamed from his eyes. He hadn't realized how much anger he had had for Joel. Joel hadn't ever truly acted contrite about what he had done. Finally, he stopped, got down off his donkey, and got on his knees and prayed. "Dear God, forgive me. When I saw how Joel still was. I was angry. That wasn't a young boy standing in that room but a mean-spirited, cruel, and conniving adult. I'm sorry he has always been so self-centered, self-seeking, and a wastrel too. I pray he has a change of heart and a desire to do better. I won't judge him, but I know someday you will. Please have mercy on him. And above all, please forgive me for letting anger and unforgivingness overwhelm me. I have sinned too. Help me do what's right and to never feel this way again. I do repent. Your son has said to always forgive, and I truly am sorry. Please forgive me too, Lord. I love you, and I do want you to show me what else I should do on Joel's behalf and my own. Amen."

Demas sat up and just closed his eyes as more tears flowed down his face. Finally, they stopped, and he remounted the donkey and went home to the farm.

After dinner, he told Matthan what had happened. Matthan just hugged him for a while. Then he said, "My son, for you are my son in many ways, God will take care of Joel and the rest of us. We must always remember that the Lord is in control. We must always let him handle what we can't. Pray for Joel to change his heart and thinking. If he does, then God has answered your prayers. But let all the anger and bitterness that you've had go. You answer to God for your own sins just as Joel will answer for his, and me too. And that is something I'm so grateful to God for. Just think that if you had to be responsible for others' sins, no one would ever go to heaven. I'm proud of you, Demas. You knew immediately that you had done wrong. And whether you should have or not, we're still on earth, and Satan takes every opportunity to weaken us and to stray from God. You've repented, asked for forgiveness, and will be stronger the next time something happens. Everyone does, so just keep trying and trusting."

"You've always been like a second father to me, Matthan. If you want anything, just let me know."

"My boy, you always have." With this, they parted for the night.

The next morning, as the men sat drinking coffee, Matthan asked Demas for a favor. "Last night, I suddenly felt a need to go to the temple and sacrifice. Could we go tomorrow and stay with Lazarus and then go the next morning? We can get our lambs from the flock there."

"I would like that too, my friend, but can you ride that far?"

"I think so. Lazarus and I have been good friends. One day, he was showing me an old chariot that he had acquired. The more we talked, he suggested that he hang a sling in the chariot, and then I would be comfortably seated while traveling. So I bought it from him, and I have used it when I go anywhere. I believe that I can ride in it, and it would be good for me to get out again."

"I should have known. Lazarus is the most gifted and inventive person that I've ever met. Yes, we will go to Bethany tomorrow."

Just then, Demas's youngest brother walked in. "Thank God you're here," he said. "Can we take a walk? I have something to discuss with you. You're the head of the family now, and I need to ask your advice on a problem that I have."

Demas looked at Matthan, who just shrugged. "Of course," he said, and they walked outside. "What's the matter, Gabriel? I don't think we've ever had a good talk before."

"Demas, I want to stop being a Pharisee. I'm not comfortable with the temple hierarchy and the views of the priests. I've been listening to a young rabbi whom I believe to be a great prophet. He comes and goes irregularly, but I always listen to him when he does come and speaks. It's as though he is voicing God's desires for us. I know that you will be disappointed in me, but I believe everything that he says. His name is Jesus. I can no longer believe the temple priests and their ideas, so I want to leave. Is there someplace where I can go and work like everyone else in the family?"

Demas shook his head and hugged Gabriel. "You are an answer to my prayers. I know of Jesus. I have everything that he has said and done written down. I have scribes with him continually, and they send me his teachings constantly. Gabriel, I know that you have heard Father's and my story of the birth of God's son in Bethlehem over thirty years ago. I know that that babe is now the Jesus whom we are talking about. I believe in him. Of course, you can leave your studies. And I have a place for you too. You can go into training at our friend Lazarus's business center in Bethany as soon as you are ready. Matthan and I are going there tomorrow morning, and you can meet him. He's a friend of Jesus and has had him and his disciples stay with him when he comes to town. Oh, and by the way, when David, your nephew, and I came down previously, he, our guards, and I were baptized by John the Baptist in the Jordan. I believe in Jesus, and though I have never seen him, I've been promised that I would someday."

"Gabriel stood still and stared at Demas. "He was the babe born when you and Father were tending sheep in the fields overlooking Bethlehem. I've heard that story so often, but I've never connected it all together. I am so glad that we will see him again."

"Me too! My whole life has been predicated on that promise. Come, let's tell Matthan. He believes in Jesus too."

The next morning, the three men left for Bethany. They went slowly so that Matthan wouldn't be shaken up too much. Lazarus was all smiles as he stepped out to greet them.

"Looks like the Shophans have come to visit. Come on in. Martha just made coffee."

As they talked, Demas saw a camaraderie building itself between Lazarus and Gabriel. It looked like things were working out for all of them. Lazarus asked, "What did Gabriel have to do to leave his position at the temple?

"Well, not going back will tell them something. Then when Demas doesn't send any more money, then that will pretty well put an end to my training. But I have already told many that I probably wouldn't be returning. In truth, I don't think that they will care. I was becoming a thorn in their shoes with all my suppositions about Jesus's ideas. I will miss Joseph of Arimathea and many like Gamaliel. I believe that they believe in Jesus too."

"Well, if you want to read everything that Jesus has said, both Matthan and Lazarus have copies of all the scrolls that my scribes have sent. Jesus knows who sent them and allows them to go along with his inner group."

"So when do you want me to work, Lazarus? I guess if I learn enough, you and your sisters will be able to go to Salamis whenever you want."

"Well, I'm not in a big hurry. Besides, it will be nice to have another man around. David is in training too, even though he is already doing most of the traveling. His eventual job will be to take over his father's job. But I think Demas still has many years to enjoy his travels."

Demas snorted, and then everyone was laughing.

The next morning, Demas, David, Matthan, and Lazarus went to the temple to offer sacrifices to God. Afterward, Matthan wanted to rest, so the other men circulated and talked to old friends. When they came back, Matthan was walking around talking to acquaintances too.

Demas went up to him and asked if he was okay. Matthan smiled and then said, "Jesus passed through and healed me. I feel wonderful."

"Where is he?" Demas asked.

"He was leaving when he saw me and stopped to talk. Then he healed me and left. Oh, Demas, he is the son of god. I just know it."

Demas turned to Lazarus and said, "Do you think he will stop at your place?"

"Maybe! But he comes and goes like this frequently, and he doesn't always come to my house. He could be pretty far away by now. Be patient, my friend. If he said he would see you, he will, but he will choose the time and place."

"Then let's go and see if he's with your sisters."

It was amazing how well Matthan was doing. The trip to Lazarus's home and then to the farm went quickly. Matthan was in the best shape that he had been in years. Everyone was so happy for him to be so well. Lazarus told Demas that a caravan for Tyre was due in at any time, so Demas spent two more days on the farm and then went back to Bethany. He was ready to go home. Gabriel enjoyed the work and liked the sisters. Everyone and everything was going well, so when the caravan came in, he was off to Tyre. Matthan was retired and enjoying his new health. Theo and his wife were so happy for Matthan. He was the children's grandfather as far as they were concerned.

Chapter 44

Demas spent a few days with Samuel and Elizabeth telling them about Matthan's full recovery by Jesus. Samuel was totally enthralled. He was glad that Demas had purged himself of his angst against Joel too. He told him that it wasn't good to have anger like that eating him up. Then Demas was on the boat to Antioch. Jonah told him that Baba had retired and hoped to see him at the next Passover. He assured him he would be back for it.

Things at home had gone well. He told the family everything that had happened. They were happy for Matthan, but his brothers still had some anger for Joel. However, he quieted their feelings and said Joel would answer to God. It wasn't their place to judge him, so they stopped complaining about him, and things returned to normal. Then he told them that Gabriel had quit the temple and was working with Lazarus. That caused a small stir. Mariam was the most interested and asked when he would be coming for a visit.

There were so many children now that it was hard to find very much quiet. When it became too much, he would go see Joseph and Shela and then go fishing. Joseph had built a small boat, and he and Demas would just sit for hours out on the river; if they caught fish, that was fine, but the quiet was better.

Months passed, and he got a note from the tribune saying that Joel had done fairly well, but he got into a fight that caused the death of two of his soldiers. Joel had been condemned to be hung on a cross just before Passover. Did he want to come and see him before it happened?

Demas was actually sorry for Joel and said he would come to Jerusalem and get his body and bury him with his parents on the farm. More than anything, he felt that he would see Jesus this time. It was as if God was encouraging him to go. David was home and said that his youngest brother and Lazarus were doing very well. He then asked Mariam if she wanted to go with him, but she didn't feel up to it. Roxanne was busy as ever, so he planned to go by himself.

He was concerned for Jesus more than anything. Jesus had to move around constantly to avoid the temple priests who wanted him dead. Even the scrolls he was receiving had him worried. Jesus never hid, but his teachings had a finality and sadness in them. Over a hundred people followed him, but the twelve men that he called his disciples were always around him. Surely, God would protect him. The temple hierarchy was hounding him, and there was no doubt that his life was in jeopardy. He would go down a couple of weeks before the Passover. He too had felt it in his spirit.

So he sailed down to Tyre. His Uncle Samuel might want to go to Passover with him. Two weeks later, he was coming into Tyre, but Samuel didn't greet him as usual. After he landed, he made his way to Samuel's house. As he approached, Samuel came out and asked, "How did you know?"

Demas didn't know what had happened. "What's wrong?"

"You don't know then! Lazarus died. Four days later, Jesus came and raised him from the dead. I was just writing to tell you and get the news off to you."

"This is good news and bad news. The temple priests can't have a witness like Lazarus, whose death can be confirmed, walking around. I'll leave for Jerusalem immediately. Hold a ship for him and his sisters. It's time for them to go to Salamis."

"We'll leave in the morning. Reznik is here, and we can go in his caravan to Bethany. I think we are seeing the hand of God in this, don't you? I want to come with you. We can get them packed and gone before anyone realizes that they aren't around anymore. Thank God that Gabriel will be able to take over. He can say he bought the place, and Lazarus and his sisters left. There's something that is going to happen this Passover. I want to be there too. Jacob can't come. His wife isn't doing too well. So, nephew, it's just you and me, the Jews, and the Romans."

The next morning, they were on their way to Bethany. They didn't talk much; even Reznik was quiet and somber. On their last night together, Reznik sat down with them. "I feel you should know that I was baptized by John the Baptist just before he was taken and then killed. He told me that my life would be totally changed and that I wouldn't be traveling as I had been for too much longer. He encouraged me to not worry, that the change for me would be a blessing from God. I've read many of the scrolls that you've sent out. I've known Lazarus and his sisters for a long time. I'll take a part of the caravan and return to Tyre with them. Then meet up with the rest of the caravan in Damascus. Would you allow this so that they can be safe?"

Demas and Samuel were both totally surprised. Then Demas agreed. It was a good plan. The family would be safe in their new home very soon.

The next night, they were in Bethany. Lazarus knew that somehow God would protect and provide for him and his sisters. They were already packed and ready to go. They could see God's hand in all of this. Martha had found a cook and housekeeper for Gabriel. The men who were working there liked Gabriel, so he knew that they would continue working for him. But no one had realized how quickly things would happen. Lazarus and his sisters would be gone, and who better to handle the questions of the priests than one of their own, a former Pharisee.

At daybreak, they we're loaded. Demas told Reznik to stop in Antioch and tell his family what had happened after he left. Demas then told Lazarus that their new house was already built and waiting and also that he had had a workshop so that Lazarus would have a place to keep on working on his creative ideas. They stood and watched as the small caravan disappeared.

Later after breakfast, Demas and Samuel left for the farm. Demas knew that Matthan would be surprised but pleased to know that the family was on their way to Salamis. But hadn't they always been able to disappear when danger surrounded them? The good Lord was certainly watching over them all.

Matthan was overjoyed to see them. He wasn't surprised that Lazarus and his sisters were already gone. He had been a part of this family too long to not know how quickly they could handle situations as dangers arose. He handed Demas a note that the tribune had sent to him. He quickly read it and shook his head. "Well, old friend, Joel has done it again. He was doing better and then got into a fight. Two soldiers were killed. Joel will be going to the tree just before Passover." It was signed by the tribune.

"I'm truly sad for him. I guess I'd better go and see him. I really did have hopes that he would change. May God have mercy on him! I'll go tomorrow to the prison and then stop to see how it's going with Gabriel. I'll be back for dinner."

The next morning, Demas rode out on a horse. He was in Bethany before he had realized it. Gabriel met him as he came in. "I had a feeling that I would be seeing you soon. Some of the temple priests just left. They wanted to talk to Lazarus, but I told them that I had bought the place and that Lazarus and his sisters left. They asked where he had gone, and I said I hadn't asked. They seemed relieved that they were gone. Then they asked me why I had bought the place. I told them because it was for sale. They really don't like me, but what could they do? Basically, I'm out of their hair. I guess they just weren't happy about me being so near. Oh well, this is how it is, so if they aren't happy, that too is too bad."

"Gabriel, you have a strange sense of humor. Do you know that? Frankly, I wish I could have seen their reactions to you being here now. You must have truly impressed them in school."

"Not really. Depressed would be the better word. I challenged them on everything and anything that I couldn't reference in the scrolls to their explanations. The one that really got to me was when they had personally had those things imparted to them by God himself. Demas, it was time for me to get out of there, and I'm quite content here already. By the way, what are you doing back so soon? Checking on me?" He grinned.

"No, I had a note from the prison tribune saying that someone I had known in childhood was going to pay the most painful death possible before Passover. I've come to say good-bye and get what I need to claim his body. His parents are buried on the farm. I plan to bury him next to them. It finishes something from my childhood. Someday I'll tell you the whole story. I'll go now to the prison and see Joel and then be back here in the afternoon."

"Good luck. I don't like that place. It always made the hair on my neck stand up when I passed it. I'm glad that you don't need me with you."

His horse had been watered, so he mounted and headed for Jerusalem. He didn't know what to say to Joel, so he prayed about it the whole way. When he arrived, the head officer of the prison said that the tribune was with the governor and said to give you these papers. He said that you would need them later.

"Thank you. Where can I go to see Joel?"

He was led into the same room as before. There weren't any benches, so he sat on the floor and waited. Soon the door opened, and Joel stumbled in. He glared at Demas and then said, "Come to torment me, Demas?"

"No, Joel. I came to say I've forgiven you and am sorry that your life has ended this way. I had been carrying that anger toward you for too long. It's gone now, and I truly am sorry for how it will end. You're a Jew, Joel, whether you care or not, and God will forgive you too if you repent. I really hope that you do. There won't be any more opportunities to do so. I hope you make the right decision now. With that, Demas turned and rapped on the door. Without turning, he said, "I pray that God will be with you always." As the door opened, he walked out as tears flowed down his face. He got back to Gabriel's, and Gabriel took him in his arms to comfort him.

"Things happen like this, and we very seldom understand. But God knows how all things will work out. Here are all the spices and linens that you will need to prepare Joel's body. You will be unclean after you prepare him. You won't be here for Passover, but your friends, family, and I will sacrifice and pray for you both. Go home now and get prepared."

Gabriel led Demas to his horse and packed the burial items on a donkey. Demas felt like a child as his brother helped him mount his horse. "Go with God, Demas. Pray and trust God to give you understanding and peace. Remember, he will never leave you or forsake you whatever happens." He kissed and hugged Demas and prayed for him.

Demas had no memory of the journey back to the farm. Matthan and Samuel helped him into the house.

"I have had a grave dug next to where Joel's parents lay. We have a place where you can prepare him. Samuel and I will go on Passover and pray for you both."

Demas went into a room and fell exhausted on his bed. That evening, Demas joined his family and friends. "We'll leave early tomorrow. You stay with Gabriel, and I'll get Joel and return here. I know that you want to help, but this is something that I have to do alone. I'll be unclean and unable to celebrate Passover with you, but please sacrifice for Joel and me. We must keep the faith regardless of our own desires. I will be fine. I'll see you when my time of uncleanness is over."

The others agreed, and the next morning, they started off. As they neared Bethany, the weather changed. The air was heavy. *How fitting,* Demas thought. Then as they came into Bethany, Gabriel was at the gate, waiting.

"They have killed him," he said. "They have killed Jesus." The men dismounted and gathered around him. "How? What has happened?"

"Late last night, they arrested Jesus in the garden of Gethsemane. He was beaten and taken to Pilate. He could find no wrong in him, but the priests insisted. Since it's the habit to release a prisoner for Passover, the priests riled everyone up to ask for the thief and murderer, Barabbas, to be released instead of Jesus. So Pilate washed his hands, absolving himself, and did as they asked. Jesus was crucified with Joel and another thief this morning. They are on the crosses as we speak!"

Suddenly, the ground began to shake, and it poured rain down in great drops like huge tears. It thundered, and the men took shelter within the house. "He's dead. I know it," said Demas. "God is pouring out his wrath. What will happen now?"

"Brother, according to the scriptures, we didn't understand what would happen, but he knew, and the scriptures are fulfilled. Now we will see what else will happen."

Around the ninth hour, the rain ceased. Demas had to go get Joel's body, so he left for Golgotha where the crucifixions usually took place. As he went up the hill, one cross was empty. There was a sign over it, saying, "The King of the Jews." *What has happened to Jesus,* Demas wondered. Then he saw Joel. His legs were broken to hurry his death. Some men were taking down the other body as he walked up. "Where is the body of Jesus?" he asked.

"Joseph of Arimathea took his body down and is preparing his body for burial. What do you want?"

"I came for the body of that thief there. I have the paper authorizing me to remove him. I'm going to bury him next to his parents in the family grave."

"We'll help you. They have to be down before the start of Passover."

"Thank you. I have cloth and a donkey to take him home on."

The men lowered Joel's body. Demas wrapped him, and the men put him on the donkey. Thanking them, Demas started for home.

The whole way there, he kept wondering about Jesus. Jesus had promised that Demas would see him, but now it was impossible. He was dead and being buried too. *He must have meant when we all are in Paradise,* he mused. *Oh, Lord,*

I will always believe in you and trust you, even if I am slow-witted in understanding.

He found the shed, and David had laid out what he would need to prepare Joel's body. The grave was just a few steps away. Two hours later, the body was anointed and wrapped, so Demas carried it to the grave. "Rest in peace, Joel. I'm truly sorry that this happened." Then he laid him in the grave and covered it. He then returned to the cabin and grabbed some things and headed for one of the hills where the sheep were allowed to range free. With the dogs to guard, the shepherds could sleep. He found a good spot where he could see the shallow valley. He built a fire and then sat down on a big rock to relax. But his thoughts kept going back to Jesus. *He said that I would see him, but I didn't. And it hadn't sounded like it would be in a resurrected life. Well*, he reasoned, *what will happen will happen!* Just then, he saw a man walking toward him. *He must have seen my fire*, Demas reasoned. "Hello. Come sit by my fire." He offered.

The man came up and thanked him. Then Demas said, "I perceive that you are a Jew. I am unclean right now, for I have just buried an old acquaintance. But there is a stream nearby if you need refreshment."

"No, I am fine. I too have just been made unclean myself. We can share this time together. You seem disappointed or sad. I can well understand. The living have a hard time accepting the inevitable. We are born, live, and then die."

"I am upset over the death of my friend, but I am more upset over the death of God's son who was crucified too. He said that I would see him, but I never did. I have to assume that he meant when we go to heaven."

"Not necessarily." Then the man quoted verses from the prophets and expanded on their meaning. Demas was enthralled by the man's knowledge and wisdom. In a way, the man explained many things that made perfect sense. He led Demas through the Word of God, and as he talked, Demas understood for the first time. He was relieved, and all his frustrations and pain ebbed away. He truly had joy in his heart. He had told the man about his life and how he had kept missing Jesus all these years, and now he was dead. But now he realized that it was a physical death and not a permanent or total loss. He would see Jesus, and he knew that nothing was ever totally and completely over, even in physical death. The man had such clarity and love in all that he said. Demas turned and offered to give him a drink and something to eat, but when he looked back, the man was gone. Demas looked all around, and there was no one there. Then he looked up into the night skies. There was a bright star lighting the heavens. He could almost hear the angels singing as they had in Bethlehem so long ago. Then he knew.

His soul was joyous. Tears ran down his face, but these were joyous ones. He knew, his visitor had been Jesus. He had come to reinforce Demas's faith and to remove all sadness from his soul. "Thank you, Lord. I am well-pleased." And soft music filled the air, and the grasses seemed to dance and wave all about him.

But there is no ending, for God's love goes on forever.